PIPELINE

PETER SCHECHTER

HARPER

An Imprint of HarperCollins*Publishers*

This is a work of fiction. The characters, incidents, and dialogue are drawn from the author's imagination and are not to be construed as real. Any resemblance to actual events or persons, living or dead, is entirely coincidental.

HARPER

An Imprint of HarperCollins*Publishers*
10 East 53rd Street
New York, New York 10022-5299

Copyright © 2009 by Peter Schechter
ISBN 978-0-06-168742-6

First Harper paperback printing: March 2010
First William Morrow hardcover printing: March 2009

HarperCollins® and Harper® are registered trademarks of Harper-Collins Publishers.

Printed in the United States of America

Visit Harper paperbacks on the World Wide Web
at www.harpercollins.com

10 9 8 7 6 5 4 3 2 1

Praise for
PETER SCHECHTER's
electrifying thriller

PIPELINE

"*Pipeline* reads like the best of David Baldacci and Daniel Silva. It's a smart, scary thriller that shows why the U.S. energy crisis and the new Russian belligerence make for a toxic mix. . . . Peter Schechter knows the way the world works—and how it can go dangerously wrong."

Brian Kelly, Editor, *U.S. News & World Report*

"*Pipeline* brings the wonderful talents of Peter Schechter together in a tour de force thriller about the intersection between politics and energy. Schechter's ear for dialogue and creating characters who live and breathe is outstanding."

Peter Bergen, *New York Times* bestselling author of *Holy War Inc.*

"Peter Schechter's new book reads like it jumped off the front pages of the world's newspapers. . . . *Pipeline* does what I've been doing—educating Americans about our need to replace oil with natural gas as we move to renewable energies. *Pipeline* is a work of fiction. But not by much."

T. Boone Pickens

"A slam-bang start. . . . A cautionary tale about international politics and the dangers of underestimating an adversary. . . . *Pipeline* succeeds. . . . [Schechter] explores the complex inner workings of global energy needs and limitations, and he puts present-day political decision making in a historical perspective. . . . *Pipeline* makes a strong case for considering these issues now."

Washington Post

By Peter Schechter

PIPELINE
POINT OF ENTRY

To my dear mother
It is as I whispered: "We will always remember."

And to Rosa, Alia, and Marina.
You are the faces of sunshine.

The darkest places in hell are reserved for those who maintain their neutrality in times of moral crisis.

—Dante Alighieri (1265–1321)

Don't buy the house; buy the neighborhood.

—Russian proverb

IN THE NOT TOO DISTANT FUTURE . . .

PROLOGUE

Hannah held her mother's hand, the little girl's honey-colored eyes bouncing with anticipation as the manager of Charlie's Chocolate-Ice-Cream Foundry turned the store's lock.

Since opening two months ago, the all-chocolate, all-the-time ice-cream shop's twenty-three versions of chocolate ice cream had become an enormous hit. Pulled by a sharp advertising campaign, kids had been dragging parents from all of Los Angeles's far-flung districts to the seaside neighborhood for a fix of cocoa ice cream.

Though Hannah's kindergarten had let out for summer break last Friday, it had taken only four days of Hannah's determined whines to break down her mother's opposition and get her to agree to the crosstown journey from Hollywood Hills. Traffic had been unusually light on the freeway—eerily light—but Hannah's mother didn't dare turn off the *Baby Beluga* sing-along disc to tune to the all-news traffic and weather radio station. Hannah's mother knew better than to toy with the few, precious moments of respite from Hannah's kinetic curiosity and happy, nonstop chatter.

With the light traffic, they had arrived fifteen minutes early in front of the ice-cream shop's brown—chocolate—facade. Hannah's mother suggested they stay in the car's air-conditioning until opening, but Hannah couldn't wait. Hannah's mom winced at the onslaught of chocolaty metaphors as they sat on the group of cocoa-colored benches just outside the shop's windows. Hannah's Gap-purchased skirt was too short to pad the back of her thighs from the hot burn of the seat's wooden slats and the little girl jumped up with a yelp. The benches had been in the sun for only a few hours, but were already boiling.

"Okay, here's some butt protection," said Hannah's mother with a smile as she spread out the white towel she had dug out of her gym bag on the car's backseat.

Hannah's mother looked around. She was surprised that they were alone. Elementary schools in L.A.'s school district were now on vacation and she had expected hordes of similarly manipulated parents to be congregating outside the ice-cream shop.

Within minutes, both Hannah and her mother were covered in beads of sweat. It was only June and California was already sweltering. Since last Friday's school dismissal, temperatures had reached 105 degrees every single day. There was no change in the forecast for at least a week—a stagnant high-pressure system was stuck like glue over the West Coast. With her daughter starting a junior tennis camp next week, Hannah's mom wiped the sweat streaking off Hannah's face with a Kleenex and wondered if it was healthy to keep kids outside in this heat.

Hannah's mom banished the thought from her mind. The alternative—keeping Hannah home and bouncing off the air-conditioned walls—was too difficult to contemplate.

Hannah, though, didn't seem to mind the heat. She had unsheathed her coterie of nonstop questions and was already poking and prodding her mother with unrelated queries on every possible subject. Have you heard of American Girl dolls? Do you think I can have one? At what age can I have a cell phone? Did you know that Luke—you know, the Luke from school, Mommy—has parents that were divorcing? What is divorcing?

Hannah's mom did her best to answer each question and keep her face locked into one of those falsely patient parental smiles. But the oppressive heat made it hard to concentrate on the meandering onslaught of Hannah's questions. She looked down the convection waves shimmering off the already-boiling concrete street and caught a glimpse of a long-haired, sandaled man walking toward them on the sidewalk. He was looking down at something in his hand.

Hannah's mom heard the jingling sound of keys coming from his fingers. God, let this be the ice-cream man, Hannah's mother begged inwardly.

"G'morning," he said with a smile. His white T-shirt was drenched in sweat. "I hope I'm not late. Overslept this morning. But I only live two blocks away."

He looked at Hannah and smiled. "This is the right day for an early morning ice cream, isn't it? And you're lucky to be the only ones. Yesterday we had a twenty-minute wait."

Hannah jumped off the bench. "Are you the man from the store?" As he grinned his assent, Hannah looked at her mother with a beaming smile and just hissed a "yessss" as her fist pumped up in the air.

Wiping the sweat on his brow with his left sleeve, the man used his right hand to insert the key and turn the lock.

"Come on in and let's choose your ice cream!" the man shouted in mock excitement. For a guy only in his twenties, he had a good way with kids, thought Hannah's mom.

The sandaled feet had taken only two steps into the store before they stopped cold. Hannah was so close behind him that she bumped into his back.

The first thing the three noticed was the ovenlike temperature. Unusual heat is a noticeable thing, but it's an eyepopper when it emanates from an ice-cream shop.

The manager of Charlie's Chocolate-Ice-Cream Foundry and his two clients adjusted their eyes to the darkened store and immediately saw the catastrophe. A squishy brown muck covered nearly every inch of the shop floor. In the astonished silence, they heard the steady drip-drip of murky liquid spilling out of the air-conditioning slats at the bottom of the long line of spanking-white refrigerated ice-cream freezers.

The glass windows of the ice-cream cases were covered in condensation. Cleaned four times a day with computer-screen wipes, there was now no way to see through the usually crystalline glass into the round containers of twenty-three flavors of chocolate.

"Oh, shit," muttered the store manager, oblivious to Hannah's presence. He rushed forward toward the cases, his sandals squeaking through the oozing, mud-colored liquid that was now splashing onto the top of his foot and in between his toes. As he lifted one of the sloped glass-paneled doors of the first refrigerated case, a rush of vapor drops converted into a little torrent of water streaking downward into the ice cream.

"Oh my God," moaned the manager of Charlie's Chocolate-Ice-Cream Foundry. "Please tell me this isn't happening. There was eight thousand dollars' worth of ice cream in this store!"

Hannah's mom felt a knot tighten in her stomach. A native Californian, she had lived through the state's traumatic 2001 crisis. It hadn't been all that long ago—but time could never diminish the harrowing memory of that late-summer morning. Dressed in business attire, Hannah's mom had walked with the rush-hour crush into the crowded elevator in the seventy-three-story building at Number Fourteen Century City Plaza. She had been on her way to her very first job interview when the elevator—along with nearly every other electricity-driven machine in the state—had jolted to a stop. Fourteen people had been stuck together in a ten-by-fifteen-foot elevator car for eleven hours, the first hour's good humor quickly replaced by a dark, groaning human hell of feces, urine, and vomit.

The horror would never leave her.

Yes, Hannah's mother intuitively knew what was happening. She now understood the light traffic and empty storefront. Los Angelinos had stayed at home, bracing themselves.

She was knocked back to attention by Hannah's sobbing yells.

"Mommy, what's happening? What's happening?"

Hannah's voice was now becoming very loud and was bordering on the hysterical.

"Look. Look! The ice cream ... it ... it ... it's all melted."

UNITED STATES

Anthony Ruiz heard the phone ring. But at this hour, he was simply not able to translate the shrill tone into the usual reflexive actions that required opening his eyes and stretching out his arms to pick up the receiver.

The answering machine in the hallway of his one-bedroom Foggy Bottom apartment collected the call. Satisfied that this momentary sleep interruption had disappeared, Anthony Ruiz turned over onto his stomach and relaxed.

Until he heard the voice booming from the answering machine's speakers.

"Tony, it's Tolberg, wake up. Your cell phone is off. Turn on CNN and call me back in the office."

Tony Ruiz's eyes unlocked as his body riveted into an upright position. He looked at the clock and saw that it was 1:27 A.M. Jeezus, what the hell was Isaiah J. Tolberg, the president's imposing chief of staff, doing awake at this hour? thought Ruiz. Notwithstanding his graying hair, folksy mannerisms, and sartorial elegance, the sixty-eight-year-old White House chief of staff ran President Gene Laurence's office with an iron fist. At the White House, everyone, including the president, addressed the former six-term senator from Kansas only as "Senator."

Tony Ruiz reached for the phone and stuck his index finger into the air, ready to jab in the requisite seven numbers that would get him Tolberg's office in the White House's West Wing. But he stopped after the first three digits, remembering the message's admonition to first turn on the television.

Ruiz zapped the remote on his way to the bathroom and punched in CNN. Standing over the toilet, he strained to hear the television's volume over the gurgling of his urine hitting the toilet-cleaner blue of the bowl's water. Within seconds, he understood the urgency of Tolberg's call.

"Shit," Tony Ruiz gasped.

The voice on the tube was that of a female reporter—her voice strained with tension. Tony furrowed his brow, from the bathroom recognizing CNN's Los Angeles correspondent. He knew the voice; her didactic delivery was engraved in his mind. During the campaign, CNN's California correspondent had been the only reporter to ever have successfully rattled President Eugene Laurence's cage with a battery of questions designed to raise doubts about Laurence's easy demeanor. The questions had implied that the candidate suffered from an intellectual laziness that had him floating above tough issues while others did the hard work. The interview had been patently unfair.

Twenty minutes into the exchange, Laurence had interrupted his hour-long interview commitment, gotten up, and walked off the Los Angeles set. "You may be in charge of the questions," the future president had snapped, removing the microphone from his lapel. "But I'm the guy with the answers. And I'm out of here."

Tony Ruiz, the president's special advisor for domestic affairs, had been left to clean up the mess with CNN. To this day, on Laurence's orders, there was only one big exception to the administration's excellent relationship with the press. CNN's Los Angeles correspondent.

Yes, he definitely recognized the reporter's voice.

Ruiz shook himself back to attention and listened to the

dialogue between the California-based reporter and CNN's anchor.

"Ryan, in the last two days, the situation here in California has escalated from the occasional neighborhood blackout to a growing panic. We're in the dark here in Los Angeles. The entire city is without any electricity."

Ruiz finished relieving himself and padded back into the bedroom. He took one look at the television and saw CNN's Anna Hardaway's face on the screen. She was standing in front of a hospital; blue emergency lights were flashing around her on the street.

"We're transmitting to you off our truck's generator and we'll keep going as long as we have juice, Ryan. Los Angeles County General, which you can see behind me, is also on a generator. Hospital officials have told me that they can function without electricity for another eight to twelve hours. But that is hardly reassuring to this city's residents who, at ten thirty P.M., are now without air-conditioning and suffering the stifling ninety-degree heat that has overtaken this metropolis."

Ryan Foxman, the New York–based bearded anchor of CNN's *Executive Office Hour,* interrupted Anna's reporting. Foxman's show was the network's top-ranked business broadcast. Ruiz guessed that Foxman was the only recognizable face the network could find at that hour to anchor the emergency transmission.

"What are city officials saying to the residents of Los Angeles, Anna? Are they being reassured?"

"Well, Ryan, you have to remember that this city's citizens can't turn on their televisions at this time." Anna Hardaway sounded a tad exasperated with her anchor's question. "You and I are being watched everywhere else in the United States, just not here. But I've heard reports that people all over this city are in their driveways and in the streets listening to their car radios."

"Of course, Anna. That was a silly question," said Foxman. Tony Ruiz couldn't remember ever hearing a news anchor admitting to a stupid question. This guy got points for honesty.

"I guess what I'm really asking is *what* are officials saying?

How long will it be before power is restored?" queried Foxman, now posing his question with precision.

"That is the eerie thing, Ryan. Nobody is saying anything. When the rolling blackouts began two mornings ago, city officials and spokespersons at WEPCO, Western Energy Power Company—they are the state's largest and this city's *only* electricity company—went out of their way to explain that citizens were going to face just a few days of rolling blackouts due to the incredibly hot weather and unusually dry spring. Twenty-four hours ago, it sounded as if they were still in control, with a plan in place to meet the surge in energy demand—"

"And now?" Ryan Foxman's voice interrupted the reporter.

"Now we can't get an answer. The mayor's office will only say that Mayor Steve Villas is in emergency meetings. We've called the governor's office in Sacramento and those calls have not been returned. And CNN's Roger Fenton, standing by at WEPCO's offices, just called my cell phone to tell me that, except for lights on the top floor, the building is locked up, tight and dark."

Anna Hardaway looked genuinely worried.

"Ryan, it's been three and a half hours since the lights went totally out in Los Angeles and nobody is saying anything. Anything at all."

Those last three words were enough for Tony Ruiz. He wouldn't bother calling Tolberg back. Ruiz threw on a pair of khaki trousers and a white shirt and on the way out grabbed his blue blazer from the coat hook. He needed to get to the White House.

WASHINGTON, D.C.
JUNE 14, 2:15 A.M.
THE WHITE HOUSE

Tony Ruiz's blue Subaru flew down Pennsylvania Avenue. At this hour, Washington's downtown streets were empty of traffic. Halfway there, Ruiz irately realized that he had forgotten to brush his teeth. Tony Ruiz was fastidious about personal hygiene.

With good reason. The only son of an immigrant Mexican apple picker, Ruiz had grown up dirt poor in Washington State's Chelan County. For over twenty years, Tony's mother and father came and went from their native Veracruz to Washington State at harvesttime. When Tony was eight, Steve McCain, the farm's owner, told Mario Ruiz that he had enough work to last throughout the year; he asked Mario to stay in America with his family.

As the car stopped at the only red light between his apartment building and the White House, Tony thought about how that small exchange between an American farmer and an illiterate Mexican seasonal worker had changed his life.

Young Tony graduated as president of his high school class, in the shadows of Lake Chelan's glacier-filled Cascade Mountains. Four years later, Mario and Rosario Ruiz attended Tony's graduation at the Washington State police academy, and Rosario made a no-holds-barred Mexican banquet for Chelan County's entire police force on the day her son joined their ranks.

Tony Ruiz had never considered doing anything but police work. It had been a dream job. His dark good looks and Latino charm had made him popular on the force. Three years and a few days after the death of the beloved twenty-year-veteran president of the local Fraternal Order of Police, Deputy Tony Ruiz had been elected president of the union by acclamation. Once again, Rosario Ruiz had celebrated her son's professional milestone by cooking for the forty-five employees of the county's police—*chiles* in walnut sauce, *sopes* with meat and bacon, *queso fundido,* and oxtail tacos.

The rest of the story was all about the serendipitous alignment of stars. The next year had been an election season in Washington State. Ronnie Masterson, the state's elderly sitting governor, was running for reelection. Seeking to bolster his law-and-order credentials, the governor had asked the state's Fraternal Order of Police for their support. Tony was a big fan of the governor and, in a large Seattle convention hall full of cops, he had risen to endorse Masterson.

Toward the end of his three-minute speech, Tony's voice had become louder. Slamming his fist, he had described Masterson to his fellow police officers as a down-to-earth politician who solved problems. Without ideology—Masterson wasn't about right or left, he was about right or wrong. Tony Ruiz ended his first-ever speech by asking his colleagues to "get behind the old man; he's got our type of common sense."

A former speaker of the state's House of Representatives and deputy governor, Governor Ronald Masterson had more power in his hands and people at his command than any state politician in memory. Nobody had ever dared call him an "old man."

So when Tony Ruiz finished, he heard a collective gasp. No applause. The hall had held its breath in absolute quiet. Only one sound had broken the silence. From the front of the room, Governor Ronnie Masterson himself was doubled over in laughter.

Ronnie Masterson had been reelected that year with over 69 percent of the vote. The campaign slogan—affixed on every poster and narrated on every spot—was The Old Man Has Our Kind of Common Sense.

From that moment on, Tony Ruiz had become part of Masterson's tightly knit circle of informal advisors. A few years later, when Gene Laurence's presidential campaign had come to Washington State, Governor Ronnie Masterson had introduced the presidential hopeful to the young deputy Tony Ruiz and told him the story. A smiling Laurence turned to his aging campaign manager, Isaiah J. Tolberg. "Now what do you think of that, Senator?"

"What I think is that we need to bring this boy on to our campaign," answered Tolberg.

The rest was history. Eleven months after a bruising political campaign, Mario and Rosario Ruiz had been invited to president-elect Eugene Laurence's swearing-in ceremony below the magnificent porticos of the United States Capitol. They had accompanied Tony as he got his White House pass. They had been right behind him as he walked into his West

Wing office for the first time. Mario's lips had trembled as his nearly illiterate eyes stumbled slowly over the official-sounding words on the doorplate: ANTHONY RUIZ, SPECIAL ADVISOR TO THE PRESIDENT FOR DOMESTIC AFFAIRS.

At that exact moment, a hand had come to rest on Rosario Ruiz's shoulder. She turned to face the president of the United States.

"Señora Ruiz, how glad I am to meet you. Thank you for letting Tony come to Washington, D.C., with us," said Gene Laurence, his eyes twinkling. "Now, Tony tells me that every time he's had a new job, you have cooked a Mexican meal for his employers. Why haven't I gotten one? You're going to owe me."

Tony Ruiz shook off the reveries as he approached the White House gates. A uniformed Secret Service officer ordered him to a halt and shined a powerful flashlight into the car.

"Oh, hello, Mr. Ruiz. Forgive the bright lights; I didn't know who it was at this time of night."

It took Ruiz five minutes to park, enter through security, and take the west elevators to the first floor. As he walked straight down the hallway to Isaiah J. Tolberg's office, Ruiz saw right away that the place was in full swing.

"Hey, Senator. I didn't call you back. I turned on CNN and figured I should just come."

Isaiah J. Tolberg was a man who stood on tradition and formality. Even at this time of night, he was polite. Over his white shirt, the Senator was wearing only the vest of his usual three-piece gray suit with thin black pinstripes. His blue necktie—adorned with interspersed small yellow ducks and gray metallic rifles—was tied tight under his collar. This was the first time in two years that Tony Ruiz had seen Senator Isaiah J. Tolberg without his suit jacket.

"Good evening, Anthony. I'm very sorry to have interrupted your rest. I appreciate your loyalty."

The two men were separated in age by nearly forty years, but genuinely liked each other. Tolberg was more at ease with Ruiz than with many of the other experienced Washington hands who populated the West Wing's offices. Tony often thought that Tolberg appreciated the fact that the Senator's old-fashioned demeanor never bent Tony's youthful informality. After all, Tony Ruiz was only twenty-nine years old.

"No sweat, Senator. What the hell is happening in California?"

"'Hell' is the right word, son. Fasten your seat belt; I have a feeling that the next few days are going to get very bumpy."

WASHINGTON, D.C.
JUNE 14, 3:45 A.M.
THE WHITE HOUSE

Tony Ruiz worked his computer's mouse at full steam. Seated at his desk down the hall from the chief of staff, Ruiz skimmed through the developing avalanche of news from California. Ruiz had gotten Tolberg to give him a quick rundown on California's energy problems. It was amazing that the chief of staff of the world's most powerful executive office knew little more than what was being reported by the nation's news bureaus.

"I need you to take the next hour or so to read everything on the Internet. Check out the *L.A. Times*, *New York Times*, *Wall Street Journal*, *San Francisco Chronicle*. AP, Reuters. Everybody. I want to know what is being said. They probably have more information than we do," ordered Tolberg in a surefire staccato. "Be back here at four A.M. because we're getting on a conference call with Bob Mieirs and Cyrus Moravian," he said, referring respectively to the secretary of energy and the governor of California.

Shortly before 4:00 A.M., Ruiz entered Tolberg's office for the second time. An oversize mug of coffee was in his hand. He sat down on the other side of the large walnut desk filled with piles of paper and silver-framed pictures. All the arrayed items created a disconcerting barrier effect between the desk's two sides.

Tony winced when he saw that some of his coffee had sloshed out of the mug and onto Tolberg's worktable. A small line of black droplets was heading straight for one of the larger paper piles.

Ruiz didn't have a napkin. He prayed that Tolberg couldn't see over the desk's obstructions.

Ruiz briefed the chief of staff on the news reports. They all told the same story, though the *L.A. Times* also had a source quoted on background that the governor was flying to Los Angeles. Tony quickly came to his conclusion.

"The gist of the coverage, Senator, is that Los Angeles has been one-hundred-percent dark since about eight-thirty P.M., their time. And the sense is that the electricity crisis is escalating. As you know, California gets its juice mostly from hydroelectric power and natural gas–fired generating plants. Some of the outlets have quotes from energy experts pointing to a sudden, acute, natural gas shortage. Others say that the dry spring in California has exhausted nearly all of the state's hydropower.

"Somebody above my pay grade has got to give you an opinion on the validity of those arguments, Senator. But one thing I sure can tell you about is the political part. There is an absolute information vacuum. Nobody knows what is happening because nobody is talking to the press. The governor, the mayor, and the utility are all battened down. They aren't saying it yet, but the sense I get is that the press feels they were lied to in the past twenty-four hours."

Isaiah J. Tolberg's hands covered his eyes in an exhausted grimace. Cyrus Moravian, California's governor, was an old friend. The Senator and Governor Moravian had been political allies for nearly twenty years. They had served on a number of blue-ribbon panels together. They were golf partners. Their wives were close.

"Why the hell didn't Cyrus warn me? I can't believe he didn't know this could happen. What in God's name is going on out there?"

Mary Jane Pfeiffer, the Senator's twenty-year secretary, knocked quietly on the closed door. Tony always suspected that she must practice her North Carolina accent when she went home at night. It just wasn't possible to talk that way naturally.

"Senator, it's four A.M. I've got the conference call parked. Now, y'all need something before you start? I reckon that at this hour of the morning, I'd recommend some chocolate chip cookies and a glass of milk."

A glass of milk? Tony thought she was kidding. This was the hour for either a stiff Scotch or more coffee. To his shock, the sexagenarian White House chief of staff was a taker for the milk and cookies.

"As always, Mary Jane, your suggestions are wise. I'd like that very much."

The Senator reached toward the phone and punched a button.

"Good morning. Isaiah Tolberg here. I'm accompanied by Tony Ruiz. Who is on the line?"

As the secretary of energy and the governor of California identified themselves over the speakerphone, Ruiz noticed that Mary Jane Pfeiffer had quietly slipped back in with the Senator's snack. On her way out, she let her hand fall below the Senator's line of sight and slipped Tony a couple of sheets of paper towel. Looking at his slopped coffee oozing across the desk, he accepted with a sheepish grin.

"It's four A.M. here and if you don't mind, I'm going to dispense with the usual niceties this morning. Cyrus, would you kindly tell us what the hell is going on in your state?"

That introduction was pretty short and severe for Tolberg. No thank yous or pleases.

Anybody who knew Isaiah J. Tolberg would know that the mouse had just roared. The White House chief of staff was an extremely frustrated man.

"Isaiah, I know it's an ungodly hour. I appreciate your being there for us." The voice was that of Cyrus Moravian.

"I wish I could tell you to go to bed. But I don't have good news. As you know, we've got a total blackout in Los Angeles. I'm headed down there right after this call."

Tony Ruiz nodded at his boss. The *L.A. Times* had the story right. The fact that the governor was flying to California's biggest city in the middle of the night was not good. It could only mean the situation was not under control.

Tolberg interrupted the governor. "Does that mean that the statements by the mayor and WEPCO over the past twenty-four hours were false? These aren't just a few rolling neighborhood blackouts?"

"Senator"—the governor was now more formal—"as best I can see it, those declarations were—umm—premature."

Isaiah J. Tolberg's brow furrowed. He waited for the governor to continue.

"I'm afraid that we're being hit by a 'perfect storm.' It hardly rained in the West this winter; hydroelectric power stations are producing one-tenth of their normal capacity. And the blistering heat blasting the whole western part of the United States has come way earlier than expected. They're burning more natural gas than they've got. Senator, the power companies are scrambling, but they don't have any juice to supply."

"So you're telling me that this will last for days?" asked Tolberg.

"No, Senator, it's worse than that. This will now spread to the rest of the state."

Tony Ruiz looked at Isaiah J. Tolberg, aghast. California was going black.

It took a full fifteen seconds before Tolberg could pull himself together to ask a question. It was to Bob Mieirs, the secretary of energy.

"Bob, what can we do to help the governor?"

"I'm looking into options, Senator. But there are no easy answers. As the governor said, California's energy comes from hydroelectric production and natural gas generators. Right now, they don't have enough of either."

Nobody said anything, so the energy secretary went on.

"You see, natural gas is increasingly seen as the future, the new energy currency. Gas is used in the United States for many things, but mainly for electricity production. Half of U.S. homes are heated with gas. It represents about thirty percent of the total energy consumption in the United States. But though I don't have the statistics in front of me,

I'll bet that in California it's double that. As you know, in the late 1990s, California began to phase out oil- or coal-fired electricity plants because of their effect on the environment. Natural gas is cleaner—it emits thirty-five percent of the greenhouse gases of oil and half the carbon dioxide of coal."

"Can we divert energy from the grids east of the Mississippi to the west? Or can we pipe excess gas from somewhere else in the country to California?" Tony Ruiz's questions injected themselves into the phone lines.

"I wish it were so simple," came Mieirs's tired answer. "I can give you long technical explanations, but the basic point is the same. Electricity needs in the rest of the world and in the United States are exploding. We don't produce enough natural gas to supply our own needs, so we have to import. Utility companies are outbidding each other for juice. There is no quick fix.

"Bottom line, gentlemen. This will take some time."

SACRAMENTO, CALIFORNIA
JUNE 15, 10:30 P.M.
CALIFORNIA STATE PRISON, SACRAMENTO

California Department of Corrections supervising officers Pete Studley and Robby Henderson were in the executive suites of Facility GP IV watching television coverage of spreading incidents of looting in Los Angeles. The total outage in Southern California was now over twenty-four hours old.

Munching on one of the kitchen's prized double-bacon cheeseburgers, Robby Henderson threw a glance Pete's way.

"So far, these incidents of violence are all centered in poor neighborhoods. But middle-class folks are soon gonna start breaking store windows to feed their families. When that starts happening, the shit will have officially hit the fan."

The executive suite's elegant name was an inside joke among the institution's corrections officers. It was the nerve center of General Population Facility Four—GP IV, for short—the largest of ten separate housing facilities on the sprawling two-hundred-acre campus of the California State Prison, Sacramento. On basic metal desks, the executive suites contained banks of closed-circuit televisions that monitored nearly every inch of the building. Three chairs—their arms' outer edges gnawed by years of being slammed into the metal desks—were arrayed haphazardly in the cramped room.

The correctional facility's modernistic smooth gray cement walls housed about three thousand inmates, nearly a thousand more bodies than its architects had originally envisioned. The prison was a level-four institution. It contained men of terrible violence—murderers, predators, gang members, transfer prisoners considered too much "trouble" at lesser penal institutions.

Approximately one-third of the prison's inmate population was serving life sentences. Over a thousand of the men had committed at least one murder. Almost all of them had committed assault with a deadly weapon. Sacramento State, as inmates called their "home," was the end of the line for the worst of the worst.

Unlike most other prisons in the United States, Sacramento State did not have granite walls. Instead, it bragged of a death-wire electric fence, embedded between two fifteen-foot-high chain-link fences, which administered a five-thousand-volt lethal dose to even the slightest touch. Nobody had ever escaped.

Pete Studley was a twenty-year-plus veteran, part of the original cadre of corrections officers who had been on staff at the prison's inauguration in 1986. The Sacramento native was appreciated by his colleagues for his unusual combination of clear leadership and good-natured humor. Divorced for over a decade, Pete had volunteered for the night shift five years ago once his second child had gone off to college. This made him the night duty senior officer.

When Robby Henderson was assigned to the prison's moonlight duty eighteen months ago, Pete's first words had been crystal clear.

"There are twenty-six officers guarding one thousand six

hundred and seven inmates on the overnight at GP IV. With those odds, we do things by the book. The schedule is God, Jesus, Muhammad, and the Buddha all rolled into one. I don't care if you are eating, shitting, or talking to your dying mother on the telephone; there are specific times for lockdown, lights out, assessment walks, and general inspections of the arms closet, radio units, and the television monitors. Miss a single moment—by even a minute—of my schedule and you're out. Other than that, we'll have a blast here."

In the last year and a half, Pete Studley and Robby Henderson had become close. Henderson's wavy blond hair, surfer-boy build, and aw-shucks demeanor were deceptive. In over twenty years in California's correctional force, Pete had never worked with anyone who had a work ethic that came even remotely close to Robby's.

"It's ten thirty, Pete. I'll do the check." Robby Henderson laid down his half-eaten meal and reached over to grab the microphone. He had to lay it back down instantly when he realized that his fingers were still oozing with the mayonnaise that had dripped off his bacon burger. Tightly coiled wires snapped the mike back across the table.

Robby Henderson grinned sheepishly at Pete as he wiped the white gluey liquid off the transmitter.

"What a slob," muttered Studley, feigning a grimace of disgust.

"Hall One, radio check," Rob Henderson now dictated into the newly wiped microphone.

"Hall One, all quiet." The response came quickly.

"Hall Two, radio check," Robby droned on.

And so it went, sixteen times. Four floors, four halls.

The sixteenth all-clear signal was from Tom Rivers, fourth floor, north hall.

"Boss, bio break please," came Tom's voice over the radio.

Robby looked over at Pete, who shrugged, again pretending good-natured frustration.

"Tom Rivers's gravestone will say: 'This man pissed an awful lot.'"

"Okay, Tom, we'll reserve your favorite urinal for you,"

Robby cracked over the microphone. He could well imagine his fifteen hall officers snickering at the comment.

Minutes later Tom Rivers's smiling face appeared next to the executive suite's glass-enclosed walls. He waved as he went down the hallway to the officers' bathrooms.

"Get Snyder and Robinson to do the munitions inspection, Robby," Pete Studley ordered. "They haven't done it in a couple of weeks. Gotta remind them what a weapon feels like."

Robby had already started on the second half of his bacon burger and once again his hands were infused with dripping mayonnaise. This time he cleaned them before grabbing the microphone.

"George, Robby here. Will you guys do the arms closet today?"

No answer.

"George, this is the executive suite. Come in, please."

Silence again.

Pete Studley now leaned forward, his polished boots firmly on the ground. George Snyder knew the drill. On Pete Studley's watch, even a few seconds' delay was an officer's death knell.

"Get Robinson," Studley ordered.

Robby Henderson was about to open his mouth when he realized that the green light of the communications equipment was off. Three years ago, all internal communications equipment in California's prison system had been placed on fully separate electrical circuits. The idea was to ensure that communications were always on a fail-safe backup system.

The system was now down.

Studley jumped out of his chair and crossed the length of the executive suite in just a few long strides. He made it to the radio console.

Just as he got there, all lights in the prison disappeared. The prison's closed-circuit television monitors then emitted an initial low whine as they darkened to a tiny central white spot.

"What the fuck is going on?" Studley shouted as he

grabbed the backup battery-charged walkie-talkies. "This is GP Four. We've got a serious problem. I've lost all energy in the complex."

Studley's heart started racing when he heard the chaotic jumbled response. Six or seven radios talked at once. Not only from his own hallway officers; Studley recognized voices from corrections officers posted at different locations in the prison's sprawling acreage.

"No lights . . . towers."

"Monitors down in GP Two."

"Unable to sound alarm."

"Telephones nonfunctional."

Pete Studley and Robby Henderson didn't see it coming. But they heard it.

The sounds were unmistakable. First they heard the quick, trampling cadence of large numbers of running footsteps. The sound was like that of the pulsating panic that would occur if someone yelled "Fire!" in a packed movie theater. The two officers could make out the strange, high-pitched tremble of the metal railings installed along every inch of GP IV's granite corridors. The reverberations were caused by the stampeding feet of out-of-control humanity.

Next came the gunshots. The *tap-tap* of pistol fire from different corners of the building seemed to accelerate to a frenzy before going suddenly silent. The popping sounds were unreal, almost playful. But there was no doubting the reality of the emotion-charged, throaty sounds of screaming men. The noise was overwhelming, the agonizing decibels ricocheting off the building's bare cement walls. Outside the building, somewhere on the campus, automatic weapons were being discharged.

Pete Studley and Robby Henderson did not need to exchange a word. They knew where the noise came from; the crushing roar of oncoming humanity was a direct result of the malfunction of the prison's electronic cell locks. The two men unholstered their .38-caliber Smith & Wesson sidearms and pointed each barrel to the door.

Neither stood a chance. They may well have killed four or five of the inmates pouring through the door, but they could not get the rest. Of all of the guards on duty that night in GP IV, only Tom Rivers survived by cowering in the oasis of the men's-room stalls. The bodies of Pete Studley and Robby Henderson were found twenty-four hours later, beaten to a pulp.

All four eyes had been gouged out of their sockets by sharp-nailed human fingers.

WASHINGTON, D.C.
JUNE 16, 11:00 A.M.
THE WHITE HOUSE

President Eugene Laurence strode into the White House Cabinet Room at a brisk clip. His lanky, patrician good looks communicated a constant aura of success. Gene Laurence was New England blue blood through and through. People guessed his origins by just one look at his preppy shirts, penny loafers, and the bifocals perched on his aquiline nose.

But unlike most of his eccentric Boston upper-class brethren, Gene Laurence had an easy manner. He was a rare breed, a break from generations of genetically selected disdain. Gene Laurence actually liked other people.

Laurence's political communications machinery fanned the flames of his outgoing and friendly reputation. They habitually had him entering his next appointment late on the pretext that he was "unable to tear himself away" from ongoing conversations—Gene Laurence could talk to anybody, cabinet secretaries, policy wonks, a housewife, or a group of hospital nurses.

Laurence was a people guy. His political persona hovered above his administration's reputation for toughness.

For all its bragging about constitutional checks and balances, America was a country with an imperial presidency. Very few world heads of state had concentrated within their office the arsenal of political, economic, and military power that the White House's resident had.

And it showed. Wherever the president went, martial

music played, flags were raised, audiences stood. Even inside the whirlwind pace of the West Wing, the president's entrance into a room demanded that everyone—from senior cabinet secretaries and members of Congress to Supreme Court justices—immediately rise to their feet.

Not today, though. The minute he walked through the Cabinet Room doors, the president knew his day would only worsen.

This morning, the six men and two women presently in the Cabinet Room did not even notice the president's arrival. They sat, clustered and spellbound, in front of a television tuned to CNN. Upon entering, President Gene Laurence said nothing. He was instantly transfixed by Anna Hardaway's face. With no makeup and ragged from exhaustion, the reporter stood in front of bedlam at Los Angeles International Airport.

There were people everywhere.

Her reporting was half fact, half emotion. As with CNN anchor Bernard Lewis's award-winning 1991 transmission from Baghdad as the bombs rained down on the city, President Laurence had the immediate impression he was watching history in the making.

"We're sliding into full-scale dread here in California," reported Anna Hardaway, her voice a low monotone. "I'm speaking in the plural today because this reporter isn't— can't be—impervious to what is happening across the state. The blackouts, which began three and a half days ago in Los Angeles, have spread like wildfire. San Diego, Sacramento, Fresno, Long Beach, Santa Ana are now also without power. But I want to point out that CNN's David Mallaby in San Francisco told me just a few hours ago that the lights are still on there.

"I'm standing in front of LAX, usually one of the nation's busiest airports. All flights into and out of California have been canceled. Security, air traffic control, baggage belts are all out of order. The chaos you see behind me is repeated in homes and offices everywhere.

"Our modern lives are dominated by electricity. And

people across California are finding out what it means to live without power. We can't reach anybody here; families are unable to talk to each other, offices are incapable of making business decisions. Cell phones are on their last remaining charge and slowly petering out. The Internet is no longer available. Telephones work, but many homes have cordless telephones and most office telephones use electrically powered switchboards.

"And since we can't reach other people, we're without information. Car radios are still working, but that can't last long as automobiles begin to run out of gas and lose battery power."

CNN cut to anchor John Randsom at headquarters, in Atlanta. His lips quivered as he tried to formulate the right question. Like most Americans, he felt he was watching his country melting before his very eyes. Any and all questions would sound banal. So he just asked her to continue.

"Please go on, Anna."

"John, we Californians are prisoners in our state. Cars are unable to be filled with gas, banks are unable to dispense money, and grocery stores are unable to sell food because their cash registers are shut tight. Traffic is gridlocked, as automobiles have been abandoned on freeways because streetlights just off the interstates' thousand exits don't work. We've had a few, sporadic reports of food looting in supermarkets, but I can't imagine that won't become more widespread as families across this huge state start to panic."

Anna Hardaway's attention was suddenly diverted by somebody on her production team.

"Hold on, John," she said into the camera. Hushed whispering could be heard from her microphone as Hardaway leaned halfway out of the camera frame. In a voice clearly not meant for the audience, CNN's spectators heard her emit a plaintive "Oh my God.

"John, I have CNN's Katherine Wu on my cell phone, standing by in Sacramento. I don't want to risk losing her, so I will just put my microphone near the phone's speaker."

Anna Hardaway fumbled as she unlatched her lapel mike and placed it on the cellular phone. The transmission was poor, but the voice could be made out.

". . . reports of a massive problem at California's huge maximum-security facility here in Sacramento. I'm unable to make it to the prison because police have all roads blocked. According to my sources, sudden electrical failure at the California correctional facility resulted in a terrifying malfunction of the jail's locks. Rather than fastening the jail's doors, the power outage instead caused the bolting mechanisms of the prisoners' cells to release. The result has been a massive prison break. Anna, we're talking about thousands of the most hardened criminal elements in the state.

"Reports are scarce and shocking. But from what I can tell, utter bedlam occurred when the jail lost power around ten thirty last night. Prisoners poured out of their cells, killing anything on their way out of the facility's buildings. This modern jail does not have walls—it has a high-voltage killer electric fence. But presumably that fence failed last night.

"It's our understanding that the correctional facility is a war zone. We have heard that hundreds, maybe even thousands, of prisoners and corrections officers were shot dead—some by escaping criminals, others by panicked guards using automatic fire. There is no way to know how many are dead. But, more worrying, there is no way to know how many murderers, gang members, and other violent elements escaped last night."

Holding the cell phone and microphone in her hand, Anna Hardaway was ashen. She was unsure whether her reporter was done. But the voice continued.

"Sacramento is a city now gripped by fear . . ."

"Turn it off," ordered Gene Laurence's voice from the other side of the cabinet table.

The eight persons in front of the television jumped to their feet, embarrassed that they had not seen the president of the United States entering the room.

They had all heard the reporting from California. It hung over the room like a dark cloud. Gene Laurence stuck out his index finger and just pointed to the chairs around one end of the long, elegant conference table. Isaiah J. Tolberg took the seat next to Laurence. To Tolberg's left sat the secretaries of energy and defense and the attorney general. Across the table, the secretary of state and the directors of the Central Intelligence Agency and the Federal Bureau of Investigation pulled out chairs.

Tony Ruiz was already leaning back in one of the smaller seats arrayed along the room's back walls, directly behind Tolberg, when Gene Laurence interrupted his motion.

"Sit down at the table, Tony. This isn't a formal cabinet meeting."

"Thank you, sir," stuttered Ruiz. Seeing the disapprovingly raised eyebrows of Attorney General Mort Levinson, Ruiz surmised that he wasn't the only one surprised by the president's invitation to his twenty-nine-year-old domestic advisor.

"Okay, talk to me, Senator," said the president, looking only at Tolberg. His lips were tight.

Tolberg was dead serious. He had not slept a minute the previous night.

"Mr. President, you saw the CNN report. It's accurate. Most of California's cities are without any power and San Francisco will go down before the end of the day. I don't have to tell you the consequences; you can imagine them. Hospitals are on generators that will peter out in the next twelve to twenty-four hours. There are practically no communications inside the state—that means no emergency communications either. We've had reports of various deaths in nursing homes; the elderly are unable to withstand the hundred-degree heat. Needless to say, sir, offices are closed, airports are shut, and vehicular transportation is at a standstill.

"This will get worse before it gets better. The prison break is a disaster that is only just beginning. We've heard numbers like over a thousand killed on prison grounds. That means that roughly two thousand prisoners are unaccounted for. The only thing that the TV reporter had wrong is that there is already massive looting in San Diego, San Jose, and South L.A.," added Tolberg. "Violence is inevitably going to escalate when the escaped inmates of Sacramento State start mixing with the general population. California is a tinder-box about to explode."

"Don, first things first," interrupted the president, looking at Don Romer, the secretary of defense. "We need to control the violence. Do we mobilize the National Guard?"

"Done, sir. I spoke to Governor Moravian an hour ago and he signed the mobilization orders. I've also spoken to the governors of Oregon, Arizona, and Nevada. They are will-ing to help. If we make the request, and Governor Moravian approves, they will mobilize their National Guards and send them across the border into California."

"How long will it take to get the situation under control?"

"It's going to take a while, Mr. President. Getting troops into the streets will take three, maybe four days."

The president winced.

"Fast, Don. Make it faster."

He turned to Bob Mieirs, the secretary of energy, and raised his eyebrows.

"We're working on it, Mr. President," said Mieirs. "Util-ity companies all over the country are diverting grid energy westward. Natural gas headed to the northeast from New Orleans is now moving to California. The secretary of state," Mieirs said, raising his hands in a sign of gratitude toward Roselee Rainer, sitting across the table, "has spoken to our friends in Mexico. They are going to accelerate gas into California and Texas in the northern pipelines from Hermosillo and Chihuahua."

Bob Mieirs paused, exhausted. He ran his fingers through his short brown hair. He hadn't yet broken the bad news.

"I'm going to need two days to get the gas to California. Once there, it will be another two or three days before the juice converts into distributable electricity."

The table looked at him, aghast. Five days! California could not last that long.

The president paused for a moment. Looking at Tolberg, he started issuing a rush of orders.

"Isaiah, help me out if I miss something. Roselee, your people at State need to be clear in our messages to the rest of the world. This is a screwup, a hiccup. But it will pass. The United States is, one, open for business, and, two, still vigilant and still strong. And call President Alvarez in Mexico to thank him.

"CIA, I want to know in real time if you pick up any chatter from any Middle East groups about hitting us when we're busy with this.

"FBI, mobilize everything you have. No leaves. Vacations canceled. Get agents from all of California's bordering states into your offices in Los Angeles, San Francisco, and Sacramento, fast. The prison break is now a federal affair.

"Tony, get to Moravian's people and tell him that the governor has an open line to this office. We'll try to get him everything he needs. Start with generators for hospitals. Coordinate with Secretary Romer to get copter flights started. Helicopters that go in with generators come out with the sickest patients and take them to military hospitals in Nevada and Oregon."

The list went on and on. Pens were scribbling. The yellow pads in front of the assembled group of the most powerful men and women in the world were chock-full of notes.

This was Gene Laurence's first major crisis. And the government officials in the room were impressed. The president of the United States was completely in charge.

A few minutes later, Laurence was done.

"Now, before you go running out of here, I want to spend fifteen minutes trying to understand how the hell this happened. The citizens of the United States are going to want some answers."

WASHINGTON, D.C.
JUNE 16, 12:00 P.M.
THE WHITE HOUSE

"At its most basic, Mr. President, we're in a gas crisis," said Energy Secretary Bob Mieirs. "It's simple, really. Gas has skyrocketed in price due to a huge decline in our domestic gas production at exactly the time we're going through a colossal, nationwide increase in electrical demand. The camel's back just broke in California.

"Gas has a lot going for it—there is more of it than oil in the world and it's cleaner. But we do not have much flexibility to expand the domestically produced reserves of the United States. Too much of our natural gas is in environmentally sensitive federal lands. If we try to drill there, we'll be tied up in court for years by environmental groups."

"Damnit, Mieirs, stop telling me what I can't do," said President Gene Laurence. For the first time, he lost his patience.

"The American people expect some answers," exclaimed the president. "And they expect reasonable solutions. Some solutions may take time. Others may take a longer time. But one thing is as clear as water. Too many of my predecessors punted on energy. We can't pretend any longer. There are Americans dying today because we can't get them electricity. We can't just keep hoping the market is going to take care of the problem. Some problems need to be solved by government."

He pounded his fist on the table. "This administration is not going to Band-Aid California's energy problem and hope that the next guy in this chair fixes it.

"So, Mr. Mieirs, how do we assure a long-term supply of natural gas for our electricity plants?"

Up to this moment, Bob Mieirs had been the picture of efficient calm. Small droplets of sweat now appeared on his temples.

"Well, Mr. President, there are a number of answers to your question. I'll give you mine: importing more liquefied natural gas—called LNG—from friendly countries. For instance, some of the biggest natural gas deposits are in Latin America. LNG liberates natural gas from the 'prison' of a pipeline. LNG is natural gas that has been cooled and liquefied to the point where it can be loaded onto special boats and shipped to market. And the freedom to load, transport, and off-load somewhere else makes natural gas behave as if it were a liquid—just like oil! LNG is a pipeless way to connect the world's gas consumers to the large gas producers."

Secretary of State Roselee Rainer jumped in. "Lots of people like that idea—I do too! I'll give you an example. Some of the largest gas reserves in the world are in Peru and Bolivia. In my book, it's a lot better to buy energy from democratic, Western-leaning Peru than from an autocratic desert dictator, right?"

Bob Mieirs was moving quickly to answer the question.

"The answer is an unqualified *yes*! However, as you would expect, there is a 'but.' Once you get the LNG on big tankers, they need to go to an off-loading facility at a port. But, until recently, our country hasn't wanted to build new facilities—they're big, ugly, and environmentally controversial. For years the United States has been dependent on the few—four, to be exact—old receiving locations currently in operation. The main one is in Louisiana, a second is in Boston, but it's used exclusively in winter, as that's when New England's natural gas market spikes with heating needs. And last, the revamped and recently reopened facilities in Cove Point, Maryland, and in Savannah, Georgia.

"So, even if you wanted to import a lot more natural gas, you couldn't. There aren't enough places to bring it in," concluded Mieirs.

"Wait a moment, Bob," interrupted Attorney General Mort Levinson. "We've got environmental laws in this country. You may not like them, but a lot of people think that protecting our environment is a smart investment. I'm one of them. You're not going to lay the blame for the lack of facilities at the feet of those of us concerned about the environment. That's just not right. There are some damned good reasons for not building those plants. And it's our job as citizens and leaders of this country to be well aware of the environmentally hazardous nature of huge off-loading platforms for natural gas."

Bob Mieirs was about to answer but the attorney general wasn't finished.

"And furthermore, those plants are a magnet for terrorists. We can't just build new potentially exploding bomb sites without really thinking through the security that each of these new terminals requires. Remember that this administration was elected—first and foremost—to protect the citizens of the United States."

Mieirs sighed. He had heard all this before.

"I get the security issue. But, you see, natural gas doesn't burn like petrol. If bombed, the off-loading sites will burn fiercely, but they won't explode. People often think of house explosions and think that a huge tank of LNG would be a hundred times worse, but in reality, it's different. For example, think of a gasoline vehicle versus a diesel vehicle . . . the gasoline will explode and combust, the diesel will burn but not explode. This makes LNG much safer than oil— both for shipping and storage. And if there is an accident with an LNG tanker that spills, surface areas may initially suffer from the extreme temperature of the very cold material, but unlike oil, there will be no sludge left for cleanup because the gas dissipates into the air.

"Look, I understand our reluctance to build off-loading facilities around our coastlines, but we've got choices to make. We're going to have to build some new facilities. People will have to hold their collective noses. But we can also take a lesson from the private sector's playbook. In this globalized world, we can off-shore some of the environmental and security risks by outsourcing natural gas facilities to Mexico. Specifically, to Baja, California. There are already a number of new facilities under construction on the peninsula. And Baja is closer to California than Louisiana."

Just as Mieirs finished his explanation, Martha Rawlings Packard raised her pencil in the air. True to her military background, the director of central intelligence sat ramrod straight in her chair.

"Martha, does the CIA agree?"

General Packard's career at the Defense Intelligence Agency had been legendary. As the DIA's youngest and first female commander, General Packard had impressed and alienated half the brass at the Pentagon with her incisive analyses and tart recommendations. You did not want to tangle with General Packard.

She was a supremely attractive woman; jet black hair

curled backward in a bun behind perfectly chiseled feminine features. And she knew it.

It had been hard for most of her male military colleagues to ignore her looks. General Packard's uniforms always somehow seemed more tightly fitted and contoured. More like Donna Karan than Fort Dix. She seemed to thrive in the wake of the water-cooler gossip that frothed around her. But nobody—not one person—ever disputed her brains. She was the smartest DIA commander in history. And that was why Gene Laurence had appointed her director of the Central Intelligence Agency.

"I don't disagree, sir. But it may not be enough."

"Let's have it, General," said the president.

"First I want to say that, as we are seeing in California, assuring our country's supply of natural gas is one of our foremost security concerns for the next fifty years. You are right, sir, to want to face the problem. The fact that thirty-five years after the Arab oil boycott, the United States still depends on Middle Eastern oil will be described by history books as the single greatest act of political folly in our history. We have come to depend on a region that is fundamentally anti-Western and deeply anti-American.

"And with one-hundred-plus dollars a barrel, our oil dependency is locking in dictatorship, violence, and extremism. There is no reason for the petroauthoritarians in Saudi Arabia, Iran, Iraq, Sudan, and Venezuela to moderate their voices or their hatred. We will continue to pay them—and they will continue to buy off their populations with undeserved billions—because we don't have choices."

She looked around. She had everybody's attention. As usual.

"Well, natural gas gives us a choice. Gas balances the equation. As the secretary of energy just told you, there are lots of views about the way to assure the long-term supply of gas for the United States. I want to give you another one. It involves Russia.

"Now, when I finish, my colleagues will think I'm crazy. I'm used to it. But what is happening in California is proof that we need to think differently. Strategically.

"These are the basics: Russia is the world's largest gas producer. It produces hundreds of times more gas than everybody else. Most of its gas is in Siberia. Today it goes to Europe through a series of expensive pipelines that took a lot of foresight and risk to build.

"Now guess what is closer to the Kamchatka gas fields in Siberia than London or Paris," continued Martha Packard, her voice a controlled didaction. "Still thinking? I'll tell you. Alaska. In my native Alaska we've been talking about a transcontinental Eurasia-American transport link via the Bering Strait for years. Now the idea is gathering steam. Have you ever heard the governor of Alaska speak on the subject? I recommend you talk to him, Mr. President. He's pretty eloquent."

She looked at her incredulous audience, unperturbed.

"Think out of the box," Packard ordered. "The French and the British built the Chunnel to connect continental Europe to the British Isles. The project was unthinkable just fifty years ago. Why can't we build a link across the sea from Russia to our continent? It's a huge project, but not impossible. It will solve our gas problems for the next fifty generations. It will build a rapport—which we sorely need—with the Russian government. And, needless to say, sir, it will give you an unprecedented political legacy."

Tony Ruiz knew he shouldn't speak, but he couldn't hold back.

"Sorry, I don't get it. You just told us that we're in debt to a bunch of bad people because the guys who were in this room before us never dealt with the problem. Everything I read about the Russians isn't much better. Why would we jump under the sheets with them?"

The room froze. Presidential assistants—especially young ones—did not usually talk in high-level meetings. And they certainly didn't challenge a senior official.

For a moment, General Martha Rawlings Packard was about to ignore Tony's question. Her nose rose slightly in disapproval. Until Isaiah J. Tolberg spoke up.

"That is exactly what was going through my mind. As usual, Tony's questions are straight to the point. The last I heard, Russia was holding up gas deliveries to Ukraine. Bullying the Georgians. Shutting down newspapers. Threatening the Europeans. As Mr. Ruiz asks, why would we get into bed with them?"

General Packard's look of displeasure relaxed.

"Tony, the key rule of international relations is that one—to use your phrase—jumps under the sheets with people you need, not with people you like. It's different from, you know, us," said the general with a sly smile. "Russia is determined to again become an international power, and with their natural resources, there isn't much anybody can do to stop them.

"So the choice is ours. The Russians can be our feared opponents and antagonists. Or we can entice them with the allure of something so big that they won't be able to resist it. Then they become our ally."

The director of central intelligence paused for a moment.

"And we get our gas," she said, her voice a controlled whisper.

KURSK OBLAST
EIGHTEEN MONTHS EARLIER, 10:20 A.M.
DANIEL UGGIN'S HOME

A year and a half before anybody could have imagined the unprecedented meltdown in California, a man named Daniel Vladimirovich Uggin awoke in his native Kursk with a hangover. A bad one.

Orthodox Christmas—commemorated on January 6 by the Russian faithful—was still ten days away, yet the town's end-of-year parties had already shifted into high gear. The bash at his equestrian hunting club the previous night had gone on until four in the morning.

The party had started at a normal enough time. The twenty or so fellow hunters rode together often; they had done this for years. Kursk was a town of noble military tradition, producing generals and admirals who were hallowed names in the czar's armed forces and later the Soviet Red Army. Daniel's grandfather, Brigadier General Anatoli Uggin, founded the hunting club just before dying for his country in the First World War. To be a member, the male head of every household had to attend a day-long shooting party at least twice per year. A century later, no member had ever violated this rule.

Mere association with the Kursk Equestrian Hunt Club, however, did not necessarily mean that its members were good shots. In fact, Daniel Vladimirovich Uggin and his comrades usually returned to the stables with little other than big smiles at the end of a Sunday spent in the State Central-Chernozem national park, a beautiful huge forest-steppe chunk of land perfect for riding, hiking, and camping. Occasionally, one of the riders had an otter or a badger slung over his horse, and the exceptional catch was always cause for celebratory rounds of vodka.

At thirty-four years of age, Daniel had made an extra effort to go easy on the previous evening's vodka. He had joined in all the toasts and had even offered a few poetic odes of his own to friendship and family. Unfortunately, the multicourse country dinner of pork dumplings, roasted venison stuffed with sweet and sour red cabbage, and braised boar with sweet onions had been accompanied by delicious red wines from Georgia.

Like most Russians, Daniel Vladimirovich did not really believe that wine counted as alcohol.

At the stroke of twelve, Piotr Rudzhin—Daniel's best friend since the seventh grade, when Piotr had forced Daniel on a grade school suicide mission to ignite stink bombs in the trash bin of their despised mathematics teacher—suggested a horse race to State Central-Chernozem park's entrance gate. Piotr, a mammoth, handsome blond statue of Russian manliness, had always been able to command attention. His talent for convincing and cajoling was legendary, no matter the consequences.

Daniel had been only the first of many to fall for the wiles of Piotr Rudzhin's charms; few could resist the smile, the bearlike embrace, and the piercing eyes. Piotr had catapulted this charisma into a burgeoning political career. First as a young two-term elected representative to the Kursk Oblast's Duma—or parliament—where his oratory and leadership were quickly noticed by the authorities in Moscow. Then, eight years ago, he had resigned from the local duma, packed his bags, and boarded a plane to Moscow. Piotr was now the deputy minister for internal affairs for the Russian state.

But, somehow, notwithstanding the long hours and late nights of Moscow's fast lane, Piotr Rudzhin never seemed to forget where he came from. There he was last night. Hugging, kissing, shouting, drinking. And, as usual, coming up with ideas that could only lead to trouble. The notion of a midnight horse race sounded scarcely better than the seventh-grade sulfur-bomb plot. But within minutes of beginning a fiery discourse on friendship, Piotr Rudzhin had them running off to saddle the horses. Daniel had no choice but to go along.

It had been a terrifying ride. The night had been cold and black; the yells of the riders had amplified and ricocheted through the trees and woods. The horses had strained and whined in the emptiness. Though the riders had started together, within seconds each one of them had found himself utterly alone. The twenty-minute trail to the park—well known to each one in the daytime—had seemed to disappear into the forest's black ferns.

As the horses accelerated, the reverberation of the galloping hooves had taken over the night. The men, seeing only the vapors of their breath billowing into the black darkness, had swerved and reined relentlessly to the right and left to avoid trees that had seemed to suddenly jump out from the dark. The crashing volume of the horses' weight trampling the frozen ground had been pierced by the occasional scream of a rider slapping into the low-hanging branches of swinging brush.

Lola, Uggin's eleven-year-old chestnut mare, had finally made it to the State Central-Chernozem park's closed gates in a careening gallop. Reining her to a halt, Daniel had struggled to slow his accelerated pulse and had squinted into the black to see who else had made it. Three others had already arrived; Daniel had come in fourth. Sixteen other riders in transfigured states of asphyxiating shock had poured in over the next fifteen minutes. Faces were scratched by the sharp ends of pine twigs, clothes were torn; but miraculously, nobody was seriously hurt. Needless to say, Piotr had arrived before anyone else, his loud laugh booming through the empty state park.

Daniel Vladimirovich now sat up in bed as the morning light poured through the window. He rubbed his temples and wondered if the horses were feeling half as bad as he did.

He looked at the clock and registered the late hour. Moaning softly, he realized that he was already an hour late to work. The trespass was serious, but not grave. On these festive holiday mornings, few colleagues showed up on time. Daniel Vladimirovich Uggin was the manager of Volga Gaz's westernmost national operation. Usually, he liked to set an example of punctuality and orderliness at the office, but the days leading up to New Year's and Christmas were slow.

Daniel Vladimirovich Uggin had just wiped away the sleep from his eyes when he saw his wife's face peek into the bedroom.

"Daniel Vladimirovich, it's ten twenty A.M." Uggin grimaced at the sound of his wife's reproaches. He knew it was not over. "I would have awakened you earlier, but you got in at five in the morning. Did you think I wouldn't notice?"

Daniel Uggin had shaken his head from left to right in silent acceptance. He was gesturing to himself. "Of course you noticed," he muttered under his breath.

"You've had two calls from Moscow already and I lied both times," Anne-Sophie said in her lilting German-accented Russian as she walked into the bedroom. "I told them that someone had called about some possible leaks in the pipeline and that you were out looking at the situation. I told them not to bother to try your mobile phone because there was no service beyond a certain point outside town."

Daniel Vladimirovich Uggin smiled at Anne-Sophie. He stood up and walked over to give her a thankful kiss.

"You are marvelous!" Uggin mouthed the words slowly, for more effect. "You tolerate the silliness of my hunting club. You don't get angry at me for coming home at dawn. And then you even lie for me!"

He had paused in mock thought for a moment and concluded, "That is what I want written on my tombstone: 'This man had the world's best wife.'"

Anne-Sophie smiled back. Ten years of marriage and two

kids—Katarina and Giorgi—hadn't shaken the sense of humor that united them.

"Who was it who called?" asked Uggin, slowly forcing himself into professional mode.

"She said she was Viktor Zhironovsky's secretary."

The name was like an electrical jolt. He had met the president and chairman of the board of Volga Gaz a few times at company meetings. But this was the first time Viktor Zhironovsky had ever called.

And Daniel Vladimirovich Uggin had slept through it. Twice.

Uggin sat up straight and looked at his wife. A moment of anger clouded his mind as he thought that she should have woken him up. But the irritation quickly dissipated. She was right to have let him sleep. It would have been more embarrassing to speak with the president of Volga Gaz with a sleepy voice. She had weighed the choices and made a decision. He respected that.

"You did the right thing, darling. But now I've got to move," said Daniel, heading to the shower.

Daniel Uggin took a moment in the hot water to mull over his unusual household. These days, sophisticated Russian cities like Moscow and St. Petersburg were magnets for foreigners—tourists, businessmen, cultural exchange students, and, increasingly, foreign spouses were a common sight. But tolerance of outsiders in Russia was a recent phenomenon. During the seventy years of Soviet rule, foreigners had been shunned, monitored, followed, and suspected. Daniel Uggin had been one of the first—and certainly in Kursk, he was *the* first—to marry a non-Russian in the aftermath of the Communist Party's collapse.

He had met Anne-Sophie Perlmutter in the midnineties at the jazz festival in Montreux during glasnost, the heady rush of freedom that had accompanied the collapse of the Soviet dictatorship.

Taking his first-ever trip outside Russia, Daniel had opted to head to Switzerland for the ten days of concerts with his favorite musicians—Chick Corea, Miles Davis, Gato Barbieri, Pat Methany, and many other jazz luminaries. The

young Russian civil engineer, who had never before tres-
passed beyond the Soviet Union's borders, was awestruck
by the music, lush mountains, opulent restaurants, and the
festival's well-heeled patrons.

But something else had happened in Montreux.

Listening to the bossa nova beats of João Gilberto, the
Brazilian musical superstar, from the grassy expanse in
front of the towers and turrets of the majestic Château de
Chillon, Uggin had noticed a number of kiosks setting up
shop near the concert site. None of these makeshift store-
fronts sold souvenirs or trinkets; instead each had hawked a
political opinion.

Uggin had been to many markets at home. But he had
never seen a marketplace of ideas.

There had been a storefront for the Swiss Jazz Society. The International Federation of the Red Cross was
a few meters away, with brochures about its emergency
relief work. The International Society for the Protection
of Aboriginal Peoples had volunteers ready to explain the
menace of development to indigenous societies. La Societé
Francophone de la Langue—the Francophone Language
Society—had proselytized about the dangers of the spreading English-language culture. The European Renewable
Energy Consortium had advocated passionately for wind
turbines and solar panels.

Daniel Uggin had been overwhelmed by the diversity of the
causes and the clear devotion of their followers. Like many
other typically cynical products of Soviet repression, Daniel
had never believed deeply in anything. The devotion of these
volunteers to their causes was completely foreign to him.

One look at the woman in the kiosk belonging to the
World Environmental Trust had unleashed a sense of excitement that he had never felt before.

She was not a traditional beauty. She was too tall and her
breasts were too small. But she was so attractive—blond
hair, radiant green eyes. Wearing a well-starched white
shirt, tight blue jeans, and blue tennis shoes, a line of very
small, perfectly formed seashells had swung in a loose circle

necklace around her well-exposed throat. But Daniel Vladimirovich Uggin had seen none of it; he had been mesmerized by the green eyes.

Daniel Vladimirovich Uggin could never have imagined that this first exchange of shy smiles between them would discharge a love affair so deep that German-born Anne-Sophie Perlmutter, recently graduated with a degree in environmental economics from the University of Frankfurt, would become his wife in less than fifteen months.

Twenty minutes after his shower, Daniel turned the key of his dark blue, Romanian-made Dacia SuperNova and began roaring through Kursk's streets. Kursk Oblast was a relatively small state in the Russian union but, throughout Russia's history, Kursk's significance had outweighed its small size. It had always been the transportation junction to Western markets—years ago, Kursk's railway hub had controlled the passenger and container traffic to Ukraine, Poland, and onward to Europe. Today it was the geographic residence of Volga Gaz's gas pipeline to Ukraine. Through those metal pipes flowed 80 percent of Russia's gas exports to Europe.

In almost no time, he parked in front of Volga Gaz's small downtown headquarters. Daniel walked—no, flew—right past Svetlana Adamova, his six-year secretary. Svetty, as everybody called her, was about thirty years old. Her exact age could well have been five years on either side of thirty, but there was just no way to know given her daily usage of pounds of facial base to accentuate her pale skin and dark hair. A woman whose very large breasts lived under the constant duress of exceedingly tight blouses, Svetty was of Ukrainian descent—there were a good many ethnic Ukrainians in Russia's border region.

She followed him right into his office.

"Good morning, Daniel Vladimirovich. Rough night? I heard about the riding expedition. It's all around town," she had said, smirking at him.

"The town is too small, obviously," he had answered with a grin. "Get me—"

"Yes, yes, I know. He has called here too. They said your

wife told them that you were inspecting a possible leak. Obviously, a lie. I knew you were partying until four in the morning."

He looked up at her, horrified by the thought that she had righted his wife's little distortion. Svetty had put on her most wounded and offended look.

"Of course I didn't tell them the truth. Do you think I'm stupid?"

Uggin felt a twinge of guilt for having allowed the thought to even cross his mind. One thing was for sure. Svetty was not stupid.

"Sorry, sorry. Okay, let's call Zhironovsky back. We can't let the chairman wait; he's called at home and at the office."

Svetty smiled, satisfied with his apology. When men apologized to women, they were so thoroughly profuse about it. It was endearing, she thought to herself. A pity it did not happen often enough.

Daniel Vladimirovich Uggin tried to concentrate on mundane things while he awaited the call. He turned on his computer and logged onto Volga Gaz's system. There were a few, mostly uninteresting e-mails; clearly, many people in the company were on holiday. This only heightened the mystery of the chairman's insistence. What was it that could not be advanced in writing?

Svetlana's voice came over the intercom. "I have the chairman's assistant on the line."

Uggin scooped up the white telephone—it had an extra-long coiling wire connecting the handset to the set, an item he had personally installed to satisfy his constant need to pace. "Uggin speaking," he barked into the phone.

"One moment and I will connect you to Chairman Zhironovsky."

An instant later, a low growl could be heard on the phone. Like the warning sound a dog made if one came too close to its food bowl. Zhironovsky.

"Chairman, it's a pleasure to speak to you. I'm sorry it has taken me so long to call you back. I hope your office was informed that I was out of cellular range." Uggin hoped to

God that this would suffice. He did not want to lie directly to the old man.

"Yes, yes, fine," snapped the voice from Moscow. Uggin felt an initial wash of relief. It looked like he would not have to do more explaining.

"Listen to me carefully, Daniel Vladimirovich. I want you to hear every word of what I am going to say. I will say this only once. Furthermore, we will never exchange a written word about this. This subject will remain between you and me—you will not talk about it with anyone. Is this understood?"

Uggin stopped pacing. He sat down, picked up a pencil, and dragged a white piece of notepaper closer. He put the pencil down, then picked it up again as his mind raced between taking notes or not. He finally decided to write.

"It is clearly understood, Chairman."

"Good. Now here are my instructions. As of midday today, your pumping and collection stations in Kursk Oblast will register a reduction of the gas flow heading toward Ukraine. The flow will continue to diminish throughout the day. Do not call or notify anybody about this. Do not report it. Do not mark this down on the logbooks. Am I clear so far?"

Uggin looked down at his notes. He had written nothing; the paper was blank. He was in such a state of shock that the pencil had not moved. Did the chairman know what he was saying? Uggin struggled to remember the relevant numbers. Ukraine consumed about eighty billion cubic meters of gas a year; half of its gas came from Russia. Most of it was needed for heating in the frigid wintertime. Right now.

Even worse—Uggin's mind was now racing—the Ukrainian pipeline fed Russian gas to homes and industries in western Europe.

Damnit, what were the numbers? As an engineer, he always knew his numbers. Why couldn't he remember now! Wait, they were returning. Nearly 40 percent of Germany's gas consumption was Russian. Twenty-five percent of France's consumption was Russian. Thirty percent of Italy's.

Uggin forced his attention back to the telephone. Zhironovsky was still talking.

"Once your last metering station in Russia registers the gas at below two cubic meters per second, I want you to shut the system down. Everything. Stop the pumps. Close the collections stations. Not one centimeter of gas leaves Russia as of midnight tonight. Am I understood?

"Uggin, listen to me carefully. You will not accept a contravening order on this matter from anybody but me. You may get calls from God knows where. Perhaps the press. Foreign government officials. Others here in Moscow. People will scream bloody murder. I don't care whether you take these calls or not; perhaps, like today, you will instruct your secretary to tell people that you are again out of cell phone range. Only *I* will have the authority to instruct you to reopen the pumps."

Silence invaded the phone line. Uggin's brain was in swirling confusion. Clearly, the chairman had not thought through the consequences of this order. Perhaps there was a break in another gas line that required immediate need elsewhere in Russia. But surely there were other ways to redirect gas without such a radical approach.

"Daniel Vladimirovich, I pay you to execute the orders of Volga Gaz. I do not want to be questioned about any of the issues that are now going through your head. I will ask you again and I expect an answer: Am I understood?"

"Yes, Mr. Zhironovsky, you are understood," Uggin answered. His mouth formed to ask a question in the politest of terms. He never got it out.

"Good. I will be in touch." Viktor Zhironovsky had hung up the phone.

**KURSK OBLAST
THE SAME DAY, 12:05 P.M.
VOLGA GAZ LOCAL HEADQUARTERS**

Daniel Vladimirovich Uggin sat frozen at his desk after hanging up with Viktor Zhironovsky. He stared blankly at his office's white wall, in front of his eyes. He was a midlevel employee at Volga and he had no choice but to execute his orders.

Uggin tried to shake himself out of his stupor. He hardly knew what to do next. Vainly hoping that the telephone call with Viktor Zhironovsky was a figment of his alcoholic evening, he logged on to the Volga Gaz intranet system with his password. He searched and clicked on the small icon at the top-right-hand corner of the Web site entitled Management. Once again, he was prompted for identification. He tapped in his employee number and password. This part of the Volga intranet site was reserved for management only.

Uggin moved quickly along the ultrasophisticated computer site. He knew exactly where to go. He clicked the pipeline metering portal and a map appeared of Volga Gaz's crisscrossed network of pipelines. Every time Uggin logged on to the pipeline metering map, he was newly impressed with the company Volga Gaz had become.

Notwithstanding its listing on Moscow's stock exchange, 51 percent of Volga Gaz was owned by the Russian State. It was, in effect, the state-owned gas company of the country with the world's largest reserves of natural gas. Through savvy purchases, sheer gumption, and considerable controversy, Volga had wrangled its way to control of over 85 percent of Russia's gas production and 100 percent of its gas exports. By owning the Russian pipeline network, it had muscled out any potential competitors. It had become—in short—the world's largest gas producer. Now it was busy buying both "upstream" gas fields in Siberia and "downstream" production and distribution facilities in western Europe. Volga Gaz was a company on the move.

Daniel Vladimirovich moved his head closer to the computer to identify his largest trunk line into Ukraine, the Urengoy-Uzhgorod pipeline. There were other gas lines that passed through his district of control, but the "U-U," as he had nicknamed the Urengoy-Uzhgorod pipeline, was all he needed to see.

The U-U pipeline—56 inches in diameter—traveled thousands of kilometers southwestward from the Urengoy gas field, in the northwestern Siberian Basin. Urengoy was the second-largest field in the world, with 300 trillion cubic feet of natural gas. Along the way, the pressure in the pipeline was secured by over 100 pumping and compressor stations that squeezed 1,500 pounds per square inch of pressure into the line to keep the gas moving at the fast clip of 6 cubic meters per second. It was an amazing feat of construction and engineering.

Uggin hesitated a moment before the maze of color-coded zigzagging stripes prior to clicking on the blue line that denoted the Urengoy-Uzhgorod pipeline. The Volga service network kept a real-time monitoring of the gas flow's speed through each line; with merely a click of a mouse, senior managers could look up the flow rate in any Volga-owned pipeline. What he saw made his blood freeze. The U-U was now at half its usual rate of speed. There was no doubt about what was happening. The gas was slowing to a trickle.

He had followed the news about the increasingly acerbic dispute with Ukraine's government over gas pricing. Negotiations on escalating cost increases for Ukrainian gas purchases had fallen apart. Like most educated people, Daniel Vladimirovich had suspected it wasn't price that ultimately separated the two sides. Rather, recent Ukrainian elections had led to a pro-Western government in Kiev. He had known that what really bugged the Kremlin was political, not financial.

Yet Daniel Uggin also understood—very, very clearly—that any opinions regarding Viktor Zhironovsky's orders and motivations were completely irrelevant. His career and future would hang on the actions he would take in just a few hours.

Suddenly, one thought occurred to him: Piotr! Chairman Viktor Zhironovsky had been very clear that he was not to talk to anybody about his orders. But Piotr Rudzhin was now a senior government official. As vice minister of the interior, Rudzhin commanded the Russian federal police, the district prosecutors, and the criminal magistrates. Most important, Rudzhin was his dear friend; he would know what to do. Perhaps he could even find a way to turn the decision around.

Yes, of course. Rudzhin! Piotr had an answer for everything.

Daniel Vladimirovich donned his otter-fur hat and once again flew past Svetlana, slowing just enough to bark a few orders.

"Svetty, do me a favor. Call Piotr Rudzhin and tell him I'm on my way over to his house. Tell him that I need to talk to him alone for an hour—that I need some advice. Oh yes, tell him that I will need coffee and cigarettes."

That should get Piotr's attention. Rudzhin, like many Russian men, chain-smoked. But Rudzhin would know that Daniel smoked only when nervous. He would immediately understand the coded urgency of the message.

Piotr's parents' house was only a ten-minute drive from Volga Gaz's office. When home for the holidays, Rudzhin stayed with his mother and father, his verve and energy reinjecting a pulse of life into the frail old couple's home. Well into their eighties, the elderly pair was rightly proud of their famous son. They planned their lives around Piotr's well-programmed visits, parading him from one table to the next in the town's coffeehouses and restaurants.

Daniel Vladimirovich pulled up to the building, bounded out of the car, and pushed open the door of the old, four-story apartment complex. The parents lived on the third floor. Uggin ignored the elevator. He took the steps two at a time and started counting. His eyes and mind concentrated on the stair count and, just as his left leg stretched onto the fifty-fourth step, he slammed into Piotr Rudzhin, waiting for him on the third-floor landing.

He hugged his friend and planted a loud, needy kiss on both cheeks. "Piotr, thank God you were here. I just told them to call you and ran out of the office."

Daniel Vladimirovich tried to calm down.

Rudzhin laughed his deep bellow. "What a night, eh? Come on, Daniel, admit that you had fun." Rudzhin took his friend into a huge bear hug as they walked into the living room.

The home was hot, airless, and dark. It smelled of age. It wasn't so much that the apartment itself was old, but rather that the inhabitants had long ago lost the energy to clean the plates, change the sheets, replace the lightbulbs, and scrub the bathrooms with the same intensity as before.

There was a sense that time had just stopped in the apartment.

"It was great fun yesterday," Rudzhin giggled on, once they were seated. "And everybody from the old gang was there. Misha looks twenty years older with his bald head, but he still drinks like a fish. And Bela, he looks happy with that young new wife . . ."

Rudzhin stopped in his tracks. He had noticed that his friend Daniel wasn't listening. Piotr did a U-turn in the conversation. "Daniel, I'm all ears. I got the message that you wanted cigarettes. That's enough for me to know that something is up."

Daniel Vladimirovich Uggin took a deep breath. He started right in. "Something has happened at work, Piotr. Something really worrying. I need to tell you about it."

"You can tell me anything, friend. It will stay with us. Can I help fix this problem? "

"Listen, listen. I got a call from Viktor Zhironovsky this morning. It had to be serious if Zhironovsky himself was calling me. He's never done that before. And it was the strangest conversation."

Uggin proceeded to tell his friend everything. Oversleeping. Zhironovsky's three calls. His tough warning about taking orders only from him. Volga Gaz's computers already registering diminished gas speeds in the trunk pipelines to Ukraine. And, finally, the clincher. That by midnight, Uggin would have to shut the compressors down.

It took ten minutes to tell the story from start to finish.

"So, when the gas slows to between one and two cubic meters per second, I am supposed to shut down the gas flow into Ukraine. Stop it completely," Uggin had concluded.

Piotr Rudzhin let the last line hang over the old living room, like a blanket of ash. He reached over to his pack of Marlboros and lit a cigarette with a single, determined stroke of a match. Smoke slowly seeped through his nose. Daniel's arm stretched out for the cigarettes too.

Piotr Rudzhin got up and paced slowly to the far window of the living room. He looked out and took two drags from the cigarette. The ash burned hot. After a few moments of silence, he spoke.

"So what? Just do it," Rudzhin sentenced.

Daniel Uggin was aghast. He couldn't believe what he had just heard from his friend.

"But? But?" Uggin sputtered, realizing that he was repeating himself. "Piotr, are you sure about this? For seventy years of Soviet rule, foreigners took us seriously only because we had a nuclear arsenal big enough to destroy the United States and a military big enough to march into Europe, right?"

Uggin took a breath before continuing.

"Fifteen years ago, we Russians decided that we no longer wanted to be the world's principal adversary. We were on our way to becoming Europe's new, dynamic partner. There have been mistakes, sure. But we've come a long way from where we started just a few years ago. Don't you worry that shutting off the gas—tonight—could turn the clock back?"

He wasn't finished. Everything that had crossed his mind since speaking to Zhironovsky now came pouring out.

"You've known me a long time. I'm good at the gas transportation business, not the political discussion business. The numbers are clear; by 2030, Europe will import two-thirds of its gas from Russia, as compared to one-third today. For the twenty-five EU members, dependence on our gas will rise from fifty percent to eighty percent. When I shut that line down tonight, apartments in Paris, factories in Dusseldorf, and churches in Rome will feel the effect in two days. And what about the Ukrainians? For all practical purposes, they have no heat source other than our gas in the middle of winter."

"Daniel Vladimirovich," Piotr spat out, spinning away from the window. "This is bigger than you. Just do what you're told."

Daniel's expression of shocked surprise must have made an impression on Piotr Rudzhin because he suddenly stopped his chastising scold. Rudzhin knew Daniel well. Uggin never thought about politics; he was a mechanical idealist. Daniel's engineering mind loved machines and calculations. If Daniel was having doubts about Zhironovsky's orders, it could only have been because Daniel had not understood the deeply patriotic reasoning behind the chairman's commands.

Piotr's expression changed. A bulb lit up in his mind. Actually, what had crossed Rudzhin's brain was less a thought than the realization of an opportunity. Daniel's friend smiled. The more Piotr considered the notion, the better he liked it.

Right then and there, Piotr Rudzhin had made a lightning-fast decision to recruit his old schoolmate. He knew Daniel Uggin was a patriot, the son of a decorated general, the grandson of a Russian hero. Russia ran through Daniel's blood. It had taken only a few seconds for Piotr Rudzhin to become convinced that some well-delivered patriotic words and a few hints of economic enticement would be enough to convince Daniel to join him in Moscow's cause.

He pointed to a chair.

"Daniel, let's talk about this for a moment," Rudzhin said quietly, his tone now gentle and mentoring. "Try to think bigger. You must understand that many of us in Moscow are seriously concerned about our country. Think back. In the past fifteen years, we have lost fourteen republics that were previously part of our nation. It takes time to rebuild. And meanwhile, relations with the West are getting tense. They say our television news programs are government controlled. They whine that our elections are not democratic enough. They don't want us in the World Trade Organization. They don't like how we handle Chechen terrorists who murder our children."

Rudzhin stubbed out the cigarette in the ashtray. It smoldered on.

"They complain, pretending to be disinterested bystanders to our domestic issues. But just how innocent are they? The British harbor our criminal oligarchs and refuse to extradite them. The Americans refuse to buy our gas or oil unless we allow their companies to participate in the exploration— their vice president says we use oil and gas as 'tools of black-

mail and intimidation.' Perhaps they don't care to remember
that they are far less subtle—after all, the Americans blackmail and intimidate with their military, their guns, and their
precision-guided bombs."

He had more to say.

"It's not only the Americans and the British, though. The
French are so afraid of energy dependence on Russia that
they are willing to coddle the Arabs in Algeria—the same
Arabs who are eating them from the inside, like a cancer.
The Germans complain that our cheaper gas is supporting
governments that abuse human rights, like our friends in
Belarus.

"Don't they use their banks, their companies, and their
armies to leverage their interests? We have resources too,
Daniel Vladimirovich. We have riches. What is wrong with
using our assets to make friends, do business, and protect
our interests?"

Daniel Uggin had never seen his friend like this. He had
listened to Piotr's speeches on road improvements, his pet
issue while a member of the local parliament. But this was
the first time Daniel had ever heard Piotr Rudzhin speak like
a national politician. He was impressed.

"Think about it, old friend." Rudzhin was going on.
"Americans can invade Iraq. France sends troops to the
Ivory Coast. Germans have military combatants in Kosovo.
Sure, we are one hundred and forty-one million Russians.
But many of our citizens are still poor and uneducated. We
need people like you to help us. Work with us; tomorrow,
after you turn your valves off, let's talk about other things
you and I can do together. Like old times, eh?"

Daniel was intrigued. But he had questions.

"Should we be responsible for freezing the Ukrainians
and slowing down the economy of western Europe? How
smart is that? Won't we just push all of them to go elsewhere
for their gas in the future?"

Rudzhin laughed and slapped his friend on the knees. The
spark in Rudzhin's eyes had returned.

"I'm going to tell you something in confidence. Nobody
will let it go that far. It's just a warning. It's a little spitball

from across the border to remind friends that sometimes they become too impolite. It's a way to ask them—tell them—to settle down and play nice. It will be over soon."

Piotr Rudzhin stood up and smiled broadly. He played with Daniel's hair on the way to the door. Rudzhin could see that Daniel was interested.

They embraced each other again in the doorway. "Call me tomorrow, Daniel," Rudzhin whispered in his ear.

Daniel Vladimirovich Uggin shuffled back to his car. He felt better. Piotr had made him understand the broader context. And somehow, the mere fact that Piotr was at his side provided Daniel with a balm of reassurance.

At 4:30 P.M., he opened his office door to tell Svetlana not to pass through any calls. Jerking his mouse forward to cajole his computer to life, Daniel logged back on to the managers' site of the Volga intranet. He once again checked the metering for pressure on the Urengoy-Ushgorod pipeline. The gas was running a full 85 percent below normal levels.

Daniel Uggin took one deep breath. Only one. He looked for and found the three boxes on his computer, interspersed at ten-centimeter distances along the pipeline's image. These represented pumping and compressor stations in his district—the cybernetic distances translated to the geographical reality of one station every seventy or so kilometers.

His mind paused one last moment to marvel at the sophistication of a modern energy system. In the past, each pumping station had to be manned by a duty clerk who manually turned the pumps' engines on and off. These employees no longer existed. Nor did the valves to turn off the flow of oil through the pipeline. All those things belonged to yesterday's technology, as old as black-and-white movies. Today the gas was controlled by his computer. There were no valves to turn, no switches to flick.

He clicked on the first box and a dialogue box jumped onto the screen. He had two choices—to run a systems analysis on the pump or to shut it down. He chose the second. Daniel Vladimirovich Uggin did the same operation for the remaining two pumping stations.

All that was left now in the Urengoy-Ushgorod pipeline was the remaining gas in the twenty-three kilometers from the last pumping station to the Ukrainian border. It wouldn't last more than a couple of hours.

Daniel Uggin wiped the sweat from his forehead with a tissue. He knew that something big had just happened. Something really important. But at that moment, in the reflected light of his computer screen, there was no way he could have known that this December afternoon would become marked forever as his life's inflection point.

After this day, everything would change. His life, his work, and his marriage.

GERMANY

Nearly naked, Blaise Ryan looked at her reflection in the antique mirror above her room's commode. Almost unwittingly, her eyes roved just left of the mirror and were caught dead center by the stern stare emanating from Princess Karolina von Hessen's two-hundred-year-old portrait. The princess's pale, serious face and small, beady eyes looked down at the suite's temporary occupant in stern disapproval.

For an instant, Blaise thought of throwing her lacy black shawl over the gilded gold frame of the painting, but then decided it wasn't worth the effort. Blaise pulled her red hair back in a tight ponytail. She allowed just a couple of front strands to swivel diagonally across her gray eyes.

Notwithstanding Princess Karolina's aloof gaze, Blaise always liked her occasional visits to the Hotel Hessischer Hof. She loved the hotel's serious worldliness and its Biedermeier furnishings, most of which were still owned by the family of the princes of Hesse. "I'll teach you how to do 'sexy,' Princess," Blaise muttered as she purposefully left the breast-level closure on her starched white shirt unbuttoned. The shirt was a favorite. Somehow its cotton managed to expand and contract with each curve of her still-lithe thirty-six-year-old body.

Satisfied with what she was seeing in the mirror, Blaise looked around and winced at the hurricanelike situation of the bedroom. But this was no time to tidy up; it was 6:00 P.M. when she walked down the hallway toward the elevator. It would be up to the efficient German housekeepers to return some order to the suite during the evening's turn-down service.

She was glad to have gotten out of California's electricity mayhem. The blackouts were over—for now. But Blaise was particularly grateful to get away from the unrelenting headlines and hurling accusations that had become steady fare in the crisis's aftermath. Throughout the twenty days of full or partial blackouts, she had worked on two or three hours of sleep a night.

As the vice president of communications for the World Environmental Trust, California's moment of pain had been a unique opportunity to advocate for a new energy policy—for once people would be listening. Her job had always been polemical; she was more than accustomed to fighting politicians and energy companies. Blaise's fights had never lacked urgency, but they had always seemed a tad theoretical—conservation, sustainable development, water management. Yet the past weeks had shaken her to the core.

She had felt woefully inadequate as lines of television and radio journalists had appeared at her office's threshold seeking interviews. It had been hard to talk policy and regulatory standards when supermarkets were closed, banks were shut, and offices and schools were locked. Everyday life for California's fifty-plus million citizens had been radically altered—over two thousand people had actually died—because of her country's inability to face its energy addiction. She had labored to sound determined and relevant for journalists doing pieces on "the aftermath." But for the first time in her life, her crusade for the environment had seemed nearly immaterial when compared to Californians' daily suffering.

Blaise had needed a break badly; Germany was the perfect antidote. It felt like light-years away from the mess in her home state.

And her trip could not have had a nobler purpose, thought Blaise as she gave the porter two euros for hailing a taxi. Few people merited this effort more than her best friend, Anne-Sophie Perlmutter, and Anne-Sophie's magnificent father.

Not even her own parents got this treatment.

Anne-Sophie's dad, Hermann Perlmutter, was about to celebrate his seventieth birthday, a date the elderly gentleman's only daughter had begun planning long ago. In a well-organized conspiracy, Anne-Sophie had planned to secretly fly her family from their home in Russia to Germany for the celebration.

Hermann's wife had passed away just before his daughter left for high school at the age of fourteen. The surprise party was the least a daughter who lived so far away could do for her father.

Anne-Sophie had told guests months ago to save the date. Blaise Ryan was just one of the invitees from the far-flung corners of Hermann Perlmutter's life. The guest list was varied, reflecting the genial nature of a man whose entire existence revolved around his passionate love for his family, his job, his life, and a good soccer match. It included the waiter from his favorite neighborhood bar where, on Sundays, Hermann watched the games of his beloved Bayern München team. Hermann's longtime boss, the recently retired, fifteen-year head of the taxation department of the German finance ministry, would be there. So would friends from his university days who were still in daily contact a half century later.

Many of Anne-Sophie's friends—young people thirty or forty years his junior—had been touched at some point in their lives by Hermann's interest and friendship. None more so than Blaise Ryan.

Blaise had met Anne-Sophie in ninth grade at the Geneva International School, an elite international baccalaureate lakeside academy that accepted a select number of day students and even fewer, mostly ultra-rich, boarders.

The third floor of the school's old mansion had been the girls' area, populated by a multitude of nationalities. The academy had boasted an unusual number of Turkish girls from Istanbul's European neighborhoods. It had been hard to keep up with their daily changes of Versace, Gucci, Valentino, and Pucci outfits. Boys, on the other hand, had been corralled in a building on the far opposite side of campus— it was the headmistress's outdated view that physical separation would hinder teenage sexual encounters.

The males generally had been less ostentatious in their material exhibitionism than the girls. Somehow the guys, even the rich ones, had preferred old blue jeans and plain white T-shirts. Shehu Ali Kindabe, the Porsche-driving eighteen-year-old son of the sultan of Sokoto, Nigeria's highest Islamic authority, had been the single exception to this rule.

Blaise Ryan's San Francisco–based parents had been the epitome of the successful high-technology couple. Her mother had been the senior corporate vice president at Tabernacle Technologies; her father, the CFO of Star Microsystems. A lot of intelligence and passion had blossomed in the household, but there was precious little time for parenting. As soon as eleven-year-old Blaise developed an affinity for choir, her parents had jumped to enroll her as a boarder in London's School for Artistically Gifted Children. Blaise had sung for three years, had become tired of the repetitiously rote chorale instruction, and had petitioned her parents to transfer her to a regular international school. As London's international school had no slots, Blaise had ended up in Geneva.

Blaise glanced over at the taxi driver's license and noted more than four *c*'s in his unpronounceable Eastern European name. She thanked the Lord that the taxi driver's Croatian or Slovenian ancestry impeded any conversation in English. The quiet gave her time to lean back in the seat and remember the first time she'd met her German roommate, Anne-Sophie. She had gotten on her tiptoes to give Anne-Sophie her first formal European peck on each cheek. Blaise had considered Anne-Sophie a strange combination: the body of a lanky basketball player and a face like a porcelain doll. The two girls had shared a room for three years. During that time, a friendship was born that would be tested by time, distance, and events. The sisterhood of the Geneva International School was glue that still bonded them impressively years later.

Anne-Sophie had always been different from most of the other students at school. She had been far more serious about her studies. From the beginning, Anne-Sophie had felt a responsibility to prove her worth to her classmates, teachers, and, most important, to the school's administration, which had accorded her one of the few available scholarships. Anne-Sophie was from a middle-class German family—her father a senior civil service tax inspector with Germany's Ministry of Finance—and had been unable to afford the upscale tuition costs of the Geneva boarding school.

As a result, Anne-Sophie had bonded with few students. Blaise had been one of the exceptions. The charm of the Californian's giddy brilliance and restless idealism had been impossible to resist. The two girls—one rational and studious, the other instinctive and irrepressible—became inseparable friends.

With Blaise's home so far away, there had been no way for her to return to the United States over short school breaks. Anne-Sophie had invited Blaise to come home with her to Frankfurt for the first long weekend in late October. That trip would prove to be the first of many visits to Hermann Perlmutter's home. Blaise had seemed to gravitate toward confidences with her best friend's rational and patient father over the ins and outs of her own mother and father's schizophrenic parental presence.

Treating him almost as a surrogate father, Blaise had ended up confiding in Hermann on a range of subjects: school, careers, drugs, and men. Blaise had confessed years later to a speechless Anne-Sophie that she had sought her father's confidential counsel on a suspected pregnancy that later turned out to be a false alarm.

Hermann had never told his own daughter about that conversation.

Blaise noted the taxi's crossing of the Main River and immediately began to pay attention. She recognized the surroundings. Warmth stirred inside as the taxi drove through Sachsenhausen, Anne-Sophie's neighborhood. Blaise remembered Anne-Sophie's stories about how much she had loved growing up in the old quarter. The neighborhood had been perfect for kids. It was a mix of elegant town houses and parks on the riverbank with lots of cafés and boutiques on the elegant Schweizer Strasse.

Blaise felt a strange but serene sense of coming home as the taxi pulled to a halt in front of the flowered garden of the Perlmutters' small home—after all, it had been years since Blaise last walked into the house.

Anne-Sophie had married Daniel Uggin and moved to Russia a decade ago. The two girlfriends had deftly used Blaise's myriad business trips to see each other with some regularity. Blaise had even taken Hermann out over the years to a couple of elegant, boozy dinners on a number of her trips to Frankfurt. But she had never actually been back to the Perlmutters' Frankfurt home.

Blaise let the warm feeling sink in as she paid the driver's fare. But the quiet introspection came to a quick, crashing halt as she heard Hermann Perlmutter's booming voice from the doorway.

"My California girl is here. So now we can really start drinking!"

The taxi drove away just as the Perlmutter clan came pouring out the door. She could see Anne-Sophie's tall blond silhouette bounding down the stairs. Hermann, slightly taller than his daughter, was next and nearly as fast. Now seventy, he had lost none of his athletic looks. Katarina, age nine, and Giorgi, age six, were right behind them. Blaise felt arms pulling her into embraces, and her ears filled with the sounds of kisses that landed on and missed her cheeks in equal numbers as she was swooped from daughter to father.

"Wait, wait. I'm not the one being celebrated here. This is

embarrassing," protested Blaise. Hermann and Anne-Sophie just laughed. Both knew that Blaise Ryan was never embarrassed by any sort of attention.

Finally, arm in arm, the three started back to the house. Daniel Uggin, Anne-Sophie's handsome, dark, Russian husband, was in front of the door. It had been ten years—at the wedding—since Blaise had last seen him. But in the past months, Daniel had been the subject of many long, late-night phone calls and worried e-mails between the two high school friends.

Blaise took a long look at Daniel. He seemed older, more serious.

"Nice to see you, Blaise." Daniel Uggin's smile was perfunctory. Distant. Then again, how could he not feel like an outsider in this lovefest?

She made a mental note to sit next to him at dinner.

The meal was wonderful. Anne-Sophie had arrived only the previous day, but that had been enough time to put together a sumptuous five-course feast crowned by Hermann's favorite warm desert, a chocolate soufflé with a Grand Marnier vanilla sauce. Bottles of champagne were followed by bottles of wine, which were followed, in turn, by bottles of schnapps. Each one of the twenty guests made more than one toast to Hermann's health and life. Blaise soon lost count of the raised glasses and wasn't about to be left behind. Jet lag had no effect on Blaise Ryan. At the supper table, she told dramatic stories about her environmental wars, asked impudent questions, and teased relentlessly to the delight of the guests.

Seated next to Daniel throughout the dinner, Blaise had used the punctuation of the meal's laughter and toasts to launch furtive glances in the direction of Anne-Sophie's husband. He seemed unusually somber. Rarely smiling, Daniel was a man physically present but mentally absent. His distance and disengagement were palpable, even toward his wife.

That wasn't how Blaise remembered him. At Anne-Sophie's wedding, Daniel Uggin had been the personification of warmth, especially with Anne-Sophie. Throughout the ceremony and the wedding's long dinner, his hand had never left hers. His eyes had never wandered far before returning to her reassuring twinkle.

Prior to arriving in Germany, Anne-Sophie had given Blaise warning of her husband's unusual behavior—defined by Anne-Sophie in one of her e-mails as a sudden and utter disinterest in anything other than his work. Seeing Daniel's removed soul in real life shocked Blaise.

Uggin's removed comportment was the only black mark on an otherwise perfect evening. This had been a night to celebrate Hermann; one look at his beaming face told Blaise that it had been a success. Few men deserved all this admiration more than this one, she thought.

After midnight, the guests slowly started fading away. When the last person walked out the door, Anne-Sophie sent her father upstairs with a kiss. She invited Blaise and Daniel to join her in the living room—as far away from the dirty dishes as possible—for a small glass of kirsch, a cherry firewater designed to melt away the toxic repercussions of a long dinner. Initially, the conversation was easy and light.

But all the pleasantries came to a screeching halt when Blaise asked about Russia. "How are things in Russia? It's a place I can never understand."

"What's so difficult about understanding us?" answered Daniel. "Do you think we're that different from you?"

If Blaise had known Daniel better, she might have been able to read the defensiveness in his voice.

"No, of course not." Blaise laughed. "It's just that Russia is a box of contradictions. Lots of money. Lots of poverty. Lots of sophistication. Lots of authoritarianism. It's a strange place."

"What are you talking about?" Daniel's voice now turned to frost. "Did you talk this way when you were in school with my wife? Grow up. Life is not perfect. Things are tough in the real world. There are enemies. Opponents. People who want to set us backward."

Blaise's face said it all. She was totally taken aback by the huge personalization of Daniel's attacking response.

"Please . . . please forgive me if I've offended you," Blaise stuttered.

Anne-Sophie stepped in. It wasn't right of Daniel to unleash an attack against an old friend. It was embarrassing. Maybe she would have felt differently had things been normal at home. Who knows? But a deep anger rose from within.

She reached out to touch her husband's arm. She enunciated gently. But firmly.

"In my little existence in Kursk, I don't see a lot of the big-city things in Russia. But I'm different from most people there because I also read the *New York Times* and the *Frankfurter Allgemeine Zeitung* online every day. Many foreigners—and many of them are friends of Russia—are worried that the promises of democracy and reforms are being disappointed."

Blaise now felt empowered by Anne-Sophie's defense.

"There is concern, Daniel," said Blaise, "that your country is being taken over by dark interests. The oil and gas industry and the government seem to be merging into a single, monolithic entity. And oil and gas monies are used for payoffs. For pressure. For foreign policy. For buying people. For politics. For power."

The veins on Uggin's neck became enlarged. There was no longer any way to stop the blowup. It had begun with Blaise's innocent, offhand comments and was now going over the edge with no warning, no flashing signals.

"Here you are, an American and a German, lecturing me on Russia," Uggin spat out. "You want to understand our history? Just look at what is happening in this living room. If you want to understand us, to interpret our desires and fears, all you have to do is eavesdrop on this conversation. Four hundred years of chiding, lecturing, wars, and condescension. We have had enough."

Blaise hesitated at first. But she couldn't stop herself. "Daniel, give me a break. No country is perfect. This is not about comparing one place with another. I'm an American and I live my life complaining about U.S. policies. Good Lord, I spent the last twenty-five days saying that the horror we Californians just went through was a direct result of our government's twenty-year lack of leadership.

"But open your eyes. You guys want to get rich without making anything. When is the last time you bought something with a 'Made in Russia' sticker on it? You don't make textiles. You don't make computers. You don't make cars. You don't make refrigerators. You just sell oil and gas to pay for huge numbers of government workers. After losing fourteen republics, the new Russia has a smaller population than the old Soviet Union. And yet there are more government employees today than there were under communism. More than half of Russia's middle class is employed by the state or by state-run corporations."

"If we are so inept," snapped Daniel, "if we don't produce anything, if we don't merit your attention, why the hell are Americans putting missile-defense structures in countries at our borders? Why does your press spend so much time criticizing us? Why are French troops in Chad or American troops in Iraq all right but having Russian troops near Estonia is a danger to worldwide stability?"

Anne-Sophie was having a hard time with his Russian defensiveness. "I love my life in Russia. I love my children, my neighbors, and my home. But why is it that Russians react to criticism by criticizing others? You have to see the bad things too. One hundred protesters were arrested in St. Petersburg last week. In most countries, protests of that size don't even make the newspaper. But in Russia the government can't even tolerate a hundred people with placards. Journalists are intimidated. From one day to the next, news programs that have been on the radio for years don't broadcast any longer."

Daniel Uggin shot up from the table, knocking down his empty glass. "Anne-Sophie, this is a personal affront to me. You have been living in my country for ten years and suddenly I've discovered that you seem to hate it. Where has this come from? Are you so angry that Volga Gaz has made me a busy man and that I'm at home less than in the past? Remember, the company you find so dangerous is now providing you with a much better life. Instead of appreciation, you and your school friend are attacking my country, my job, and me.

"I'm going to bed," Uggin declared. He looked at Anne-Sophie and raised a warning index finger in the air. "And I expect you to get up now and come with me."

She got up, but was going nowhere.

"Daniel, please sit down," Anne-Sophie said, her voice flat to restrain the incredible surge of bitterness. "You know better than anybody that since I was eighteen years old, I've spent whatever few years of my short life fighting the blind greed of multinational corporations. They use people, abuse the environment. They are oblivious to everything but profit. And Volga Gaz is a multinational corporation on steroids, Daniel. In a year, Volga Gaz will be the publicly traded company with the world's highest market cap. It's just paying for the worst habits of the Russian State.

"I'm glad you are happy working for them." Anne-Sophie was punching out the words. "But don't ask me to admire the company just because it pays your salary."

Daniel Uggin and his wife were standing up in Hermann Perlmutter's living room. Blaise was unsure whether to stand or remain seated. The scene was horrible.

"Please sit down," Anne-Sophie begged him.

Without a word, Daniel Uggin turned around and walked up the stairs to the bedroom.

**FRANKFURT
JULY 14, 12:40 A.M.**

Blaise looked over toward Anne-Sophie, aghast. All she could see was Anne-Sophie's glassy stare.

"I'm so sorry. This is my fault. I had no idea that I was going to ignite this storm. You had told me that things weren't going well. But I never imagined this. Please, Annie, forgive me," said Blaise.

Blaise had known that, after nearly a decade of envy-generating, problem-free matrimony, Anne-Sophie's marriage was suddenly suffering a dark turn. Anne-Sophie's increasingly alarming calls and e-mails had given her ample warning. But marital difficulties were one thing. Daniel's aggressive attacks were an entirely different matter.

Anne-Sophie's eyes looked toward Blaise's.

"Can I walk you back to the hotel?"

"Are you nuts? It's at least an hour's walk and it is past midnight. You've put this amazing party together. Let's get you to bed. I'll call a cab and we'll talk tomorrow."

Anne-Sophie laid her hand on Blaise's arm. "No, I want to talk to you now. I want to walk."

Blaise quickly understood that this was not a polite gesture. Anne-Sophie needed to unload.

The two women left the house and turned left. They walked slowly.

"Blaise, the last thing I want to do is burden you with problems. But I don't know who else to turn to."

Blaise stopped cold in the street. The breeze whipped her red hair across her face.

"Talk, girl," she ordered.

Anne-Sophie sucked in a breath of the cool evening air.

"In a way, I'm glad this happened. I had already told you a lot in our phone calls. But now you have seen for yourself what I'm going through." Anne-Sophie paused a long moment before continuing.

"Ten years ago, I made a choice. I knew what I was doing. I agreed to become a foreign wife in a tough place because I felt with all my heart that Daniel was the man I wanted to spend my life with. You know the beginnings, Blaise. I moved to Kursk and Daniel took a job with Volga Gaz.

"For nine of the ten years of our marriage, we were a happy family. Katarina and Giorgi were born. We lived comfortably. There was no way to save on Daniel's Volga Gaz middle-management salary. But ours was a family that thrived on closeness and intimacy as internal combustion. We weren't concerned about money because there was never any realistic expectation that meaningful resources would ever enter our lives."

Blaise felt her soul tightening. She could see where this was going. Daniel had a lover. Goddamnit. How could Daniel do that to her friend!

"It isn't what you are thinking, Blaise. I don't think he has another woman." Anne-Sophie smiled weakly. They knew each other well.

"Over the past year and a half, things have changed. Slowly at first, then faster. Daniel was suddenly called to Moscow by Piotr Rudzhin. Remember, you met him at the wedding; he was Daniel's best man. Rudzhin has become a government big shot. When Daniel returned from Moscow, he announced that he had been promoted to district director. Two deputy directors were hired under him."

"So what's the problem? All this sounds good," Blaise said, interrupting her friend and instantly regretting it. Anne-Sophie needed time to get it out.

"I was ecstatic too. We got a new house. I drive a Saab now. It all seemed too good to be true. But within months, Daniel began to travel—first a little and now up to three weeks a month."

Anne-Sophie described the changes in her husband. When he was home, Daniel often spoke to Piotr Rudzhin, long evening conversations, and then went to bed exhausted, hardly able to speak a word to the woman who only a few months earlier had been his best friend. Anne-Sophie felt her husband was sliding away from her.

"Wait, wait," Blaise interrupted, irritated by what sounded like the prototypical whining-wife syndrome. She could hardly believe it. Anne-Sophie was a strong woman; what was wrong with her? "Anne-Sophie, you can't blame him for throwing himself at his job. I'm an expert. I know what it is like to be obsessed by work."

"No, you wait, Blaise. Let me finish."

For the second time, Blaise regretted her inability to keep her thoughts inside her head.

"Okay, sorry. I will shut up. I promise."

"It's not the absences," Anne-Sophie continued quietly. "It's the fact that the man has changed. He has become obsessed with Russia—you just heard it. He spouts conspiracy theories about how the world wants to damage his country. He didn't even want to come to my father's party and only changed his mind at the last minute."

For a moment, Anne-Sophie stopped walking.

"No, Blaise, I'm not a simpleminded, complaining wife. I'm a wife who is worried that her husband is mixed up in something beyond his control. And within just a few hours of our arrival here in Frankfurt, things became worse, not better."

"What happened?" asked Blaise. The two women resumed walking past Schweizer Strasse's shop windows.

"Two things. On the airplane, I saw Katarina and her father quarreling across the aisle about his passport as the plane was descending. He was organizing his papers and I guess Katarina took his passport to look through it. She's nine—she'll grab anything. I couldn't hear what they were saying. But she told me later on in the bathroom that her father had gotten angry when she asked why he had a Bolivian visa. That's when he grabbed back the passport."

Anne-Sophie saw the quizzical look in her friend's eyes.

"Blaise, look, maybe you need to be married to understand this. But for ten years I had a husband who told me everything. And now I discover that he is something very different. Bolivia? Give me a break, why would he not tell me this? Sure, he told me that he was traveling beyond Moscow—to St. Petersburg, Yekaterinburg ... even as far as Vladivostok. But why would he keep Bolivia a secret?"

"Maybe he will tell you this weekend?" Blaise did not sound very convinced.

"So here is the second thing." Anne-Sophie rolled on, ignoring Blaise's vacuous comment. "Within an hour of arriving at my father's house, he makes a call. At first, I was really irritated because I thought he had used Hermann's phone to call Russia. Christ, my father is a retired tax collector. He can't afford extra expenses. So I went to the phone and punched redial. It was a local number. The woman on the line answered in German, 'Mr. Pieter Schmidt's office.'"

Now Blaise was looking far more interested. They had

stopped at a crosswalk to wait for the traffic light to change. It had turned green but Blaise wasn't moving.

"Does he know anybody here?"

"He knows my family. That's it."

"Who the hell is Pieter Schmidt then?"

"I don't know, Blaise, but before dinner this evening he told me that he was going to go shopping for a present for my father tomorrow morning, at ten A.M. He didn't ask me to come. He didn't ask me what I thought he should buy."

Blaise didn't know what to say. So she asked an obvious question.

"And you are thinking that he didn't really come to Frankfurt for your father's celebration, but rather to see this Pieter Schmidt, right?"

"Yes." Blaise thought it was unusual that Anne-Sophie was not looking at her. She was staring out into the night's dark distance.

Then Anne-Sophie's reluctance hit her.

"And you want to know who he is, right?"

"Yes."

"And you are asking yourself how you accomplish this, right?"

"Yes."

"And you've concluded that the only way to do it is to follow your own husband."

Anne-Sophie looked at her. A single tear was streaking across her left cheek.

"Yes."

Blaise took a deep breath.

"Here is what we're going to do, sister. You are not going to follow him. I will. If he catches you behind him, it's the end of your marriage. If he catches me, it will be serious, but you can steadfastly say that you knew nothing. You can blame me for ruining our friendship. You need to keep open a viable option to deny that you had anything to do with this."

"I can't ask you to do this," said Anne-Sophie. Her green eyes were drier, but sadness made them glassy and opaque.

"You haven't asked. I'm telling you what is going to happen tomorrow. I'm doing this. Not you.

"We're not discussing it anymore," Blaise Ryan added, her voice jagged with unmistakable finality.

FRANKFURT
LATER THAT DAY, 12:05 P.M.
HOTEL HESSISCHER HOF

It was midday when Blaise again gave the Hessischer Hof's porter another two euros for hailing a taxi.

Blaise had awakened early that morning in her hotel room, filled with doubts. The instant her eyes opened, she had begun to regret her promise of a stupid sleuthing investigation of her best friend's husband. In the early light of day, Blaise had wondered if she was getting involved in something that was none of her business—even after last night's blowup.

But, regrets or not, she had gone through with her detective work. One thing Blaise Ryan's friends and enemies both agreed on was that she was loyal to a fault. There was next to nothing Blaise Ryan wouldn't do for a friend.

As she gave the taxi driver the Perlmutters' street address, she thought about what she had discovered. Thank God her heart habitually overrode her brain. The past four hours had completely changed her mind; she was now certain that Anne-Sophie's suspicions were well grounded.

Blaise should have known better than to doubt Anne-Sophie. Too often in the history of their friendship, Blaise had been the one to request help. Over a decade ago, Anne-Sophie had closed her eyes and figuratively jumped off a cliff for Blaise. It had been both a physical and a mental leap into a void. Blaise had recognized always that her friend's participation in her flamboyant plan had cut deeply against the natural grain of Anne-Sophie's quiet character.

Yes, she was glad to now be the one offering assistance to Anne-Sophie.

Blaise tilted her head back and smiled inwardly as she thought back to Anne-Sophie's role in the best day of her career in the environmental movement.

It had been thirteen years ago. In Madrid.

She replayed the headlines in the *International Herald Tribune* with a grin: "Protesters Take Over the Madrid Meetings of the International Monetary Fund and World Bank." There had been a picture—front page, above the broadsheet's fold—of Blaise, Anne-Sophie, and four other women hanging from the sparkling ceiling of Madrid's conference center. The photograph had spoken a thousand words.

The six female bodies had hovered in midair, immobile and twisting at the midpoint between the convention center's floor and ceiling. Suddenly a whooshing sound had filled the room and a huge canvas had fallen from the ceiling and had remained suspended aboveground, held aloft by the rope each airborne body held in her hand.

The speech by the World Bank president had skidded to a midsentence stop. Not even the farthest person in the room could have failed to read the huge banner as the sun shone on its gigantic print.

THE WORLD BANK DOESN'T ERADICATE POVERTY
IT CREATES INEQUALITY
HARMS THE ENVIRONMENT
AND MAKES PEOPLE POORER

Blaise remembered the bedlam that had ensued. Security personnel had run back and forth in the conference hall, but nobody had seemed to know how to get up to the ceiling. Police had poured in. Some of the ministers, fearing a terrorist attack, had gotten up from their chairs and started moving toward the door. But the sight of the suspended bodies and banner was like a magnet. People moved, but nobody left.

The World Bank president had stuttered, trying to continue his address. The words had come out of his mouth, but were no longer being projected into the hall's audio system.

His voice had become a barely audible whisper. And yet suddenly another voice, that of a woman, had begun projecting loudly into the hall.

The protesters had cut him off and taken over the loudspeakers.

"My name is Blaise Ryan and I am one of the directors of the World Environmental Trust."

People around the room had looked left and right, desperately seeking the speaker. Accustomed to polished presentations, all eyes had gone to the podium, but all they could see was a small man tapping pathetically into a silent microphone.

Suddenly, the governors and ministers had realized that the voice belonged to one of the bodies hanging in midair above them. All eyes had zoomed upward.

"We are here today not to interrupt your meeting, but to use your meeting as a megaphone to address the citizens of the world's wealthier countries. Forgive us the intrusion, but we had no choice.

"Our fight is with an international institution financed principally by taxpayers from wealthy countries. By espousing policies that destroy the social fabric of many countries, this institution has failed. By aligning with corporations that profit from development by destroying the environment, this institution has failed. By fomenting a torrent of debt that countries cannot service, this institution has failed.

"We call on European, American, and Japanese voters to demand that their governments cease supporting the IMF and the World Bank."

The next day's *International Herald Tribune* report on the event had begun with the following sentence: "Today World Bank President Anthony Wolfberg must be asking himself, who in God's name is Blaise Ryan?"

Blaise smiled in nostalgia. Her eyes were closed and her head rested against the taxi's leather seat back. Of all her protests and marches, of all the press releases and television appearances, of all the polemics she had created throughout her life, that morning, hanging on the rope in Madrid with

PIPELINE   +   75

Anne-Sophie, was one of her fondest memories.

Right now, those reminiscences felt like a long time ago. Reality was not so warm. Blaise shuddered as she thought about what she would soon have to tell Anne-Sophie.

The taxi arrived in front of the Perlmutters' home just after 1:00 P.M. Her friend was waiting at the door. Blaise could tell that Anne-Sophie was anxious for news.

"Look, I started out by doing a favor for you, a favor I did not really believe in. And now, to my amazement, there is a connection with something I know a lot about. It's a very weird coincidence."

Anne-Sophie looked at her in astonishment. She had literally no idea what Blaise was talking about.

"Okay, okay. I know I'm not making sense. I'll start at the beginning."

Blaise took a breath. She was dressed in her trademark tight blue jeans and an open-necked azure linen shirt. The choker of small blue stones around her neck rose and fell with her respiration.

"As of nine this morning, I waited on your street in a taxi," said Blaise, pointing to the spot a hundred or so feet down the tree-lined road. "Unless you were dead wrong and he was just headed to the shops on Schweizer Strasse, I figured that I would need to have ready transportation. I asked the bellhop to find me a woman driver on the hotel's taxi line. She was Turkish. I handed her a hundred dollars and said that we were going to follow my husband because he was having an affair. She went on for five minutes about how all men should be stoned to death.

"Anyway, as you know, Daniel left home around nine forty-five and walked the two blocks to Schweizer Strasse and turned right. For a moment, it occurred to me that we were pathetically paranoid women. Here he was, ambling past the boutiques just as they were opening up. But, after a block, he looked around and raised his hand for a cab.

"Here's where it becomes just factual. He drove the twenty minutes into the city. He got out on Hanoverweg 12. It's a four-story building. There was no doubt about where he was going because the whole building is the corporate headquarters of Anfang Energie. There was a guard at the door, so I didn't go in."

"What else?" Anne-Sophie asked breathlessly.

"Nothing else. I didn't wait for him because I figured that he would want to get back quickly from his 'present-buying' expedition.

"But I found out something that is pretty important," Blaise added with staccato precision. She felt sorry for her friend; none of this could be easy. After all, she was reporting on the results of a detective enterprise that centered on Anne-Sophie's husband.

"I went back to the hotel, said good-bye to my Turkish lady, and walked to the Hessicher Hof's business center. I got on a computer and Googled Anfang Energie. They have a decent, but restrained, Web site. Pieter Schmidt, whose number Daniel called yesterday, is the CEO of Anfang. The company was started by his grandfather and it remains a private company.

"They have a long history of oil-exploration activities; they specialize in the former Soviet Union. Big investments in Kazakhstan, Uzbekistan, Azerbaijan. Those projects look to be years old, so they must have had pretty good contacts in Moscow or they would never have gotten into those places during Soviet times.

"But here is the clincher, Annie. Anfang's site is very proud of the fact that they are in the midst of their first large bid in Latin America. They are tendering an offer for a large project in Peru, called Humboldt."

She saw the recognition on her friend's face.

"Yes, the same Humboldt project that dominated my professional life for so many years. The same Humboldt project that got me into trouble after my stupid mistake in Peru. I had stopped following it closely when we lost the fight over the first phase. Don't you think it's a weird coincidence that this company is working on Humboldt?"

Anne-Sophie's eyes were a blank. Besides the odd connection with a project that had been near and dear to Blaise's heart, Anne-Sophie could not see what was so interesting about the Peruvian link.

"Come on, think about it. Your husband is a natural-gas engineer with a visa to go to Bolivia. I worked on Humboldt long enough to know that Peru and Bolivia are competitors in gas production. Why has your husband gone to see Anfang Energie? If they're the people who want to get Peru's gas to market, the Bolivians would be their diametrically opposed competitors."

Neither woman had any more answers. They were at the end of the line. Neither knew what to do or even what questions to ask.

But both were left with the overwhelming feeling that Anne-Sophie's marital difficulties had caused them to inadvertently discover something very important.

LIMA
AUGUST 1, 8:30 P.M.
THE PLAZA DE ARMAS

Senator Luis Matta's office was already streaked in darkness when Susana Castillo, the senator's thirty-four-year-old press secretary, walked into it for the second time in a half hour. Her message was the same. This time it was delivered with unusual terseness.

"Senator, it's eight thirty P.M. already, go home. You've had a week of this crazy pace—in at the crack of dawn and out in the dark of night. I know this is an important time, but it won't help if you get sick."

His suit jacket was off, the tie loose around his neck. But even after a twelve-hour day, the senator still cut a striking figure.

Luis Matta smiled a tired grin of appreciation. In addition to Susana, a few other loyal staff would be at their desks. He knew they would not leave until he left. This was loyalty at its very best. He was honored by it.

The senator got up. Slowly. Every day, a new ache seemed to spring up in his still-good-looking four-decade-old body. The pains were like garden weeds. One day here, another day there. None was serious, all were irritating. Now it was this weird pounding around the balls of his feet.

He shrugged off all the throbbing and knotting, attributing it to stress. He did not need a medical specialist to figure this out.

"What is the latest news from California?" Over the last month and a half, Matta had kept the television in his office on throughout the day. He had been transfixed by the California meltdown. Understandably so. The natural gas from his country could one day go a long way toward avoiding a recurrence of that tragedy.

"Our ambassador in Washington flew out there the day before yesterday. I was copied on his report to the foreign ministry. He was in shock. It's been six weeks. But signs of the calamity were everywhere. Burned-down houses from people who tried to cook with flammable liquids inside their homes. Cars still abandoned on the side of the freeway. Entire neighborhoods ransacked by looting. More dead than in the World Trade Center bombing."

Susana paused. "It's hard to imagine that this occurred in the world's richest country."

"Yes, I know," Matta whispered. "It makes what we are doing all the more important. I had wished that what happened in California would be a uniting factor. Something that would make all Peruvians understand how necessary Humboldt is."

Matta paused, a dejected smile on his lips. "That hope lasted about thirty seconds. Instead, it's all happening again, all the accusations, the name-calling, the hatred."

She was the only person on his staff to whom he opened up. She was his alter ego, sounding board, complaint department, personal advisor, and coffee companion. All those assets came in a package that also exuded a dark-eyed passion and a deep sense of humor that gurgled out in flashes of laughter and smiles.

Matta knew how lucky he was and winced whenever the occasional panicked thought of Susana's departure crept through his mind. He knew she might have to leave soon. Susana Castillo was an only child; her father had died a decade ago. Now her mother was sick with cancer. It would be only a matter of months before Susana would depart to take full-time care of her parent.

Matta ordered his brain to refocus back into the room.

"It's hard to believe this issue is so divisive. This is a big moment for Peru. Decision time is close. My meeting tomorrow with President Garzón kicks off the legally required thirty-day period. Next week the minister of justice submits the law to Congress. Our hearings start in one month. Seven days after that, we choose the operator. God, the next weeks will be a killer." Senator Matta was pulling his hand through his hair.

Matta got up from behind his desk and ambled over to look out his third-floor window to the wide plaza below. In the window's darkened reflection, his jet black hair, combed and fixed back with expensive sculpting foam, juxtaposed loudly with his broad white teeth.

The Senatorial Office Building was located just off Lima's famous Plaza de Armas. A cocktail of sights and smells, the imposing three-block square was a World Heritage Site. Much of Lima's history pulsated through the huge plaza. Inca temples had stood here. Spanish conquistador Francisco Pizarro had been assassinated on the square's southern corner.

Yet today, the Plaza de Armas was a mixture of colonial grandeur and lowly poverty. Among the magnificent cathedral and the imposing government buildings, thousands of dark-skinned, indigenous salespeople milled about, hocking sticks of gum, shoes, pots, underwear—anything. At the square's center, congregating around the fifteenth-century bronze statue of a trumpeting angel, women wearing the traditional ponchos of highland Indians to protect themselves against Lima's August chill stood over huge vats of boiling water, cooking fresh corn on the cob.

The Plaza de Armas was a vast Wal-Mart for the poor, set on the stage of pompous architecture.

The Congress buildings were off to the left. Sixty-four million dollars had been spent to renovate the massive structures. Public reaction to the investment in heritage preservation was, as almost everything else in Peru, highly polarized. On the one hand, the work had been beautifully done, restoring the colonial grandeur of the buildings, to the delight of architects, historians, tourists, and, of course, its elected officials. On the other hand, the rebuilding had produced endless column inches of populist criticism about erroneous spending priorities.

Stop whining about the press, thought Matta to himself. Journalists couldn't help themselves. After all, they had had their fairness genes surgically removed at birth.

He walked over to the handcrafted, tropical-wood coffee table to collect some stray papers he would just have to finish at home. There were no photos in the room other than the photograph of Alicia and the girls at a playground. Unlike many of his colleagues, his office did not boast a collection of pictures of himself with other senators, presidents, actors, and sports figures. He hated the pavilions of narcissism so common in most politicians' offices; they were little more than dark caverns filled with pictures of them with this or that important person. Luis Matta found the spectacle grotesque.

Susana looked at him in admiration. She was keenly aware that she was working for a politician skyrocketing to the top. Already editorials and commentaries in the newspapers were speculating as to whether Luis Matta would run for president in a year and a half. She also knew that next month's hearings on the second phase of the Humboldt project were a key inflection point for Luis Matta's political career.

"It's exhausting to even think about another round of Humboldt hearings," said Susana. "I've hardly recovered from the fight about phase one two years ago." She regretted engaging him in conversation, but it was just one of those things that staff working for powerful politicians the world over could not resist. They knew the boss had to go home, had to rest, had to disengage. Yet an important politician's senior staff was psychologically unable to pass up an opportunity for one-on-one political engagement.

Luis Matta stopped on the way to the office door. Susana

was right. The first round of hearings had been controversial enough. Humboldt was Peru's biggest-ever infrastructure scheme. Named after the meandering German explorer of the nineteenth century, Humboldt's first phase had been an engineering feat—a twisting and winding pipeline designed to pump and transport millions of cubic meters of natural gas from an extraction point in the pristine Amazon jungle, across thirteen-thousand-foot Andean peaks, through a desert, and into the capital.

And a few months ago, the gas had begun to flow. At Lima's gates, Humboldt's natural gas was now being converted to electricity that switched on the lights and turned over the machinery of the majority of Peru's homes and factories. Humboldt had been one of the most polarizing issues Matta had ever worked on. But it was already proving to be a success.

"Twenty-four months have gone by and the feeling of irreparable polarization still sticks in my gut," grimaced Luis Matta. "I have never seen two sides of any issue—environmentalists and social activists in one corner, business and government in another—ripping each other apart with such hatred and venom. Now it's going to start all over again."

Phase two was Humboldt's second pipeline, this one leading northeast. Two companies—Constable Oil from Oklahoma and Anfang Energie from Frankfurt—had prequalified to bid on the construction of a line to bring Peru's leftover gas to a spanking-new, modern port. There, next to the Pacific Ocean, the companies would liquefy and load the gas on ships headed straight north, up the continent's coastline, to quench California's unending thirst for energy.

It would mean billions in income for Peru.

Like the last time, Matta's job would be to ensure that the new Humboldt pipeline had the best possible technology and used the most modern practices. His duty would be to slow down the coalition of ministers, bankers, and investors who sought to build as fast as possible, while accelerating the environmentalists and social activists who wanted to slow the project under an avalanche of impact studies and analyses.

That meant moving forward with all deliberate speed,

marrying the project's implementation schedule with world-class experts to ensure that the work would be completed safely and with the greatest possible respect for the environment.

Essentially, an impossible task.

Susana wished that she hadn't engaged the senator in a rehashing of the project and its poisoned atmospherics. She knew now where he was going. She recognized it from a mile away. Once he got started, he could not be stopped. The recriminations always ended up with a frenzied and furious assault on the American woman.

"And then there was Blaise Ryan," said Matta, right on cue. "I felt the wrath of the proponents and the detractors; both were horrible to each other. But, of the four billion citizens on this planet, none is more unreasonable and unpleasant than Blaise Ryan.

"I saw Ryan last night on CNN with that excellent Los Angeles correspondent who reported during the California crisis," Matta continued, referring to Anna Hardaway. "At least I'm not the only one in her crosshairs. Ryan was laying into the Laurence administration, saying that this president was following in the timid footsteps of past governments and refusing to take measures to move the economy to alternative fuels. As usual, her criticism was devastating."

Matta paused and pursed his lips in a wry smile. "I felt sorry for Laurence. But at least Ryan was taking a break from attacking me. It won't last long. I'll soon have to face her again."

His frustration was rhetorical. He had no choice but to oversee the divisive process again. There was no way to avoid it; the gas held too many promises for his country.

Susana took his elbow and moved him closer to the office's door in the hope of whisking him out. Wisps of her black hair were swishing and swinging against her neckline. Her smile revealed perfect teeth.

"Senator, how is it possible that somebody with such thin skin has been so successful in politics? You can't allow yourself to be dragged into a psychological funk every time somebody calls you a name. You are doing your job—

making sure that Peru takes advantage of its huge natural resources. Don't pay attention to all the noise."

Matta felt a rise of irritation. She wasn't out there—in front of cameras and reporters, staring at the packed, cavernous hearing room. He locked in on her dark eyes.

"Susana, I know you mean well, but telling a politician not to pay attention to what others think is silly advice," Matta said, immediately regretting the acerbic, icy tone. She didn't deserve this. Back off, he told himself.

Astonishingly, the thirty-four-year-old Susana kept Matta's cold stare at center keel of her pupils. She did not back down an inch.

"Senator, I was there. I was at the hearings. I saw how they treated you. And I know what that woman did. We all know that Blaise Ryan will stop at nothing to get what she wants. I know that she offended you deeply. I know you don't deserve that type of animosity."

Susana sucked in a mouthful of air. "But it's high time you got over it."

Senator Luis Matta was taken aback by her bluntness. Ever since her mother had become sick, Susana's usually reserved recommendations to her boss had occasionally become laced with an acerbic, sour quality. Her criticism bothered him. Damnit, he did not want to get over his resentment toward Blaise Ryan. He enjoyed being angry and hurt about it. In a peculiar and perverse way, hating Blaise Ryan gave him even greater determination.

He decided not to engage. "Come on, let's go home. We'll have too much of the real thing tomorrow. Do me a favor, call Hugo downstairs and tell him to bring the car to the side door."

As he walked out into the darkened hallway, Matta stopped short. He chastised himself for having forgotten to ask about Susana's mother. Matta regretted how the crushing press of political life tended to drain away his ability to connect on a personal level.

"How is she?" Matta asked, turning around.

"The same, Luis. Thanks for remembering." Susana didn't have to ask who the senator was referring to. Her mother had been sick with lymphoma for over a year. The doctors had tried all the obvious chemotherapies, but nothing had worked.

"Her only hope is still the bone marrow transplant."

"When can that be done?"

Susana shrugged and turned away, not wanting him to see the lump in her throat. Her welling emotions were equal parts sadness and anger.

"It can't be done safely here; we just don't have the technology in Peru. And I don't have a spare million dollars. Believe it or not, that is what the bone marrow transplant and a three-month hospital stay would cost a foreigner without U.S. health insurance to do in Houston."

She looked straight toward him now, her eyes flashing anger. "It's so unfair, Luis. I love working for you—it's the most interesting job anybody could ask for. But do I need to remind you of the salary of a Peruvian senator's communications director? If I had gone to work for a Spanish bank or an American oil company, I might have had the money to pay for my mother's treatment. Or they might have helped me get my mother to treatment at their headquarters."

Matta walked back into his office feeling more than a twinge of guilt. Susana Castillo was usually a highly rational woman—the senator was sure that deep down she understood that he would do whatever he could to help. But in rare emotional moments such as these, he could feel Susana's desperation pointing in his direction, subconsciously accusing him of not having pulled the right strings or cajoled the right person to get her mother treatment.

He made a mental note to call the U.S. ambassador to see if there was any way to skirt the costs. He doubted it, but it was worth a try. He would also call some of his campaign's financial contributors; perhaps he could get a collection going.

Matta took Susana in his arms. There was little even one of the most powerful politicians in Peru could do to help his trusted advisor's mother.

Thank God he had at least remembered to ask.

LIMA
AUGUST 1, 9:00 P.M.
THE PLAZA DE ARMAS

Hugo Flores had been the senator's chauffeur for over ten years. Luis Matta had "stolen" him from his job at the Mercedes-Benz offices in Peru when the German car company's local, longtime manager retired. A small, dark sixty-year-old with a chiseled aquiline nose and elongated black eyes, Hugo looked like an artist's rendition of his Incan ancestors.

Hugo wasn't family, but his presence was comforting and familiar. He wasn't a friend, but Matta listened to his advice. Hugo had seen the ups and downs of Senator Luis Matta's political career.

As Luis Matta walked through the side door of the Senate building, his pupils adjusted to the spreading darkness outside. Eyes squinting, he finally made out a sparkling Pacific blue Mercedes diesel sedan. The car was not new, but given Hugo's years of employment with the German car manufacturer, it just seemed to rejuvenate and regenerate under his care. This diminutive Peruvian, with barely a high school education, had even taught himself to speak and read German.

"I must read the owner's manual in its original language," Hugo had reasoned during his job interview with the senator.

When the senator had offered him the position a decade ago, the question of a Mercedes was an absolute precondition. "I'm honored, Senator, to work for you. But it has to be with a Mercedes. I will not drive anything else," Hugo Flores had dictated to a younger Luis Matta. Most people would have been turned off by a driver laying down the law. Not Matta. He was amused and impressed; it demonstrated that this was a man who knew what he wanted.

Hugo was now waiting for the senator beside the Mercedes, the rear passenger door open.

Luis Matta felt a passing twinge of exasperation. For the last ten years, he had punctually reminded Hugo at least once a week that, when alone, there was no need to stand outside and open the car door. That totaled about 520 reminders to Hugo that Luis Matta was not the type of employer who required that level of fastidiousness.

Hugo had never paid the slightest attention.

"Hugo, I may have mentioned this before," said Matta, with a small grin, denoting the initiation of the well-worn exchange between the two men. "There is no need for you to open—" The senator's voice of mock seriousness got lost in the baritone of Hugo's deep, bellowing laugh, which was terminally silenced by the closing car door.

"Yessir," he giggled as he slid into the driver's seat. The "yessir" was meaningless. It was only an acknowledgment that he had heard the senator, not that he would abide by his instructions.

Hugo slowly advanced the car out of the curving driveway. The Mercedes slid by the building's main entrance just as two well-dressed men—one pale and blond with elegant European facial features, the other larger, darker, and with an unkempt stare in his dark eyes—walked out from behind the large main doors of the Senate building.

Luis Matta recognized both immediately. The smaller man was Ludwig Schutz, Manager of Anfang Energie's Latin American operations. Since registering his company's official bid for the Humboldt pipeline business, Ludwig had become a regular visitor to Matta's Senate office. It was part of the game. The senator was the senior player in the Humboldt decision, so it was Schutz's business to drop in, solicit the senator's views, and ask if there was anything else he needed. Matta would carefully answer that his support would go to the best and least expensive proposal. They both knew how to dance this jig.

The larger, dark man now dialing his mobile phone was Oleg Stradius. Matta had met him only once before, with Ludwig, in his office. He had said next to nothing during the entire hour-long meeting. His business card identified him only as Anfang Energie's head of security.

Matta felt a creeping irritation. Clearly, the men had been inside the building lobbying other senators. He had no doubt they were offering money and influence to whoever would listen—and he knew that a few of his colleagues were not beyond playing one company against the other to see what they could squeeze out. But, for the most part, Luis Matta was certain that his committee was not on the take; its thirteen senators would decide upon the best and most responsible course for the country.

Winter had arrived in the southern hemisphere. As Lima's cold, damp air hit the visitors, Senator Luis Matta could see the weather-driven shudder that crawled across Ludwig Schutz's nearly translucent skin. Against his better judgment, Matta found himself feeling sorry for the two energy company executives. Foreign visitors seemed to always forget that Lima was a foggy, chilly place.

"Hugo, pull over. Let's offer these gentlemen a ride," Matta ordered.

Hugo quickly maneuvered the car to the sidewalk. The senator rolled down the window and smiled at the German, trying to raise the collar of his business jacket.

"Ludwig, you look like you need a rescue."

"Senator, it is a pleasure," he said, snapping to attention with German formality. "I appear to have forgotten that Lima's winters are nearly as unpleasant as those in Stuttgart.

"We seem to have lost our driver," Schutz added, explaining his forlorn situation.

No surprise. Notwithstanding the capture of the last of the leaders of the Shining Path, Peru's murderous Maoist terrorist group, ten years ago, the police still did not let any unofficial cars anywhere near the Senate building. Visitors were always in front of the building frantically working their cellular phones to find drivers or taxis parked blocks away.

"Forget it," Senator Matta answered. "Jump in, I'll take you."

"Senator, you are too kind. We are going to our hotel, the Miraflores Park Plaza," said Ludwig Schutz with obvious relief. But the smile did not last. The German's face quickly stiffened, worried that he was trespassing on unwritten diplomatic lines by inconveniencing a senior senator.

"Please do not worry yourself, Senator. I'm sure we will

find our car," he said, trying to correct his too-quick initial acceptance of the senatorial ride.

"Come on, Ludwig. Don't be silly! My house is right on the way. Hugo can drop me off and then take you to the hotel," Matta said, getting out of the car to allow the two European energy executives to get in.

This was too much for Hugo. One thing was his boss's protestations about his overanxious cares when he was alone. Quite another was seeing the senator open the car door for two foreigners. Hugo was out of his seat like a rocket.

Matta lived in the posh Miraflores neighborhood, less than fifteen minutes away. The hotel was just ten minutes farther down the road. Though it was late and Matta wanted to let Hugo go home, it would be no more than a short detour. At this time of night, there was no traffic.

The three men settled uncomfortably in the Mercedes's backseat. Oleg Stradius took the place of a person and a half. The man was like a celestial black hole—his huge presence created a massive gravitational displacement, but it was impossible to peer inside the dark core. Except for polite pleasantries, he said nothing.

Ludwig Schutz was clearly accustomed to the larger man's reticent silence. It did not seem to bother or distract him one bit. Ludwig Schutz and Luis Matta chatted amiably about world news, avoiding any mention of the project. It was a show in elegant restraint, two men brought together by the one thing they were not talking about.

Hugo got off the highway and entered Miraflores. Traffic tightened up as they passed the neighborhood's beautiful, large, tree-lined square. Along the streets, the cafés and bars were chock-full of young customers, draped over each other, smiling, smoking, drinking. Matta thought to himself that it was hardly different from what he used to do as a teenager, but somehow young people today exuded a sexual energy that he couldn't remember from his own youth.

The streets off the huge plaza led to the hotel and restaurant district. One after the other, elegant cars and well-dressed diners awaited entry into Lima's restaurants. In the last fifteen years, Lima had become a gastronomic mecca.

A new generation of chefs, graduated from European schools, had thrown off the stranglehold of French gastronomic rigidity. They had reinvented Peruvian cuisine with high-intensity sophistication. The food created by this courageous band of nationalist culinary pioneers in the capital's ultramodern new restaurants had become increasingly creative, turning traditional Peruvian menus into mouthwatering cascades of foams, reductions, and fusions.

As Hugo turned right onto the side street that led to Matta's house, Ludwig straightened out, arched his spine, and twisted his body so that he was nearly face-to-face with the senator. His back squarely blocked his colleague. It was a carefully calibrated gesture of intimacy.

"Senator, forgive me for ruining your generosity by talking shop," Ludwig began, with his usual formality. "I must tell you that I am concerned about what is happening in Bolivia and how it will affect our business in your country. As you know, Senator, your countrymen like to believe that the Bolivians will never get their act together quickly enough to pump their gas out of the ground."

Matta nodded. There was no doubting how true that statement was. Neighboring Bolivia had considerable reserves of natural gas that could compete with Peru's exported gas. Furthermore, its gas fields were more accessible, making extraction easier than his own country's far-off Amazonian resources. This meant that if Bolivia were able to get its gas out and transport it to market, it would be cheaper than Peru's. If that were to occur, the exciting prospects of Peruvian gas would swivel from opportunity to crisis.

"You see, Senator, Peruvians rarely give Bolivia a second thought," Ludwig continued, now warming to his business. "Your newspapers dismiss Bolivia's landlocked poverty. Your politicians shake their heads disapprovingly at its political mess. Your businessmen are appalled by Bolivia's constant state of upheaval. And your elites think that the ultranationalist peasant movements next door will never allow the sale of Bolivia's 'national resources' to foreign capitalists."

Ludwig adjusted his spectacles slowly. "Most Peruvians just don't believe that Bolivia could get its gas to market before you. Am I right, Senator?"

Matta hesitated for a minute and concluded that this was one of those questions that did not require answering. Ludwig was obviously trying to say something important and Matta was not about to interrupt. With a block to go, the car was nearly at his house and Matta did not want him to stop. The senator wished for a way to send Hugo a secret message to slow down.

"I say this with the utmost respect, Senator, but this image of Bolivia may be condescending and, more dangerously, it may be completely wrong." Schutz was now staring at Luis Matta intensely. He knew he had Matta's full attention.

"You also know that Russian oil companies are very interested in expanding their Latin American operations?" Again, it was more a statement than a question, another rhetorical query that did not need an answer. And Schutz did not wait for one.

"Well, Volga Gaz has already completed its agreement with the Bolivian government and it's my understanding that negotiations are well advanced with Chile to take Bolivia's gas out through Chilean ports," Schutz finished.

Matta's entire body briefly froze. He heard his own heart rhythmically pumping as his mind slowly coiled its neurons around the implications of Ludwig's message. If the Bolivians got their gas to market first, there would be no room left for Peru's gas—it would still take time for the Americans to build the necessary off-loading facilities.

California's recent energy debacle had amply proved how desperate the United States was for more gas. But no matter how great the need, the U.S. market just could not absorb both countries' gas right now.

Luis Matta wanted to ask one, three, five, a hundred questions. But he ended up asking none because the car braked to a smooth stop in front of the senator's house. Luis Matta's throat cleared to instruct Hugo to wait a second, but he was too slow. Hugo was already out of the car and opening Matta's door. The three men climbed out of the backseat and shook hands on the narrow sidewalk in front of the senator's home. The conversation was over.

Schutz looked at Matta intently as he held his hand.

"You are kind to have rescued us from the cold, Senator." He drew closer. Now he was whispering.

"Speed, sir. For all of us, you need to move the decision along faster."

LIMA
AUGUST 1, 9:15 P.M.
MIRAFLORES

Senator Matta waved Hugo off. The chauffeur usually waited until the senator entered the house. Not today; Luis Matta needed a minute alone.

He drank in the hulking beauty of the old Spanish-colonial home. The big house was wonderful. Matta loved to stare at its bold facade of concrete steps leading to twelve-foot-high double wooden doors, each adorned with three-hundred-year-old wrought-iron knockers in the form of fists.

He knew he could not stand outside alone for very long—Alicia and the girls would be waiting for his arrival to eat dinner. Yet he could not go in just yet. The drive with Ludwig Schutz needed to be thought through.

So Luis Matta allowed his orderly mind to slowly return to neutral under the large mango tree that shaded the house's entrance. The leaves and the hanging fruit swayed slowly—the mangos would be ripe for eating in less than a month—as the Pacific wind accelerated its chilly, humid, nightly encroachment on the city. Standing very still outside the house, Luis Matta could literally feel the tree's limbs groaning, in and out of the streetlight, as their shadows crossed his face.

Matta disdained disorder of any type. Physical disarray was enervating, but mental confusion was unforgivable. He breathed slowly and forced the pieces back into order. If what Schutz said was true, losing the Humboldt export market to Bolivia would signify forsaking a decade of development in

Peru. It automatically meant reduced investments and fewer jobs, schools, hospitals, and social services.

And, let's be honest, it would also be the end of "Mr. Humboldt's" political career, he thought.

His slow, analytical dissection of Ludwig Schutz's news came to a screeching stop when a shriek from inside the house pierced the quiet creaks of the straining mango tree.

Matta had been caught. Outed. Found, in front of the house, by the dual cascade of living and breathing chaos that was his personal creation.

His two daughters.

"Papi is home!" the renewed yell again surged from inside the house and pierced the night. Matta couldn't help a big smile from crossing his face as he threw the mango tree a farewell glance, half expecting it to topple over from the force of the fast-expanding, high-decibel shock waves. Everything else, including Ludwig Schutz, would have to wait.

The large wooden doors opened and out poured two rushing nine-year-old girls, giggling mercilessly. Their radar was locked on his elegantly dressed clothes. Laura and Sara were fraternal twins—Matta always insisted on being specific about this because one neither looked nor behaved anything like the other. Most people refused to believe they were twins at all.

"Papi"—Sara's body hit the senator first—"I have to tell you something."

This phrase was used indiscriminately to introduce both the gravest as well as the silliest of monologues. It was a universal attention-getting statement. Matta leaned over and listened intently.

"I went to Carlota's house after school today," Sara said, in total rapture, referring to the new girl in her class. "And I have to tell you something."

"Yes, I know you do." There was no use reminding her that she had just said that; he asked the gods of patience for their blessing.

"She is boring," Sara declared. "Boring," she repeated, in case her father had not understood.

Matta had ceased long ago to be shocked by the capacity

of little girls to emit vast declarative statements that completely contradicted vast declarative statements emitted just twenty-four hours earlier.

"But, Sara, yesterday you told me that Carlota was 'incredibly nice' and that you wanted to invite her to your birthday party."

"Papi!" she groaned. "Papi!" Laura joined in in a plaintive tone.

Both were instantaneously irritated by his confusion. Nine-year-old girls did not believe that consistency was a requirement for interesting conversation. Yesterday Carlota was all right. Today she was boring. What was important was why Sara found her boring, not the fact itself. And the senator was ruining the story by asking stupid questions. What was his problem?

"You know why she's boring?" asked Sara. "Because she wanted to do homework rather than play. Can you believe that?"

He couldn't. Sara was right. Carlota was boring.

The three of them walked in the door, still being held open by one of the retinue of housekeepers employed by his wife, Alicia. She was new; Matta couldn't remember her name. Father and daughters were all raveled up in each other's arms and they had to disentangle to fit in the doorway. Matta smiled at the nameless woman at the entrance.

Alicia was sitting alone in the living room. The public rooms of the old Spanish-colonial house were huge. There were a total of five sofas and three coffee tables assembled decoratively around Alicia. The color scheme was a sedate green-gray—just how teak looks right before the sun bleaches it irretrievably. Large Persian carpets padded the room in tranquility.

She sat barefoot, in the corner of one of the sofas, legs curled under her, drenched in the light of a Roche-Bobois chrome standing lamp that swiveled over her and then pointed its impeccable silver light downward. She was reading *Architectural Digest*.

Alicia was dressed in a light blue blouse and tight blue jeans. Her pair of suede ankle-length boots was neatly arranged on the floor, next to the sofa. At forty, Alicia's body was still thin and tight from daily exercise with a trainer who came every morning at 8:00 A.M. Seeing her husband, she swished away a strand of shoulder-length sandy brown hair that had fallen over her slightly elongated, almond-shaped Incan eyes. Matta rarely tired of seeing her strange mix of European and Indian features. Often the mix of blood fell short. In Alicia, the races merged to perfection.

"You're late," she chided.

Good God, thought Matta. More criticism. This day will never end.

LIMA
AUGUST 1, 11:00 P.M.
THE MIRAFLORES PARK PLAZA

Just a few hours after Senator Luis Matta sat down to dinner with his family, an international conference-call operator was connecting three countries. It was 7:00 A.M. in Frankfurt and 8:00 A.M. in Moscow.

"The board will come to order," ordered a high-pitched voice with a clear German clip. Pieter Schmidt was Anfang Energie's CEO and chairman. His grandfather, Wilhelm Schmidt, had founded the company six decades ago.

"Thank you for your punctuality," Schmidt continued. "As usual, the board will speak in English to facilitate communication. We continue to prefer no interpreters or any other outsiders on the call.

"We expect a quick agenda today—I am sure that is a relief to our colleagues in Lima where it is the middle of the night." The nasal voice allowed some humor to drift into his ordered speech. "First there will be a discussion as to the final disposition of our purchase. Then there will be a report from our Latin American operations. I do not expect us to go for more than an hour.

"I give the floor to Professor Alfred Weiss, our corporate chief legal counsel."

"Thank you, Mr. Chairman, and thank you, gentlemen,

for participating," began the lawyer. Like any good lawyer, his delivery was in a monotone. No highs. No flats. No emotion.

"I have ended my research and consultation on the question put to me at the last meeting of the board a week ago," continued the lawyer. "Under German law, we are a private company. Thus we are not bound by the regulatory constraints faced by public companies traded on the Frankfurt stock exchange. As you know, public companies must report all 'significant events' that could affect the share price of the stock. Technically, we do not face the same requirements."

A deep baritone interrupted the professor. The accent was Russian, unmistakably that of the chairman of the board of Volga Gaz. "Good, this is as I thought. And this is the way it must be."

"Mr. Zhironovsky, with your permission, allow me to finish the report," Professor Weiss retorted quickly. Anybody who had had anything to do with Professor Alfred Weiss knew how much he disliked interruptions. But everyone on the call noticed that, behind the lawyerly tones of the attorney's disdainful certainty, the pitch of his voice rose by a few octaves. He was clearly nervous.

"I said previously that we were not technically obligated to report the sale of Anfang Energie. I use the word 'technically' because there are clear precedents in German law that, when the purchaser is a foreign entity, disclosure is a far more preferable and transparent route. There are a number of regulatory entities—the German Federal Trade Commission and the Parliament's Energy Committee have been particularly activist in their approach to the sale of German energy entities to foreigners—that could initiate an embarrassing and unwanted investigation after the fact."

There was a split second of silence. The tinkling of ice in a glass resonated loudly into the conference call. Professor Weiss was taking a sip of water. He cleared his throat and continued.

"Even if you believe that regulators would not have sufficient legal arguments to review our transaction, there are political reasons that might spur scrutiny from the German government. Clearly, recent events in Russia, particularly in the energy sector, have caused some worldwide concern. Obviously, I am referring to the events in Ukraine less than two years ago. Rightly or wrongly, these experiences have raised the level of caution of Western governments and investors about doing business with Russia. The last thing we want is to have our politicians debating whether the Russian government is extending its reach into Germany through the purchase of our company."

"Professor Weiss, we have your opinion. Thank you. It is enough," snarled the Russian voice.

"One last thing," Weiss tried, but he could not finish.

"No more!" This time Viktor Zhironovsky was shouting. "Four months ago, Volga Gaz paid eight hundred and ninety-four million euros for Anfang Energie and you were happy. Members of this board all made a lot of money. You are also continuing to make huge salaries to run the company. If there were doubts about the sale, you had a long time to consider those before signing the documents. It's too late. My decision is not to make public any news about the sale. If any one of you has a problem with that, you can resign now."

The seven men on the conference call all stared at their speakerphones. Nobody spoke. Anfang Energie, a German family company of sixty-three years, had been sold one hundred and eighteen days ago. The men on the call had, indeed, made millions. But today was the first time they realized—truly understood—that they were no longer in charge.

Pieter Schmidt was not about to allow his board of directors to get into a useless fight with its new owner. He knew what to do. Germans were highly formal and legalistic people. Even if Viktor Zhironovsky was now the final arbiter, he knew his board's Teutonic sensibilities would be assuaged by some official act. Hopefully, Zhironovsky would not interrupt.

"I put this issue before the board now," Schmidt intoned. "The motion is to indefinitely postpone any official disclosure of the sale of Anfang Energie after hearing counsel's opinion that there are no mandatory reporting requirements.

"I vote yes," he added quickly.

Slowly, one yes after another crawled across the phone line. Pieter Schmidt smiled inwardly. He had hoped Zhironovsky would stay silent. This was not the moment for him to gloat. Schmidt moved the agenda forward quickly.

"Very good. Now we can go on to a report from Latin America."

Ludwig Schutz cleared his throat.

"We are pleased with our progress, gentlemen. It is our opinion that we will be able to report with some certainty in the next weeks. The decision-making process is in its final stages and culminates with Senate hearings on Humboldt's phase two in thirty days. Senator Luis Matta is in charge of those hearings. There is considerable press coverage of Humboldt and this will accelerate the public pressure for a quick resolution."

Schutz was not finished. "The hearings will also be noticed in Bolivia. I spoke to Mr. Uggin, our colleague in charge of Volga Gaz's negotiations in Bolivia. I understand that he could not be on the phone tonight but he has asked me to tell you that the Bolivians are nervous about Peru's timing. Like me, he believes that the faster the Peruvians move, the more quickly the Bolivians will be spurred into action. He has assured me that the events in the next days should give them a good reason to speed up their negotiations with Chile."

Schutz was concluding. "Mr. Uggin and I are in complete agreement. Both sides are unwittingly headed toward a race against each other to approve their respective gas deals. And that, gentlemen, is exactly what we want."

Ludwig felt that he should be getting some praise from his board of directors at this point in the conference call. None came. He was a little disappointed.

Zhironovsky's voice interrupted. "Where are the Americans? What is Constable Oil doing?" The Russian was asking about Anfang Energie's competitor for the Humboldt contract.

Perfect, thought Schutz. That is exactly the question I want. The call was suddenly looking up.

"Mr. Zhironovsky, we have access to excellent intelligence about what is happening in Senator Matta's office. This knowledge permits us a real-time understanding about what is going on. There are some risks associated with buying information, and it is, of course, not something we do with pleasure. But the pressures of the business require some—how shall I say—extraordinary actions.

"Already, our investment has yielded information worth gold," continued Schutz in a steady tone. "We now know that Constable Oil delivered a twenty-year term sheet to the Peruvian government for the export of the liquefied gas. This is less than our offer of twenty-five years. We also heard about their proffers of royalty payments."

"And?" growled Zhironovsky.

"They are lower than ours, sir."

"Thank you, Schutz. This was an excellent report. The trap is set," boomed Zhironovsky's voice. "If things in Peru go as well as you promise, Volga Gaz will control the principal South American gas fields in thirty days. The Americans are counting on this gas to avoid another California; they won't know what hit them. In a month's time, Russia will have the ability to turn the gas flow on and off at will. This power can allow California a sigh of relief or it can spread the shortage to the entire western part of the United States.

"Ah yes, thanks to all this good work, the world will shortly become a very different place in America's eyes," Zhironovsky concluded with a chortle.

The accolades were finally coming, thought Ludwig.

**MOSCOW
AUGUST 2, 1:00 P.M.
THE CDL RESTAURANT**

The CDL restaurant, at 50 Povarskaya Street, was less than fifty yards from the Barrikadnaya Metro stop. But as he maneuvered his Saab 9000 Turbo past the parked procession of chauffeured vehicles and toward the mansion's statuesque entrance, Deputy Minister of the Interior Piotr Rudzhin knew that the restaurant's proximity to the subway was meaningless. Nobody having lunch at this restaurant would be arriving by public transportation.

Czentraliny Dom Literatov—or CDL—translates roughly into Central House of Writers. A place of legends. The building itself was over a hundred years old. The structure had once functioned as the one-time meeting place of Moscow's Freemasons, but was later inaugurated as the club of the Russian Writers Guild, frequented by many famous Russian writers such as Alexander Pushkin and Leo Tolstoy. The restaurant played an important role in Mikhail Bulgakov's anti-Soviet satire *The Master and Margarita*. In the novel, the devil pops into CDL with his cat for dinner and defines the place as "inexpensive and not bad at all."

Inexpensive! How times can change a menu price, thought Piotr Rudzhin with irony.

Today, the restaurant no longer fed the literati. Instead, it now catered to the deep pockets of Moscow's nouveau riche. In the decade and a half after the fall of the Soviet Union, the country had generated millions of unregulated, undeclared, and untaxed rubles for a whole generation of bureaucrats turned oligarchs, young mafia families, and fast-moving politicians. While the nation's countryside still bore the stigma of imprisoning large swaths of Russians in an unbreakable cycle of rural peasantry, its cities were exploding with wealth and opulence.

Piotr Rudzhin irritably slowed his car behind two other expensive vehicles in line for CDL's valet service. His Saab 9000 was a wonderful vehicle, but he normally wouldn't be caught dead behind the wheel in Moscow's horrendous traffic. Rudzhin instantly regretted having allowed his chauffeur the day off to attend his daughter's wedding.

As Piotr awaited his turn for the restaurant's valet, his bad-tempered thoughts were interrupted by the vibrations of his cellular phone. He reached into his suit jacket's inside pocket. It was Uggin.

"Daniel, I've been waiting for your call. Where are you?"

"At the airport in La Paz. I board in fifteen minutes."

"Right on time, old friend. I'm about to meet the big man for lunch in five minutes. Quickly, what can you tell me?"

"It's done, Piotr. I've got copies of the papers." Uggin was making an effort to control his obvious elation.

"That is great news. Fabulous. I'll tell Zhironovsky." Piotr Rudzhin could not believe how well his decision to recruit his school-yard friend was working out. "How hard was it?"

"It was a mess. These Bolivians have more inferiority complexes than a teenager with acne. You would think that the royalties from Volga's gas contracts would have them dancing with joy. No. Instead they were offended because the Chileans were charging them too much money to transmit the Bolivian gas to Chile's northernmost port. Who the hell do they think they are? They're a little landlocked country—they should feel lucky that the Chileans agreed to allow the gas to cross the border."

"You told them that?" Rudzhin was momentarily aghast.

"Of course not, you dope," laughed Daniel Uggin. "You would have been proud of me. I did two round-trips to Santiago to negotiate a better transfer price for Bolivia's gas. It was like Kissinger's shuttle diplomacy for Middle East peace. Anyway, I got the Chileans to agree to a thirty percent discount off their original offer. And I told the Bolivians that was as good as it was going to get. Bottom line, Piotr, the Bolivians signed. The gas will go to a liquefaction plant in Antofagasta in northern Chile."

Uggin's good news had Piotr Rudzhin in a broad smile.

"I heard that Schutz was very upbeat on the conference call three days ago," continued Daniel. His voice became serious as he allowed a pause to invade the phone line.

"Piotr, you trust this guy, right? I mean . . . Schutz isn't Russian. Do you believe him? I have to go back in a week. Do you want me to go to Lima and make sure?"

Rudzhin marveled at his friend's brimming-over energy. Rudzhin had suspected that Daniel's quietly efficient, technical background would be an asset. But Uggin's involvement was working out a thousand times better than he'd imagined. He could never have guessed that he would have to be curbing Daniel's enthusiasm just eighteen months after the discussion in his parents' apartment in Kursk.

"No, Daniel. As much as I would like to have one of us look at the situation in Peru personally, I think we have to stay out of that country. It would be a grave risk to awaken any Peruvian suspicion of Russia's involvement."

"Okay. As long as the old man and you are comfortable, I'm fine too. In that case, I'll see you tomorrow evening. Is our lunch with Zhironovsky still on for Friday?"

"Absolutely. Fly well, Daniel Vladimirovich."

Rudzhin hung up the phone. His lips curled into a smile as he considered Daniel's transformation, nothing less than amazing. In a way, it was much like his own makeover, which had begun upon his arrival in Moscow.

Just a few years ago, Piotr Rudzhin was an average up-and-comer from a provincial town. Elections to the Kursk Oblast Duma had made him an important figure in the neighborhood, but the local legislature had been insignificant on a national scale. Now, less than seven years later, he was powerful and wealthy—an increasingly commanding figure in Russian politics—and sought out as an ally by the oligarchy.

Rudzhin leaned forward and took a quick look in the rearview mirror. A blond lock curling over his left eyebrow needed some attention. Swinging the hair backward with a shove of his index finger, he again thanked his lucky stars for Viktor Zhironovsky. Without his powerful mentor, Piotr Rudzhin would not be who he was today.

Viktor Zhironovsky and Piotr Rudzhin's close relationship was a perfectly Russian friendship. It reflected modern Russia's peculiar political balancing act. On the one hand were the infinitely rich oligarchs and robber barons, handpicked by Boris Yeltsin's family, who had profited from the sale of Russia's state-owned assets. To the untrained visitor's eye, these men and women had created a new, post-Soviet Russia that was modern, sleek, and sophisticated.

On the other hand was the infinitely brutish Russian State. There was nothing modern—or even post-Soviet—about the Russian government. The bureaucracy—filled with mediocre officialdom—still understood only the language of fear and raw muscle. The top echelons were controlled by the Siloviki, politicians from the "power ministries"—the old security and military apparatus—who under Yeltsin had formed a de facto higher-level inner cabinet.

Moscow cocktail parties were hyperopulent affairs in enormous reconverted homes that served only Johnnie Walker Blue and Cristal champagne with hors d'oeuvres made a few hours earlier in one of Alain Ducasse's Paris restaurants and flown to Moscow on a private plane. No matter how festive, the parties ended up as swollen rivers of gossip about the endless jostle for power between the oligarchs and the Siloviki bureaucracy. The two sides were caught in a perpetual cycle of fear, retribution, blackmail, and corruption.

Those with the money and the power distrusted and despised each other, but the system remained in balance. That's why it worked. Politicians did not seek executive positions in the private sector. And few self-respecting college-graduating Russians of any intellect or education would remotely consider a career in government.

Crossover between the opposing ends of the Russian fulcrum was rare and unnecessary.

In Russia, professionals and businessmen "partnered" with politicians and government leaders. Sure, this public-private partnership was a lucrative one—the business baron ensured a good life for the politician; the politician guaranteed contracts for the businessman. But, though the burden of corruption was a heavy one, the alliances between those in and out of government successfully protected Russia from the grabbing hand of foreign interests. Oligarchs and government fought incessantly among one another, but they agreed on one thing: Russia always came first.

Moscow was a city of power, important friends, big decisions, beautiful women, and high intrigue. Once you had it in your hands, it was hard to let go, thought Rudzhin. But he knew that political life in Moscow was like dancing on a knife's blade. For most of his seven years in the city, Rudzhin had never been entirely certain of his position.

Until Viktor Zhironovsky had invited him last winter to Courchevel, the exquisite Alpine ski resort nestled geographically in the three-corner border that united Italy, Switzerland, and France. On that day, all his doubts dissipated. Rudzhin knew he had made it.

Piotr remembered his elation at having been chosen as one of Zhironovsky's guests at his famed alpine home in the French Savoy region. The "chalet" was a huge fifteen-thousand-square-foot eclectic structure. Art Deco meets Alpine mountain chic. It had indoor and outdoor swimming pools, a ballroom, a Jacuzzi that accommodated ten relaxed bodies, a cinema that sat twenty-five guests, a bowling alley with three automated lanes, and its own indoor ice rink. A large bronze sphinx guarded the oval-shaped, gravel-strewn driveway to the house.

More than five thousand Russians flocked to Courchevel every January, after Orthodox Christmas, to admire the panoramic view of the snow-capped glaciers. Those Russian visitors had either their own homes or stayed in hotels such as the Cheval Blanc, where the inn's suites went for more than $20,000 per night. The hotel organized a yearly "Millionaire's Cup" ski competition on the town's most difficult slopes. Zhironovsky's guests were regularly invited to participate. It was always an amusing day, with caviar served at the finish line. This year, the first prize had been a beautifully designed white-gold box with meteorite fragments found in the Central African Republic.

Courchevel had brought home for Piotr Rudzhin the meaning of a recent *Forbes* magazine article about Russia's moneyed elites. The magazine had counted sixty billionaires in Russia today, forty-seven of them residing in Moscow. Amazing for a country that only fifteen years ago had no millionaires, let alone billionaires.

The thoughts of Courchevel fizzled away as the CDL's parking attendant rapped on his car's hood. Irritated by the interruption, Rudzhin stepped out of the car, handing the keys to the valet attendant dressed in a gray morning coat, white bow tie, and top hat. As the keys exchanged physical possession, Rudzhin lifted his right index finger in front of the young man's face and wagged it very slowly; barely a millimeter separated Rudzhin's fingertip from the attendant's nose.

The implication was crystal clear: Hell hath no fury if something amiss were to happen to the Saab 9000.

Piotr Rudzhin entered the magnificent building and checked in with a matronly woman dressed in a cheap-looking black-and-white polyester outfit. Rudzhin noticed the white footwear often favored by Eastern European working women. The shoes were a type of cheap, open-toed ice-skating boot with a broad wooden heel and a wide open toe through which one half of the woman's foot, clad in raw-colored, semisheer hose, jutted out.

This was the footwear of choice for legions of Russian hotel maids, waitresses, bartenders, store clerks, and any other woman who worked standing up. These boots were everywhere. Oddly popular and spectacularly ugly.

The poorly dressed woman at the CDL's door carefully scanned a list of names written in cramped pencil strokes. Though he clearly saw his name, Rudzhin resisted the urge to lean over the counter and point to his luncheon host's name, next to his. This rude imposition would have caused a bureaucratic faux pas of galactic dimensions.

Finally she grunted. Her eyes revealed disappointment. Unfortunately, here was yet another man she would have to let in.

"Mr. Zhironovsky is waiting for you in the Pushkin Room. This is on the second floor on the far left side."

Piotr Rudzhin buttoned his blue Armani suit's middle closure and walked slowly through the bottom floor's bar area—a lounge with sofas and love seats, antique balustrades and opulently displayed heraldry—toward the marble staircase. It was hard for the customers lining up at the caviar carriage—staffed by a gesticulating white-aproned man in a tall chef's hat—not to notice the towering, athletic figure with the thick shock of blond hair walking by. Even the caviar chef, constructing perfect centerpieces of beluga, blini, and pelmeni favorites onto oversize plates, noticed that he momentarily lost his customers' rapt attention.

Rudzhin strode up the stairs and looked around. One floor's decoration outmatched the next. Piotr could not help but marvel at the high ceiling and wooden balconies that seemed to circumnavigate the second-floor dining room. Tables covered with white damask linens were set with enormous care. Three wineglasses, one water glass, and one vodka glass horizontally crowned each setting of Christofle tableware.

One of the waiters silently greeted Piotr Rudzhin with a formal bow and stretched out his white-gloved hand in the direction in which they were to walk. Rudzhin followed and stepped back as the waiter opened the second-to-last doorway at the end of the large dining hall.

The transition was amazing. The large dining room gave way to a small space of resplendent elegance. A chandelier made of thousands of individually cut pieces of crystal swooped low over the round lunch table exquisitely set for two. Next to the dining table were two leather couches, each a warm brownish red. The sofas were separated by a low mahogany coffee table on which rested a large picture book of St. Petersburg's architectural treasures, an ice bucket with a chilled bottle of Beluga Gold Line vodka, and a cigar humidor stocked exclusively with Cuban Lonsdales. The walls were of warm wood paneling. Borodin's *Nocturne* played softly over acoustically balanced speakers.

Viktor Zhironovsky, one of the richest and most powerful political men in Russia, sat comfortably on one of the couches. A lit cigar was resting in the ashtray as the chairman of Volga Gaz nonchalantly swept through the day's *Izvestia,* one of Russia's most respected newspapers. A few years ago, the newspaper had been the first acquisition in Volga Gaz's burgeoning media empire.

"Am I late?" Piotr Rudzhin immediately blurted out, concerned to see the chairman so clearly comfortable. He must have been here for at least a half hour, Rudzhin thought. He glanced at his watch.

"Calm down, Piotr. I'm early. I try to be here before all my lunches. It's one of the few places where I can find both a little beauty and a little quiet. And you know what? There is another benefit. This room has no cellular reception. If they want me, they have to drag themselves over here!"

Rudzhin was not entirely sure who "they" were. But, obviously, whoever had a claim on the chairman's time was in danger of being put on the list of "them." Not a good list to be on.

Rudzhin went over and leaned down to greet the seated man with a kiss on both cheeks. Chairman Viktor Zhironovsky didn't have to get up. Notwithstanding Rudzhin's political successes, the gestures of respect would flow only one way in this meeting. Zhironovsky was the elder.

And infinitely more powerful.

Viktor Zhironovsky changed the subject. Though the informal tone of his voice remained the same, it was clear that he was all business now. "Tell me a little about life at the Ministry of Interior. What is the gossip these days?"

Zhironovsky poured a small amount of vodka for his guest and handed the tiny glass over to Rudzhin with a smile.

"Mr. Chairman, what could I possibly tell you that you do not know? You are being humble," teased Piotr, raising his glass to the chairman's health. He understood that this was Zhironovsky's way of testing him. His value as one of Zhironovsky's political understudies would increase if he was able to deliver some nuggets of information that the chairman did not have.

"No, Rudzhin, you would be surprised," Chairman Viktor Zhironovsky intoned modestly. "My life is becoming hostage to natural gas—price, extraction, transportation, delivery, export, distribution. All the time. Twenty-four hours a day, seven days a week. Of course, it's all important. But this wonderful underground gas of ours is an all-consuming affair. It would be nice to hear a little about other things."

Rudzhin smiled. He marveled at the chairman. Even when the two were alone, Zhironovsky could not stop working the network. He did a lot more than natural gas—Viktor Zhironovsky was building a company whose control and influence was extending beyond energy and into the media and politics.

Zhironovsky was the closest advisor to Russia's popular president Oskar Tuzhbin. There had long been rumors that Zhironovsky would be Russia's new president when Tuzhbin ended his second term in two years. In a particularly Russian twist on democratic government, the new buzz around town was that President Tuzhbin and Viktor Zhironovsky would swap jobs.

The younger Rudzhin admired the fact that Zhironovsky never took any information for granted. Like a shark in search of food, he was perpetually on the move.

"Let's see, Mr. Chairman. I can think of three things of interest from this morning. First, I got a good preview of the new crime statistics that will come out next Monday. Not a good thing, sir. The Militsiya report a nineteen percent increase in aggravated assault, a fourteen percent increase in robbery, a twenty-one percent increase in street muggings, and even a seven percent increase in murder. Our economy grows. The country is clearly more prosperous. But crime is going the wrong way."

"Christ," said Zhironovsky, shaking his head. "You see, I did not know that. The president thinks he can get away with blaming crime on Chechen mafias and gangs. But this won't fly. For God's sake, we are going to have to find a way to strangle the street crimes. People need to feel safe in the street. Thanks for telling me. I'll talk to the president.

"Okay, so what is the other stuff?" Zhironovsky insisted. He was impressed and wanted more. Clearly, Piotr was getting early warning access to important information.

"The lottery for the European Cup was held five minutes before I left the office. Dynamo Moscow plays Manchester United in Manchester for its first game." Rudzhin's wry smile showed that he was pleased with himself. He knew the chairman was a wild soccer fanatic and, given what had just been said about cell phone access in the restaurant, chances were good that Zhironovsky wouldn't yet have this information.

"Shit!" Zhironovsky reached for the newspaper, folded it into a tube, and whipped the leather couch. "How do we always get this bad luck? Can you explain to me how we get Manchester United as our first pick? Why can't we get Belgrade Sporting or Bucharest Steaua as our first game? You want to know what the problem is with being Russian? It's bad luck. The Italians, or Spaniards, or Germans don't have bad luck. Only we do. Bad luck and cold winters.

"Shit!" Zhironovsky spat out again. "There are two pieces of bad news, Rudzhin. You are making an old man lose his appetite before we sit down for lunch."

Viktor Zhironovsky looked at Rudzhin with newfound admiration. What was the third piece of news his young friend would have?

"Well, the last bit will make you smile." Rudzhin looked him straight in the eye. "I just finished a phone call with my old friend Uggin."

Rudzhin took in a breath to allow for a dramatic pause.

"Yes, Mr. Chairman, Uggin has succeeded in getting the Bolivians to sign a gas deal with Chile. Bolivia is on the cusp of being able to get its gas out to the Pacific. Meanwhile, in Peru, the legal process for Humboldt's formal approval began right on time, three days ago. This means that the president submitted the bill to Senator Luis Matta and the Congress now has thirty days to approve the contract. We expect no delays. And, as Schutz said, we are well positioned to win."

Viktor Zhironovksy's mouth curled into a huge smile. This was indeed a third piece of information that made him very, very happy.

"Good news, Rudzhin. Very good!" Zhironovsky's brow then furrowed in momentary concern.

"Is there . . . do you think . . . that anybody suspects that Anfang . . ."

Rudzhin cut him off, waving his hand in the air.

"Absolutely not. There were no questions. No requests for clarification. Not even a hint. Our links to Anfang Energie are completely confidential. And our negotiations with the Bolivians are done."

He looked at the chairman with a smirk.

"We have successfully provoked a race between Peru and Bolivia. We'll see which country gets their gas to market first. When Anfang wins the Peru contract, it won't matter to us which country wins or loses. In either case, Volga Gaz wins because we will effectively own the production from both of Latin America's most important gas producers."

Zhironovsky lifted his vodka glass in Rudzhin's direction. He swilled down the clear liquid. "To you, my dear Piotr."

Rudzhin smiled broadly at the gesture. Compliments were rare from this man.

"Mr. Chairman, I wish to tell you that I am very pleased with Uggin's work."

"Agreed. He has shown his loyalty. He did well on the Ukrainian shutdown. And he is now doing a good job. But, Piotr, reassure me. You know how much our effort in Latin

America means to me. Are you sure he's trustworthy? He married a foreigner, you know."

Rudzhin looked Viktor Zhironovsky straight in the eyes. "He is my oldest friend. I trust him completely. Full stop."

But Rudzhin knew this probably wasn't enough for the chairman of Volga Gaz. He would have preferred not to tell him, but it was important that Zhironovsky understood that he too was a thorough man.

"And . . . I plan to take out some insurance."

Nothing more needed to be said. Zhironovsky's eyes spoke the deep admiration for his younger colleague. The chairman was a believer in covering all the bases. Rudzhin had just done that.

"Good, then on Friday we'll stick to our plan of taking him out for his congratulatory lunch." Zhironovsky leaned forward as his eyes retracted in concentration.

"Now let me tell you about something else. Sit back, because you won't believe it."

Zhironovsky poured more vodka before continuing.

"The day before yesterday, I was asked to attend a meeting with the American governor of Alaska. Governor Whitley is a nice man, elegant, late fifties, educated at Berkeley, and of the same political party as President Eugene Laurence. But there is also something unusual about the governor.

"You see, the governor likes Russia," Zhironovsky continued. "He always has. He is one of the few Americans who believe that a strategic alliance with Russia would be good for the United States."

The chairman could see that his young friend was intrigued.

"Governor Whitley reports that the bedlam and chaos of the energy blackouts two months ago in California have made a profound impression on the White House. He says that President Laurence sees himself as the man history has destined to resolve America's long-term energy problem."

Piotr Rudzhin interrupted, his voice laden with concern. "So the American president is going to promote a major program of renewable energy, right? This is what I feared would happen after California. The more the Americans realize their dependence on outsiders for energy, the greater their political clamor for conservation and renewable resources."

Zhironovsky raised his hand outward, imitating a policeman's signal to stop traffic. The older man was smiling.

"Actually, my young friend, you are dead wrong. And this is what is so interesting. According to the good governor of Alaska, it seems that America's politicians are drawing very different conclusions. Because of its worldwide abundance and its clean burn, the lesson they seem to be learning from their California crisis is that natural gas must replace oil as the key energy currency of the future."

"There cannot be better news," Rudzhin said, his eyes widening in surprise.

"Yes, there can," Zhironovsky answered fast, revealing just the slightest irritation that the cadence of his good story was interrupted. "And I'm about to give it to you.

"You see, given their realization of natural gas's growing importance, it seems that Governor Whitley's long interest in a Bering Strait crossing—first a pipeline and then rail transportation—is suddenly being taken very seriously in Washington. Remember, dear boy, the influential female head of the CIA is from Alaska too."

Rudzhin was stunned.

"Mr. Chairman, how real can this be? It seems outlandish."

"According to Governor Whitley, they are dead serious. Why shouldn't they be? They need gas and we have more of it than anybody else in the world."

"The notion seems almost unreal—" Zhironovsky did not let Piotr finish his thought.

"Look, we build pipelines across frozen Siberia. The Brits and the French build a tunnel in the English Channel. Technology has made the issue of length irrelevant in discussions about bridges and tunnels. The engineering here is easy; it's the politics that are complicated."

"How will this affect our Latin American project?" Rudzhin interrupted again, nearly breathless. The whole thing was too much for him to digest in one fell swoop. He was thinking out loud, not the right thing to do with Viktor Zhironovsky. Piotr Rudzhin should have known better than to continue.

"Do you think we should slow down in Latin America?" Rudzhin asked anxiously. "If a Bering Strait crossing is truly a possibility, we may need to reconsider our intentions in Peru. We have always known that, if Anfang's connection to Volga Gaz gets out, the political aftershocks would wipe away any possibility of advancing our work in Latin America. It was a risk we were willing to take from the beginning. But do we now want to expand that risk to this new project? Do you think that we may be overreaching, sir?"

Viktor Zhironovsky's eyes turned suddenly cold. His green irises were like light beams locking in on Rudzhin.

Rudzhin immediately regretted the tone of his question. He knew the instant it came out that he had crossed a line.

Zhironovsky looked sharply at his younger colleague. Never allowing his eyes to move from Rudzhin's, the plump, white-haired chairman uncrossed his legs and slowly got up from the sofa. He began pacing the length of the room, engrossed in thought. But his eyes never loosed their grip on Piotr Rudzhin.

Circling behind Rudzhin's sofa, the old man lined himself up behind the young deputy minister of the interior. He stopped, and silence enveloped the room. Piotr Rudzhin felt an iron grip press in on the right side of his neck, just at the edge of the clavicle. Finally the chairman spoke. The tone was somewhere in the decibel range of a low-pitched growl.

"Piotr, I will consider that question not to have been asked. Don't let our closeness fool you into thinking that you are intimate with me. I like you. I have helped you. I will continue to help you. But you are not my advisor. You are not my confidant. You are not my friend. You will learn from me. But do not ever doubt me. If you doubt me in private, I can only conclude that you could also doubt me in public. And that is not possible. Do you understand that, Piotr?"

Rudzhin felt an iron thumb digging under his neckline.

"Yes, Mr. Chairman. I understand you very clearly."

"Rudzhin, understand that we Russians live under constant threat. We had an empire—first czarist, then Soviet—

which we proceeded to lose. Not once, but twice. Under our belly, we have Islamist countries that used to be part of our national territory. Today, they pray five times a day for our destruction. To our east, we have a billion and a half Chinese. To our west and south, we have the Baltic countries, Georgia, Ukraine, Bulgaria, and Romania. All of them formerly under our control. All are flirting with the United States and Europe today because they want investments, money, and membership in the European Union."

Zhironovsky had more.

"But, most of all, Rudzhin, the United States is masterminding the expansion of NATO right up to our borders. They are sticking their missiles into our asshole. They expanded their NATO military alliance to Bulgaria, Estonia, Latvia, Lithuania, Romania, Slovakia, and Slovenia. Now they talk of Ukraine and Georgia joining the alliance.

"Who do you think they are allying against, Rudzhin? They say, 'Don't worry, we're just modernizing the alliance.' Horseshit! Against whom is all this military expansion directed? We all know it's against us, Rudzhin. We're the target. We're the bull's-eye."

Zhironovsky walked back around the room to his seat on the sofa in front of Rudzhin. His breathing was labored, but his eyes were less wild now. Nonetheless, they signaled a steely determination.

"A few years ago, we succumbed to the illusion that Russia had no enemies. We paid dearly for this, Piotr. As Russia's leaders, we have a responsibility to push back. To show that we have cards and that we're willing to play them. And, my young friend, the biggest, nastiest, loudest card we have is gas. Lots and lots of expensive gas."

Rudzhin took advantage of a pause as the old man threw back the rest of the clear liquid in his vodka glass.

"Chairman Zhironovsky, please don't mistake my questions for doubts. You know the endless admiration and appreciation I have for you. You know that I am with you, sir. I too believe that the blessings of our natural resources give us a unique opportunity to reassert the strength of our country. My only question is whether we should find a way to slow down the Latin American effort until we know whether this new opportunity of the Bering Strait will bear fruit."

Zhironovsky was much more relaxed now. Rudzhin's soothing words had had the right calming affect.

"Piotr, my dear boy, you will see that age brings the wisdom to assess the risks and opportunities of every move. Less than two years ago, we shut the Ukrainian pipeline down for nearly three weeks and everybody worried that this would send Europe into a frantic frenzy to build alternative pipelines from Algeria and Libya. Nothing happened. But the French and the Germans got the message. Last year, we told the Byelorussians, who became too intimate and comfortable with us, that they would have to pay market price or we would shut the gas down. After what happened in Ukraine, they believed us.

"I don't play children's games, Rudzhin. Russia doesn't play children's games. Remember this, Piotr. This isn't about a few little movements on a chessboard. The crisis in California has given us a strategic opening. In one fell swoop, we now have a chance to rebuild and strengthen our country and weaken the Americans at the same time. There can be no reconsiderations or second thoughts."

Zhironovsky was now on a roll.

"No, Rudzhin, this is not about economics. It's about power. For the past year, you have helped me to plan and implement a secret takeover of Latin America's largest natural gas fields. Once we get the Humboldt contract, it won't matter if the Americans find out that Anfang Energie is a cover for Volga Gaz. It will be too late to do anything about it. They will scream. They will protest. But the gas fields in Peru and Bolivia will belong to us. And we will control the movement of liquefied natural gas on tankers to California for the next fifty years.

"Everybody had been aware of a coming natural gas shortage in California. But the stupid Americans can't make long-term political decisions. Our analysts were smart enough to understand that bringing liquefied gas to America's shores on boats was their only medium-term answer. That is why we wanted Peru and Bolivia. The natural gas in those two countries can provide nearly the totality of America's liquefied natural gas imports. They'll soon be investing billions in loading facilities and infrastructure to take the Latin American gas. There will be no turning back; they will be stuck with depending on us."

Zhironovsky paused, sucking in a deep breath of air. Piotr Rudzhin took advantage of the split-second lull to try to further placate the chairman.

"Your plan has been impeccable every step of the way. Our financial offer for the operation of the Bolivian fields was done in the open, as Volga Gaz. You were absolutely right that the Americans would not protest our bid; they didn't see a single foray into one Latin American country as a threat. And you were also correct about our need to disguise our Peruvian bid under Anfang's corporate cover. Control of a single Latin American country's large gas fields is one thing. Control of both Bolivia and Peru's fields at the same time is quite another. The Americans would have taken us down."

Zhironovsky waved his hand in the air. He didn't want interruptions.

"Stop looking at the tactics, Rudzhin. Don't get fixated on the little movements. If you want to go further, learn two lessons, Rudzhin. Learn them now.

"First, never forget that the beauty of life is in the strategy. It's the end result that counts. The destination. History won't give a damn how we got there. What the books will write about is the audacity that suddenly put Russia in control of a huge percentage of the liquefied gas needs of the United States of America.

"They will write about that day as the time when the world's power equation shifted," said Zhironovsky, his voice ponderous.

"Now here is the second lesson, boy. You need balls to seize an opportunity. Roman generals had a name for knowing how to take advantage of the enemy's smallest battlefield mistake. They called it carpe diem—seize the day.

"This is what we will do now with the Bering Strait. We are going to behave very elegantly with our American friends. We are going to show interest. We are going to say the right things about building a whole new alliance and we will talk about global interdependence. Something as huge as a project to cross the Bering Strait might never happen at all; and if it turns out to have been a dream, we will still have them by the neck in Latin America.

"But God have mercy on the Yankees if they really want to build a chunnel between our countries." Zhironovsky smiled. "Because when they make this great battlefield mistake, the liquefied exports from Latin America and the piped gas across the Strait from Siberia will make up nearly one hundred percent of America's gas needs. All of it controlled by Russia. We will have the power to detonate a thousand Californias with a mere snap of our fingers."

Zhironovsky looked at the ornate ceiling of the CDL's Pushkin Room.

"History will write about that day as more than just a 'shift' in power. History will identify that exact moment as the end of the American empire."

MOSCOW
AUGUST 3, 5:40 P.M.
THE HOTEL BALTSCHUG KEMPINSKI

The next day, Daniel Uggin's flight from La Paz, with a change of planes in São Paulo, landed punctually, late in the afternoon, at Moscow's Sheremetyevo airport, the city's largest airfield. For a man who just eighteen months earlier had no more than a handful of plane rides under his belt, flying had now become second nature.

As Sheremetyevo's mechanical doors slid open, Uggin looked around and saw a man dressed in a gray suit walking his way.

"Oleg from the ministry of the interior, sir. Very nice to see you. I have instructions from Deputy Minister Rudzhin to pick you up and take you directly to the hotel to relax. Later, Mr. Rudzhin has arranged a social gathering for you. The deputy minister and his friends will be waiting for you at GQ around midnight."

Uggin was pleased with the attention. Tomorrow would be an important day; Volga Gaz's big boss had invited him to lunch. By now, he had become accustomed to the occasional business meeting with Viktor Zhironovsky. But this was to be the first meal with Volga Gaz's chairman. By Russian standards, it was a breakthrough.

He followed Oleg across the busy hall and outside toward a waiting Mercedes-Benz. A man jumped out of the driver's seat and took Daniel's bags. Oleg opened the rear door and Daniel got in, immediately scooting behind the driver to allow Oleg to take the seat next to his. Instead, Oleg closed the door and swung into the front seat.

Sheremetyevo was the closest of Moscow's three airports from the city center, so the ride had taken under an hour. Daniel smiled as the car made the turn into the Hotel Baltschug Kempinski's elegant driveway. When he was in Moscow, the hotel became Daniel's home away from home. Andrei, the Baltschug Kempinski's outstanding concierge, always made sure he got his favorite room—suite 914 was one of the rooms designed by Her Royal Highness, Princess Michael of Kent; it had one of the most panoramic views of the Kremlin and the Moskva River as it wound its way through the city.

After leaving his suitcases in the suite, Daniel took a stroll to bring some life back into his limbs, still numb from the fourteen-hour flight. He returned to his room and napped for two hours exactly. His room-service dinner was followed by a long, hot shower. At 11:45 P.M., Daniel descended in the elevator to find Piotr Rudzhin and his friends.

He walked out of the Baltschug Kempinski's ornate lobby and strolled the half block down Baltschug Street to the marble-columned seventeenth-century mansion that today housed GQ Bar. Though it was still hours before the GQ Bar would reach its usual 3 A.M. frenzied pitch, he noticed that the sidewalk was already littered with sports cars, Bentleys, Rolls-Royces, and the occasional Ferrari.

Daniel Uggin's eyes had to adjust to the cavernous lounge, attempting to quickly find his friend. He tried—and failed—to avoid being distracted by the women. Despite its name, this fashionable joint venture between the American men's magazine and Arkady Novikov—Moscow's king of fine, ultratrendy dining—was known as a favorite gathering place for the city's best-looking beauties.

Trying to make his way toward the balcony, Daniel walked past the smooth, glossy bar crowded with a jumble of dressed-to-kill hipsters. As he walked through the noisy lounge, he automatically registered the time. It was shortly past midnight. That was the hour that the soothing, dining-time piano music was replaced by a DJ spinning international hits. Uggin recalled a sign at the bar's entrance announcing this week's guest disc jockey as a music genius from St. Tropez. Daniel looked up at the glass-enclosed elevated cabin and smiled as the French DJ pumped his fist rhythmically in the air, his long brown locks framed by oversize headphones.

As he stepped out onto the far quieter balcony, he saw his friends. The elegant terrace, just minutes away from the lights of Red Square, jutted right over the banks of the Moskva River. Sofas and plush cushions were arrayed al fresco in a purposely haphazard mélange of jumbled furniture. Silken white fabric, hung from almost invisible dark wiring, swayed to and fro in the soft summer breezes. The sofas and aisles, abuzz with laughter and conversation, were crowded with stylish patrons dressed in the latest fashions.

Tonight Rudzhin had asked a couple of friends to join them for an easy evening of after-dinner drinks. The group was uncomplicated—Antoni owned a prominent Moscow-based real estate agency, clearly a good business in a city recently identified by London's *Financial Times* as having the most expensive living accommodations in the world.

Antoni's fiancée, Andrea, was the top recruiting agent for Fashion Twins, the city's hottest modeling agency. The last fifteen years had brought the world an explosion of modeling talent from Russia. The disheveled Soviet Union had morphed into one of the primary breeding grounds for the planet's top-money runway women.

Tonight Andrea had come accompanied by her two best

friends—Nina and Dariya—both high-cheeked, blond god-
desses with similarly streaky, diagonally modern haircuts.
They were drop-dead gorgeous.

Comfortably seated with a Johnnie Walker Black Label on
ice in his hand, Daniel's mind rewound momentarily back to
the fight with his wife in Germany. Drinking in the high
style around him, Daniel Uggin thought about the argument
in Hermann Perlmutter's living room. It had been brutal.
Ugly. Daniel regretted the tone, but not the substance.

He was thankful, though, that in the last weeks, things
with Anne-Sophie had receded to a cool truce that, at the
very least, returned some semblance of normalcy to their
home.

Daniel Uggin was in an introspective mood this evening.
How could he not be? The previous night's long, first-class
transatlantic journey, the elegant meals in Moscow's best
restaurants, and tonight's high-flying scene at the GQ Bar
all testified to the vast changes in his life. But perhaps what
impressed him most was how quickly he had become accustomed to his new fast-lane status.

Daniel Uggin had met many of Piotr Rudzhin's Muscovite
friends in the past eighteen months. Piotr had been generous
about introducing Daniel to the big city. Rudzhin always had
a dinner, a drink, or a reception to attend and would always
bring Daniel in tow.

The small group gathered around the GQ Bar's sofa was
one of Daniel's favorites. They were easygoing, without the
flitting pretensions and floating pomp of the highfliers at
many of Rudzhin's parties. It was nice to spend an evening
with people who had nothing to do with work.

He had met Dariya, one of the models, on an earlier trip.
She was now seated to his left. Her skin was perfect—a
pale creamy color shimmering with translucent beauty. Her
blond hair and high cheekbones accented a smile showing
magnificent white teeth. The multiple-pleat black skirt was
hemmed below her knees. However, its conservatism was
deceptive. When she crossed her long legs, the skirt pleats
turned out to be hidden slits, revealing endless miles of legs

ending in medium-heeled sandals with tan-colored straps that crisscrossed, Greek style, up her silken calves.

Dariya was in the midst of laying into Piotr Rudzhin for a derisive comment about the uselessness of the press.

"Piotr, should you say these things if you're now the deputy minister? It's just not right. I don't know anything about politics, but your friends in this government need to stop overreacting to criticism. I just worked six weeks at the Paris fashion shows—you should see how those French journalists talk about their politicians. But here we close newspapers and fire television personalities just because we don't like what they say. It makes the government look paranoid. You guys need to grow up."

Dariya noticed the sudden heavy silence around the table. If she was either embarrassed or worried, it didn't show.

She flashed a brilliant smile.

"Come on now, how many people here agree with me that Piotr is of a new generation. He's our hope. He needs to teach those old guys," she concluded, looking directly at Rudzhin.

It was a classy performance. She had gotten everybody to agree that the government was paranoid while lauding Piotr Rudzhin as one of the few exceptions.

Daniel Uggin leaned over toward Dariya. He was amused to find himself a little nervous about talking to such a powerfully beautiful woman.

"Do you always have such strong opinions?"

She smiled.

"I'm a Russian woman. I'm genetically programmed to have strong opinions."

Dariya's tiff with Rudzhin and her quick answer about Russian women impressed him. Laughing at her joke, he looked at his surroundings. Just a few years earlier, the possibility of an evening like this would never have occurred to him—the GQ Bar, the flashing smile of a beautiful model, the elegant Muscovites. It was all still so new.

Yes, the past eighteen months had brought deep transformations. In just over a year and a half, he had become a very different man.

Uggin felt a shake on his shoulder.

"Daniel ... Daniel, we're leaving," said Piotr Rudzhin with a laugh. "What the hell were you thinking so seriously about?"

Daniel Uggin was jolted back to attention, wondering how long his thoughts had wandered away. He smiled sheepishly as he found the group already standing up. Except for Dariya.

"Where are you going so early?" Uggin asked with a grin. He tried to change the subject away from his daydreaming.

"There's still a long week ahead. And I've got an eight A.M. meeting at the ministry. Nina is off to St. Petersburg, and you, my friend, have an important lunch tomorrow. I guess you're the only one who can sleep late."

As Uggin rose from his chair, Rudzhin enveloped his friend in a huge bearlike embrace and whispered a quick, "See you tomorrow." It was followed by a quiet admonition. "Get there early, Daniel. You don't want to be late; this will be an important meeting."

"I don't have to work tomorrow," Dariya whined, still frozen in her chair. In mock protest, she was the only one who had not gotten up. "Why does everybody have to leave?"

With a great show of feigned sadness, the model began to gather her things.

Suddenly, Daniel Uggin heard himself speak, but he did not know where the voice came from. He recognized it as his own. It was forming involuntary words that he did not mean to utter.

"Dariya, I'm not going anywhere. My room is a two-minute commute to the hotel. And my first meeting tomorrow is only at lunchtime. So if you don't mind having me alone, I'd be honored to buy you a last drink."

"Yes, yes." Dariya was beaming a smile. She looked at the departing group with mock seriousness. "You see, this is a gentleman. These days, you have to go all the way to Kursk to find some manners in Russia."

They spent the next hour together seated on a plush sofa. With the barely audible ripple of the Moskva's waters just under them, they talked easily about her career, her travels, and her modeling shoots. He told her about his Kursk youth with Rudzhin. Dariya's conversation was surprisingly relaxed; it had none of the tension that many non-Muscovites found typical of the city's residents.

The few truly beautiful women Daniel had met in the past months commuting to the capital were like a flash of searing light. The heat of their beauty was magnetic, but it repelled any proximity. Not Dariya. Her bright personality was like a landing beacon. She was accessible, her smile welcoming. There was nothing hidden. No pretense of mysteriousness.

She curled her legs on the plush sofa and swiveled her body toward him. She held her chin in her palm, her blond hair and blue eyes reflecting the light of her effervescent smile.

"You're a nice man, Daniel Uggin. It's lovely to meet somebody who doesn't feel that humanity has to bow in respect as you pass. The problem with these rich and powerful guys in Moscow is that they expect the world to serve them."

As she said the words, her hand left her chin and slid over his palm. Lightly. Just barely touching. He felt his heartbeat accelerate.

She was looking into his eyes. He felt her hand sweeping again over his. His skin tingled.

Dariya leaned over and kissed him—just barely. On the cheeks.

"Yes, you are a sweet man. You are not even sure what to do when a girl tries to seduce you," she said, her smile crashing all barriers.

Uggin could not say anything. She giggled.

"Okay, Daniel Uggin, I'll do all the work. I want to stay here. With you. All night. Tonight."

They walked the half block to the Baltschug Kempinski, into the Art Deco elevator and then down the corridor to his ninth-floor suite. What ensued was one of the most beautiful nights Uggin had ever spent with a woman. It was long and sweet and loving. It went slowly. They undressed each other deliberately. Each article of clothing came off gradually, the unhurried pace heightening the need to belong to each other.

She put him on his stomach and kissed every part of his body. Slow, languid kisses that made him feel as if this woman belonged only to him. His back. His buttocks. In between his thighs. Her tongue went to his ankles and then to the soles of his feet, ending in between his toes.

They made love four or five times. Each time ended in heightened levels of tenderness. And each time they wanted more. There were no demanding bursts or any panting violence. Their two bodies relished the slow rhythm of their loving.

In the morning, Daniel ordered a room-service breakfast of waffles with cinnamon sugar, cappuccino, and orange juice. It came on silver platters resting on white linen. The waiter set the round table for them.

"Is it too much for me to ask you to call me when you come back to Moscow?" Dariya said to him, sipping her coffee. She was dressed in a plush white cotton bathrobe.

He hesitated for a split second. She caught the pause and held her hand up toward him in a gesture asking him to stop talking. Her free hand caressed his arm.

"Daniel, I've seen the ring on your finger. I won't ask for anything. I don't want you to feel you have to tell me anything. All I want to say is that we had something lovely together last night. If we promise not to ask each other questions, maybe we can have last night over again."

Uggin smiled. He couldn't resist her. A model of this caliber could easily have been arrogant and deceitful. Instead, she was caring and elegant.

She dressed, and after long, passionate kisses left Daniel alone. On the way out, Dariya slipped a folded piece of paper into his business jacket, draped over the dresser chair.

"I want to see you again. I want you to understand that clearly. That is my telephone number," Dariya said, pointing to his jacket as she receded into the hallway. Daniel lingered at his room's door long after he heard the ding of the elevator around the corner. He felt strange. But he had no regrets.

Uggin finished dressing, went downstairs, and bought a newspaper. He needed to kill an hour before going to Zhironovsky's lunch. Nestled in a hotel lobby easy chair, he tried to analyze what had happened the previous evening. But he was unsure of how to unwind the twisted confusion of his feelings. Daniel Uggin closed his eyes and decided that he wouldn't make the effort. It had been wonderful. Enough said.

At about the exact time Uggin was relaxing with a newspaper in the hotel lobby, the cellular telephone of the deputy minister of the interior vibrated mercilessly. Piotr Rudzhin looked at the display on his Motorazr phone and his lips grimaced in disdain.

"Yes?"

"It's me," said the high-pitched voice of Andrei, the Baltschug's concierge. "I got it all on video."

"Okay."

"Jesus, they went at it until five-thirty this morning. I think it was six times. You've got to hand it to her; I don't know how she does it. She figures out the target and what he wants. Then she acts out the part. Six hours later, the guy is in love. It's amazing."

"Amazing," Rudzhin said, grunting his agreement. "Thanks for calling."

Rudzhin flipped the phone to its closed position. He didn't like what he had just done. And he hoped to God he wouldn't have to use it.

Rudzhin shrugged his shoulders. There was no choice. A man in his position needed insurance.

MOSCOW
AUGUST 4, 12:50 P.M.
VOLGA GAZ HEADQUARTERS

Ten minutes before Daniel's appointment, the car stopped in

front of Volga Gaz's twenty-four-story building on Pavelet-skaya Ploshchad, a posh square in Moscow's business center. A pleasant-looking attendant waited outside to greet him, directing him to an elevator with the key turned to the off position pending his arrival.

Uggin was feeling good. All this attention was pleasant.

As the elevator doors opened on the penthouse floor, he was handed off to a well-dressed, officious-looking woman in her midfifties. She was slightly overweight and, notwith-standing a shy demeanor, was clearly in control of the chair-man's suites. She introduced herself as Gudrun Bashemov, one of Viktor Zhironovsky's personal assistants. Daniel Uggin immediately picked up a familiar lilt in her spoken Russian.

"You and I have something in common, Mr. Uggin," said Gudrun, identifying the recognition in his eyes. "You see, like your wife, I'm German. I was born in Berlin. I married a Russian and moved here fifteen years ago. Moscow has been wonderful to me."

Gudrun flashed a sweet smile that was all welcome and caring. She showed him to a seat in the ultramodern wait-ing room. The room had a Zen-like feel. The walls were off-white, with no hangings. The furniture was a sleek com-bination of metals and dyed leathers from Ligne Roset in Paris. A number of large Persian rugs adorned the hardwood floor. A low glass coffee table with oversize books on Volga Gaz's projects was centered in the middle of the collection of couches and love seats.

Gudrun was about to offer Daniel a coffee when the eleva-tor doors opened and Piotr Rudzhin rushed out. He gave his friend a big embrace and looked quickly at Gudrun.

"Gudrun, can we go right in?"

Again, the sweet smile flashed on Gudrun's pretty face.

"Of course, Piotr. Please be my guest."

Uggin was impressed by Piotr's clear intimacy with Zhi-ronovsky's office. Daniel had been aware that the two men worked together, but this was the first time Uggin had real-ized their level of close familiarity. He followed Rudzhin into a richly paneled office. A huge floor-to-ceiling glass window framed one entire end of the office. The view was breathtaking. The domes of the Kremlin and St. Basil's Cathedral were in the glass's dead center.

Next to the window was the chairman's large steel-and-marble desk. Exquisitely lit paintings and sculptures dotted the room's walls and shelves. An elegant sitting area—with leather couches in the same modern style as the outside waiting room—was already set up with small vodka glasses and tiny bite-size sandwiches. The fireplace, just a few feet to the left of the sitting area, was stacked with wood, awaiting winter.

It was August, but Daniel noticed the fireplace. He had never seen one in an office before.

Viktor Zhironovsky got up from behind his desk and slowly made his way to greet his visitors. Though overweight, the sixty-eight-year-old chairman's step was agile. The few strands of white hair left on his balding head bounced freely as he kissed Piotr Rudzhin on both cheeks.

"Uggin, Rudzhin! Delighted to see both of you. Come, let's have a drink before going to lunch," Zhironovsky said, directing the group to the couches.

"Now, Uggin, I've heard this story of the two of you in school. How is it possible that you are still a friend of Piotr, after he led you on the seventh-grade stink-bomb mission that got both of you expelled? Your judgment concerns me, my boy. I wonder about your ability to choose friends." Viktor Zhironovsky bellowed in laughter as he slapped Daniel on the back. The chairman's nearly transparent blue eyes were dancing.

The three sat down and after a white-gloved waiter filled the vodka glasses, Zhironovsky immediately turned serious. The blue eyes lost their joviality and became impregnable.

"Now, before we go to lunch, I have a couple of things to say," Zhironovsky announced, looking straight at Daniel. "Uggin, you have done an excellent job for us so far. Rudzhin recommended you for our Latin American plans, but—trust me—I did my own digging before accepting. And I found four qualities that interested me."

Daniel was completely taken aback by Zhironovsky's directness. He had expected to answer queries about his trip to Bolivia, not talk about himself.

"The first is that you are a childhood friend of Rudzhin's. This is critical. One discovers quickly in politics that old friendships are irreplaceable." Zhironovsky's cold eyes zeroed in on his visitor. Daniel felt increasingly uncomfortable. So far, the chairman's words were positive, yet he couldn't help feeling that he was under intense scrutiny.

Uggin shook himself to attention as Zhironovsky kept the list going.

"Second, you are a mechanical engineer and have been a loyal employee of Volga Gaz for over thirteen years. You did your job when I gave you tough orders on the Ukrainian issue. I appreciated the loyalty then. I appreciate it now. Third, I found out that you come from an impressive military family that sacrificed for Russia—your father and grandfather were both high-ranking officers in the Red Army and, indeed, your grandfather died defending our Russian land in the First World War. Russian patriotism runs in your blood, my boy."

Uggin wondered again where all this was going.

"Fourth, notwithstanding your family heritage, you're a modern Russian. You speak English and German, you have traveled, and you have even married a foreigner."

Daniel looked at Piotr, next to him. His arms were crossed, his face impassive. Uggin was completely taken aback by Zhironovsky's recitation of his family background. Not sure of what to say, Uggin opted for silence. Zhironovsky moved right on.

"Those are four important qualities. Over the past eighteen months, I've seen that I made the right choice by investing in you. Now, let's go further. I want you to come to Moscow. With your family. And I'm offering you the position of vice president for international affairs. It comes with a big salary increase. And, of course, you will get a place to live, a car and driver, and, Uggin, a very generous expense account."

Daniel Uggin was floored. This was a huge honor. Now Piotr was smiling. He recalled Piotr's admonition of the previous night to get to the meeting on time. Rudzhin had known all along what this meeting was about.

Zhironovsky continued, his voice lower, now treating Daniel as an intimate.

"Let's be frank, Uggin. Luck has made Volga Gaz into a huge company. Our country has enjoyed what I like to call a 'triple boom.' In the last ten years, we have had increased gas reserves, increased production volumes, and increased prices. These three stars do not align often. We Russians should consider ourselves extraordinarily fortunate.

"Here in Moscow, our job is to prove that we know how to convert luck into opportunity. Volga Gaz has to become stronger, bigger, and more agile. To be successful, we will need to be tough. This is not just a goal for our company. It's also a Russian goal, a national objective. That is why some of the most important officials in the Kremlin and I are working together. It is why your friend Rudzhin is here. We all know that Volga Gaz's future is not a private problem; it's a patriotic mission.

"And we need . . ." Zhironovsky paused for a moment before concluding the half sentence. "Let me be clearer—we demand your participation."

Uggin was overcome by a range of strange emotions. Floored by the chairman's words, he had never in his life felt as important as he did at this very moment. Viktor Zhironovsky, the man who controlled a huge part of Russia's economy and was, potentially, the nation's future president, had just declared in the most absolute terms that he *demanded* Daniel Uggin's help.

Daniel Uggin was just enough in control to know that he was participating in a life-changing moment. But it was hard to keep the jumble of feelings in check. Zhironovsky's appeal imbued him with a strange new feeling—a sense of destiny. Proud to be chosen for his professional capabilities, he also felt he was embarking on a mission greater than just a job.

Uggin gathered his thoughts.

"I'm honored, Mr. Zhironovsky, at the trust you are willing to place in me. It is a very exciting opportunity. Of course, I have a million questions."

Zhironovsky cut him off with a wave of his hand as he stood up.

"Yes, yes. But those we will deal with over lunch."

MOSCOW
AUGUST 4, 1:45 P.M.
VOLGA GAZ'S CORPORATE DINING ROOM

Right on cue, the two French doors at the far end of Viktor Zhironovsky's office were slid quietly open by a waiter in a black tuxedo and white gloves.

"Come, come," Zhironovsky commanded as he sheperded his guests into the intimate, exquisite dining room. "Only my best guests eat here. I call this the 'Taipan' room. Do you know what that means? It is Chinese. It translates into 'he who wields real power.'"

The dramatic floor-to-ceiling glass walls, Tibetan rugs, and Ming vases played off the simplicity of the ebonized wood floor. The dining table could fit ten guests, but only one end of the table was elegantly set for the three men.

As soon as they sat down, Viktor Zhironovsky ordered the waiter to bring a bottle of champagne—Cuvée William Deutz Rosé 1999—to celebrate Uggin's promotion. Daniel Uggin had trouble keeping his ogling stares under control. He did not know whether to be more impressed by the chairman's knowledge of champagnes or by the opulent surroundings of the dining room.

A small menu, printed in fine cursive on thick notepaper, was placed in front of them. The food courses and wine pairings were titled in both Spanish and Russian. On the bottom was the signature of Juan-Estaban Arcos, the world-famous Spanish chef and producer of avant-garde, experimental delicacies in his small restaurant north of Barcelona. In the past years, Arcos had been fawned over as the world's most original gastronome by prestigious international foodie magazines; his restaurant had a two-year waiting list.

Zhironovsky saw Uggin struggling to understand the menu. It included maddeningly unintelligible courses such as seaweed tagliarini with Bay of Biscay scallops, a cappuccino of foamed duck's liver mousse and seared tuna made into a Tower of Babel with golden beets and salted jicama.

"Daniel, I trust you're not a traditionalist when it comes to eating," Zhironovsky intoned in a mock chide. "I truly hope not because this month I have Arcos's best sous-chef cooking for me. And he is even crazier than his boss. But if this is too wild for you, don't worry. By the time you are back at this table, the menu will have changed."

The chairman picked up on Daniel's inquisitive look.

"You see, my dear Uggin, I hate getting bored. My guest chefs rotate month to month. In September, Jean-Paul Arnaud will send his top assistant from his three-star Hôtel de la Poste in the Loire. Yes, you will find the Frenchman far more subdued and steady than this Spanish madman. On the other hand, it will be a less amusing experience."

Lunch went on at a leisurely pace, the unusual courses coming and going. Dessert was a densely fluid crème caramel served in a martini glass. The still-impeccable waiter communicated the chef's instructions on the dessert's consumption. It had to be drunk in a single go so as to enjoy the thick liquid's phased temperatures, which began very warm at the top and finished ice cold on the bottom.

Finally, espresso was served in small rose-colored cups of fifteenth-century Chinese porcelain. Exhausted by the extended meal, Daniel Uggin wondered how Zhironovsky could do this every day. Just as Uggin's mind began to calculate the calories consumed and the cholesterol created, he heard Zhironovsky's voice directed toward him. The chairman's tone was suddenly serious.

"Now, my boy, Piotr and I do have some business to discuss with you," said Zhironovsky, folding his napkin on the table and looking at Daniel Uggin.

"Of course, Mr. Chairman. How can I help?"

Zhironovsky glanced at Rudzhin.

Taking the cue, Piotr started right in.

"I'll be direct, Daniel. No beating around the bush. Our Latin American trap is set. If things proceed on schedule, in a few months Russia will control the gas fields in Peru and

Bolivia. It is imperative to keep our Peru cover with Anfang a secret, at least until we sign the contracts with the Peruvian government; longer, if possible. But after that, it will be impossible to turn back the deal, even if the connection between Anfang Energie and Volga Gaz becomes public."

"The Americans won't know what hit them," interrupted Zhironovsky. "At the time of their greatest need to expand the United States's access to natural gas, they will find that Volga Gaz is the operator, manager, and provider of their most important source of liquefied gas. It will completely change the quality of Russia's relationship with the Americans."

Rudzhin looked at Daniel before continuing. He could see his friend's concentrated interest.

"But something new has happened, Daniel. And we must strive to take advantage of the situation," Piotr whispered, shifting forward, his body now close to Uggin's.

"You see, we've become aware that the crisis in California has had a deep psychological impact on the Americans. We all knew that the September eleventh terrorist attacks have made the United States far more cognizant of its dependency on Middle Eastern oil. But for years the concern never spread beyond oil. What happened in California in early June has now made the Americans realize that they are similarly vulnerable to natural gas shortages too."

"This is a good thing for us, isn't it?" asked Daniel. "It will only make them more anxious for access to the liquefied gas from Latin America, won't it?"

Zhironovsky was smiling. "Good questions," he muttered under his breath.

"Absolutely," affirmed Rudzhin. "But the fact is that it will take time to build new off-loading sites in the United States. And, even so, the liquefied gas from Latin America won't be enough to meet their growing needs."

Uggin was now puzzled. He couldn't see where this was going.

"You looked perplexed, my friend. And rightly so. You see, the Americans are now in a panic. President Laurence's administration wants to be the one to ensure that there are

no more Californias in America's future. So they are looking for more gas. From other sources. With dependable
partners."

Rudzhin paused for a second before posing a rhetorical
question.

"And who do you think has all this gas?"

"Well, we do," answered Uggin dutifully. "But—"

Rudzhin raised his hand, signaling Daniel to silence.

"And where is our gas?"

"In Siberian fields, of course." Daniel was now feeling
that this exercise was slightly infantile. "But—"

Again Rudzhin raised his hand, with a broad ear-to-ear
smile.

"And what is Siberia close to?"

"Nothing," Daniel started to answer and then stopped himself. Slowly, his mind was bending in a certain direction.

Zhironovsky watched the exchange with amused glee. He
saw Daniel Uggin struggling against an answer that simply
couldn't be the right one.

"Go ahead, young man, I know what you are thinking.
Don't worry about sounding silly. Say it."

"Well, sir, Siberia is close to nothing. But it's so big—
seven time zones—that, actually, it's close to everything."

"Ah, yes." Zhironovsky beamed. "This boy is good . . ."

Rudzhin took over the conversation once again.

"Daniel, you still can't quite bring yourself to say it. So
let me. Siberia has ten of the twenty largest gas fields in the
world. Just eastern Siberia alone—Sakhalin and Kamchatka,
in particular—contains more gas than most other countries'
fields combined. And eastern Siberia is a lot closer to Alaska
than it is to Moscow or Paris or London."

"So, are you telling me . . . ?"

"Yes, you're right. The Americans are interested in reviv-
ing the notion of a Bering Strait crossing."

Uggin was incredulous.

"I thought this idea was dead," he exclaimed. "We haven't
discussed this since Czar Nicholas the second brought up
the idea before the First World War. Wasn't he the first one
to talk about it? And that was only because he was furious

that his grandfather had sold Alaska to the Americans for $7.2 billion thirty-eight years earlier."

Zhironovsky leaned forward, the veins on his nearly bald forehead bulging. His blue eyes shone with intensity.

"Uggin, I like you even more because you know your history. And the tides of history could shift again in the next few weeks. From the American point of view, a Bering Strait crossing could be the perfect solution to their problem—a physical connection to the one nation that can supply them with all the natural gas they could ever need. Furthermore, it feeds right into all of their myths—conquering new boundaries, believing blindly in technology and engineering—you know, all the silly things the Americans believe about themselves."

"And all with a nation that is not Muslim; that too is important in America these days," added Rudzhin.

"Will they really want this?" asked Uggin. "After all, we're not exactly their favorite friend now."

"They will want it. Badly. So badly that once they have given it some thought, they won't be able to get it out of their heads. The Americans are shortsighted; they won't see that a long-term dependency on Russia is a strategic trap. They can't get beyond their big cars. Their crazy use of water. Of electricity. Spend, spend. Consume, consume. The United States is incapable of change. It survives on a mountain of overconsumption and debt. They can't change their culture, so they will jump at any chance to keep things the way they are."

An eerie silence came over the table.

"So how do we help the Americans come to the conclusion that a bridge across the Bering Strait is their panacea?" Uggin asked quietly.

Zhironovsky looked at him dead center.

"That is what we want to talk to you about."

The ornate grandfather clock, timed to strike on the hour, chimed three loud gongs.

Zhironovsky licked his lips. A half hour ago, he had ordered a bottle of eighteen-year-old single-malt whiskey and most of it was already gone.

"Uggin, what we are going to discuss here is highly confidential. The only other people who know what we are talking about are the president and the director of the FSB," said Zhironovsky, referring to the Russian security agency.

"There is no greater national security priority in this country. Do you understand?"

Daniel Uggin nodded somberly, grateful for the confidence.

"If this is serious, we will have the United States by the balls. A Bering Strait crossing could mean a permanent change in the power equation. We would demand an end to antimissile systems in Eastern Europe. We would require the Americans not to interfere in our relations with difficult neighbors such as Georgia or Ukraine. We would insist on a cancellation of Japan's nuclear plans. NATO would have to dissolve. China would be put in its place.

"You see, Uggin," said Zhironovsky, waving his hand in a wide arc. "The possibilities are endless.

"But, as your question implied, we have to help them come to the right decision. We cannot just hope that they come to the correct conclusion alone."

Zhironovsky saw Uggin's puzzled look. Zhironovsky's hand came to rest on his arm.

"President Eugene Laurence called President Tuzhbin the day before yesterday. He asked if we would receive a high-level delegation led by General Martha Packard, the director of the CIA. It seems that she is a believer in the possibilities of a Bering Strait crossing. She is coming at the end of this month and her purpose would be to engage us in a discussion of the crossing's feasibility."

"This is incredible," Uggin nearly shouted. "They are really serious about it." He worried for an instant that his outburst would be misconstrued. "It's not that I did not believe what you have told me, Mr. Chairman, I'm just so surprised by how real this is."

If Zhironovsky was concerned, he didn't show it. He continued.

"Since Tuesday afternoon, Rudzhin and I have sat in numerous meetings with our intelligence colleagues. And we have all concluded the same thing. General Packard is a very important conduit. Her presence denotes America's seriousness. But . . . we think she is not enough. She is from Alaska; everybody knows that the Alaskans are historically close to Russia.

"So we will graciously accept General Packard's leadership of the American delegation. But we will also ask for somebody to join her directly from the White House. We will tell the Americans that we think someone from the president's political staff should be at the table during our discussions. It must be somebody who has access to the president, is trusted by Tolberg, the powerful White House chief of staff. And who doesn't need to filter his opinion through the snail's-pace of the U.S. interagency process."

"And we know exactly who we want," interrupted Rudzhin, a little disappointed that Zhironovsky was doing all the talking.

"Piotr is right. We know who we want. A young man. Single. Very smart. Comes from a poor background. A Mexican. His name is Anthony Ruiz. Now, mind you, we cannot ask for him directly, but if we phrase the request correctly— you know, we will suggest a politically creative person who is close to the president; someone young, not tainted by the Cold War era—we think it could end up being Mr. Ruiz."

"And why do you think this Anthony Ruiz is so important?" asked Uggin.

"I meant what I said about him. They tell me that he is, indeed, capable and young and therefore has no memory of the decades of antagonism between our countries. He made it to the top. And you know the Americans; they love anybody who embodies their American-dream story. It is true that while Ruiz doesn't have the weight of a cabinet secretary, we believe he could be an important voice in favor of the project. He is respected in the White House as an advisor untainted by Washington's cynicism. That is why Chief of Staff Tolberg has come to depend on him.

"But in addition to all these qualities, our intelligence services believe he has other 'assets.' He is young, therefore receptive. He is anxious to leave his mark. He does not have international experience. From a poor family. No university degrees. Our people believe he could easily become impressed by things he has never before encountered."

Uggin still didn't know what all this top-secret information had to do with him. But he had a sense he was about to find out.

"If we can get Mr. Ruiz here, we want you as his escort. Your job is to become his friend. Make him an enthusiastic supporter. Take him to dinner. Show him the town. And together, we will find a way to make him stumble."

UNITED STATES

"You have got to be kidding," exclaimed Tony Ruiz for the second consecutive time. He stared at Rajpour Rosenblatt, his mouth agape.

Rosenblatt leaned back in his oversize red leather chair and pulled firmly on his bow tie. The scientist's dark eyes twinkled in merriment. Impressing Washington's government types with facts and technical figures were the moments he loved most about living in the nation's capital.

"At first, I thought it was as dreamy as *Star Trek*. But then, the whole idea of a transcontinental crossing has mushroomed at the White House. People are taking this thing seriously, Raj. Isn't it just some wild hype? I grew up on the West Coast and never heard of this," protested Ruiz.

"Look, Tony, there are people in Washington, D.C., who have never visited the Capitol building. Trust me. It's completely feasible from an engineering point of view."

It was not what Tony Ruiz wanted to hear. But he listened;

after all, he had been the one to call and ask for an hour of the renowned scientist's time. Tony had been lucky to find the scientist in town during the mid-August lull that invaded Washington's summertime.

There was no question that Rosenblatt knew his stuff. The son of a prominent Indian businesswoman and the Jewish dean of the faculty of Applied Mathematics at Cornell University, the dark-skinned Rosenblatt was considered one of the foremost engineering experts in the United States. At the president's request, Rosenblatt had chaired an advisory committee that had just produced the definitive report on the state of the nation's aging public infrastructure.

"Tony, take those civilian blinders off for a second. The weather is bad and the food is foul up there. But neither of those two things has anything to do with engineering. Crossing the Bering Strait by bridge or tunnel has been talked about for a long time. It's perfectly doable."

Notwithstanding the engineer's chiding tones, Ruiz genuinely liked Rajpour Rosenblatt. They had worked together on the political impact of the infrastructure report. As long as it didn't stretch or obscure the truth, Rosenblatt was one of only a few scientists willing to work with politicians on the messaging and communications of his scientific opinions.

"Okay," said Tony Ruiz, "I'll shut up. But the whole thing sounds like science fiction to me."

"Drink your coffee and listen," said Rosenblatt, smiling. He looked up at the ceiling before starting.

"The latest scientific consensus for a Bering Strait crossing is to build a tunnel—it would be the world's longest—between Cape Dezhnev, Russia, and Cape Prince of Wales, Alaska."

"Why not a bridge?" interrupted Ruiz, forgetting he had just promised silence.

Rosenblatt shot Tony a tough stare.

"Sorry, sorry. I won't interrupt." To prove his good faith, Tony Ruiz balanced the yellow pad on his knees and clicked his pen. He was ready to take notes.

"Lots of people have talked about a bridge," Raj continued. "A bridge would be easier to build. And it wouldn't be much longer than the Lake Pontchartrain causeway in New Orleans. That causeway is today the world's longest bridge.

"But a bridge is exposed to the elements. And notwithstanding my joke about the weather and food, winters are a serious matter up there. We're talking about temperatures that could go down to minus seventy degrees Fahrenheit. That means maintenance is nearly impossible between November and April. And then the end-of-winter ice floes present a whole special problem of their own. Specially protected piers would be needed to keep the bridge stable during the springtime ice bombardment."

Tony nodded. Made sense.

"A tunnel has none of those problems. Sure, it's more expensive than a bridge; people are talking about a twelve-billion-dollar price tag. But that isn't outrageous for a sixty-four-mile construction. The project would actually be three separate tunnels, the middle section beginning and ending on the two Diomede Islands halfway into the strait. Maximum depth would be only about one hundred and eighty feet. The tunnel would be composed of natural gas and oil pipelines, fiber-optic cable, and an unmanned rail link for container traffic. The whole thing would take about ten years to complete."

Rosenblatt paused.

"Questions?" he asked.

"What, you're done?" choked out Tony Ruiz. "That's it? It can't be that simple."

"Tony, I'm sparing you the engineering details. But, yes, it's that simple. The Chunnel connecting France and England is about forty percent smaller than this project, but it's under some of the roughest winter waters in the world. Though longer, the engineering for this tunnel is more reasonable because it won't be a passenger link; there are none of the human-safety issues."

Tony was about to say something but Rosenblatt held up his hand.

"Look, Tony, close your eyes and think about it. Big building projects have been bold strokes that propelled the history of civilization forward. Big infrastructure has opened frontiers, brought economic opportunity, and changed societies. Roman aqueducts brought water to parched cities and wiped away cholera. The bullet train brought Japan's disparate areas into the national economy. The Tennessee Valley Authority ended centuries of flooding in the Midwest. The Chunnel is the symbolic end to England's isolation from the rest of Europe. Those were big ideas. So is the Bering Strait crossing.

"Furthermore, there is a Russian company that has already moved on the project. It's called WorldLink. They announced plans to start negotiations with the U.S. government a year ago. The press release said they want to sell the United States and Russian governments controlling equal shares totaling fifty-two percent of the project. The rest they expect to get from private investors."

"Come on! Who is going to invest in this?" snapped Ruiz, sarcasm dripping from his voice.

"Lots of people. WorldLink is so bullish about the tunnel's success that they are talking about adding an extremely high-voltage electricity cable to the mix. The Russians produce more electricity in their two Okhotsk Sea generator plants than they know what to do with. They rightly figure that transporting electricity eastward is cheaper than sending it west across Siberia.

"No, Tony, this thing will attract a ton of investors," Rosenblatt mused, leaning back deeply into his leather chair. "WorldLink is predicting profitability in under a decade. That is far better than most toll highways in this country. And those toll-road projects get fast funding from banks and investment funds."

"Jesus, Raj, the way you talk about this pie-in-the-sky elephant project makes this something completely different. This is real."

Rajpour Rosenblatt leaned forward and took in his young friend's eyes.

"This is one hundred percent real."

Tony Ruiz nestled back in his chair. He threw a dejected stare across the scientist's light-colored pine desk. It was impressively uncluttered. Rajpour Rosenblatt did not fit the banal stereotype of the messy, absentminded professor.

"Okay, you've convinced me now that this Bering Strait tunnel is technically possible. But I gotta tell you, Raj, I still don't get it. Why would we do this? Why in God's name would we *want* to do this? We're hooked on oil like a junkie is hooked on heroin. And now, rather than finding a way to wean ourselves off expensive, polluting oil, we're going to go get hooked on expensive, polluting natural gas. It's like telling the same heroin-addicted junkie to try a little cocaine."

Rosenblatt said nothing, so Tony continued.

"It hasn't been two months since California went to hell and back. Shouldn't our government policy be to promote alternatives to carbon fuels? Shouldn't we be creating incentives for nuclear, wind, biofuels, hydropower, and hydrogen-cell energies? Shouldn't we be inciting conservation—higher fuel standards, hybrid cars, and ethanol gas?"

Tony slammed his palm on the desk. The force made the yellow notepad balanced on his knees slip onto the floor.

"And instead of doing any of that, we're now talking about adding a new gas dependence on Russia to our already large oil dependence on the Middle East. These Russians don't seem all that much better. To me, they're just another gang of authoritarians to whom we're going to pay billions of dollars."

Tony threw a pained stare at the senior scientist across the desk. He eyes begged for some support. For any small sign of reassurance that he was right.

It didn't come.

Rajpour Rosenblatt looked at him blankly.

"Good questions, Tony. They're the right ones to ask. But I'm not the guy to answer them. All that is way above my pay grade. I'm just here to tell you what you don't want to hear. Namely, that crossing the Bering Strait is a near certainty."

WASHINGTON, D.C.
AUGUST 17, 1:00 P.M.
THE WHITE HOUSE

Anthony Ruiz pushed away the papers on his desk and un-raveled the aluminum foil covering the White House cafeteria's poor imitation of a pizza. He was still mulling over his morning meeting with Rajpour Rosenblatt when he absent-mindedly picked up the remote and turned on the television. Since the California crisis, the television in his office had never strayed away from CNN.

Seeing a close-up of Anna Hardaway's face on the screen, Tony was reaching for the remote to zap the CNN reporter away when the camera angle widened to include a shot of her guest. Hardaway's reporting of the crisis had been prize-winning journalism; it had been so good that the network had now graduated her to anchoring in-studio interviews. Tony didn't have a problem with Hardaway's reporting. But he just couldn't stand hearing another withering analysis of California's situation.

Sitting next to Anna Hardaway was a good-looking, red-haired woman with a winning smile. She was dressed simply in a starched white shirt and elegantly fitting blue jeans. Dark high-heeled pumps covered her feet. Something about the woman was supremely attractive.

She's hot, thought Tony Ruiz, slowly lifting his right hand off the remote as the left hand wiped a string of mozzarella from the side of his face. Tony's mind struggled to place the actress, but he realized it was an impossible task. Months had gone by since he had watched a television series or seen a movie.

Once the woman began to talk, however, it took less than five seconds to realize that she was not an actress at all.

"Anna, that isn't the right question," the redhead was saying as she leaned over her host's desk. Her posture was so emphatic that she seemed nearly face-to-face with the interviewer. "Don't ask me how the United States is going to find more energy to avoid another California crisis. Haven't we learned anything from what has happened there? It can happen again—maybe in a year, maybe in a decade. Maybe even tomorrow. How many people have to die before we understand that the question to ask is how our country slows its use of energy? The issue, Anna, is not finding more sources of the same carbon fuels. The issue is how to consume less!"

Over the past weeks, Tony had tuned out the pundits and the editorialists. Opinions had been everywhere—a dime a dozen—in the aftermath of California. As usual, the media onslaught had cheapened the tragedy, turning it into an opinion circus. But there was something mesmerizing about this particular woman. She had an unusual combination of looks, energy, and smarts that kept him watching. Who the hell was she?

"My guest is Blaise Ryan of the World Environmental Trust," intoned Anna Hardaway. "All right, Blaise, let's ask the question you want to answer. How does America consume less?"

"Political will, Anna. Leadership. Decision. Clarity. And guts. All things we haven't had in our politics for twenty-five years. It's high time somebody at the White House understood that we can't go on importing fossil fuels as if there were no tomorrow. How long is our political leadership going to allow our country to become ever more dependent on foreign sources of oil and gas? People have died, Anna. And, even today, there is nothing coming out of the White House except for a stunning silence."

Notwithstanding the quasinuclear attack on his boss, Tony couldn't figure out if he was more enthralled by Blaise Ryan's incisive clarity or her down-to-earth good looks. He was so taken by her nearly feline gray eyes that he didn't hear the phone until the third ring. He picked it up irritably.

It was Mary Jane Pfeiffer, the chief of staff's secretary, with the bad news that he would have to rip himself away from his trance over Blaise Ryan. Isaiah J. Tolberg wanted to see him right away.

"You wanted to see me, Senator?" asked Tony two minutes later. He was holding on to Tolberg's heavy door, leaning inward. Ruiz's feet were still planted in the corridor; only his head leaned into the chief of staff's office.

Without looking up from a briefing paper on his desk, Tolberg waved Ruiz in. Hand raised in the air, Tolberg pointed to the brown leather sofa near the office's far wall. Tony sat down and waited for the chief of staff to finish.

From the very first day at the White House, Ruiz had been impressed by the modesty of the offices of senior White House officials. People would have been surprised to find that some of the country's most powerful men and women worked in understated surroundings. Yet, even without regal size or opulent furnishings, every nook and cranny in the White House's West Wing offices still managed to denote power.

He looked around Tolberg's office. A glass coffee table surrounded by leather sofas and easy chairs dominated one side of the room. The chief of staff's large, dark desk and an adjacent round conference table with four chairs filled the other half. It could have been the office of any important corporate executive. But the dark furnishings, the freshly cut flowers, and the thick plush of the blue carpet instantly communicated that this office was just a few feet away from the workplace of the world's most powerful leader.

Tolberg closed the file and slowly rose from behind the desk. Notwithstanding his usual elegance, the chief of staff looked tired.

"We have to talk, Tony," said Tolberg, closing the door on his way to the sitting area.

Tony Ruiz's back stiffened. This was only the second time since beginning his work at the White House that Tolberg had shut the door.

Tolberg sat down slowly, never removing his eyes from Tony's. Tolberg's stare was sharp.

"Tony, I'm going to shoot straight with you. I trust you absolutely; but some of what we're going to talk about today doesn't leave this office. Understood?"

Ruiz nodded seriously. His mind sped through the possibilities. There was surprisingly little about his job that was top secret.

"All right," said Tolberg. "It's been a little over two months since we first watched the events in California explode onto our television screens. The consequences were much worse than we ever expected. Everybody in this building—everybody in this country—has been touched by the human tragedy. Two thousand four hundred and sixteen people died in those twenty hot California days.

"Yes, half of those deaths happened in the Sacramento jail breakout." Tolberg continued reciting numbers as if they were a mantra. "The other half was made up of unnecessary tragedies. Most of them elderly, newborn, or infirm. There were also the ninety-seven persons killed in the firefight during Los Angeles's looting. And the horror of sixteen people murdered in Sacramento's Rising Meadows neighborhood by three escaped convicts."

Tony Ruiz wondered where this was going. Tolberg didn't have to rerecite the numbers. He knew them by heart; they had been seared into his brain. Tolberg and Ruiz had personally spent twelve gut-wrenching July days in California, part of the twenty-person wave of White House officials sent to attend funerals, console families, and assess the damage.

Even President Eugene Laurence had spent five full days in the state. He had been determined not to repeat the same mistakes his predecessor had committed in the aftermath of Hurricane Katrina.

"Yes, sir," Ruiz whispered. Tony knew by looking at Tolberg that more was coming.

"Here's the thing, Tony. I just got off the phone with Mieirs and Governor Moravian. It might happen again. Soon. In the next seven days. The country's eastern grids can't supply any more juice without brownouts on the East Coast—and they're just not going to risk doing that to their customers. Mexico's gas has helped; but it's not enough. The last two months have still been hotter than hell in California; we've even got wildfires in the mountains outside Los Angeles. For all practical purposes, the heat has wiped away any of the benefits of Governor Moravian's mandatory energy-conservation policy."

Tolberg paused for a moment, looking at the ceiling. "The

only goddamn piece of good news is that the weather is supposed to break in two days. They're calling for rain and substantially cooler temperatures."

Tony's mouth was agape, aghast at the possibility that the blackouts would return.

"What . . . what is the governor going to do?" Tony knew the stuttered query was a stupid one. But he couldn't think of anything else to say.

"He's going to wait twenty-four hours for a confirmation of the weather. If the meteorologists are wrong and the heat continues, he is going to get ahead of the crisis and warn the state's citizens. It's political suicide to connect himself so personally to the crisis, but he feels strongly that it's the right thing to do."

Silence filled the office as the two men stared at each other. They were both thinking the exact same thing. Neither dared utter the words.

Finally Tolberg said it. Straight out.

"I know what you're thinking, Tony. And you're right. Moravian is not the only one who will be committing suicide with that warning. He'll be taking us down with him."

Tony nodded. It couldn't be any clearer. If Governor Cyrus Moravian went on the air to warn Californians that another energy crisis was imminent, the entire country would clamor for President Gene Laurence's head. No matter how close a friend of Tolberg, Moravian's speech would do everything possible to shift the blame to the federal government's lackluster response to the tragedy in the nation's largest state.

It wasn't that the governor was malicious or vindictive. It was just politics. That's the way things worked.

"What is the president saying, sir?" asked Tony meekly.

"The president is royally pissed off. He feels that this hot potato has been handed down over six presidents since Nixon. He wants—he needs—something clear and decisive. He knows that there are only long-term answers. But what makes him furious is no answers at all. There can't be another energy crisis in California without a clear direction from this president."

Tony smiled.

Tolberg looked at him, irritated. "What is so funny, young man?"

"Senator, have you ever heard of a woman called Blaise Ryan? She's an environmentalist. By the way, she is also absolutely gorgeous. I was just watching an interview with Ryan when you called me in. She was saying the exact same thing. That solving this would come down to leadership. Guts. It's precisely what you are telling me the president thinks."

"She may be well synchronized with our boss, Tony. He wants us to focus like a laser beam on new energy solutions. He wants big ideas, out-of-the-box thinking. Bold strokes. And he wants options on his desk by September fifteenth."

This was the second time in less than a minute that Tony had a feeling of déjà vu. First, the president was thinking like Blaise Ryan. Now, Tolberg was sounding eerily like Raj Rosenblatt. Only a few hours ago words like "big" and "bold" had punctuated Rosenblatt's explanations.

"Since our meeting in the cabinet room two months ago," Tolberg recited with precision, "the president has become very interested in the CIA director's description of a new transcontinental connection through the Bering Strait. President Laurence has made the rounds. He's done his homework with Governor Whitley in Alaska, the CEO of Exxon, Russian experts, energy specialists. We had Raj Rosenblatt here for a quiet coffee the day before yesterday."

"Shit," said Tony sheepishly. "I went to see him on my own today. He never said anything."

Tolberg smiled knowingly. Raj was a pro; he had said nothing to Ruiz of his meeting with President Eugene Laurence.

"The president is taking this seriously. He called President Tuzhbin last week. They had a long conversation and agreed that the next step was to send a confidential high-level delegation to Moscow. President Laurence wants Martha Packard to lead it. She's off in about twelve days."

Isaiah J. Tolberg paused for a moment. Tony cocked his head, wondering what all of this had to do with the president's domestic affairs advisor.

"Tony, the president wants you to go."

Ruiz jumped off the sofa, his eyes wide open in surprise. It was a reflex reaction.

"Me? Why should I go?"

"Please sit down, young man," chided Tolberg with a gentle smile. Ruiz did as he was told.

"Most people would be flattered that the president would choose them for a sensitive foreign mission. Your reaction is surprising, Tony."

"Senator, I'm a former cop from Chelan County. Of course I'm flattered. But I know nothing about energy. Nothing about Russia. Nothing about engineering. Nothing about confidential foreign missions. And to boot, Packard doesn't like me; you had to save my butt that day in the Cabinet Room when I asked a question she thought was impertinent. So why the hell does the president want *me* to go?"

"Because, Tony, you do know one thing better than almost anybody around here. You have a Ph.D. in Gene Laurence. You are fiercely loyal to the president. And, while Packard is thinking her big strategic thoughts about U.S.–Russia relations, your job will be to look out for Gene Laurence's back. That is reason enough, isn't it?"

Tony Ruiz nodded his assent. But his mind was whirling. He had trouble thinking straight.

"Packard's trip is a fact-finding mission," Tolberg enunciated with clarity. "We're not going to agree to anything. Not signing any documents. The objective is to assess whether the Russians and the Americans can become partners in a historic enterprise.

"There is, candidly, also another reason the boss is anxious that you go," continued Tolberg matter-of-factly. "President Laurence had a preparatory conversation with President Tuzhbin the day before yesterday. They both specifically agreed that somebody like you should accompany Packard."

Ruiz was out of his seat again. Now he had two damned presidents asking for him!

Tolberg stuck out his index finger and pointed it downward, toward the sofa.

"Tony, the Russians did not ask for you by name. How could they? Tuzhbin has no idea who you are. But Laurence liked his thinking. Tuzhbin wants somebody there who does not represent part of the bureaucracy. He wants somebody there that is Laurence's personal emissary. Somebody the president trusts one hundred percent."

"So, why don't you go, Senator? That sounds like a description of you, not me."

"Because both presidents also agreed that this person should have a fully open mind to a new era of relations with Russia. Somebody who isn't deformed by the tensions of the Cold War. Somebody who didn't grow up during the fifties, sixties, and seventies believing that Russians were rapacious communist bears.

"And that, young man, sounds like a description of you," Tolberg concluded with a smile.

WASHINGTON, D.C.
AUGUST 17, 1:45 P.M.
THE WHITE HOUSE

Tony Ruiz was silent for a moment as he tried to put some order in his brain.

For the first time in his short political career, he didn't know whether to believe Isaiah J. Tolberg. The president and Tolberg had obviously spent a large part of the previous week secretly vetting the notion of a Bering Strait crossing. The chief of staff's protestations that the Russia trip would only be a fact-finding mission with no authority to conclude or sign any agreements sounded hollow. Tony wondered if the CIA's Martha Packard clearly understood that her trip was limited only to "finding facts."

It occurred to Tony that it was possible he was being used. In the coldest light, the president's desire to have him go to Russia could be explained as an attempt to dress up the mission as more than just a CIA trip. Ruiz's presence in Moscow would be one of an inexperienced political participant without the credibility to torpedo Packard's agenda. Yet, if anybody would ask, Tony's presence on the delegation would lend an aura of White House control.

Tony banished the painful thought from his mind. The notion was nonsense. Even if true, there was no way to communicate his reservations to Tolberg.

But beyond the personal doubts about why he had been chosen for this trip, Tony had serious substantive issues with the project itself. Those he would not—could not—keep silent about. He decided there and then to put his misgivings on the record.

"Senator, of course I'll go. And of course I'm flattered. Nothing is more important to me than to have your confidence and the president's trust. I believe in this administration and I believe in Gene Laurence."

Ruiz took a breath.

"But since you're asking me to do this, I want to be honest with you."

Tolberg leaned his head to the left. "Go ahead, Tony."

"Frankly, Senator, I think this whole Russian idea is off-kilter. You see, I think—"

Tolberg interrupted him.

"Tony, we've done our due diligence. Everybody we've spoken to thinks this is an expensive, hugely daring—but technically feasible—project."

"Give me a minute, Senator," retorted Tony Ruiz. "Hear me out. The engineering is not the part that has me worried. Rosenblatt has convinced me that the science exists to make it technically achievable.

"What concerns me are the politics."

Tony straightened up. If he was going to take a run at Tolberg, he might as well go the full monty.

"A moment ago, I told you, Senator, how impressed I was with the environmentalist woman on television. Her point was that searching for fossil fuels is like Don Quixote tilting at windmills. It's a mirage. She is right, Senator. She talked about the need for guts and leadership. I'm no expert, but I'm smart enough to recognize that something is wrong. This

Bering Strait scheme is guts and leadership in the wrong direction. For a whole host of reasons.

"First, we're going to invest billions with a country that is our former mortal adversary. I recognize that the Russians are no longer our enemies, but they're not exactly our friends either. Why in God's name would we go into business with these guys and make ourselves dependent on their natural resources? Nothing I've read about Russia today would make me think they're a good long-term business partner for us.

"Second, we're already dependent on Arab desert princes for oil. We've seen what dependence does. It makes the elite in those countries richer, more entrenched, and less democratic. And it certainly has not made those countries friendlier to the United States. Now we're going to enrich the Russians by giving them billions for their natural gas. If we do that, at least let's not delude ourselves into believing that any of this is going to make them our friends.

"Third, there is a grim environmental problem looming on the horizon. If we're serious about climate change, adding a gas dependency to an oil addiction is not the way to start. If the president is looking for big and bold, we should be considering incentives for noncarbon fuel industries and specific measures to force—yes, I said force—conservation."

He dared not look at Tolberg. He knew that if he met the Senator's eyes, he would not be able to go any further. Tony Ruiz took a deep breath and lined up for his final shot.

"Big and bold. That's what you are looking for, right, Senator? Well, big and bold is a policy that *together* advances green conservation and promotes energy independence from petroauthoritarians everywhere, no matter whether they live in the desert or the tundra. Anything else isn't anywhere close to bold."

There it was. He was done. As Tony's shoulders relaxed, the thought crossed his mind that his job could be "done," literally as well as figuratively. Ruiz's eyes moved timidly in Tolberg's direction.

What he saw surprised him. The dapper chief of staff was smiling broadly, his eyes dancing with pleasure. Isaiah J.

Tolberg got up off his chair, came around the coffee table, and sat down next to Tony on the leather couch. He swung his cuff-linked sleeve around Tony's shoulders.

"Young man, that was about as fine a political speech as I've ever heard anybody deliver. You will go far. That brain of yours works. But, oh boy, so does that tongue. Excellent.

"But as good as that little sermon was, the lesson you haven't yet learned is the one about political costs," said Isaiah Tolberg, unwinding his arm from Tony's shoulders. His tone was fatherly. "It's a hard lesson to learn in theory. One has to personally suffer the cutting bite of political failure to really internalize the teaching.

"But I'm going to give you a tutorial now, Tony. You can have all the right arguments. All the right policies. All the right analyses and prescriptions. You can be one hundred percent correct. And still, in politics, it's possible that the smartest path is not to move ahead.

"Let's take your geo-eco strategy. If I followed correctly, your point is that conservation helps both the climate and helps wean us off foreign oil. Do I have it right? Well, the question is, how do we really get Americans to conserve? I'll tell you how; there's only one way to do it. We would have to tax carbon fuels like oil and natural gas. Gasoline would need to become too expensive for commuters to buy it for guzzling SUVs. Natural-heating gas would have to cost more than solar panels. Alternative energies would require help to compete against fossil fuels."

Tolberg looked at Ruiz with a disarming smile.

"So, how much tax do we need, Tony? What do you think? Two or three dollars on top of the average four-dollar price per gallon of gasoline and home-heating propane?"

The instant Tony Ruiz nodded his assent, he realized he had fallen into Tolberg's trap.

"Well, what do you think will happen to this president if, after the California crisis, all he can come up with is a two-dollar gasoline tax?" Tolberg's voice dripped with sarcasm. "Can you imagine the conservative talk shows—they would have a field day. I can hear Rush Limbaugh now: 'Gene Laurence doesn't think California suffered enough. He watched people die in the Golden State and now wants to punish Californians with a two-dollar gas tax.' Do you know how long we would last? I'll tell you. Five minutes. We would be eaten alive, Tony. Chewed up and spat out."

Ruiz's eyes looked downward. He knew Tolberg was right. His previous misgivings about the White House's chief of staff gave way to a renewed admiration for the older man's incisive political acumen.

"It's all about the moment, my friend," Tolberg continued, pressing his point. "Politics is about timing. Your plan was the right one if we'd had the guts and the inclination to launch it a year ago. Now, after California, we can't ask people to suffer more."

Tolberg got up. The meeting was over.

"All good ideas, Tony. Good ideas with bad timing. Pack your bags. You're off to Moscow in twelve days."

LANGLEY, VIRGINIA
AUGUST 17, 5:45 p.m.
CIA HEADQUARTERS

General Martha Packard picked up the phone slowly. She didn't like unscheduled calls from the White House. Twenty years in Washington had taught her that impromptu interruptions from high-level civilians almost never brought good news.

Her caution would be proved right. Again.

"Senator, nice to hear from you," she lied. "What's up?" Martha Packard was not one for small talk.

"General, I'm so glad to hear you're well," said the voice of President Eugene Laurence's chief of staff. It was clear to Packard that Tolberg had elegantly engaged her nonexistent phone manners. She ignored the taunt.

"I've been speaking to the president about your upcoming trip to Moscow. We're all intrigued, General. Your success over there could shape the rest of this president's term in office. The stakes are big enough for this to be Eugene Laurence's principal legacy—it could well be what history books will remember about this president."

Packard didn't answer. The general did not like the rhetorical warm-ups all Washington politicians thought were a necessary beginning to every conversation. She looked down irritably at the coffee spot just to the left of her medal of valor. General Martha Packard went to work in uniform. She was not the first former military officer to become the head of the Central Intelligence Agency. But she was the first one to refuse to occupy the traditionally civilian position without resigning her military commission.

If her silence made Isaiah J. Tolberg uncomfortable, he certainly didn't show it.

"Now, the president feels that a mission like the one you're undertaking has such big political ramifications that it might be worth expanding our delegation beyond your ample expertise to include some additional political brainpower."

Packard felt every muscle in her body tighten. Tolberg was in full Washington-speak mode. In English, his words meant, "We don't trust you to go alone." She knew what was coming. Tolberg was joining the trip.

"So the president has asked Tony Ruiz to join you in Russia. I've just talked to him and he is willing to go along."

"What?" Packard choked, unable to contain her irritation. "You're sending a twenty-nine-year-old former policeman with me to negotiate with the most suspicious and conspiratorial humans on the planet? That isn't possible."

"Tony's presence is, General, what the president desires," answered Tolberg without missing a beat. She couldn't tell through his thick formality if he was irritated with her sharpness.

"Well, Senator, the White House may think that Tony Ruiz is a nice fellow. But he has no experience. Hell, I don't even know if this Washington State kid ever crossed the border to Canada. He also talks too much; his interruption in the Cabinet Room a few months ago was inexcusable. Remember that while we Americans like brash youngsters, it is a quality foreigners don't appreciate.

"No," the CIA director concluded. "I don't want him on the plane. He can't come."

"General Packard, I don't believe I was asking for your permission. You are leading this delegation. And you are the person who first brought the idea of a transcontinental crossing to the president's attention. But you're traveling at the president's behest. And he has decided that he would like somebody from the White House to join along. Tony is his choice."

Packard was furious. This was her mission. Her idea. Her launching pad to a political future. She wasn't about to share the limelight with a bit player.

And notwithstanding the elegant words, she knew Tolberg had just tried to put her in her place. She wasn't about to roll over and take it.

"Senator Tolberg, don't pull this civilian one-upsmanship on me. Like you, I've been around the track in this town. My trip to Moscow could instantly transform our relations with the second-mightiest nation on this planet *and* solve our energy needs for the next fifty years. This isn't a school field trip; there can be no mistakes. I'm not about to have an under-thirty White House chaperone with me on one of this country's most important missions."

She could hear Tolberg hesitating. She took advantage of the silence and pressed further.

"The Russians need to hear us speak with one voice. They don't do well with confusion, sir. They should have one clear interlocutor. This is a CIA trip. The presence of somebody from the White House, even if I am clearly the mission chief, has the potential to create misunderstanding."

Packard thought this last bit was particularly convincing. So she decided to end magnanimously.

"There will be ample time to consider the political issues upon my return. If I'm successful in Moscow, we'll need to think a lot about how we announce the transcontinental link. And I respect the president's desire to make Mr. Ruiz an integral part of those discussions. He will be very helpful at that stage, I'm sure."

Leaning back in her deep desk chair, she knew she had

won this skirmish. General Packard never ceased to be impressed by how much time and energy in Washington had to be spent beating back the small incursions into one's own territory. It was an enormous waste of effort; but there was no doubting she was very good at it.

Silence permeated the secure phone line. She said nothing, patiently awaiting Tolberg's verbal retreat. But when he spoke, she could not believe what she was hearing.

"General Packard, you've known me for a long time. Unlike you, I don't like to be blunt. I've always believed adults should be courteous in their professional interactions. I don't believe in rapping people on their knuckles to get a message across.

"However, it's obvious I haven't been clear enough with you. President Gene Laurence believes that having a White House presence on this trip would be beneficial. Notwithstanding Mr. Ruiz's young age, President Laurence has developed an enormous respect for his political insight. As a result, the president has asked Tony to accompany you to Moscow. I am calling you to advise you of the president's decision, not to ask your opinion on the subject.

"Now, General Packard," continued the chief of staff with ice in his voice, "I would like to ask you if all this is clear enough?"

Martha Packard closed her eyes and swallowed hard. She could not believe that the director of central intelligence was being forced to accept the presence of an underage agent from the president's office.

But she had no choice.

"Yes, sir. Crystal clear."

GERMANY

Anne-Sophie Perlmutter let her weight slip deep into the plane's window seat the minute the Frankfurt-bound Lufthansa Airbus 320 lifted off from Kiev's Boryspil State International Airport. Overwhelmed by the feeling of losing control, she tried to close her eyes.

A few hours ago, Anne-Sophie had careened down the highway from Kursk to Kiev. The Ukrainian capital was the closest airfield to her house with direct flights to Frankfurt. Over flat farmland and across the Ukrainian border, the drive had taken less than three hours.

As the airplane climbed through Eastern Europe's overcast skies, Anne-Sophie could feel her hands tremble. The rivets that had long held up the load-bearing fixtures of her life were now buckling. Her existence had become like a runaway freight train, plodding at a steady speed down tracks that led to a precipice. So far, she hadn't been able to find a way to alight. Hopefully, this trip to Germany would provide a road map.

Five weeks had passed since the fateful argument at her

father's house. Since then, not a single word about the fight had again crossed Daniel's and Anne-Sophie's lips. The two had bent over backward to be polite—particularly in front of the children.

But the lifeblood was seeping out of the couple's relationship. The caring was draining away. Like water in a bathtub. Sucked into invisibility, gone and irretrievable.

She had tried to find a dialogue with Daniel. But he had hardly engaged. His responses had reverted to a standard monotone—neither hot nor cold. Still, Anne-Sophie had decided on a final effort, if only out of respect for over a decade together. She needed to tell herself that they had attempted to repair it.

It didn't go well. The conversation that was supposed to be about reconstructing a way to live together had instead turned into the final rupture. Over steaming cups of coffee and croissants at Kursk's turn-of-the-century Ustinov Café, Anne-Sophie's attempt to reglue their marriage had unraveled into another bitter exchange about his job and Russia.

And that was before Daniel had sprung yet another one of his surprises.

"Stop exaggerating Russia's problems," he had admonished her a half hour into the conversation in a voice that dripped with irritation. "In the year and a half of working for Zhironovsky, I've come to understand that our gas is a powerful weapon against those who want to do us harm. These guys in Moscow are sophisticated. They are using gas to send a message to the world."

"What is that message, Daniel?" asked Anne-Sophie impatiently. She had struggled to remain composed against yet another reappearance of his paranoid xenophobia.

"The message is that the fall of the Soviet Union doesn't mean that Russia can be mistreated. We are the largest country on the planet. A world power. And we require respect. The mistake of the communists was to believe that military power and nuclear weapons were the only way to get the world's respect."

She hadn't known what to say to him. But Daniel clearly had more. It was his big revelation.

"Zhironovsky has offered me a job at headquarters, in Moscow. He told me last week that we should move there. He has given me a new assignment. And I said yes. This move will solve a lot of the problems between us. You need a big city. You need to see foreigners. You need to take your mind off your little life in a little town. I can go now and you can come at the end of the school year, with the children."

He had been excited to share the news about the family's move. He had talked on, needing his wife to understand the alluring heights to which he now had access.

"My new job will be to take care of Volga Gaz's international issues. And, if we are successful, we will push the Americans down a few notches. If our project works, the Americans will suddenly wake up one day and find themselves depending on Volga Gaz for a huge part of their gas needs."

Daniel Vladimirovich Uggin's mouth had curled into a wide smile. "We're going to force the Americans to look at Russia in a far different light.

"So you see, Anne-Sophie," Daniel was saying, "we're moving to Moscow."

Yesterday's coffee was the very moment Anne-Sophie Perlmutter would always remember as the end of her marriage. The realization had hit her like lightning when her husband dictated his unilateral decision to move. There was no bridging the gap. She was stuck in Russia with a man who had fallen *out* of love with her and *in* love with his country and his job.

A thousand questions had zoomed through her mind—separation, moving, and, above all, the children. But she had held her tongue. She needed time. She had to get away.

"Moscow?" she lied, forcing a smile to cross her lips. "Hmm? Moving to the big city? That is something I never thought of. It could be just the right thing. Let me think about it and we can talk in a few days.

"Can I change the subject?" Anne-Sophie had asked, forcing an easy smile to her lips. "My father called to tell me he wasn't feeling well. He is getting tests done on Monday and Tuesday at the hospital. I would like to go for a few days.

You're home for the next few days, right? Do you think that is okay? I can catch the Lufthansa flight from Kiev tomorrow afternoon."

None of it was true. Her father was fine. But knowing the conversation might go wrong, Anne-Sophie had already planned this trip. Blaise would pick her up tomorrow. What forethought, she had said to herself, waiting for Daniel's answer.

He hadn't hesitated. Daniel had clearly been pleased that Anne-Sophie hadn't rejected outright the sudden notion of moving to Russia's capital. "Darling, you haven't told me anything about Hermann! I'm sorry he isn't well. Yes, of course, of course.

"Leave the children with me. Go to your father."

FRANKFURT
AUGUST 21, 4:00 P.M.
FRANKFURT AIRPORT

Anne-Sophie squinted right and left as she walked through the terminal's electronically rotating glass doors, pulling her small Samsonite suitcase behind her. The bright sunshine blinded her.

Traffic was a constant mess at Frankfurt's Rhein-Main airport. Named after the two rivers that converged in Germany's business capital, the airport was one of the world's busiest. The terminals' access roads were a jumble of cars, buses, taxis, shuttle vans, and masses of passengers struggling to reach their assigned lanes. Vehicles serving airport destinations such as terminal transfers, parking lots, and local hotels were directed to the near curbside. Taxis and private cars to downtown and other places in the Frankfurt metropolitan area picked up passengers fifty yards away, on multiple concrete islands accessed and connected by pedestrian crosswalks.

Elite units of Germany's border police in instantly identifiable yellow shirts walked in between cars eyeing drivers and vehicles approaching the terminal. They were heavily armed with submachine guns and protected by gray bullet-proof vests. The border police did not mingle or talk to the traffic cops whose shrieking whistles and frenzied gestures moved the endless flow of cars pouring into the airport.

The chaos at Frankfurt Airport was not the picture of Teutonic orderliness one would expect in Germany's financial center.

Anne-Sophie studied the crisscrossing directional signs that distributed passengers to their preferred means of transportation. Picking her way through the airport shuttle services to the passenger pickup islands, her attention was caught by one particularly noisy car whose horn would not stop blowing. She smiled as she recognized the driver. Not even Italian or Turkish immigrants would risk the social opprobrium that inevitably befell anyone making this much noise in Germany.

Only Blaise Ryan could be so oblivious to the rules of German etiquette.

Anne-Sophie picked up her pace and ran toward the noisy gray Ford Focus. Contrary to all rational expectation, the fact that the Ford had found its passenger did not diminish the driver's need to make noise. In fact, Anne-Sophie noticed that her proximity to the vehicle only increased the driver's rate of pressure on the car's horn.

Anne-Sophie threw the Samsonite next to the compact roll-away suitcase already in the open trunk and jumped into the passenger seat. She threw her arms around her old friend. The two women embraced and kissed each other multiple times on both cheeks.

"Get your seat belt on and let's get out of here before one of those border police guys comes and arrests us. God, they look scary!" Blaise accelerated the car forward and zigzagged between the maze of drop-offs and pickups arrayed in front of them. Within just a few minutes, the Ford had accelerated to over 150 kilometers an hour.

"I just love your autobahns," said Blaise, gray eyes gleaming through the streaks of red hair falling over her eyes. "There is no speed limit, and whatever the car is telling me right here is meaningless because I don't read kilometers. I'm oblivious."

Typical Blaise. She knew exactly that 150 kilometers per

hour equaled over ninety miles per hour. But with Blaise, the truth was something that could be temporarily blurred. Not to mislead, but rather as a useful social tool to enhance pleasurable conversation.

"Don't act so innocent. You know exactly how fast you are going," giggled Anne-Sophie. Somehow the combination of blue sky, sunshine, and her friend's California smile was already lifting the burden off her shoulders. "Where are we going?"

"To Heidelberg. Only an hour's drive. You came one-tenth of the distance that I flew last night. Don't tell me you're tired. I landed about four hours ago—I've stood in a long line at passport control, had breakfast, and bought some expensive underwear in that silly shopping mall underneath the airport."

To prove her purchase, Blaise pulled one hand off the Ford's steering wheel to hitch up her already short skirt, revealing newly minted, orange-colored La Perla thong panties. "I also read the newspaper, rented the car, went into a smelly bathroom at the rental agency to brush my teeth and do up my hair, drove around for an hour, and now . . . here I am, so happy to see you!"

"Put your hand back on the wheel, you crazy woman." Anne-Sophie was in full-scale cackle now. "Heidelberg? Why Heidelberg? Shouldn't we just call my father and say we're here and go to his house? Anyway, I haven't been to Heidelberg in fifteen years. I don't know anybody there."

"Good," snapped Blaise. "That is another reason on a long list of good reasons to go to Heidelberg. It's close. It's beautiful. I've never been there and have always wanted to go. We'll be alone because, as you just told me, you don't know anybody. It's the inspiring home of philosophers like Friedrich Hegel and Karl-Otto Apel. And God knows we need to do some thinking. Enough reasons?"

Blaise glanced over at the woman sitting next to her. Anne-Sophie was a shadow of her former self. She was too thin, nearly gaunt. Her sculptured face read exhaustion. Blaise wasn't surprised—even in faraway San Francisco, the two women's daily e-mail exchanges had given ample warning of Anne-Sophie's state of mind.

Blaise's right hand reached over to stroke her friend's cheek. Though Anne-Sophie smiled broadly, Blaise's quick look away from the windshield had picked up the gathered clouds of sadness in her friend's eyes. The soft touch of Blaise's hand was designed to remind Anne-Sophie that, behind the laughter, there was a soul mate who knew her. Loved her. Felt with her.

For a second, Blaise's grin disappeared as her hand returned to the steering wheel. "The most important reason we're going to Heidelberg is because you and I need some time alone. We need to talk, friend."

HEIDELBERG
AUGUST 21, 6:00 P.M.
THE PHILOSOPHENWEG

In German, it is called the Philosophenweg. A tree-lined, flower-strewn walk on the northern side of the broad Neckar River, the Philosopher's Lane was a burst of cross-river fairy-tale views toward the turrets and domes of the old city's ramparts and castles. For seven hundred years, philosophers from Heidelberg's Ruprecht Karls University have walked, talked, debated, and disagreed across from the magnificence on the other side of the Neckar.

Heidelberg's original name came from the famed fruits of the great hill behind the old town—Heidelbeerenberg, or Blueberry Mountain—but it was the beautiful storybook cityscape that had given it the reputation as Germany's most romantic town. It was not a coincidence that the city's most popular bumper sticker was *Ich habe mein Herz in Heidelberg verloren.*

I lost my heart in Heidelberg.

This was a place where people spilled their hearts, opened their souls. Blaise had chosen well.

An hour ago, they had checked into the Goldener Hirsch—the Golden Stag—an elegant, small hotel where Blaise had prepaid for a suite for two nights. Once in the sumptuous three-room chamber, Anne-Sophie and Blaise raided the minibar, pulling out a small bottle of champagne and a bag of cashews.

They had burst out laughing at Blaise's imitation of the harsh look of the stout woman who had checked them in at the hotel's reception desk. With hair mounted in a large beehive at the top of her head, the matronly clerk clearly had disapproved of the new, apparently lesbian, guests. The fat lady had resented the fact that the room's prepayment meant she was left with no choice but to give the lodge's best quarters to this undesirable gay couple.

Blaise had traveled far longer, so Anne-Sophie had insisted that Blaise be the first to, according to the hotel's overwritten brochure, "luxuriate under our enormous showerhead's wide barrage of independently delivered water pixels." They had lounged in the hotel's thick white bathrobes while waiting for room service to deliver the apple strudels ordered for a snack. They had made a pact with great fanfare on the run-of-show of the rest of the day's activities: It would be a quick snack, a long walk, and a big dinner.

Now, at 7:30 P.M., the two women were a half hour into their stroll on the Philosopher's Lane. The sun, still warm, but low in the western sky, extended their shadows far ahead of their bodies. Anne-Sophie told her friend about yesterday's coffee with Daniel. She ended with his plans to move to Moscow.

As Anne-Sophie talked, Blaise noticed how her friend, in only thirty minutes, had imperceptibly moved the conversation from a sad recount of a dying relationship to a discussion of how to end a marriage.

"What kills me is that the gentle, idealistic man I loved has replaced me with an infatuation for the bureaucratic equivalent of the caveman—the Russian State," said Anne-Sophie. Her sadness was pierced by a bitter sarcasm.

"My husband is the only university graduate to be found in Russia's eleven time zones who believes the government is honest and well-meaning. There are two Russias, Blaise. One is the Russia of the new capitalism—it's a treacherous cauldron of oligarchs, gamblers, and real entrepreneurs who are changing the landscape, creating jobs and wealth. And the other Russia is the state. It is made up only of thugs and the mafia.

"Nobody with an education wants to work for the government. Nobody. Except for Daniel."

"So, since that disaster at your dad's house five weeks ago, are you any clearer on what he does for Volga Gaz?" asked Blaise.

"I know you think I'm stupid, Blaise. But I don't know. They have something planned against the Americans. I don't know what it is, but yesterday he was bragging about pushing the Americans 'down a few notches.'

"I find everything out by accident. I know about Anfang because my best friend spent a morning spying on him. I find out about Bolivia from my nine-year-old daughter. I discover he is moving to Moscow over breakfast in a café. Everything is smoke and mirrors."

For once Blaise Ryan didn't have words. It didn't matter because Anne-Sophie had more to say.

"Sit with me here. Let's take this bench and look at the view." Anne-Sophie guided her friend to the wooden seat directly overlooking the river. The old city, drenched in the waning sun's orange light, dazzled in front of them.

"I need to confess something. You have come such a long way, but I asked you to meet me not only because I need a good shoulder to cry on. I also need Blaise Ryan's creative mind. You see, I've come to realize that I need to get out. Out means out of Russia. Out from under his constant paranoia. But I can't go without the kids; I won't leave my children in Russia, Blaise."

"Did the kids come up in yesterday's conversation?" asked Blaise, putting a gentle hand on her friend's shoulder.

"No. If I tell him I want to leave, I am afraid he will divorce me and keep the children. He will say that it's important to 'make them Russian.' That is what he is about now. Russia! Russia! Nothing else matters."

Anne-Sophie looked at Blaise, her eyes hard. "To get out with Katarina and Giorgi, I need to find out more about what my husband does. I need leverage. Negotiating power. I need to force my husband to choose between job and family. Once he is face-to-face with those stark options, he'll choose the job."

Blaise looked at her friend quizzically, surprised that this was not turning out to be the two-day, tear-filled consolation session she had expected. Instead, her friend sounded like a determined woman with a plan.

"How are you going to do that?"

"Well, I think that this German company, Anfang, is the key. Two months ago, you already found out a lot on the Internet. But we need more. And companies here are like companies in the United States. They need to abide by the law. They need to file statements. Documents are public.

"Yes, Blaise, I need to start by knowing everything there is to know about Anfang. And that is why you're here, my dear friend. I will need advice about how to handle the information we get."

Anne-Sophie's eyes shifted forward in a determined stare. "And I have a plan to get the information. Want to hear it?"

Blaise Ryan was too taken aback to say anything intelligent. Eyes wide open in utter astonishment over her friend's hard-hearted conspiratorial tones, Blaise just nodded in the affirmative.

Anne-Sophie outlined her plan in twenty minutes. Blaise Ryan was rarely surprised by life. But today she was flabbergasted. She had come halfway across the world to console a dear friend who had married into a Russian world that had suddenly locked her out. She had fully expected to see Anne-Sophie near an emotional breaking point.

Instead, she now faced a woman determined to go to war with Russia's most powerful elements.

FRANKFURT
AUGUST 24, 1:00 P.M.
HERMANN PERLMUTTER'S HOME

Three days later, Blaise sat alone at the dining table of Anne-Sophie's childhood home watching her friend talking in German on the telephone and scribbling notes. Until today, she had never previously bemoaned the fact that German was not one of her languages.

Surrounded by half-eaten sandwiches of Appenzeller cheese and Black Forest ham, Blaise desperately tried to discern the gist of Anne-Sophie's half-hour phone conversation with her father. Each furrow of Anne-Sophie's brow, each movement of her hand, each muttered "ja, ja" exasperated her further. It drove her crazy not to understand.

Finally, Anne-Sophie put down the phone. She walked back to the table in deep thought. She was clearly not happy.

"So? Did he find out anything? He must have because you were on the phone with him for thirty-five minutes," Blaise blurted out.

"You know my father. He can charm everybody, make anybody talk." Anne-Sophie smiled sadly. "Yes. He found out what we needed to know."

"Come on, stop delaying. What is it?"

"Okay. He did just what we asked. He went to his old office at the tax collection bureau in the ministry of finance and got his secretary of thirty years to do the digging for him. At first, they didn't know what to look for, so they scoured through Anfang's articles of incorporation."

"What was in them?"

"Almost nothing of interest. The company was created in 1923 by Pieter Schmidt's great-grandfather. Schmidt remains the CEO. The articles of incorporation have been amended six times over the years for small, unimportant reasons. The last amendment was in 2000."

"All right, what happened next?"

"They then pulled Anfang's corporate taxes; they were due in April."

Blaise could tell by Anne-Sophie's voice that whatever Hermann had found wasn't good news.

"They didn't file their corporate taxes this year," Anne-Sophie intoned.

"What do you mean, they didn't file a tax return?" Blaise insisted. "Anfang is a big company, they must have completed a return."

"Well, they didn't," Anne-Sophie retorted, looking down at her notes to find a specific notation. "Instead they filed something called a Form T-161."

Blaise didn't have to tell Anne-Sophie that what she had just heard was the equivalent of gibberish. She waited for her friend to go on.

"My father says that Form T-161 is titled 'Notice of Cessation of Operations.' It is the form Germany's tax authorities require when a corporation winds up its business and ceases to exist. This form is the way out-of-business companies advise the Finance Ministry not to expect any further tax payments in the future."

"I don't get it, Annie. This company exists today. We have their address; I saw their building."

"Blaise, if you would stop interrupting me, you would be able to get the whole story a whole lot faster," Anne-Sophie admonished.

"What? What?"

"It seems that companies filing Form T-161 are required to provide a formal explanation for the cessation of business. The reason Anfang Energie is no longer going to pay corporate taxes in the Federal Republic of Germany is that they've been sold. To a foreign company."

Blaise started to sense what was coming.

"Anfang Energie was purchased by Volga Gaz in January of this year. Anfang exists only in name; it's now a wholly owned subsidiary of Volga Gaz."

"Jesus," whispered Blaise. "But why isn't this public?" She looked at Anne-Sophie in puzzlement. "Why isn't there any knowledge of this?"

"I asked my father the same question. It seems that, as a closely held, private company with no outside shareholders, Anfang Energie has no legal requirement to disclose the sale. It was a private transaction."

"But obviously the company's attorney is a nice German lawyer, a detail-oriented stickler." Blaise smiled. It was perfectly Teutonic. The attorney had filed the T-161 because he wanted to be sure that the ministry wouldn't chase down Anfang for any tax payments this year.

"Yes, that is exactly what happened."

It took only a few seconds for the initial elation of having found out that Anfang was just a cover for Volga Gaz to give way to real worry. Now that they knew the truth, what were they to do with the information? The two women fell into a ponderous silence. Without saying so, both wondered the exact same thing. But each of them came to a diametrically opposite conclusion.

Anne-Sophie was the first to talk.

"Blaise, there is nothing more to think about," she said, her hands cutting the air in agitation. "I have to go back to Kursk. I have to tell Daniel that I know he has hidden his life from me. That he is involved in secrets and conspiracies. Right here, in Frankfurt. In my own country! I have to tell him that this is not the family life I want for my children. And then I have to ask him for a divorce."

Anne-Sophie was in a furious spin, fixating on the need to leave Daniel. She repeated over and over again that it was impossible to live under the same roof with a man who was a veritable stranger. A man who hid what he did every day.

The more Anne-Sophie talked, the more worried Blaise became. Really worried. Blaise didn't know why her mind was always so efficient at clearly reading the dangers ahead. Perhaps it was because years of brawls with corporate higher-ups had accustomed her brain to think suspiciously. Whatever the reason, it made no difference. The only thing of importance was that Anne-Sophie wasn't thinking straight.

Blaise now decided that there was no choice but to speak up.

"Stop for a moment," Blaise whispered. "You have to take a step back. As painful as this is, you need to try to see this with some distance. You're not thinking clearly enough about what Hermann found out this morning."

Anne-Sophie looked up sadly.

Blaise swallowed hard. "I don't think that going back to confront Daniel is a very good idea."

"What?" shouted Anne-Sophie. "There isn't any other choice."

Blaise raised her hand, demanding silence. "Hear me out

for a moment. We've fallen into something much bigger than just you, Anne-Sophie. It's not just about *what* Daniel is hiding. The real question is *why* he has kept the details of his job, his travels, and his relationship with Anfang Energie a secret. And if you ask yourself that question, the answer is frightening."

She saw that her friend was now paying attention.

"Let's review what we know. We know that Anfang Energie is bidding for a large project in Peru called Humboldt to export natural gas to the United States. Don't underestimate the importance of Humboldt; this isn't just any little energy project in South America. There are huge financial and political interests involved here, lots of them coming from my own country. The United States is desperate for natural gas. Remember, I've seen firsthand what failing generators and empty pipelines have done to people's lives in California.

"We also know that Daniel has been traveling to Bolivia. Your daughter found the visa stamp in his passport, right? This probably means that, in some capacity, Daniel has been involved in Volga Gaz's partnership with the Bolivian gas company. Peru and Bolivia are in a race to get their gas to market first. So, supposedly, Bolivia and Peru are big competitors in the gas-export business.

"Supposedly," Blaise repeated before continuing.

"But now your father has discovered that this competition is a sham. Anfang Energie and Volga Gaz are actually one and the same company. If Anfang wins the Humboldt bid, the Russians will virtually control the eastern Pacific Ocean's natural gas routes to California."

Anne-Sophie interrupted, struggling with her anger to pay attention. "But if Peru and Bolivia are such fierce competitors, why would they allow the same company to bid on both of their gas-export projects?"

"You've hit the nail straight on, Annie. You see, I don't think either country knows of the connection between Anfang and Volga Gaz. I know the man in charge of Humboldt. His name is Luis Matta. He is a destroyer of the environment, somebody who believes that Peru needs to develop its natural gas capacity no matter what the cost to the fragile

Amazonian ecosystems. But he is not corrupt. In his own way, he is convinced of doing the right thing for his country. Had he known that Anfang was a Volga Gaz subsidiary, he would never have qualified them for the Humboldt bid."

Blaise took a deep breath. "No, I don't think anybody knows. What we've just discovered is a massive Russian sting operation to take control of South America's natural gas."

Blaise's gray eyes took one look across the table and saw that Anne-Sophie did not get it. She was still having trouble looking beyond the concentric circles of her own problems.

"Blaise, all this superpower cloak-and-dagger stuff has nothing to do with me. I'm just a woman in a relationship that has gone sour. My husband may be involved in all of this. Or he may not. I don't care; I just want to get out. This is not how I want to live my life."

Blaise reached over to the water pitcher and poured water into her wineglass. She tried to gauge how honest she should be with her best friend. Anne-Sophie's situation pained her. But Blaise needed her to understand the danger she was in.

"Unfortunately, all this international secrecy has *everything* to do with you. You have to listen to me. Carefully.

"You're my best friend," Blaise pleaded. "I can't lie to you. I'm going to be very, very direct. You can't get out of your marriage. Not now. Not yet. You can't go back to Russia and tell your husband that you know all of this. We have inadvertently found out something that is very, very critical to Volga Gaz. If it's important to Volga Gaz, it's important to the Russian government. They won't let some insignificant marital difficulties endanger their plan."

Anne-Sophie started to protest. "Blaise, I don't care about the Russian government—"

"Damnit, Annie." Blaise's voice thundered through the dining room. "Wake up. You are in real danger, Anne-Sophie. This isn't about your marriage anymore. Daniel's superiors are tough people. If you reveal what you know, they will squash you like an insect. If you say something, if you let on to any knowledge at all, you are putting your life at risk."

Blaise paused for a split second.

"And you're endangering your children."

Right then and there, Blaise could see that Anne-Sophie finally understood. She was caught. Trapped between a man she no longer respected and a knowledge that she could not reveal.

"What do you want me to do, Blaise?" pleaded Anne-Sophie. "What am I supposed to do?"

Blaise knew that there was one road open that would not endanger Anne-Sophie. Only one option. It made Blaise shudder in disgust to even consider it, but it was clear that there was no other choice.

"I have one idea," whispered Blaise. "But I need a few days to make it happen. Meanwhile, can you go back to Kursk and pretend nothing has happened? You will have to act, lie and play a part. You will have to tell Daniel that you've thought about his offer and agree to move to Moscow. You have to go back and just be the same wife. Annie, this has got to be the biggest performance of your life.

"Can you do it? Answer me."

Anne-Sophie's head slowly fashioned an up-and-down movement. "What do you have in mind, Blaise? Can you really help?"

Blaise formulated her proposal over the next half hour. It took considerable explanation to make Anne-Sophie understand the connections. The timing. The more she described it, the more convinced she became that it could really work.

It would create just the right distance from Anne-Sophie to guarantee that nobody in Russia would ever suspect her involvement.

Senator Luis Matta let his weight fall back into the deep brown leather chair. He was a very tired man. Still, as he relaxed into the high back, Matta allowed himself a moment of satisfaction. It was the first day of September and Humboldt's hearings were beginning right on time.

Matta swiveled around to take in the panoramic perspective of the packed hearing room. All thirteen committee members were present—no surprise; none of Senator Matta's media-hungry political colleagues would dare skip this circus. Crammed in the back third of the hall, Susana Castillo was hushing eleven television camera operators and dozens of reporters and photographers into silence.

Luis Matta took in the view. It was hard to remember a similar scene in his fifteen years in politics. The hearing room was a large, ceremonial area with an imposing curved ceiling. Usually, the committee's deliberations were far less interesting—the room was accustomed to feeling empty, with only a couple of lobbyists and interested spectators thinly spread around the twelve rows of chairs.

Not today.

For this event, the chairman's staff had ordered extra chairs that now spilled into crowded aisles. At least two hundred people were crammed into the chamber. Against the glare of hot camera lights, Matta strained to focus his eyes on the faces in the audience. Once his vision penetrated the halogen onslaught's white heat, he noticed the remarkable tendency of constituency groups to always sit together. Indeed, all parties—even those who were ferocious competitors—sat in interest-group clusters.

Matta's eyes scanned the seats. Senior government officials and their staffs—there must have been two dozen representatives of the administration, he thought to himself, raising his hand in a friendly wave to the minister of the economy and the minister of energy and mines—were in the first row. Impeccably dressed bankers, who would soon be scrambling over each other to broker the enormous project's loans, clustered together elegantly on Matta's left. Representatives of international organizations—the chairman recognized the resident heads of the World Bank and the United Nations Development Programme—were squirreled away in the back, desperate not to be noticed. Oil and gas executives from the private sector—he immediately recognized Ludwig Schutz and Arnie Constable from the United States—were cramped together six rows back, in the center.

Matta moved quickly over these groups. He was missing one and squinted hard to search. His eyes finally moved to the front of the room and caught the sullen stares of the environmental organizations. They sat in the front rows to ensure that none of the politicians would miss their glowering disapproval.

Matta's heart skipped a beat as he made out Blaise Ryan's sparkling dark red hair among the environmentalists. She was there, second row, fourth seat from the left aisle, dressed in dark brown pants, a perfectly starched, flawlessly white cotton tunic with a Nehru collar and retro-Chinese Cultural Revolution sleeves with oversize cuffs. Assisted by two well-disguised pleats, the tunic bloomed outward as it passed the waistline, elegantly accenting the curves of her hips. It was hard to see through the reflection of lights pointed toward the senators on the dais, but he could literally feel the gray eyes boring their way into him.

Matta was exhausted. The work schedule of the previous weeks had been harrowing. His every step had been covered by a bevy of reporters assigned to stick to him throughout the project's decision-making process. When he had walked into the committee room a few moments earlier, he had been uncertain of lasting through the day-long hearings.

Seeing Blaise Ryan now provided him with a precise response to his exhaustion. Very few persons on the planet aroused in Matta's balanced and rational soul such a profound feeling of animosity. She was at the top of the list. Just a few weeks ago, in his office, Susana had warned him to thicken his skin. Today, he was glad this horrendous woman was here and that his skin was thin. Her presence jolted him back to attention.

Matta had always been uncomfortable with the deep controversies sparked by the gas project. It was an issue that had no middle ground. Environmental groups detested the idea of a gas-extraction facility and a pipeline thrust into the middle of the Amazon jungle. All precautions and risk-mitigation measures the government of Peru would force upon Humboldt's managers would make no difference. The environmentalists' opposition was philosophical, not practical.

Luis Matta was a politician in the best sense. He understood that heated disagreements were part and parcel of hot issues. He enjoyed the intellectual challenge of serious debate. But what he would not—could not—ever forgive was what had happened in this very room nearly eighteen months earlier during the hearings to authorize Humboldt's first phase.

During those first hearings, he had personally done everything possible to ensure that the project would meet or exceed every known international standard to mitigate negative environmental consequences. Matta's committee had legislated compensation for villagers along the pipeline's path. A special group of agronomists had been impaneled to provide advice on reseeding the delicate Andean soils to alleviate construction-related erosion. Matta had personally negotiated the creation of a social fund to help the Andean peasants in the communities along the pipeline route.

Last and perhaps most important, Matta had aroused howls of disapproval from the project's bidders when he had ruled that the Amazon would have to be treated like an offshore-drilling platform. To avoid the massive movement of job seekers and squatters into the precious rain forest, Matta had inserted language into the law that prohibited the construction of any roads to the extraction facility.

If the companies wanted Peru's gas, they would have to helicopter all their materials, equipment, and manpower to the site.

Matta recalled the huge sense of pride he had felt when he had entered into the hearing room a year and a half ago. Newspapers in Peru had heralded the tough negotiating skills of the young chairman. He had done the impossible. His committee had been on the cusp of approving a project that would assure Peru decades of energy independence, yet it would do so with world-class environmental and social guarantees for its citizens. Three days earlier, an editorial in the *Miami Herald* had called Peru's imminent approval of the Humboldt project "a case study in how to do things right."

Matta had taken his time walking to the dais on that day. Basking in accolades as he strolled down his committee room's right-hand aisle, the chairman had shaken hands with journalists, exchanged knowing words with economists from the World Bank, and embraced ambassadors who had just cabled their home governments about the Peruvian Congress's impressive work.

Yet Luis Matta's day in the sun had never materialized.

As the chairman moved slowly down the crowded aisles, a very attractive, foreign-looking woman had been awaiting her turn to greet the successful politician. Her red hair had been pulled sharply backward into a ponytail that wound its way back over her left shoulder. She had worn tight blue jeans and high heels, a starched white shirt, and a necklace of blue lapis lazuli stones that played off the translucent gray of her eyes. She had smiled placidly as he came toward her.

It had been impossible not to notice her.

"Hello," he had said in English; clearly she wasn't local. "My name is Luis Matta." He should have known instantaneously that something was amiss because she never took his outstretched hand.

"Mr. Matta, I'm Blaise Ryan with the World Environmental Trust. I'm very happy that today you'll get the results you so richly deserve for all your efforts on this project."

Matta had begun to mouth a grateful acknowledgment for her kind compliment when he saw her right hand—the one that had never taken his own hand in greeting—rise up. In her palm was a large plastic Tupperware container filled with an oozing brown substance.

He had no time to stop it.

The shit from her container had landed right on his face, the warm, wet cow feces dripping down onto his suit from his eyelashes and nose. Three other environmental activists had, without his knowledge, edged through the crowd and were now standing close by. They too emptied their own brown containers onto his head and shoulders.

The commotion had been instantaneous. People had run to help him but had skidded to a dead halt a few feet away, unsure of how or where to touch the fecally impregnated committee chairman. The sound of snapping cameras had filled the room. Television crews had disconnected cameras from their tripods and scrambled over rows of seats to get a clear angle, sending chairs tumbling onto the floor. Producers were screaming into cellular phones, demanding immediate live airtime from their newsrooms. Police had poured into the elegant hall, shoving spectators aside, desperate to arrest the perpetrators and protect the senator.

At the center of the mayhem, Matta had just stood there, stunned, entirely covered in putrid manure. The picture of the senator, utterly alone, with nobody daring to touch him, had been the lead on the evening news, the focus of the newspapers' front pages, and the cover of every weekly magazine.

As horrible as it had been, Matta's committee had reconvened a few weeks later in a closed session to push through its approval of the Humboldt project. The press had quickly moved on to the next story. Normalcy had returned. Blaise Ryan's attack had been a circus act, entirely devoid of permanence.

But still, he remembered that moment as the darkest of his political life. And today, there she was again, right in front of him. Taunting him with her presence. The gray eyes looking right at him.

He had known she would be there today. A few days prior to the hearings, a stern-looking captain from the Peruvian Judicial Police, the arm of the justice ministry charged with the protection of all federal elected officials, had appeared in Matta's office. The captain had strongly urged him to bar Blaise Ryan from the coming proceedings.

But Susana, ever the contrarian, had argued to ignore the police captain's advice. "If you prohibit her entry, rest assured that this will be the press story. Coverage will be all about her. On the other hand, if you just ignore her, the press will file stories about your orderly and efficient hearings on Humboldt's second phase, all with her sitting right there!"

He tried to calm his feelings of ire and hatred. Revenge is a dish best eaten cold, he said to himself. I am up here to move the new Humboldt project. She is down there, in the audience, with nothing to do but watch.

Luis Matta pulled twice on the cord attached to the small bell next to his chair, signaling the committee to session. As the committee room slowly hushed, he began to read his short opening statement. In Peru, by law and tradition, the chairman had to provide a short, concise explanation of the committee's business.

"Ladies and gentlemen, we are in session over the next few days to consider the expansion of the Humboldt gas project begun a year and a half ago. As you know, the government of Peru has agreed to allow gas exploration in certain restricted areas of its departments in the Amazon lowlands. Based on geological surveys, the ministry of mines five years ago divided these areas into numbered lots, each extending approximately three hundred thousand square kilometers in size, with the intent of leasing these numbered lots to private companies interested in partnering with Peru to exploit our large gas reserves.

"This committee will now hold hearings to consider approval of a liquefied natural gas pipeline which will transport gas not consumed in Peru to a coastal terminal for the purpose of exporting the gas. The gas will travel one thousand three hundred and fifty-two kilometers from the extraction sites in lots eighty-six, eighty-two, and fifty-three. The committee will also consider at this time a further lease of lot seventy-nine.

"This committee will now come to order." Matta again rang the bell twice.

That was it. Short and sweet. Unlike lots of other parliaments around the world, the Peruvian Congress adhered to strict legal formats. Big political speeches and hot rhetoric were reserved for plenary sessions on the floor of the Senate. Committees were expected to conduct business in an orderly fashion.

The rest of the day went smoothly. The morning was reserved for the two government ministers. Both expounded in huge detail on the project's benefits. The minister of the economy was the country's most powerful political personality after the president and was one of Matta's potential election rivals in a future presidential bid. Never one to lose an opportunity to campaign, the minister spent over an hour enumerating the social investments that would suddenly become affordable thanks to the large pool of new cash generated by the dollars from gas exports.

The testimony of the minister of mines went over two hours. He tediously reviewed the available geological data in each of the leased lots in order to clearly prove that Peru had the gas reserves necessary to support a project of such magnitude. Christ, thought Matta irritably, he could have shortened his presentation to less than a half hour. We all know the country is full of gas.

In the afternoon, the committee heard from private consulting experts on the engineering of the pipeline itself. The details were many and excruciatingly boring. The consultants went into the minutiae of pipe thickness, welding requirements, slope angles. It was withering stuff.

There were no questions from any of the committee members when the consultants finished their testimony. Thank God. At 4:30 P.M. Luis Matta closed the session.

Luis Matta took a moment to pause and look straight at Blaise Ryan. He wanted to look into her eyes to see the inevitable flicker of regret upon realizing that Humboldt's forward motion was unstoppable. A quick twinge of disappointment ran through his mind when he saw she was no longer in her seat.

"We look forward to the coming days of discussion," he continued. "The committee's business is concluded for today."

Chairman Luis Matta's eyes felt immediate relief as the television cameras were turned off. Six and a half hours under the pelting onslaught of the lights' high-voltage illumination was exhausting. He rubbed his eyes slowly and turned around to talk to his staff, busily picking up papers and reorganizing their files.

He looked for Susana. She would certainly have a couple of press interviews lined up.

As he slowly got up from his chair, he heard a woman's voice calling from the audience below.

"Mr. Chairman."

He didn't have to turn around. He knew. The voice spoke in English. Every instinct in his body told him to keep moving forward, but he was unable to help himself. His natural curiosity got the better of him. Matta slowly turned, his face wrinkled in a grimace. He half expected something to be flying his way.

He was pleased to find Blaise Ryan looking at him, both arms restrained by officers of the Peruvian Judicial Police. They were not about to let something happen a second time. He looked down placidly, content in the knowledge that he was safe from flying objects and even happier to see her manhandled in a police half nelson.

"Mr. Chairman, please. I *must* talk to you." The fact that

she was held by two burly police officers didn't reduce this woman's jolting attractiveness one bit. She wasn't beautiful in the traditional sense. But the stunning eyes set deep in high cheekbones, the red hair in a ponytail, the full, rounded lips combined together in an irresistible package.

Luis Matta, however, was able to resist very nicely.

Without answering, Matta turned around and started heading out the senators' entrance.

"I have information, sir."

Matta kept walking.

"Mr. Chairman, I need to tell you something personal. In confidence," the voice pleaded.

Matta stopped and turned back toward her. This was too good. She was going to apologize for her misdeeds. He immediately wondered which news outlet would carry the best coverage of Blaise Ryan's public apology.

"You have fifteen seconds, Ms. Ryan."

"It's private, sir."

"Now you have ten seconds." Matta counted. He noticed that, from out of nowhere, Susana was suddenly next to him. Looking at his press secretary, he smiled and patted her on the back. Clearly, Susana had thought that the exchange between her boss and Blaise Ryan was enticing enough to drop her busy spinning of the attendant journalists.

"Clearly, we don't agree on much," started Blaise Ryan. "I don't trust you and you certainly don't trust me. I understand that. Yet sometimes even people who consider each other a menace are forced into a common cause against an even worse danger. This may be our case. I must talk to you—in person, privately."

This miserable shit of a woman was now demanding a meeting with him. Did she not remember what she had done? How dare she talk to him without even a hint of an apology? Luis Matta considered himself a modern, rational man. But this went over the line. Courtesies—particularly from people who have given offense—were one of life's requirements.

He walked away. Fast. Fuming.

Susana caught up to him, her lungs gasping for air.

"What are you going to do?"

"Nothing."

"What are you going to answer?"

"Nothing."

They were through the senators' entrance and heading toward the building's main hallway. He kept moving, his strides getting longer and her steps now moving in a little jog to keep up. Once he was out in the public hall, there would be hordes of journalists clamoring for an interview. Their conversation would be over. She moved in front of him to block his exit.

"It's a mistake. You should see her."

Luis Matta stopped dead in his tracks and his eyes bored straight into Susana Castillo's dark pupils.

"Let's get this clear. I'm the elected official. You work for me. You and I have a very good relationship, but you need to know when to stop. There are lines you should not cross. Start learning where these lines are because you have just crossed one."

Susana Castillo sucked in air. He had never spoken to her in that tone, at that volume. Blaise Ryan was a subject that was not open to advice. She should drop it. She couldn't win every battle.

But, then again, that was not what she was paid to do. Her job was to be the last person standing to tell him the truth. Every politician needed at least one such person. Some political leaders allowed their spouses to fill the role—but Alicia had no interest in politics. So the occupation fell to Matta's press secretary.

"Then fire me, sir." Susana's usually informal language had suddenly reverted to high formality. The words, however, had punches that landed with weight.

"But until you do that, it's my responsibility to give you another point of view. You need that, Senator. Everyone talks about you as a presidential candidate; the press clucks around you as the country's new political blood. As the adulation increases, you will need me. More than you can imagine. And if it's not me, you need somebody like me to keep your feet firmly on the earth, to remind you that you are not infallible, to ground you."

She stared at him, her dark eyes flashing. Once Susana Castillo engaged, there was no backing her down.

"So, Senator Matta, you do not have to take my recommendations. Nor do you have to act on every bit of advice I give you. But you do have to listen. You have to consider my counsel. That's the unwritten contract between political leader and senior advisor. When you have decided that you no longer want to hear me out, just let me know. That will be the moment I'll leave to take care of my sick mother."

She saw his shoulders relax a bit. His eyes moved back down from their upward stare to meet hers. It was clear that her remarks had hit home. But unlike most people in her position, she understood that she no longer needed to press the point. She didn't need a reaffirmation of her importance in his political pecking order. She had made her point. Now she was ready to go back to the substance of their disagreement.

"Luis, there is no reason for this woman to seek you out privately. You are enemies. Antagonists. She has every reason to keep that hatred alive and public—it's good publicity for her and her cause. Yet she wants to tell you something in private.

"You should listen. If you don't want to be alone with her, I will set it up and will accompany you."

Luis Matta's eyes narrowed. Seconds ticked by. In six years, she had seen this only once before. Utter silence enveloped them as his mind broke a big decision up into small, digestible pieces.

Suddenly Matta's eyes came back to life. He pointed to the door and the hallway beyond.

"I don't want to do ten separate interviews with the hordes on the other side of this door. Get them together and organized for one single press conference. Tell the print journalists that you want to give the cameras a couple of minutes to set up so there is no pushing and shoving. I'll get my thoughts in order and come out in a moment."

Susana nodded. She turned around and reached for the knob to the hallway door. The masses of press would be just beyond.

"And . . ."

Matta paused for a second, just to torture her.

"Set up a time to see Blaise Ryan this afternoon in my office."

LIMA
SEPTEMBER 1, 6:30 P.M.
SENATOR MATTA'S OFFICE

Two hours later, Susana knocked quietly on Luis Matta's door and walked into his office with tentative steps. Even the ever-tough Susana Castillo was worried about this meeting.

She was surprised that the senator was nowhere to be seen until she noticed the closed door to his private bathroom. She walked over to the door.

"Luis, she is here." Susana felt silly talking in a whisper to a dark brown wooden door.

Susana Castillo heard the running of the bathroom faucet and concluded he had not heard her over the din of the water. She called out again.

"Luis, Blaise Ryan is—"

"I heard you the first time," snapped the angry voice from inside.

Thirty seconds later, Luis Matta exited the bathroom. The senator always took off his suit jacket and loosened his tie when he was not in official meetings. But as he walked into his office, Susana immediately noticed that Matta had on his dark suit. His tie was knotted tight under the collar of his white shirt.

He intended this meeting to be ice cold.

Without even a glance, Matta walked straight past her. The senator sat down behind his desk and swiveled his chair in her direction. He stared hard at his press secretary, raising a pointed finger in her direction.

"This is on your head, Susana. I shouldn't have agreed to it. God help you if this goes wrong."

She was about to answer but thought better of it. The

warning launched in her direction had actually been an indirect instruction to bring Blaise Ryan into the office. Susana swiveled open the outer office's door to allow their guest to enter. The tension could have been cut with a knife.

Dressed in the same white, square-collared Nehru tunic that she had worn earlier in the day, Blaise Ryan walked slowly across the office's foyer, toward the large desk. Susana tried desperately to read the attractive woman's body language. Ryan's demeanor was serious. She didn't smile. Her step was purposeful but her arms were close to her sides; there was no self-assured swagger. Only the gray eyes, set deep in the finely chiseled face, radiated a hot intensity.

She stopped in front of Matta's desk.

"Thank you for seeing me, Senator." Matta didn't answer. No response. All she got was a dark stare.

"I have to talk to you about something confidential," she started, glancing in Susana's direction.

After another thirty seconds of deafening silence, Matta answered slowly.

"If the insinuation was meant to ask Ms. Castillo to leave, that will not happen. She is going to stay."

Blaise nodded. Silence again enveloped the office.

Susana walked forward, to the desk. If Matta was not going to offer Blaise Ryan a chair, she would. It was ridiculous to leave this woman standing. Susana sat down on one of the two chairs from across the dark desk and stretched out her arm, signaling for Blaise to take the other.

"I'm here to talk to you about Humboldt, Senator Matta," Ryan said as she took the seat.

"Why else would you be here?" The senator's fast answer was caustic and said roughly.

"Look, Senator, I know it must have taken considerable effort for you to agree to see me. You can also imagine that asking for this meeting was no easy decision on my part. I still believe Humboldt is a profound mistake; you are facilitating a crime against the planet."

"Yes, that's easy for you to say dressed in the latest Beverly Hills fashions," Matta spat out. "But if you would swivel that red head of yours to the window, you would see a lot of desperate people outside on the square—poor people. They are the ones I'm paid to think about. And the money my country will earn from Humboldt will help provide education, health, and a fighting chance for the poor of my country."

Matta's dark eyes bored into hers. "But I presume all that is of little importance if you are a wealthy American with a god-given mission to save the planet."

Blaise drew in a breath; her left fist clenched. She was mustering every iota of patience in her body.

"Senator, for what it's worth, you should know that I regret what I did to you eighteen months ago. It was cheap drama. And frankly, it did my cause a lot of damage. Personalizing the fight against Humboldt was a mistake. I still disagree vehemently with what you are doing, but I don't impugn your motives. Nobody disputes that you have Peru's best interests at heart.

"You're doing the wrong thing for the right reason," Blaise concluded, allowing a small smile at that clever turn of phrase.

Susana knew Matta well. Only she could recognize the small signs of relaxation in the drop of his eyebrow. Outwardly though, his only answer was stony silence; the senator did not want this American woman to feel any diminution of his wrath.

"Senator." Blaise Ryan crossed her legs, her tone one of sad resignation. "My credibility with you is not high; I know that. But believe it or not, I'm here because I believe you're an honest man. And even if you hate me for the rest of your life, I know you will do the right thing with the information I'm about to give you. You need to hear what I have to say."

Susana leaned forward, straining not to lose a single word. This wasn't at all what she expected. Ryan sounded ominous, dark. She glanced toward her boss. He too was now leaning forward, arms folded on the desk. Like most politicians, Luis Matta was an inquisitive man. And now, his curiosity had taken over.

"I'm worried, sir, that one of your bidders is not who you think they are. I'm talking specifically about Anfang Energie, Senator. They are no longer a German company. Earlier this year, they were purchased in secret by Volga Gaz of Russia."

"What?" Matta's chair shot backward. "Is this your new tactic? You want to gum up my committee's work by soiling the reputation of one of our bidders? It won't work, Ms. Ryan. We won't delay because of your games."

Even Susana had had enough. She stood up and grimly stared down at the American woman in their office.

"That's enough, Ms. Ryan. Please leave this office."

"Please," Blaise Ryan's voice was plaintive. "Please hear me out. I imagined that you would think this is just a ruse. It isn't; I promise. Just listen to what I have to say."

She looked from one to the other. Her face was lined with worry.

"Please," Blaise repeated.

Susana Castillo wasn't sure what to do, sit or stand. On the one hand, nothing about this woman was trustworthy. On the other hand, nobody could put on such a performance. Blaise Ryan wasn't acting.

In the end, Senator Luis Matta resolved Susana's doubts.

"Sit down, Susana. Ms. Ryan, you have five minutes."

"Thank you." Blaise sighed with relief. She launched right in, worried that he might change his mind.

"I've come across information about Anfang by accident. It was a fluke. I no longer have anything to do with Humboldt; after what happened in your committee room, my superiors at the trust took me off anything to do with Peru. What I found occurred only because I was trying to help a friend resolve a personal matter. But I wouldn't have been able to put the puzzle together had it not been for the coincidence of knowing something about Peru's gas-production plans."

For the next ten minutes, Blaise Ryan told the two Peruvians all she knew. Anne-Sophie. Daniel. Volga Gaz. Daniel's trips to Bolivia and his connection with Anfang. And, fi-

nally, the discovery that the German company now belonged
to Russia's largest oil and gas conglomerate, Volga Gaz. She
leaned over to take something from her pocketbook, but
stopped suddenly when Matta and Susana moved backward
in their seats, fearing another attack.

"I brought you the proof. May I get it from my bag? It's
a tax document in German, but you'll have to trust me that
what it says is that Anfang Energie is not paying any further taxes in Germany because they have been purchased
by Volga Gaz."

Luis Matta pointed to her bag in a sign of assent. He got
up from behind his desk and began to pace around the office.
Any lingering doubt he might have had about Blaise Ryan's
intentions was fast disappearing.

"Why would they do this, Ms. Ryan?" Matta asked, looking at the German Ministry of Finance's tax document.
"Why would Anfang Energie and Volga Gaz go through this
elaborate ruse to get the Humboldt contract?"

"Everything I have told you so far has been fact. The absolute truth. Now you are asking me to speculate."

"Well, you are here, aren't you? Sitting in my office. Go
ahead."

"Senator, I think what the Russians are plotting goes
much further than Peru. It's about a conspiracy against my
country, not yours. You've seen how vulnerable we are to
gas shortages in California. What they want is to control the
Pacific transportation channels of natural gas to the United
States. They already have the Bolivian fields. If they get
Peru's gas, they'll be in command of three-quarters of South
America's gas reserves."

The truth hit Matta like a rock.

Suddenly the pieces seemed to fall into place in the senator's head. Pacing faster, his fist punching at the air, Luis
Matta began to shout. Mostly to himself.

"Now it all makes sense. Damnit. How did I not see this?
The signs were all there. Anfang's extraordinarily attrac-
tive bid. Its strange, first-time interest in Latin America.
The conversation with Ludwig Schutz in the car. Susana,

remember I told you that Schutz had urged us to act faster in order to get Peru's gas out before the Bolivians. His inside information about Bolivia was nothing but a hoax to make Anfang seem like a friend. A ruse. A miserable lie!"

Matta walked toward Blaise Ryan. Leaning his body over her chair, he looked at her dead center.

"Ms. Ryan, is it therefore your opinion that Peru is being used by the Russians to gain some sort of strategic advantage over the United States? That my country's gas could be used for some sort of blackmail of your country?"

"Yes, I'm certain that is the intention."

Matta's mind was spinning. For over four years, he had labored to make the Humboldt project a beacon of transparency. An example of the right way to do things. There had been no corruption. No underhanded maneuvers. No backroom negotiations.

And now Humboldt was being used as a pawn in a vast superpower game. He was not going to allow it. Matta had heard enough.

"Ms. Ryan, what you have revealed leaves me with two infuriating sensations. The first is that I have been double-crossed. My country has been taken for a ride. God knows, I won't allow that to happen. The second is a feeling of gratitude to you. It's the last thing I wanted. My desire was to despise you for every remaining minute of my life. You have just changed that."

He held his hand out to Blaise Ryan. She took it. Neither smiled. There was no warmth. But the blood feud was over.

"There is nothing more you can do here, Ms. Ryan. Go home to America. The rest is up to me. Thank you for telling us."

She turned around without a further word. As she reached the door, he called out to her once more.

"Ms. Ryan. One question. Why? Why did you bring this to me?"

"Senator, that is an easy question. If my friend were to reveal to her husband what she knows, I have not the slightest doubt that the Russians would do anything to silence her. Her life would be in danger. This is a dark geopolitical conspiracy way beyond her—and my—abilities. I needed to leave this to a political professional who would know how to ignite a worldwide scandal without any trace of it ever being connected back to my friend.

"You're that person, Senator," Blaise Ryan added with a wry smile as she turned around and walked out of the office.

As the door closed, Susana turned to look at her boss.

"My God, what a disaster. This will delay Humboldt by months. Do you have any doubts about her?" Susana ran her hand through her dark brown hair.

"Unfortunately, none. And forget about the delay. I'm going to rule the German bid null and void; it's a sham. Humboldt will be awarded to Constable Oil, the American company." Matta looked determined.

"What do we do?"

"Three things. First, I want a meeting with the German ambassador early tomorrow morning. He needs to authenticate the German government's tax form. We can't act until we are absolutely certain that what Ryan has given us is an official document. Second, get your press lists ready. Once we have the ambassador's guarantee that the tax form is valid, we'll call a press conference and go public with the information. I want every single foreign correspondent in Lima there. These bastards are not going to get away with it.

"Third, I'm going to call Ludwig Schutz now and tell him that I want to see him right away in his hotel. I'm going to confront the son of a bitch."

"I want to go with you, Luis. I want to see the bastard's face when we tell him that we know what they are doing."

"Yes, good. Come with me. He's lied to me before; you can help make sure I don't fall into the same trap again."

"Give me ten minutes. I'll call Hugo to bring the car around and meet you downstairs." Susana's lips were tight with determination.

They were going to face down these liars.

LIMA
SEPTEMBER 1, 7:20 P.M.
THE MIRAFLORES PARK PLAZA HOTEL

Ludwig Schutz was in his underwear leaning over the bathtub, when the phone rang. He had just poured into the running water copious amounts of the hotel-provided tube of Roger & Gallet shower gel.

Pleased with the steady rise of the bath foam, Schutz considered not answering the telephone. The day's hearings had gone well; Anfang's bid was on a steady glide to a smooth landing. An uninterrupted, relaxing bath was a well-deserved end to a good day's work.

Schutz's Germanic work ethic got the better of his doubts. Deciding to answer, Anfang's Peru representative walked over to the toilet and picked up the hotel's bathroom extension. It was strategically placed right over the lavatory.

"It's me," said a woman's urgent voice.

"Hello, my dear. How are you? I'm surprised to hear from you at this hour," Schutz responded after a moment's pause. He had trouble immediately identifying the caller over the steady cascade of the bathtub's running water. He reached over to close the lid on the toilet and sat down.

"Not good."

"Really? I thought the hearing went well."

"The problem has nothing to do with the hearing," the woman snapped. She was obviously agitated.

"What then is the—"

The caller angrily interrupted Schutz in midsentence.

"He knows it all. We both just found out. You used me, you son of a bitch. You never told me of your connection to the Russians. My deal with you was to help Anfang. I was helping a German company. Now I find out that you aren't who you said you were."

Schutz was ashen. He was desperate to turn off the bath so he could hear more clearly. Glancing at the telephone cord, he saw it would never reach the bathtub's water levers.

"How did this happen?" he asked, his voice trembling.

Ludwig Schutz's nearly naked body was suddenly cold.

"Of all people, Blaise Ryan told him. She's the environmental activist who dumped the cow shit on Matta eighteen months ago. The person Matta hates most in the world."

"But when ... how ... did she find this out?" Schutz hated the sound of his trembling voice.

"By accident. Trying to help a German friend divorcing her husband, who is an employee of Volga Gaz. The details don't matter. All that matters is that Matta is furious. He is on his way to your hotel. He is calling a press conference tomorrow."

Christ, thought Schutz. He had no idea what to do.

"You are a lying bastard, Schutz," the woman continued. "You owe me big time now. I expect you to turn your promise into reality immediately. Or your situation is going to get even worse when I tell the senator everything I know."

He tried to calm her down.

"You have just fulfilled your part of the bargain. I can't ask for more. We will have your mother to Frankfurt and into a hospital within a week. And it will be just as I promised. Everything will be at our expense."

Schutz could hear the woman settling down.

"Fine. He asked me to accompany him to your hotel. I will see you in a half hour. If you even hint at having known beforehand, I'll turn against you. You better know how to do a good job of acting." Those were the woman's last words before Schutz heard a sudden click on the line.

Susana Castillo had hung up.

LIMA
SEPTEMBER 1, 8:05 P.M.
THE MIRAFLORES PARK PLAZA HOTEL

Oleg Stradius, chief of security for Anfang Energie, was frantic. His burly frame exited the elevator, walked hurriedly down the long brick-colored corridor, and rapped loudly on his colleague's hotel room door. Schutz's call to his room had been nearly hysterical.

Ludwig Schutz opened it quickly. The chief of Anfang Energie's Latin American operations was putting on a tie.

"We need to talk. We have a problem." Schutz pulled Oleg Stradius's large frame into his hotel suite. He closed the door to the hallway and turned around.

"We have a big problem," Schutz repeated, a single drop of sweat rolling down the side of his cheek.

They both just stood in the middle of the suite's foyer.

"What is happening, Ludwig?"

"I just got a call from our source." The smaller man's hands were nearly trembling as he confessed the news.

"Matta knows it all. Everything. He has just found out about our connection with Volga. He is on his way over. He wants to throw it in our face."

"Oh my God," Stradius murmured, his eyes half closing.

Oleg Stradius's astonishment only made Schutz more agitated. Pulse racing, his mind sped demonically through the options. Matta would be there in a half hour. There was no way to get out of the meeting. What the hell was he going to do?

"How did he find out?" shouted Stradius.

The question interrupted Schutz's effort to slow his speeding brain. For the first time in his professional life, he felt events spinning out of control.

"It was the American environmentalist woman, the one who hates him. Blaise Ryan. She has the whole story. All the connections."

"What? Why would she go to him? They despise each other." Schutz could see that Stradius was as confused as he was.

"Oleg, it's about some friend of hers in Russia. It's too long to explain now; we don't have time. The only important thing is that Matta is furious. He wants to call a press conference."

The German's body was now blooming with sweat. The armpits of his short-sleeved shirt were slathered with moisture. "What the hell do we do?"

Schutz paced in circles around the coffee table, trying to control his rampaging thoughts. He needed a moment to think. Forcing his Germanic brain to regain a modicum of orderliness, Schutz came to a single, overwhelming conclusion. He needed cover. This was too big a decision to take by himself. Looking at his watch, he walked to the phone and dialed Pieter Schmidt's mobile phone number. It was two A.M. in Germany.

Anfang's CEO did not answer. Schutz suddenly remembered; Pieter Schmidt was on a family vacation. On safari in Botswana. Schutz slammed down the handset realizing it would be impossible to find his boss in the African savannah in the middle of the night. The phone flew off the room's desk, crashing onto the floor. Its fitted plastic plate, which normally identified the Park Plaza's different services, spun wildly across the floor.

Stradius watched with increasing desperation. A former KGB interrogator, Stradius could function only with clear orders. Watching Schutz struggle with the phone convinced him that his colleague was out of control.

"I'm calling Zhironovsky," affirmed Stradius, pulling his cellular telephone from his pants pocket. He looked up the chairman's emergency number and punched in the numbers.

Within a few seconds, Oleg Stradius was speaking excitedly in Russian to a voice on the line. After a short pause to allow an answer from the other side of the planet, the security chief began to shout. Gesticulating wildly, his bellows ricocheted through the room. The argument lasted only another minute. Suddenly, Stradius stopped barking.

He had been cut off.

"What happened?" Schutz begged from the floor, where he was trying to reattach the plastic pad to the hotel phone. "What did he say?"

"It wasn't him. It was the security guard on duty."

"Why didn't you talk to Zhironovsky?"

"They refused to patch him through. It's three A.M. in Moscow and the security guard would not wake him up."

The two men stared at each other in stunned silence. They were on their own. Alone. The decisions they would make in the next few seconds would make or break their careers. Their futures were on the line.

Schutz understood that he had to be the one to decide. Stradius was an implementer, a mere instrument. He had no ability to lead. Ludwig Schutz was in charge and knew what he had to do.

Schutz rose up off the floor and fixed an angry stare into the large man's eyes.

"Stradius, go to your room and change. You look like hell. The senator will be here in ten minutes and I want you in the meeting. We will have to take care of this on our own."

LIMA
SEPTEMBER 2, 9:00 A.M.
JORGE CHÁVEZ INTERNATIONAL AIRPORT

The next morning, dressed in a casual brown dress and medium-heeled, tan-colored sandals, Blaise's long legs took her quickly down the airport hall toward the American Airlines Admirals Club. With all her traveling, Blaise was a platinum-level frequent flyer, permitting her constant access to airline clubs and complimentary upgrades to business class.

The security line had been excruciatingly long—slowed by passengers who were made to remove the layers of coats and sweaters that buffered them against Lima's chilly winter mornings. Waiting in the grinding queue, Blaise had noticed clumps of people gathered in front of television sets in the airport's numerous duty-free shops and coffee bars just beyond the security stations.

Blaise had suddenly felt a strange wave of worry wash over her. It hadn't been ignited by her usual legendary impatience. Instead, it had been a quick, unsettled jolt of anxiety, as if something about her trip to Lima had remained unresolved. The unease irritated her. After all, Blaise had come to Lima to do a very important job and, yesterday afternoon, she had succeeded.

She had known that it could easily have gone the other way. Her biggest worry had been that Luis Matta would refuse to see her. Given their past, the senator could well have sent her packing. But the opposite had happened. She made a mental note to e-mail the good news to Anne-Sophie once the plane landed in Miami.

Now it would be up to Matta. Once the Peruvian senator made the news public, there would be a worldwide firestorm of protest at the deceit. The Russians would become frantic with denials and backpedaling. The ensuing chaos cascading over Daniel and his friends at Volga Gaz would give Anne-Sophie enough time to get the kids out. Blaise figured that the scandal's winds would break loose in two or three days max. With some advance warning, Anne-Sophie could be out of Russia a few days later.

Blaise Ryan took the elevator down one floor to the club room and handed the American Airlines attendant her ticket. The airline representative pointed out the club's highlights—newspapers on the rack to the left and the coffee and croissants arrayed on the bar at the back.

Blaise flashed a thankful grin and took her boarding pass. As she stretched out her arm to pick up her carry-on bags, the attendant leaned over the counter and handed her an additional printed paper.

"This is on us, Ms. Ryan. You look like you could use a drink. Give the voucher to our barman and he'll make you a mimosa."

Blaise laughed in gratitude. Yes, the lady had gotten it just right; champagne and orange juice would be a fitting end to her stay in Lima.

The club was full of passengers. Finally finding a seat, Blaise lowered herself down on a cushy, faux-leather easy chair. The flute of orange-colored bubbly at her side, she reached over to pick up the *People* magazine strewn on the coffee table. She smiled at the elderly, well-dressed man in his midseventies sitting opposite her. He was reading a local paper.

The huge headline of *El Comercio* caught her eye. She couldn't read Spanish, but her perfect French was enough to convince her that something about the print was ominous.

LUIS MATTA ENCONTRADO SIN VIDA

Blaise Ryan felt a cold sweat run down her spine. It couldn't be.

"Excuse me, sir." Blaise leaned over to the gentleman across the table. "Do you speak English?"

"Of course, my dear. I'm Peruvian. But I graduated many years ago with a doctor's degree in biology from Cambridge."

"Forgive me for interrupting. I speak French and that front-page story caught my eye." Blaise pointed to the article. "Would you translate it for me?"

"Certainly, my dear. Which one? Ah yes, this one. Such a tragedy. It's been all over the radio and television news this morning. This young senator would have gone far."

Blaise could feel her hands start to tremble. "Please, please read it to me."

The old man started to read slowly, translating with precision.

" 'Hotel chambermaids at the Miraflores Park Plaza Hotel found Senator Luis Matta dead in a hotel room bed early this morning. Also dead in the same room was his press secretary, Susana Castillo. Both bodies were naked in bed.

" 'Police authorities report that the cause of death was by gunshot in an apparent murder-suicide. There are unconfirmed reports of a suicide note written by Ms. Castillo that references the anger she felt at the senator's refusal to divorce his wife.

" 'The bodies have been transferred to the state coroner's office for examination. There has been no official comment from either family or the senator's office.

" 'Senator Luis Matta leaves behind his wife, Alicia, and twin daughters, Laura and Sara, nine years old. He had become a widely known figure in Peru because of his chairmanship of the Humboldt project hearings . . .' "

The older man glanced toward Blaise. What he saw made him stop cold.

"My dear. Are you all right? Shall I get you some tea?"

Blaise Ryan didn't answer. She sat in front of him, her usually sparkling gray eyes staring emptily into space. Her red hair was combed backward into a ponytail, making it easier

for the older gentleman to see how her normally perfect lips
were now crumpling into uncontrolled tremors. Blaise heard
a rustling noise just below and slid her gaze downward. She
saw that the sound was coming from the erratic shaking of
her fingers as they rattled the pages of the magazine open
on her lap.

Blaise felt an overwhelming need to move. Leaving her
bags strewn around the lounge chair in front of her elegant
elderly translator, Blaise just got up and walked away without a word. She moved like a zombie through the lounge,
heading instinctively toward the women's bathroom.

Once inside, she just stood there. Motionless. Alone, in
front of the large bathroom mirror, hoping some order would
return to her brain. Blaise Ryan knew she was close to full-
scale panic. But she was also very aware that she couldn't
allow herself to go over the edge. Mustering every last ounce
of energy, Blaise strained to take back control over her body.
She had to think. The next few moments were critical.

Within minutes, she felt some semblance of normalcy
return. The only thing clear to her was that Luis Matta and
Susana Castillo had been murdered hours after she told them
about Volga Gaz. She surmised that the senator and his press
assistant had revealed what they knew to somebody willing
to kill to avoid allowing the information to become public.

The ramifications of that thought catapulted Blaise Ryan
into action. What if Matta or Susana told the killers how
they had come across the information? What if they now
knew about her?

That meant they were looking for her. Perhaps right here.
Right now.

Fear is a funny thing. It affects people very differently.
Some succumb to uncontrolled cowering. Others feel a cold
clarity layering through their mind. That is what was happening to Blaise at this exact moment. She felt a penetrating,
clairvoyant vision, into the present. She understood that her
immediate objective had to be to get on the plane and out of
Peru. She had twenty minutes until boarding time.

Blaise exited the bathroom and saw the elderly gentleman
still staring at the bathroom door. She walked over.

"Forgive me, sir. I had coincidentally just met that man who died yesterday, so I was unusually affected by the news of his death. Thank you again for the translation." Blaise smiled, hurriedly picking up her bags.

She headed to the club's coatroom, where passengers left their roll-away bags and overcoats. She immediately identified a long trench coat that might fit her. Her eyes now sought out a hat. At the far end of the coatrack was a Che Guevara–like cap, which would easily fit her considerable head of red hair. Regretting for just an instant the robbery of fellow passengers' clothes, she took the coat and the cap and walked to the array of twelve individual cubicles reserved for travelers seeking a quiet desk for work. She stepped into an empty one and looked at her watch.

As long as she was in the Admirals Club, she was safe. The challenge would be to walk down the airport's corridor to her gate. Presuming the killers would be looking for a red-haired woman, she hoped—prayed—that the trench coat and cap would respectively hide her legs and her red mane long enough to make it to Gate A7. This wasn't a disguise. At best, it was a distraction.

Ten minutes later, the stolen items draped over her body and head, Blaise walked out. Turning right out of the elevator, she looked up and saw that she was next to Gate A3. Four gates to go.

She passed a glass wall and looked at her reflection. Blaise allowed herself a smile. The coat and hat looked ridiculous, but they did the trick. Anybody looking for a red-haired woman would not immediately gravitate to the person with a covered head and a long trench coat. She could see movement at Gate A7. Good. That meant they were boarding the flight. With only another minute to go until she reached her departure area, she heard the call over the airport loudspeakers.

"Blaise Ryan. Miss Blaise Ryan, please return to the security area. You have forgotten some items. Blaise Ryan to the security area, please."

Blaise felt a shudder as she quickened her pace. She was not about to fall for the ruse; she had not forgotten anything at security. Her mind was splicing together quick calculations. There was bad and good news about the voice on the loudspeaker. The bad news was that Matta's killers knew she was here. The good news was that they were probably stuck at the slow security lines.

Blaise got to the gate and handed the agent the ticket. She walked onto the plane and settled in her business-class seat, waiting anxiously for the plane to fill with travelers. She glanced backward to the economy section of the Boeing 767 and saw that it was nearly full.

Blaise allowed herself to relax for a moment. Flight attendants were slapping closed the overhead bins. She was almost free.

Almost turned out to not be good enough.

Just as Blaise was about to relax, her attention was caught by a commotion at the front of the aircraft. The minute she heard it, she knew it wasn't good news.

The plane's public address system crackled. "Ms. Blaise Ryan, please identify yourself to the flight attendants." She frantically tried to decide what to do. Knowing that they could pick her out by the passenger manifest, she figured there was little choice. The last thing she needed was to be considered a problem passenger by the flight crew. She reached up to ring the call button.

A flight attendant approached her. "Ms. Ryan, there is a man with diplomatic identification at the door of the plane. He is asking to talk to you."

Another split-second calculation was needed. Again, she decided that the more naturally she behaved the better it was.

"Thank you very much," said Blaise, uncurling herself from the seat.

As she got to the front of the airplane, a tall man with a bushy mustache identified himself as Aleksander Shirakin from the Russian Embassy. He stood just to the left of the open cockpit door.

"I'm so sorry to bother you, Ms. Ryan. We knew from the congressional hearing yesterday that you were in Peru. I'm afraid I have bad news for you regarding your friend Anne-Sophie Perlmutter. She has been taken very ill and is in a hospital in Moscow. As her husband is a senior official at Volga Gaz, we've been asked to make arrangements for you to travel to see her. Please come with me."

Blaise Ryan did everything in her power to suppress the shock of hearing Anne-Sophie's name being used to pry her out of the airplane. It was clear from the man's tall story that they were betting she had not heard the news about Matta. She looked around and saw the flight attendants busily locking the food carts into the galley's storage compartments. Nobody was paying attention.

"Thank you for coming to tell me. I will call Anne-Sophie the moment I land in Miami."

This was not the answer he had expected. The tall man took her arm and pulled her to the airplane door.

"Please come with me now."

"No! I won't." The sharp tones were loud enough to turn the heads of the flight crew. Even the captain, ensconced in the cockpit's left-hand seat, turned his head.

"Come, now." The man was literally pulling her off the airplane.

"Let go of me!" At this point, Blaise could see the captain getting out of his chair.

"Good morning," the captain drawled. "Is there a problem here?" He was in his midfifties and obviously a southerner. Good, thought Blaise. Probably old-fashioned and protective of women.

"Captain, my name is Blaise Ryan. I'm an American citizen and a platinum flyer with your airline. I'm in business class, seat 4C." Blaise identified herself with all the codes needed to denote her elite status with American Airlines. So far, that was the truth. Now came the lie.

"My ex-fiancé is from Russia, Captain," she said, her voice as plaintive and teary as possible. "We broke up last night after I found out that he was cheating on me. Now he has sent some Russian Embassy goons to drag me off the plane. I don't know how I got involved with these bad people. I just want to get to Miami, change planes, and go home to my parents' house in California, sir. Please tell him to leave me alone."

The Russian was clearly caught off guard by the enormity of the lie. The diplomat didn't even know where to begin.

"She must come with me," he repeated in a monotone.

The captain placed his body squarely between Blaise and the Russian.

"Now, sir, if you're not flying with us, please step back from this aircraft. There is no reason this lady has to go with you if she does not want to."

"I'm from the Russian Embassy. She must come," he repeated sullenly.

The captain's look sharpened. "Sir, I'm ordering you off this aircraft. This is a United States flag carrier. I am the captain of this ship. Under international treaty, I'm under no obligation to give over a U.S. national to anybody once they are on this airplane. This is as good as United States territory.

"Back away," the captain barked loudly.

Once the man was off, the captain turned around to the small gaggle of flight attendants who had gathered.

"How many more to board?" he snapped at the senior purser.

"None, sir. Boarding is complete."

"Then close this goddamn door and cross-check."

Blaise gave the captain a sad smile of appreciation. Her gray eyes communicated a deep gratitude.

"My pleasure, ma'am. He didn't look like a nice guy, not at all. Take care of yourself," he said, winking as he crouched back into the flight deck.

Blaise walked slowly back to her aisle seat. She should have felt a deep, overwhelming sense of relief. But she didn't. How could she? The man from the Russian Embassy had known Anne-Sophie's name. Blaise had revealed it yesterday to Matta. And now Anne-Sophie was in real danger.

Her trip to Peru had been an utter failure.

RUSSIA

As Blaise Ryan's jet headed north to Miami, Viktor Zhironovsky was in his office literally screaming at the top of his lungs. There was no real need for Volga Gaz's chairman to shout; Piotr Rudzhin was barely two feet away. Nonetheless, Rudzhin had concluded that it would not be prudent to interrupt. He couldn't recall ever seeing Zhironovsky so upset.

"How the hell did this happen?" Zhironovsky roared, his face red with rage. "I want answers. Mark my words, Rudzhin. Heads will roll. And the first one will be your damn friend's."

"Mr. Chairman, please," pleaded Piotr Rudzhin. "What has happened is unfortunate, but—"

"Unfortunate! You call what occurred unfortunate? Is that the only word you can think of? Don't patronize me with quiet, rational understatements. It is a full-scale, one-hundred-percent disaster. Do you hear me? What has happened is a calamity."

Zhironovsky wasn't done. His bloodshot eyes spat fury.

"Listen to me, Rudzhin. There is no way to parse the blow.

Packard and the Americans arrive this evening. And we will begin our meetings tomorrow with one hand behind our backs. Half of our plan has become unworkable. Compromised. We were discovered in Peru. And by whom?"

The chairman answered his own question.

"By the wife of your friend Uggin. The national policies of the Russian Federation have fallen victim to his stupid marital problems. Do you realize the ridiculousness of this? Somehow his German bitch got information out to a friend of hers who leaked it to Senator Matta. And, on top of it, we have been forced to take severe emergency measures against a foreign official. There will be investigations. Inquiries. Medical and police reports. I've ordered Schutz and Stradius to clear out of Peru on the first possible flight. Humboldt is finished; the project will be delayed God knows how long. Now we may never get it."

Piotr Rudzhin called forth every possible ounce of patience. He had been in Zhironovsky's office for an hour and a half and the chairman had, by now, repeated the same rant three or four times. Yes, of course the situation in Lima was nothing less than a disaster. But the Americans were arriving in a few hours and Zhironovsky was refusing to think rationally. The man who had, only a few weeks ago, lectured him on strategy was now unable to keep his eye on the ball.

Rudzhin had to force the old man to prioritize.

"Chairman Zhironovsky, there is no doubt that what happened in Peru is a huge problem. But let's thank God that Schutz made the right decision last night. And, while it is true that Volga Gaz may not have a future in Peru, the important thing is that we have prevented the information from going any further. The real disaster would have been a public disclosure. That could have even derailed General Packard's visit."

Piotr Rudzhin lowered his voice to a quiet admonition. "Sir, there will be a lot of noise about Humboldt in the coming days. We must not let it distract us. We cannot lose sight of the fact that the Bering Strait is the truly big prize. We must concentrate on the arrival of the Americans."

Hearing Rudzhin actually say that the decision to kill

Matta and his press secretary was the right one seemed to calm Zhironovsky down a bit. The balding old man leaned over his desk.

"What about the American environmentalist woman? We have to do something about her."

"Yes, we must," Rudzhin agreed. At the moment, he had no idea what to do about Blaise Ryan. But there was no doubt that the woman was a loose cannon who had to be silenced. He guessed that they would have only a few days to figure that out.

"All right, Rudzhin, we will postpone a discussion of what went wrong until after the Americans leave. The minute Packard gets on the plane to go back to America, I want to hear a plan about what to do with this woman Ryan. Understood?"

"Yes, sir."

"One more thing, Rudzhin," growled Zhironovsky. "I want Uggin off the case. I don't want him in our meetings. He can't be trusted."

"I don't think that is a good idea, Mr. Chairman."

"Why the hell not?" Zhironovsky's eyes began to bulge again.

"Because there is nobody else to do his job. He has studied for the meeting. He knows what he has to do with the young man from the White House. It's too late to change him for somebody else. Is he guilty of carelessness? Yes. Of not controlling what happens in his own house? Yes. But I am convinced—totally convinced—that he is dedicated to his job and to our cause."

Zhironovsky knew that Rudzhin was right. "Then at least, at the very least, arrest the wife," snapped the chairman.

"With all due respect, sir, that too would be a mistake. All that would do would be to distract Uggin from his mission. You have my word; I will give immediate orders to transfer a team from Moscow to Kursk. They will keep Anne-Sophie Perlmutter under surveillance. She will not make one phone call that we do not hear. She will not send an e-mail we do not read. If she attempts to leave the country, we will stop her. Is this satisfactory?"

Zhironovsky just grunted. Rudzhin didn't know what that grunt meant.

"Do I have your approval?" Rudzhin insisted.

"Yes, it's enough." Zhironovsky slammed his fist on the table, his eyes boring into Rudzhin's. "For now."

MOSCOW
SEPTEMBER 2, 10:05 P.M.
THE METROPOL HOTEL

Anthony Ruiz walked around his hotel suite in disbelief at the opulence of his surroundings.

The Metropol Hotel was one of Moscow's longest-running bastions of luxury. The historic building, built in 1904 by the last of Russia's czarist art patrons, was one of the best-known addresses in town. The hotel had long served as the destination of choice for kings and queens, presidents and prime ministers.

Tony Ruiz's room was huge—the living area had two turn-of-the-century, brick-colored sofas and three large Louis XIV classical chairs arrayed in a room big enough to entertain ten visitors. The young White House advisor's lips curled into a wry grin as he pushed aside the elegant plush curtains to look out over the illuminated spires of the Cathedral of St. Michael the Archangel.

He knew what his father would say. What the hell is a Latino cop from Chelan County doing in a place like this?

The Metropol's suite was perfectly in tune with everything else that had occurred since his arrival at Vnukovo airport. Only ninety minutes earlier, Tony had been staring out the airplane window as the CIA's triple-engined jet wound down its motors. On the tarmac below, he had noticed a group of men lining up just in front of the airport terminal to greet the four-member American delegation.

Tony had pored over his briefing books on the flight. So, hurrying down the staircase ten steps behind General Martha Packard, he had recognized most of the members of the Russian greeting committee.

Viktor Zhironovsky, CEO of Russia's natural gas con-glomerate, and Arkadi Semiant, director-general of the FSB, Russia's intelligence agency, were slightly ahead of the others. Third after Semiant was Piotr Rudzhin, the deputy minister of the interior. The next two were men whose faces Tony remembered as foreign ministry officials, but he could not remember their names. Last in the six-person line, look-ing slightly out of place, was a younger, dark-haired man whom Tony did not recognize. He had been absent from the CIA briefing book.

It had been hard to follow each heavily accented introduc-tion, so Ruiz had paid particular attention to catch the last official's name. The man stretched out one hand in Tony's direction while holding an elegantly wrapped package against his chest with the other. But just as Tony took the dark-haired man's hand, the deafening roll of a snare drum drowned out the words.

Surprised by the noise, Ruiz had swung his head around to see a military band in the full regalia of the Hussar regi-ment marching toward them in goose step across the airport tarmac. Once the soldiers, outfitted in the corps' traditional enormous fur hats, had come to a halt in front of the visitors, the national anthems of Russia and the United States began to play.

The seven-car motorcade of window-darkened black Audi A8s, followed by Mercedes G-class wagons with flashing blue lights, had sped into the city with an official escort. Blaring two-toned sirens, motorcycle police had struggled to open Moscow's streets to their passing. It wasn't an easy job. Traffic was heavy with cars and buses; people were ev-erywhere.

The slow slog through Moscow's center allowed Ruiz the time to get a good look at the bars, restaurants, cafés, and shops. All of them were open, crammed with humanity. Tony was amazed by how attractive people were. Gorgeous women in miniskirts—nearly all in unusually high heels—sat at outside tables across from handsome men—nearly all with uniformly slicked-back hair. As the caravan neared the hotel, the cars swerved left, to reveal the wondrous expanse of Red Square. Tony stared out the car window, amazed by the turrets of the Kremlin's brilliantly illuminated facade.

Sitting on his suite's bed, it occurred to Ruiz that all the stereotypes of graying Soviet decay had been wiped away in that one car ride. It took just one and a half hours to convince Tony that Russia was a country in bloom, hopping with life.

As Ruiz changed into blue jeans and began to unpack, he thanked God for his hosts' warm welcome. The Russian greeting had been a pleasant contrast to the previous eleven hours. The trip over from the United States had seemed a cold hell.

In the days prior to their departure, Tony had struggled to keep an open mind about the notion of a Bering Strait link. Yet he couldn't get over his profound belief that everything about the idea was preposterous. He had seen firsthand what energy dependency had wrought in California. In the course of the last twenty years, America's foreign-energy addiction had risen from a barely manageable 27 percent to 60 percent—most of it from regions of severe instability hostile to the United States. Now he was going to embark on a fact-finding mission designed to heighten his country's enslavement to foreign energy sources. The whole thing was wrong.

It sure didn't help that General Martha Packard was to be his boss over the next four days. From the moment Tony had pulled up in a taxi at Washington's Andrews Air Force Base, the director of Central Intelligence had done everything possible to make Tony Ruiz understand that his presence in the delegation was unwelcome.

"Hello, Mr. Ruiz." The CIA director had hardly deigned to look at him as he entered the air force base's VIP lounge. Those were the first and only words Martha Packard would send in his direction during the entire eleven-hour flight.

Once on the airplane, General Packard and her deputy, Stuart Altman, were shown two of the four sleeping quarters on the aircraft. Altman was also the agency's senior energy expert; he would play an important role on the trip. But somebody had decided that neither Tony Ruiz nor Betty Angler, Packard's hugely overweight, dark-haired personal assistant, merited the remaining two private rooms. Instead, they were directed to separate seats in the plane's main section. Any excitement Tony might have felt about international travel on a government jet evaporated with one look at the modest, economy-class surroundings of the CIA plane's cabin.

Ruiz tried twice—once an hour after takeoff and again an hour before landing—to meet with the CIA director. Both times the purser had delivered Tony's request to the forward cabin. And twice he had returned with a rebuff. The first because the director was "resting." The second because the director was "preparing herself for the arrival."

What a bitch, thought Tony.

The hotel phone's shrill electronic tones jolted Tony out of his frustrated reveries just as he was debating whether to take a shower now or wait until his 7:00 A.M. wake-up call. He reached across the bed to grab the receiver.

"Hello, Tony, this is Daniel Uggin. I'm the international director of Volga Gaz."

Ruiz was momentarily confused. His silence prompted the caller to explain further.

"We met at the airport, remember? Right as the band began to play."

"Yes, yes, of course. How are you?" Tony answered quickly, momentarily embarrassed by his forgetfulness. A picture of the last man in the greeting line formed in his head.

"I'm sorry to bother you at this late hour. You must be tired from your trip. I had a welcoming present for you, but these military guys were too anxious to show their stuff," Uggin chuckled over the phone line. "They were supposed to wait for a signal before beginning to play 'The Star-Spangled Banner.' But you know what the military is like; they never follow orders."

Tony was grateful for the gesture.

"I will give it to the concierge. Is that okay?" the caller asked.

"Sure, that is great. Very kind of you."

"Good. I'll ask the hotel personnel to take it upstairs."

"Wait, wait, umm ... Daniel." Struggling to remember the man's name, Tony thought he should be polite and extend an invitation. "Why don't you come up and I'll give you a drink. I have an enormous suite and the company will do me some good."

"Well, of course. But you are our guest. I should be the one buying the drinks." Uggin laughed. "I'll be right up."

Minutes later, the suite's bell rang. Tony opened the door, clothed in blue jeans, a green T-shirt, and sneakers. He was embarrassed to see his visitor dressed in a stiff suit and tie. Shit, thought Ruiz, I should have thought to change my clothes. This international diplomatic stuff was hard.

Uggin gave Tony the present. A bottle of Beluga Gold Line vodka. Retail price was $150 a bottle.

"Unlike the French, we don't export our best products. This is liquid gold. We keep it right here. Close by." Uggin grinned.

This time Ruiz was not going to be outdone. Before leaving Washington, Mary Jane Pfeiffer, Tolberg's southern-tongued secretary, had suggested bringing along a few bottles of Jack Daniel's bourbon to pass out as gifts. "You know, those Russian good ol' boys over there really know how to throw it down. You're gonna get a lot of vodka. Let 'em taste some of our better moonshine," Mary Jane had said to him.

"I have something for you also," said Tony Ruiz, pulling a gift-bagged bottle of Kentucky's finest out of his suitcase.

Uggin smiled broadly, admiring the American whiskey. He didn't hesitate.

"Can we open this one? You know, I'm a big fan of scotch, but I've never tried bourbon."

Tony grinned as he fetched ice from the suite's minibar. He felt at a slight disadvantage because it was clear that Daniel knew more about him than vice versa. His Russian guest deftly shortened the distance between them with a quick, initial explanation of his international role at Volga Gaz. After that, the conversation became light and easy, avoiding anything even remotely related to work. They felt an immediate kinship upon realizing that both were originally from smaller cities far from the political buzz of their countries' capitals.

Daniel Uggin stayed only fifteen minutes. It was clear he didn't want to disturb his guest after the long transatlantic trip.

"Tony, I should go. You need to rest. We start in the morning at eight thirty and have three long days ahead of us. Tomorrow evening, we have a formal dinner with both delegations. But perhaps after the dinner—if you're up for it—or the next day, I hope you'll let me take you out to see how this city lives at night. Moscow, you know, has become New York on steroids."

"I saw that on the way in from the airport. You've got yourself a deal, Daniel." Tony Ruiz laughed.

The two men clasped hands warmly before Daniel headed down the hallway toward the elevators.

Nice guy, Tony Ruiz thought as he closed his hotel door and headed straight to bed. But as he closed his eyes to sleep, the thought occurred to Tony that perhaps Daniel Uggin's easygoing manner had been just a little too nice.

MOSCOW
SEPTEMBER 3, 8:20 A.M.
TO VOLGA GAZ HEADQUARTERS

Tony Ruiz had slept profoundly, awakening before the hotel wake-up call. A shower and a room-service breakfast followed in quick succession. He had already been in the lobby a good twenty minutes when Martha Packard strode purposefully off the Metropol's elevators, followed closely by the obese Betty Angler and Stuart Altman, the CIA's energy expert.

Two very contrary impressions struck Tony on seeing General Martha Packard and her trailing acolytes.

First, the fact that the group had descended in the elevator together gave him the unpleasant impression that they had just concluded a preparatory breakfast meeting without him. The woman had an agenda and she was freezing him out.

Right then and there, Tony resolved to take the first possible private opportunity with Packard to protest her ongoing efforts to keep him away. Coming on this trip hadn't been his choice. But he was determined not to be treated as the never-acknowledged Hispanic busboy by the CIA's WASP ice queen.

Immediately behind his initial jolt of resentment, a second, more amusing, thought seeped through his mind. Following Packard's steely pace through the lobby, Tony realized that this was the first time he had ever seen her—either in person or in news photographs—dressed as a civilian.

Packard's outfit was elegant. A fitted blue jacket and matching skirt that hovered ever so slightly above the knees were mixed with a white brass-buttoned shirt. An antique necklace of small silver squares and colored semiprecious stones accented her long neck. Her dark hair, combed backward and held in place by a hair band with embedded yellow sparkles, contrasted with her white skin, chiseled nose, and glossed red lips.

Jewelry, makeup, hair band. All that was impressive enough. But what Tony really had trouble keeping his eyes off of were the general's sheer-hosed legs and her dark blue, high-heeled pumps. Prior to this moment, it would never have occurred to him that this forty-five-year-old military woman could walk in anything but spit-polished, black, tie-up flat shoes.

Any thought that connected the words "Packard" and "pleasant" in the same brainwave was instantly erased by her demeanor. "Martha" and "menacing" became once again the prevailing synonyms.

"Let's move, Mr. Ruiz. Or we'll be late," she called his way as she glided past.

The ride to Volga Gaz headquarters took less than ten minutes. As the Americans alighted, they were whisked off to a fifth-floor boardroom. Tan-colored thick-leather chairs were fitted against an enormous light-colored conference table. In front of each chair was a setting that jumbled dinnerware with office supplies. The sophisticated and the mundane were mixed on place mats, as beautifully crafted, rose-colored Russian breakfast china and crystal goblets lay side by side with sharpened pencils and yellow pads.

After an initial round of greeting, Viktor Zhironovsky tapped a pencil against the crystal ware, the chiming ring filling the conference room.

"I would like to officially welcome my friends from America. General Packard, you especially. My colleagues at the FSB warned me about your legendary toughness. But they did not caution me sufficiently about your alluring beauty," Zhironovsky began unctuously.

"We have an opportunity today to create history. To bend the present into a better future. Russia and the United States are far apart in many ways. Yet one idea, one dream, one bold stroke can bring us together. What we accomplish here in the coming days has the potential to bind our two countries politically, strategically, and geographically. Shall we get to work?"

All participants—four Americans and six Russians—took their seats. A young, impeccably dressed assistant distributed reams of paper to each delegation member. The document, its contents divided into two separate English and Russian columns, was ceremoniously titled "Agenda for Negotiating an Agreement on the Historic Construction of a Bering Strait Tunnel Between Our Countries."

After just one glance at the agenda, Tony Ruiz felt the hairs on the back of his neck stand on end. In one fell swoop, his suspicions were confirmed. Tolberg had told him that the trip was to be only a fact-finding mission. Tony had doubted it then. And now, clear as daylight, the agenda he had in front of him said these meetings were real negotiations.

The title wasn't the only thing about the schedule that concerned him. The program also noted that, after long discussions on financing, engineering, environmental implications, tunnel contents, gas amounts, pricing, and political requirements, there would be a daily, end-of-afternoon, one-hour time period slotted simply as "Private Discussions Between Chairman Viktor Zhironovsky and General Martha Packard."

The truth hit him like a hammer, its implication obvious. The meetings were rigged. There was no doubt about what was happening. Martha Packard had come to Russia to ride the Bering Strait negotiation straight to a political career. She planned to use her mission to Moscow to show that she was the one person in the administration who had a long-term solution to America's energy scarcity. The CIA director would return to Washington holding a document that was a fait accompli. A done deal.

The more Tony thought about it, the clearer it became. Martha Packard intended to negotiate the Russians to near completion. She would then land in Washington with the agreement already hammered out. All that would be needed to seal the deal would be the president's approval.

Yes, yes. He could see it all in sharp focus now. Packard was going to force Gene Laurence's hand. One way or another, she was going to get what she wanted. If the president agreed to the deal, the CIA director would get the credit for being the intellectual force behind a brave new shift in U.S. energy policy. If Laurence didn't sign the agreement, Tony could already taste the acerbic headlines of leaked press reports about the president's reluctance. Unnamed press sources would paint Packard as a patriotic victim, the brilliant woman who had offered a clear solution to her country's problems only to have it spurned by a shortsighted president.

Tony shook his head in disappointment. One look at the schedule the Russians had just passed out said it all. And there was almost nothing he could do to change the course of events. He was completely frozen out.

MOSCOW
SEPTEMBER 3, 11:30 P.M.
THE CAFÉ PUSHKIN

Spread over four floors in a gorgeous turn-of-the-century mansion, the Café Pushkin was a twenty-four-hour cascade of food, drink, and sophistication. The bar, with floor-to-ceiling windows and wood-paneled walls, was packed with a heady mix of good-looking humanity. Half the crowd looked like Swiss bankers, the other half like bohemian filmmakers.

Having initially hesitated in agreeing to the outing, Tony Ruiz now felt relieved to be here with Daniel Uggin and his two gorgeous blond friends. The Café Pushkin's loud, manic atmosphere swiveled his mind away from the directed fury every nerve in his body aimed toward Martha Packard.

The discussions at Volga Gaz's offices had been an endless numerical siege. The day had been entirely quantitative. In the morning, Packard's deputy, Stuart Altman, had given a long presentation of the CIA's analysis of America's gas import requirements. Using ratios juxtaposing predicted U.S. economic growth with expanding gas needs, the American side outlined the millions of cubic feet of natural gas that could be purchased from the Russians over the next twenty years.

The afternoon centered on gas production in the Kamchatka Peninsula. Engineers from Volga Gaz had presented a withering onslaught of numbers from geological and engineering analyses of the present and future output from the various eastern Siberian fields.

Tony had tuned most of it out. Throughout the day, he had debated his next move. His choices were clear. His first instinct was to call Isaiah J. Tolberg and inform the White House chief of staff about what he thought Packard was doing in Moscow. But he doubted that the tattling would produce the one result he really wanted—to pull Packard off the trip.

There was only one other alternative, namely, to force a showdown with Packard. He had no choice, really. The only way to get Tolberg to take action from Washington was to convince the White House chief of staff that Tony had tried everything possible to rein her in. Tomorrow Altman would be going alone to a first meeting that centered on construction obstacles. The rest of the group was assembling at ten A.M. at Volga Gaz.

This would give Tony more than enough time in the morning to demand a meeting with Packard at the hotel.

It had taken nearly all day for Tony to decide what to do. In the late afternoon, Zhironovsky and Packard had, as dictated by the agenda, retired to the Volga Gaz chairman's office for private discussions. The elegant dinner for both nations' teams had been long in speechmaking but blissfully short in duration. Martha Packard may have had the sleeping quarters on the airplane, but by 10:00 P.M. she had begged off more toasts, asking for her host's understanding of her acute jet lag.

Daniel Uggin had slid close to Tony. "Are you tired, my friend? Come on; let me show you the city."

Tony knew he probably should go to bed, but he desperately needed the distraction. Nodding in the affirmative, Uggin reached for the cell phone in his coat pocket.

"I'm going to ask some friends to join us. No business. Only fun, okay?"

Now, sitting in the Café Pushkin, Tony thanked his lucky stars for Daniel Uggin's insistence. He liked the group. Besides gorgeous, both girls were spunky. One of them, Dariya, was clearly close to Uggin.

The other woman, Nina, wore an Armani dress that Tony swore he had seen the previous evening in a swank fashion magazine on his hotel room's coffee table. Her smooth, tawny-colored shoulders were totally bare. The dress she wore began in black, tightly fashioned around ample round breasts. From there, the outfit converted to broad diagonal white-and-black stripes of shiny sequins that fell straight down, but only a very short distance. Indeed, the dress was extraordinarily mini, ending suddenly at the top third of Nina's thighs. The rest was long, perfectly shaped legs.

"I have to tell you," Tony said, leaning over Nina. "I never expected Russia to be like this. In the United States, we still have this outdated image of Soviet shabbiness. But Moscow is incredibly alive. And all the people are gorgeous."

"All?" Nina asked. Her nose wrinkled in a cute smile as she fished for a compliment.

Putting a warm hand on her shoulder, Tony laughed. "All of them. But none more than both of you."

"I heard that," interrupted Dariya, breaking away from her conversation with Uggin. "So American guys do know how to compliment pretty girls after all. I was under the impression you were all tough cowboys."

"Look, let me ask you guys a question," said Tony, turning serious. "How did all this money, good looks, and sophistication happen so fast? I guess part of our outdated image of Russia is that we haven't realized the depth of the change. It's been only fifteen years since you had a repressive communist system."

"Well," said Nina firmly, "we don't exactly have a government like yours now either. Don't let Daniel's friend Rudzhin hear me; he would throw me in jail. But the fact is that these guys in charge of our country have trouble holding back their authoritarian tendencies too."

"She's right," laughed Dariya. "But, unlike the communists, at least today the government lets us dress well and eat good food in nice places."

Tony wondered why Uggin didn't join the conversation. Was he part of the government establishment? But if he was, how bad could these bureaucrats be? He seemed to be enjoying the women's antigovernment banter.

"Okay. Here you are teasing about the government. Your jokes are good natured. But I hear real complaints. Why doesn't anybody do anything about it?"

"Like what?" both girls asked in unison. They seemed genuinely puzzled by the question.

"I don't know. Write a newspaper column. Organize a march. Take a protest advertisement out in the newspaper. Convince your neighbors to sign a petition. There are lots of things to do."

Dariya and Nina looked at each other in utter surprise. Nina turned to Tony, her blue eyes sparkling with mirth.

"Why would we want to do all that? We're having too much fun."

The table erupted in laughter. Uggin held up his hand in mock seriousness.

"Enough politics. Why don't we take Tony on a walk? Let's let him feel the fun."

Uggin insisted on paying. The four got up and walked out of the restaurant. On the sidewalk, the three Russians talked heatedly among themselves. Tony couldn't understand a word but they seemed to be arguing about where to take him. Finally a consensus seemed to form.

"Come on." Uggin smiled. "We're going to show you something a little different. You've seen a bit of the chic part of the city. Now it's time to show you the quiet Moscow."

They walked a few blocks through crowded streets. At the Komsomolskaya subway station, the group descended on the electronic escalator and entered the station. His Russian friends smiled on seeing Tony's predictably stunned look. The station looked more like a baroque theater than a public-transportation stop. Long oval porticoes lined the passageway. The yellow-domed roof of the station displayed museum-quality murals in marble-encrusted carved frames. Chandeliers with crystal cuttings hung every couple of yards.

"Yes, yes." Nina giggled. "It's beautiful. Personally, I never use the subway. But I love to show the Moscow underground to my foreign friends at this late hour." Nina wrinkled her nose as she thought of the crowds commuting daily to work. "Yes, you definitely don't want to be anywhere close to here when nine million people are on the trains at rush hour."

They exited three stations later and walked the short distance to the Patriarch's Pond. It was a serene water reservoir. A couple of cafés were set back among the trees, romantically lighted with Roman candles flickering in the night's September breeze.

"We can have a nightcap at the pavilion over there." Daniel pointed to a building where outside tables with flower vases were occupied by couples deep in romantic conversation. "But let's first take a walk around the pond. Listen. There isn't a sound. And we are right in the middle of Moscow."

As they walked around the pond, Tony felt Nina's arm encircling his own. He looked over and met her blue eyes. Wisps of blond hair flickered over the left half of her face. Her lips were smiling broadly, but her eyes were fixed on his.

Tony sensed a physical surge. He could feel heat at the spot where her arm was intertwined with his. His body temperature was literally rising with every step they took together.

Tony was flattered by this beautiful woman's attention. But her close physical proximity was too effortless, too fast. It made him feel awkward. Cautious.

You're being a moron, he told himself. She is absolutely gorgeous and outgoing. He chalked his hesitation up to cultural discomfort, the embarrassment of a country Latino in the big foreign city.

After twenty minutes, Daniel suggested they go inside the pavilion for drinks. A few couples were on the dance floor, moving slowly to the music of a four-man band playing a good set of Frank Sinatra songs. Tony smiled at the heavily accented lyrics belted out by the young singer.

Once they ordered drinks, Nina looked his way with a big grin.

"All right, Mr. American. Let's dance to your music."

He followed her to the dance floor, striving to unlock his eyes from her long, tanned legs.

They swayed gently to Sinatra's "Summer Winds." Nina smiled in his direction as she moved herself against his body. His head just above her left shoulder, Tony's face was for a moment covered in her blond hair. He closed his eyes as the clean perfume of her shampoo wafted into his nostrils.

As the couple moved on the dance floor, Nina came imperceptibly closer. Every second step he could feel a new part of her body slipping against his. First her thigh against his. Then her shoulder. Her hips.

There probably had been a moment earlier in the evening during which Tony Ruiz could have stopped the forward motion of his accelerating need to have this woman. If he had given it some serious thought, he would have realized the dangers of becoming involved with a woman he knew nothing about while on an official mission for the United States government.

But after the dance, it was too late. Sitting next to Nina on the plush sofa, his mind had become a radar device, registering her every movement. When her hand rested on the couch, his brain performed meticulous calculations to calibrate the distance to his own hand. As her legs crossed, he computed the probabilities as to whether the quick swish against his pants had been intentional or not. He couldn't help himself. With every passing second, she was becoming more beautiful, more exotic.

As they got up to dance again, Nina giggled something in Russian to her two friends. This time there was nothing subtle about their movements on the dance floor. Within seconds, Nina was caressing his hair, kissing his cheek. She held him tightly as he felt her breasts against his chest. Their lips locked with passion.

To his surprise, when the song ended he looked around for Daniel and Dariya and found them gone.

"I told them to go away," she said, her eyes downcast, pretending embarrassment.

They walked, nearly hugging, two blocks until the first free cab finally pulled over. She gave the driver quick instructions and they alighted at her apartment building. In the short six-floor elevator ride, she took him in her arms. He could feel her tongue on his neck. He reached down and took her smooth thighs in his palms as his fingers stroked upward, nicking the thin line of her lace underwear.

They spilled out of the elevator. She opened her apartment and, as they made their way to her room, he barely had time to notice the home's ultra-Asian, high-tech design. In the bedroom, he nearly fell over the low, light-wood bed. The windows were dressed with shades that imitated Japanese bamboo doorways that slid silently from side to side. The walls were white.

Nina took her clothes off in front of him, leaving only her panties. He struggled fast to undress. Reaching out for his hand, she led him, naked, to the bathroom. There she squeezed a small amount of a high-powered mint gel manufactured somewhere in rural France onto a toothbrush. With her free hand she brushed a few times and then put the brush into his mouth. She moved the bristles gently, side to side, against his teeth. As she handed him a glass to let him rinse, she turned around in front of him, looking at the mirror.

In the reflection, he could see her perfect round breasts

swaying as she began a slow, rhythmic movement of her buttocks against him. She curved her back forward, leaving only his exposed skin pressing against her lace thong panties.

It did not take long for him to pick her up, turn her around, and sit her on the marble sink countertop. They kissed long and passionately and began making love right there on the counter. Slowly, very slowly, he saw her blue eyes fade and glaze in ecstasy.

At the end, they both poured into each other's arms like a tumbling tower of cards. Giggling, the two walked hand in hand to the bed and made love all over again.

At six in the morning, she made him coffee and took it to the bed. Caressing his dark hair, she smiled at him gently.

"I want to do this again."

"So do I. Can we see each other tonight?" Looking at her perfect blond face, Tony prayed for the right answer. She was beautiful, full of life. He had to see her again.

"Yes, please. When are you finished with your meetings?"

"We go all day. Can I call you in the evening?"

"I will wait for your call all day." Nina smiled. She hesitated a moment before speaking again.

"Uggin tells me your meetings are important. He said that the tunnel can change history. What do you think?"

Tony was taken aback by the fact that Uggin had been chatting so casually about their confidential meetings. His answer was careful.

"Sure, it has a lot of possibilities. But it's far from a done deal."

Nina nuzzled against his neck, her breath warm.

"We should all hope this happens. It's a good thing. It will moderate the bossy instincts of Russia's leaders. For me, that is the most positive thing."

"I guess I haven't thought of that angle. But there are also lots of problems with the idea. The world needs to find other energy sources that don't harm the environment." Tony purposely skipped the part about his misgivings with increasing America's dependency on her country.

"Well, I think the idea is fascinating," she said, suddenly serious. "And after tonight, so should you."

For a tiny instant a cold, paralyzing flash of darkness spewed out from her eyes, catching him unaware. He felt a strange shiver. In the next instant, it was gone.

"Get dressed, get dressed, Mr. Anthony Ruiz," Nina giggled. "Or that terrible CIA woman will punish you and not let you out again tonight. And that can't happen because I need to see you."

Nina called a taxi to take him to his hotel. Ten minutes later, she walked him to the elevator in a bathrobe and they again kissed deeply. Unable to let go, he walked into the elevator, his mouth still attached to her lips. They laughed and waved at each other as the elevator door closed.

Tony Ruiz hopped into the waiting taxi. Ordering the driver to the Metropol Hotel, Tony let his weight recede into the cab's vinyl backseat. What a night! He had never met anybody—any woman—like Nina. She was part mischievous child, part goddess. He had slept less than three hours, yet he'd never felt more alive.

Notwithstanding the early hour, Moscow's streets were clogged. Just as well, Tony thought. He was in no hurry to get back to the hotel and face Packard. The notion of going straight from his night's excitement to a showdown with the CIA director and her cold aloofness worried him. He wondered if he was really ready to face her.

Suddenly, the thought of Martha Packard connected with a slamming jolt of horrible realization. It was like an electric stab. His stomach turned and he suddenly felt sick. Tony Ruiz shot up in his cab seat, ramrod straight.

It couldn't be. Please. It just couldn't be true. His brain suddenly echoed with one loud voice—Nina's voice. He recalled her chiding him to get dressed quickly so that the "terrible CIA woman" would let him out to see her again tonight. How had she known about Packard? How could she have known?

Tony Ruiz's mind became mush. He couldn't think straight. His fingers quivering, he tried to replay the chronological events of the previous evening in his mind. The mental pictures would not stay in order. Trying to slow his brain, thoughts jumbled together, coming and going too fast to control.

Nina clearly had wanted the night to end in her bed. Sure, he had been seduced; he had known it was happening. It had gone fast, but nothing about the evening had been suspicious or out of place. Until this morning. Until the conversation about the tunnel. Until her outspoken support of the Bering Strait project.

Until she had warned him, in that single, fast nanosecond of chill, that he had to be for it.

And then she had mentioned Packard. Sickened and pale, Tony realized there was no other way to read what had happened. The quick, offhand comment about the American intelligence chief had been Nina's cold warning. Her threat. Her way of putting Tony on official notice that he had been duped. Blackmailed.

Nina knew about Packard because it was her job to know.

The implication was obvious. The Russians probably had the whole night on videotape. The toothbrush, the sex, the caressing words, his desperation to see her again.

For one fleeting instant, Tony's mind grasped at straws. Perhaps Uggin had innocently told her about Packard's presence in Moscow. Couldn't that be possible? Wasn't that the obvious explanation?

That thought was a natural human reaction. In desperation, humans clutch at any small inkling of optimism. Tony knew that his life would be over without that single strand of hope. Finished. Devoid of that tiny flicker of confidence, he knew that his career and his soul would be distilled down to a choice between a humbling resignation or spending the rest of his life at the behest of Russian intelligence services blackmailing him into ever-deeper waters.

Alas, the thought was futile. The excuse was a sham, vanishing as quickly as it had come. Tony was in sufficient control of his mind to know that no matter how chatty Uggin was, he would never have told her about Packard. He was a

Russian bureaucrat. He didn't reveal things accidentally to just any pretty girl.

Unless the pretty girl was an FSB agent.

MOSCOW
SEPTEMBER 4, 8:05 A.M.
THE METROPOL HOTEL

One hour later, Tony Ruiz descended in the Metropol's elevators to the fourteenth floor and walked down the hall. He had considered calling ahead, but had discarded the idea.

He rapped loudly on the door. No answer. Tony hesitated momentarily. Alone in the hotel hallway, he shrugged. No choice. An hour ago, he had been nervous about having to face down a senior U.S. government official acting contrary to the president's instructions.

Instead, he was now here for a very different reason.

He knocked again. Louder.

This time he heard the locks open. Martha Packard opened the door and stared blankly at her visitor.

She was dressed in an outfit that was the photographic negative of yesterday's clothes. This time her skirt and jacket were a light brown, her brass-buttoned blouse a dark navy blue. The stockinged feet meant that she had not yet had time to put on shoes. Behind her, on the coffee table in the suite's living room, was a breakfast tray surrounded by papers piled neatly on the sofa and chairs.

"Mr. Ruiz," she said coldly, not moving an inch. "Good morning. What can I do for you?"

"We need to talk, General." Tony felt a shiver. The next ten minutes would be the most important ones in his life.

"Yes, I guess we do. I've been waiting for your inevitable outburst."

He had been prepared for a million excuses to avoid this conversation. Tony was taken aback by her absolute directness.

"Can I come in?" Tony asked.

She thought about it for a second and then silently moved away from the door. Packard motioned him to a chair.

The director of Central Intelligence sat down directly in front of him. She stared sullenly in his direction. The message was clear. He had sought out this meeting. He needed to start. Tony took a deep breath.

"General Packard, you look like a person who prefers straight talk. I will respect that. I've come here to ask you—no, sorry, to tell you—that you're overstepping your authority."

If Tony had expected some big bang after that statement, he'd been severely mistaken. Martha Packard's staring eyes were cold and empty. He felt compelled to continue.

"I did not request this trip. I was asked to accompany you to Moscow. Not because I have any particular knowledge about this country or about the subject we're here to discuss. My instructions were to protect the president. I was told that we were to come to Moscow on a fact-finding mission. Instead, I find that you are in the midst of negotiating an agreement with our Russian counterparts to build a Bering Strait tunnel. That is way beyond the White House's expectation of what this trip is all about."

For one split second, Tony thought he saw a sparkle of respect in her eyes. He decided to press the point. With a false calm, he slammed forward his conclusion.

"It's my suspicion that you are preparing to present President Gene Laurence with a deal that's a fait accompli. I believe that it is your plan to leak the details upon your return to Washington. Once the story is out, you're betting that the president will feel compelled to sign. To me, that constitutes a real danger to my boss."

Packard crossed her legs, buying time. Tony took it as a sure sign that his words had hit home.

"You're not enamored of the idea of a Bering Strait tunnel, are you, Mr. Ruiz?"

"That is an understatement," Tony snapped.

"And is your disdain for this idea grounded in reality? Or are you just another of those environmental doomsday believers who think any fossil fuel will shorten our planet's existence?"

"General, with all due respect, that is a smart-ass question," Tony answered coldly. "It would be like me asking you whether the fact that you were born in Alaska is clouding your judgment of the Russians. I hold you in greater respect than to ask that."

Ruiz could see Martha Packard looking at him with newfound admiration. He was more than holding his own.

"Okay, Mr. Ruiz. Fair enough. The Russians are not the prettiest government in the world. But they have something that we want. No, cancel that. They have something we need. We can't let another California occur in our country. One more of those catastrophes and the United States will be on its knees. We will become the world's laughingstock. We don't have choices. Alternative energies sound nice. But whatever small promise they hold may take years to develop."

"We have to start somewhere, General. We can't go on depending on foreigners—and, in particular, foreigners who don't like us—for our energy. The decision to put our future in Russia's hands may come back and bite us in the ass. Isn't it time to take a first step to liberate ourselves from foreign control of energy? The United States can't postpone tough decisions forever."

Packard stared at him for a long time. She weighed her words carefully.

"We can debate this until kingdom come. Let's be practical. What do you propose, Mr. Ruiz?"

He was ready for the question.

"Go negotiate your tunnel, General. With one condition. No press. No announcement. No leaks. Laurence can't be made to feel that he is in a trap, with no choice other than to sign. If word gets out, the deal is broken. Irreparably. If you stick to it and there is no public pressure, I'll join you in recommending that Laurence adopt the deal as long as it's joined at the hip with specific measures to foster alternative fuels."

Packard was stunned. He had expected this.

"I'm surprised," she stuttered. "I expected a fight to the death with you. I postponed our meeting with the Russians until midday, expecting to spend the next hours in furious conference calls with Washington. I even had the secretary of energy and the secretary of state on standby, ready to back me up."

Tony saw her struggling with a question she had no way of answering. If this had been a better day, he might even have been amused. He allowed himself a sad smile as he put himself in her shoes. He could imagine her question: Why was this guy capitulating so easily?

He cleared his throat, doing everything possible not to show the pit he felt in his stomach.

This would be the moment on which the rest of his career—his life—depended. The bait had been laid. She would get her damn tunnel. Now he would reveal the price, the quid pro quo.

"General, I imagine that you must be asking yourself why this little discussion went so smoothly. I can understand your surprise. You see, I actually have some advice to ask of you."

Packard was too much of a pro to ask questions. She knew when to be quiet.

"Last night," Tony continued as steadily as possible, "was an interesting one. I accepted an invitation to go out with one of our hosts. Daniel Uggin invited me out on the town. He brought with him two very beautiful women. We had a very nice time going from bar to bar. This is actually a great city."

Tony did his best to form his lips into a smile.

"Now it's my impression that the women were brought to seduce me. The cloak-and-dagger trade is your department, not mine, General Packard. But I've read my share of spy stories and I presume that the old Soviet game of sexual blackmail is still alive and kicking. Am I right?"

He saw her nodding slowly. Warily. He continued, choosing his words with great care.

"So, as tempted as I might have been to fall into one of these women's arms, I decided to come to you first and ask for your suggestions or, umm, advice. I want to be sure to do the right thing for my country."

General Martha Packard's eyes narrowed for just a

moment. Her answer would reveal no emotion. She was a senior intelligence professional. There was no need for any further explanation from Tony. She understood the half-truth.

"Mr. Ruiz, there is no doubt that you have done the right thing. Telling me what happened was your only course of action."

Tony felt every muscle in his body relax. There it was. It wasn't pretty, but it was the best he could do. He felt relieved, but heartbroken. It was a stiff price to pay for his freedom. He had not only given up his deep disdain for this putrid project, he had also confessed to the head of the CIA that he had fallen for a Russian agent's attempt to recruit him. In return for her silence, Martha Packard would always own his chit.

As tears of regret welled up in his eyes, Tony Ruiz realized that his American dream was dead. All his life, Tony Ruiz had seen his parents struggle for survival. Their son had been proof of their ultimate success; he had fought the odds and had always come out on top.

Not this time.

Though Tony Ruiz had calculated that it was preferable to be indebted to a powerful American than to a foreign power, his decision didn't make him feel any better. It was a devil's pact. Yes, Tony's quick thinking had avoided the potential of future damaging blackmail by a foreign power. But in exchange, he had acquired a lifetime of debt to a military woman he profoundly mistrusted.

CULPEPER, VIRGINIA
SEPTEMBER 4, 7:00 A.M.
THE IT'S ABOUT THYME INN

After a night of fitful tossing, Blaise Ryan had given up trying to go back to sleep once her eyes had shot open at 5:30 A.M. It was her second night at the small rural Virginia inn located an hour and a half outside the nation's capital.

This past night had gone even worse than the previous one.

Nestled just above a restaurant of the same name, the three-room bed-and-breakfast was a cute mix of country furnishings and Victorian decoration set on Culpeper's Main Street, just fifteen miles from the Blue Ridge Mountains. She had found it—and loved it—a few years back while attending a friend's wedding in the bucolic cow-studded pastures of the Virginia piedmont.

The past forty-eight hours had been the most difficult ones of her life. Blaise Ryan was a tough fighter. Years of clashing with government officials and heads of corporations had inured her to the scrapes and pains of conflict with powerful interests. In all those fights, replete with accusations and insults, she had never known fear. Bruises, yes. Humiliation, sure. Insults, of course. But never fear.

Yet in the last two days, Blaise had been filled with the unfamiliar feeling of paralyzing terror. Her life had been transformed three times over in the past months—from scrappy policy fighter to witness of the California energy crisis's pain and suffering and now to potential victim of physical violence. Those were a lot of changes in too short a time. The weight of events was doing her in.

Losing one's way in life is painful for anyone. But Blaise's moment of darkness could not have come at a worse time. She was in serious danger. She knew the Russians were looking for her. What she didn't know was what to do about it.

Too scared to leave the inn, she had survived her stay in Culpeper on only pots of coffee and the occasional croissant brought up by the worried innkeepers. Blaise moved emptily around the room—from her bed to the small country French desk to the bathroom and back again. Only the shower seemed to assuage her fears, the hot jets of water temporarily washing away the memories of Matta and Lima.

But the minute she stepped out of the white porcelain tub to dry off in front of the mirror, the dread flooded back, immobilizing her mind.

Blaise had made only one decision once the U.S.-bound flight had taken off from Lima. A few minutes after her American Airlines Boeing 767 landed in Miami, she had gone to the counter to change her final destination. Rather than returning to San Francisco, Blaise had requested paying the $100 change fee to connect to Washington, D.C. There was nobody in California who could help her. Her only chance was to get to Washington.

But once on the two-hour flight from Miami to Reagan National Airport, she had succumbed to another attack of dark desperation. What was she going to do in Washington? The only people she really knew in the nation's capital were the senior officers of environmental organizations and the few congressional staffers who supported green causes. She needed the protective guns of the FBI and the CIA. Instead, all she had were tree-hugging ecologists.

Not knowing whom to trust, Blaise had panicked upon her arrival in D.C. Though she had come to find help, seeing the people-filled airport suddenly spurred a change of mind. Surmising that staying overnight in Washington was too risky, Blaise had rented a car. Once behind the wheel, she had instinctively driven out of town and watched in a silent trance as the road signs of Route 66 flew by her windshield. Blaise had kept driving, not knowing where she was going until she saw the directions to Shenandoah National Park. That was when she had remembered the It's About Thyme Inn.

She had hoped that the quiet of Culpeper's Main Street would somehow help reboot her frozen brain. Instead, the opposite had happened. The terror of knowing she was being hunted had begun to consume every waking moment. Beyond her own fears, Blaise had trouble warding off the painful pangs of deep, lonely guilt about Anne-Sophie, whom she had not contacted for fear that a phone call to Russia could be traced. After the run-in with the Russian Embassy goon who had known her friend's name, there was no doubt in Blaise's mind that Anne-Sophie was under surveillance.

After more than an hour and a half awake, she stood now in front of the mirror, glancing momentarily at her reflection and turning away, disgusted by the lines of anxiety that traversed her gaunt face. She went back to bed. She loathed her paralysis, but she was a woman reduced to a state of utter confusion, unable to decide on any course of action.

Blaise stared emptily at the ceiling from the inn's wrought-iron bed. Without any real thought or interest, she reached across to the night table, picked up the remote, and zapped on the television. She heard the sound, but couldn't be bothered with focusing on the screen.

"Nearly two months after the lights went out here in this state, the streets of Los Angeles are still patrolled by uniformed soldiers of the Hundred-and-Second Mechanized Division of the California National Guard. Not for much longer, though. The looting may have stopped and the guns may have fallen silent, but yesterday's announcement by

Governor Cyrus Moravian that the National Guard was returning to its bases tomorrow has shaken the fragile confidence of this city's residents. In neighborhoods all over Los Angeles, citizens have gathered with signs begging the National Guard to stay. Notwithstanding the welcome rains and cooler temperatures, it's a sign—a symbol, an indication—of the still-fragile state of mind of California's residents.

"I interviewed Governor Moravian yesterday and he . . ."

Sprawled limply on the unmade bed, Blaise found herself slowly focusing on the television reporter's familiar voice. She struggled to raise her head toward the screen. Seeing CNN's Anna Hardaway, Blaise felt her mind involuntarily engage for the first time in days. Her brain was out of practice. It took a while to concentrate on the words emanating from the television. She remembered reading somewhere that Anna Hardaway had won a Pulitzer Prize for her courageous, emotive reporting during the California energy crisis.

As she listened to the journalist, she recalled her two on-camera interviews with Hardaway. Blaise had admired the fact that, throughout the ordeal of the emergency, the news reporter had lost neither her journalistic realism nor her humanity. Anna Hardaway had demonstrated a unique touch, combining a reporter's dispassionate distance with emotion-laden descriptions that had brought faraway viewers close to—almost into—California's escalating tragedy.

Blaise sat up on the bed, now fully attentive to CNN's story. It wasn't the content of the correspondent's reporting that suddenly dragged life back into her fear-induced lethargy. No, Blaise didn't really pay attention to the substance at all. Instead, an idea was forming in her mind that centered on Hardaway herself.

Out of gut instinct alone, Blaise scrambled out of bed and turned on her cell phone to look up Anna Hardaway's mobile number. Without a moment's reflection, she picked up the room's phone and began to dial, congratulating herself on having the wherewithal not to make the call with her own cell phone.

"Anna Hardaway." A voice answered the phone. Blaise could hear fumbling movements across the line.

"Anna, this is Blaise Ryan. How are you?"

"For Christ's sake, Blaise. It's four-twenty in the morning."

Blaise's eyes veered to the night table's alarm clock and saw that it was 7:20 in the morning. Feeling stupid for having forgotten all about the time change with California, she should have known that Hardaway's presence on television didn't mean she was transmitting live. But now that the reporter was on the telephone, she couldn't allow Hardaway to hang up. However impulsive it may have been, this call signified one small step in the right direction. She had to keep moving forward.

"Anna, I'm sorry about the time. I need to talk to you. It's urgent."

The reporter hesitated. "Come on, can't we talk in a couple of hours?"

"No, we need to talk now."

"Okay," Hardaway said, relenting. "Let me get the light on."

Blaise could hear more fumbling. She presumed that the reporter was looking for a pen and notepad. That's what all reporters did when somebody used the magic word "urgent" to get their attention.

Blaise Ryan was now fully alert. It was strange, she thought. Once her mind had closed on a direction, forty-eight hours of paralysis seemed to dissipate in less than one minute.

"All right, I'm back," Hardaway snapped.

"Okay, I'm calling for some advice—"

"What! You woke me up so that I could give you advice? I don't give advice in the middle of the night. I don't even talk to sources at this hour. I just made an exception. And it better be good."

"Hold on, hold on. Don't blow up. I will give you a story that will bend your mind. But there are two conditions. First, what I'm telling you is off the record and on deep background. And, though I promise that it's your exclusive story, you can't use any of it until I give you the green light. I trust you, Anna. But I won't talk unless you agree to the ground rules."

"Fine. Done. It's off the record and on deep background," Hardaway grunted. Like any reporter, she hated stories that could not be attributed to a readily identifiable source. "But I won't agree to the confidentiality. Once you tell me, I'm free to dig."

Blaise hesitated. She didn't play poker, but she thought the bluff might work. "I understand. Good night. Sorry to have bothered you."

"Wait, wait. Okay, fine. As long as I get a promise that you go nowhere else with the scoop."

Blaise smiled at the easy win before continuing. "I promise. Second is the advice part. When we're done, I need you to tell me where I go with what I know. I'm in danger, Anna. Really serious danger. But I don't know who to talk to."

Blaise knew she had her attention now.

"All right, Blaise, I'll help in any way I can," Hardaway said, her voice turning warm with concern. "What the hell is going on?"

With Hardaway furiously scribbling away on the other side of the continent, it took Blaise nearly a half hour to tell her story. As she chronicled the history of the past days, the newswoman demanded precision, peppering her throughout with an onslaught of questions. How did your friend in Russia find out about Anfang? What is your relationship with this Peruvian senator? Has there been an official coroner's report about his death or are you relying only on that first news report you read at the airport? How can you prove Anfang's links to the Russians? What is the volume of gas that Latin America will export to the United States? How much will Peru's gas help to assuage the gas deficit in California? How will the gas get here? Who is buying it?

As the questions came, fast and furious, Blaise could nearly touch Hardaway's mounting interest. She could tell that the journalist was trying to form a news story in her mind, testing it by demanding details and questioning facts. Blaise worried that she was unable to answer some of Hardaway's hard questions. But she had experience in dealing with reporters; they respected people who admitted not knowing an answer. There was nothing a journalist hated more than a source who blithely slung mindless answers at all oncoming questions.

Hardaway's queries died down as Blaise began to wind up the tale. By the time she got to the part about the man identifying himself as a Russian diplomat at the Lima airport, an unexpected silence filled the phone line.

"Jesus, Blaise," was all Hardaway could say. "Now I know why you began this conversation by asking for advice."

Silence again.

"Can you help me?" whispered Blaise.

"I don't know. I have to think about it. I'm the California correspondent, not the Washington bureau chief. I appreciate the fact that you trusted me with the story. But don't you remember that I did an interview with Laurence during the campaign that ended up with him walking off the set?

"You may have chosen the wrong person," Hardaway continued sadly, nearly apologetic. "I'm persona non grata with this administration. There's almost nobody who will talk to me."

Blaise could feel herself falling back into the dark hole of uncertainty. The one and only determined stroke she had made to liberate herself was going nowhere.

"Anna, you must know somebody. Please." It was more plea than question.

"Well, there is only one guy I can think of. I met him when he was a new campaign hire. A Latino guy from Washington State named Tony Ruiz. Really smart. Really nice. But young. He was sent to try to make nice after his boss walked out on me midinterview. I was nervous; he did a good job of calming me down. I knew I had become radioactive with Laurence. And the big shots at CNN headquarters in Atlanta were beside themselves, thinking that our network would be blacklisted by the Laurence campaign because of my tiff with their candidate."

"And?" demanded Blaise. She needed more substance if she was to pin some hope on this young Hispanic.

"And he fixed it. Within three days, Laurence's press

people offered Ryan Foxman an hour-long interview on economic issues. I'm still pissed at Laurence's huffiness and they're still angry with me. But at least Ruiz got the network goons off my back."

"What does he do now?"

"I had heard he was a domestic affairs advisor. Look, at least he's at the White House. At least I know him. And, most important, at least he'll take my call."

"He sounds perfect," Blaise lied. She knew that this young advisor was anything but ideal. But Mr. Tony Ruiz from Washington State was the only thing she had going right now. "Here is what I would ask, Anna. Get me in to see him. If he is at the White House, he has the political juice to call in somebody else who can help."

She heard hesitation. Blaise imagined Hardaway was worried that the scoop would get away from her.

"Anna, I gave you my word. The story is yours. I'll keep you in the loop every step of the way. But you have to help me get to this guy."

"Okay, Blaise. Give me a few hours and call me back," Hardaway agreed.

LOS ANGELES, CALIFORNIA
SEPTEMBER 4, 11:40 A.M.
CNN STUDIOS

"All right, that's a wrap," shouted Steve Orinbach, Anna Hardaway's cameraman, as the lights switched off. He looked at his watch. Perfect. Right on time for lunch.

"Nice work, Anna. Just the right tone." Orinbach smiled her way, his long, stringy hair falling on his face as he leaned over to break down the equipment. His tattoo-covered arms struggled to push the tripod into place.

"Wanna get a bite?" he asked without looking up. "We have to be in Westwood at two-thirty P.M. So I figure we have some time."

"Not today, sweetie pie." Anna Hardaway smiled. She loved using the most unctuous names to address her talented, punk-loving, camera-wielding toughie. It drove him nuts.

Anna walked down the paper-strewn hallway to her small office. It was a mess. Just what you would expect of a television reporter.

She immediately swished the computer's mouse to bring the machine back to life. Disappointed, she reached for her purse and glanced at her mobile phone, which had remained silent during the broadcast. Nothing.

Anna was getting worried.

After hanging up with Blaise, she had put in a call to the White House operator and left an urgent message with her name and cell phone number. It had been way too early on the East Coast to expect Ruiz to be at his desk. But she had figured that he would call back upon his arrival.

Government working hours in Washington began between 9 and 9:30 A.M. That was barely dawn in California. When she hadn't heard anything by then, she penned a quick e-mail to Ruiz requesting a return call on an urgent matter. By midmorning California time, she wrote him again. This time she decided to put more oomph in the note.

"Tony," she had written. "Need to talk. I've got an exclusive on a story that requires White House confirmation. Please contact me. This is my third message. Regards, AH."

Anna Hardaway had been sure that her use of journalistic high-priority codes would prompt Ruiz to life. Pressing Send, Anna had gone off an hour ago to talk to her producer. From there, she had walked around the corner to makeup and then ducked under the heavy curtains onto the set next door. Her piece had taken about forty minutes to produce, from start to finish. Returning to her desk, she was now frustrated to find no answer from Tony Ruiz.

Anna pulled absentmindedly at a wisp of her auburn hair, deep in thought about what else she could do to find Ruiz. The shrill tone of her telephone startled her into an involuntary jump. She grabbed the receiver, expecting a voice from the White House. Instead, it was Blaise.

"Look, I don't have good news for you. I have left three messages. Nothing. I don't know if he is traveling or if he just won't talk to me."

Hardaway could hear the gasp of fear in the phone's silence.

"I'm going to keep trying, Blaise. I promise. I will find this guy. I can't swear he will help. But you have my word that I'll find him."

There was nothing else to say.

She heard a barely audible "Thank you" as the phone was hung up. Anna Hardaway felt sorry for Blaise. Her scrappy environmentalist acquaintance had become a shadow of her former self.

Where the hell was Ruiz? She considered, and discarded, the possibility that he had not received the message. Anthony Ruiz worked at the White House. Phone. Blackberry. White House operators. These guys were connected every minute of every day.

Anna forced her mind to concentrate. Twenty years in journalism had taught her that ratcheting up the pressure was the only way to get reticent government officials to talk. A thought occurred to her.

She pulled her computer keyboard nearer and started to tap on the keys.

"Ruiz, damnit. It's important. Get back to me. Ever heard of Russian involvement in California-bound natural gas? AH."

She punched Send.

Anna made two quick phone calls to confirm this afternoon's interviews and was on her way to the ladies' room when she heard the mechanical two-tone announcement of an incoming e-mail. Glancing backward, she could hardly believe what she saw.

Ruiz. It had taken less than three minutes for him to answer the last e-mail.

Anna spun around and leaned over the chair to open the message. She immediately noted that it had been sent from a Blackberry.

"Will call your office in exactly five minutes. Pick up."

Anna Hardaway jumped up and ran down the hallway to the bathroom. She had four minutes to get back to her desk.

LOS ANGELES, CALIFORNIA
SEPTEMBER 4, 12:00 P.M.
CNN STUDIOS

The phone was already ringing when Anna Hardaway walked back into her office, coffee in hand. She glanced at her watch; Ruiz was early. The last e-mail had clearly made an impression on the young White House advisor.

"Anna Hardaway." She did her best to sound officious, pretending to have no clue as to who would be calling.

"Hey, it's Ruiz." His voice was equally nonchalant.

"Long time, friend."

"Yeah. Congratulations on the Pulitzer. Well deserved." The banter was ridiculous.

"Ruiz, I've been hounding you all morning."

"I know. Sorry. I'm not in D.C."

Anna's voice turned sober. "Can we stop circling around each other like hyenas, Tony? I need something from you. It's important. You know the subject; I put it in the e-mail."

"How the hell did you find out about the Russian natural gas negotiations, Anna? It was seriously under wraps."

Hardaway's journalistic radar bleeped. There was something strange about his response. But right then and there, she couldn't put her finger on it.

"I found out the way every reporter finds something out. I have a good source. I'm even going to let you meet the source. But I'm going to hold on to the name for a while yet. Can you confirm that the United States government knows about surreptitious Russian attempts to become one of California's main suppliers of imported natural gas?"

"Are we off the record?" he asked cautiously.

Christ, Anna thought. Here it goes again. Why won't anybody speak anymore for attribution?

"Okay, we're off the record."

"There is nothing secret or surreptitious about Russia's desire to supply natural gas to the Pacific coast of the United States. We're encouraging the conversation. You know better than most how badly we need the natural gas. The Russians have what we want. I'm in Moscow talking to them now."

"What? You're in Moscow?" Hardaway choked, her body jerking backward in stunned surprise. The revelation of his whereabouts had made her move so suddenly that the coiled phone cord sent her Styrofoam coffee cup flying across the desk. Hot liquid was slowly seeping out of the sealed container.

"You mean you know about what they did in Peru? And you're still talking to these bastards?"

"What the hell are you talking about, Hardaway?" gasped Tony. "I'm in Moscow because . . ."

Silence invaded the telephone line as the two suddenly realized they had been talking about completely different things. Anna Hardaway's radar warnings were now off the charts.

The truth was dawning on Anna Hardaway. "Jesus, Tony. We've been talking past each other. You're in Moscow on something completely different, aren't you? You're making some gas deal with these guys."

Hardaway knew she had caught him.

Had this been just any news story, Anna Hardaway would have pressed on relentlessly. She would have been all over him, like a pit bull. To get him to reveal more, she would have threatened to go on air with the revelation that a senior White House official was in Moscow negotiating a gas supply deal with the Russians. But these weren't normal circumstances. She had Blaise to think about. She had promised.

"Tony, can we take a step back? All cards faceup on the table, okay? I'm in a bind. I've got an exclusive here—well, maybe after talking to you, I've got two scoops—but I also have a pal in trouble. I'm struggling to be a journalist and a friend at the same time. Maybe the two can't go together, but I need to try. Can you work with me on that basis?"

She continued without waiting for an answer.

"Here is what I know. I've found out that a Russian company called Volga Gaz submitted false bids through sham operating companies to operate the principal Latin American gas fields. The gas from those fields was going to be exported to the United States. I suspect the Russian company tried to hide its involvement in Latin America because its real purpose is to gain some type of leverage with the United States. The senior Peruvian senator who was in charge of his government's decision to award the project found out about the Russians' secret involvement three days ago. The next day he turned up dead."

She heard Tony suck in air.

"I'm not done," Hardaway barked. "As if all that isn't good enough, our little misunderstanding a minute ago made me realize that I've stumbled on to an even bigger story. While all this is happening in Peru, I just found out my government has people in Moscow negotiating some other gas deal with the Russians. Connect the dots for me, Ruiz."

She could almost feel the whirring of Tony Ruiz's brain as it strained to compute the calculations.

"Listen to me, Anna. I can't connect the dots because what you've just told me is a complete mystery. You have got to believe me; I have never heard of these projects in Latin America. I have never heard of a Peruvian senator—alive or dead. And I've never heard of Russia operating sham companies in our backyard. None of it. Not one goddamn bit of it."

Hardaway believed him. He sounded angry and agitated.

"Can you reveal your source? How did they get this information?"

"I'll do better than that. Let me see if my source will get on the line. Can you hold and I will conference the person in?"

Anna Hardaway put Ruiz on hold and moved the computer mouse to Contacts List to look up Blaise Ryan's cell phone number. She dialed it quickly.

"Hi, it's me," Hardaway said as soon as Blaise answered the phone, still in its On position from Blaise's search for Anna's number a few hours earlier.

"I said I would call you. I'd prefer to use a landline."

"Too late. I've got Ruiz on the phone. Our thought was to conference you in. But fasten your seat belt. You won't believe it. He's in Moscow."

In a quick minute, Anna Hardaway summarized their conversation so far. She ended with a warning.

"You're going to have to make a decision here. It's your

call. This guy is in Moscow negotiating a gas deal. If you decide to trust him, do it with your eyes open. I don't know him well enough to put my hands in the fire. He lives in Washington. They double-cross people for breakfast in that city."

Blaise remembered President Harry Truman's old adage: If you want a friend in Washington, get a dog.

"What would you do, Anna? What do your instincts tell you?"

"I would trust him. For two reasons. First, because he hasn't been in Washington long enough to have been completely corrupted. Second, because I pulled his bio this morning. I had forgotten that Ruiz used to be a cop. A Chelan County sheriff's deputy."

"Okay, put me on," Blaise declared with finality. That last bit of information was hugely positive.

Two clicks later and the two coasts of the United States were connected with the coming dusk of Moscow's evening.

"Tony, you there? Okay. I want to introduce you to Blaise Ryan."

"Nice to meet you. I've heard your name before, haven't I?" The phone was silent for a moment as Tony reflected on her name. "Oh yeah, I remember now. You're the environmentalist who was beating the crap out of us on Anna's show."

Blaise Ryan felt a chill go through her body. This was not a good way to start.

"By the way," Ruiz chuckled, "two comments about that. First, you do a good interview. Second, I agreed with almost everything you said. That is between you and me, though."

Blaise sighed in relief.

"Look, Blaise. Anna has told me a lot. But I need to understand some details. How did you get into this?"

"It was a fluke. I was trying to help a friend and I tripped over this information. I know a lot about Peruvian gas because I was the leading environmental voice opposing gas extraction in the Amazon. My friend is married—badly married—to a Russian who has been involved in hiding Volga Gaz's connection to Humboldt. I know it sounds crazy, but we went from marital advice to discovering a Russian fraud—and possibly a murder—in less than a month."

"What exactly is the role of your friend's husband in perpetrating this fraud?"

"I can't answer that exactly. He has been traveling to Bolivia. He has met with the German company that is posing in Peru as an independent entity. He talked to his wife about taking the Americans down a notch or two. In the past months, he has become extremely paranoid. And rabidly anti-Western. I heard it myself about six weeks ago."

"What is this man's name?"

"Daniel Uggin."

"Oh my God." Tony Ruiz groaned. He couldn't hold back the surprise.

Anna Hardaway heard the moan, but had no way of knowing that this name belonged to the son of a bitch who had set Tony up the previous evening. She couldn't see the band of cold sweat that had begun to form on his spine. Or the shudders of his fingers.

If Anna Hardaway or Blaise Ryan had known what had happened to Tony in Moscow over the past twenty-four hours, they would have understood his anger. Uggin had not only miserably conned Tony in order to get his support in the Moscow negotiations. Now it turned out that he was also a zealot. A crusading anti-American.

It was indeed impossible for either woman to fathom Tony Ruiz's growing fury as the pieces began falling into place in his mind over a twelve-thousand-mile phone connection. The blackmail perpetrated against him had been much bigger than just the Bering Strait deal. The Russians had a much larger purpose; they were coming at America from two sides.

But Tony Ruiz was now a man stuck in the mud. He had been caught in an act of massive stupidity. There was nothing he could do with this newfound knowledge. Absolutely nothing. Packard now had him by the balls. It was impossible to wriggle himself out of his promised support for the coming announcement of a Bering Strait–generated great new era in Russo-American relations.

"Tony, you there?" Anna whispered into the phone.

"I'm here."

"So? What do you think?"

"Blaise, are you sure about Matta's death? How do you know he was killed?"

"Matta was my sworn enemy. I have been his biggest opponent for years. But the guy was not corrupt or on the take. I saw him three days ago with his press secretary—there was nothing between them. The idea that these two were involved is bull."

"How did you get in to see Matta?" Tony asked. "You said you were his big opponent; his mortal enemy."

"I asked." Blaise smiled, thinking back to her blunt statement about enemies banding together against even greater evils. "I demanded to talk to him in the most persuasive way possible. I found a way to formulate the question so that he couldn't say no."

Blaise and Anna waited for him to say something. Though the young White House official revealed nothing over the phone, something about the texture of his silence was qualitatively different. It was not the hush of hostile rejection, but rather the quiet of somebody mulling over an idea. Anna Hardaway suspected that something about what Blaise had just said had made Tony Ruiz think about his options.

"Okay. I need a couple of days to think about this. I get on a plane to come back home in forty-eight hours. I'll try to have some clear thoughts by the time I get to Washington. Blaise, can you come and see me then?"

Blaise wondered if she would go crazy sitting around Culpeper for another three days. But what choice did she have? Though noncommittal, he seemed interested in helping. There was nothing more she could ask him to do. The guy was halfway around the world. She would have to trust Tony Ruiz.

"Sure," Blaise answered.

RUSSIA

Viktor Zhironovsky was walking out of Volga Gaz's head-quarters at the exact moment Tony Ruiz was searching for a tie in the Metropol's closet after hanging up on his three-way, transatlantic conversation. Stopping in front of the open door of his waiting Mercedes sedan to connect his gold-plated Ronson lighter with the dark Romeo y Julieta maduro in his mouth, the chairman of Volga Gaz gazed at his longtime chauffeur.

"Sir?" asked the driver, waiting for destination instructions. He could tell his boss was in decent spirits. It was not hard to assess Viktor Zhironovsky's frames of mind. When there was a cigar, the mood was okay.

"I've invited the Americans to the CDL." Zhironovsky's implication was clear. The elegant Pushkin Room was always his for the asking, but the chairman only took guests he enjoyed or needed to his coveted second-floor hideout at the Central House of Writers. Tonight his American visitors clearly fit both requirements.

As he reclined in the backseat's dark blue leather, Zhironovsky drew a long mouthful of smoke from the cigar. Yes, the Americans deserved a long, boozy dinner at the CDL. The meetings were going well. The two nations' negotiating teams had taken big steps today and, as a result, his fury with events in Peru had subsided.

A few hours earlier, the chairman had completed his second private, end-of-the-afternoon meeting with the attractive Martha Packard. Today, Zhironovsky had noticed a newfound enthusiasm in her voice. He couldn't pin it down—but something about her demeanor was easier than during the previous day's meeting. She seemed released. Freer to decide.

The first day's meeting had ended positively enough, but Packard had been cautious. Her responses to the Russian proposals had been full of qualifying statements: "Perhaps." "It could be a good idea." "This might work." Her lack of decisiveness had clearly frustrated her hosts.

But things had been very different this afternoon, her language devoid of indecipherable grays. The meeting had been punctuated by clear decision making.

They had made progress. The tunnel would be a Russo-American joint venture—following the example of the international space station's successful cooperation—financed by each government's agreement to float an initial $6 billion in bonds on international financial markets. They had further agreed that a panel of three renowned international scientists culled from the Russian Academy of Scientists, the U.S. Federation of Scientists, and Europe's International College of Engineers would adjudicate, by unanimous vote, the contract to an experienced engineering company.

He had lost on his request to have the joint-venture company headed by a Russian. Packard had insisted that an American be the president of the enterprise. Zhironovsky smiled as he thought back to his feigned fury. He had barked and shouted. Cajoled and argued. But she had held firm.

The reality was that it didn't matter to him at all who would head the company. It was irrelevant. There was one and only one thing that was important: The two sides of the

Bering Strait were going to be linked. His dream to convert the Americans into a begging dependency on Russia for their energy and electricity was becoming a reality.

Tomorrow they would face difficult economic questions. Pricing for the natural gas. Commitments of quantities. Royalty payments. Environmental questions. All tough issues. Zhironovsky knew these technical matters would be mostly handled by Stuart Altman, Packard's deputy. But, he thought with satisfaction, if the CIA chief's mood tomorrow was similar to today's, they could well be signing an historic memorandum of understanding by the time the Americans left the day after tomorrow.

The vibration of his mobile phone in his coat jacket pulled Zhironovsky out of his thoughts. Shit. Cellular phones were a horrid invention. The little machines were facilitators of disorder, allowing the irrelevant minutiae of life to cascade and interrupt without advance warning.

He glanced at the phone screen with the full intention of screening out only the most important of callers. Viktor Zhironovsky grunted with misery when he saw "No Caller ID" on the display. The phone vibrated again. He decided that this was not the time to ignore a call.

"Zhironovsky," the chairman barked into the phone.

"Good evening," growled the low-toned voice. "It's Mikhail. From the United States."

Zhironovsky's round body tensed momentarily. Mikhail was one of those operators Volga Gaz routinely contracted around the world. These men belonged to the Russian mafia. They were unpleasant, but their job was to resolve difficulties. They fixed problems nobody wanted to deal with, repaired issues nobody enjoyed discussing. The Mikhails of the world telephoned either with very good or very bad news.

"Tell me," Zhironovsky ordered.

"We found your woman. She is in a little town outside Washington. She got a long call on her mobile phone and it was enough time to electronically triangulate her whereabouts. Your instructions?"

"Did you listen to the call?"

"No. That is impossible to do without major equipment that would be noticed. All we were able to do is fix her approximate location through reporting cellular phone towers."

Viktor Zhironovsky wondered if what the man said was true. It was a pity that they were unable to know anything about the call's contents. Knowing what she was up to would have facilitated a decision. But the mere fact that the environmentalist woman was in the Washington area was disconcerting enough. She was far from her native California.

To Viktor Zhironovsky, this call was proof—once again—that if you wanted something important done, you had to do it yourself. Rudzhin had wanted to wait until the Americans left to decide what to do about Blaise Ryan. Now, instead of being at home in San Francisco, she was waltzing around Washington. Free to talk to anybody she desired. Thank God he hadn't listened to Rudzhin.

Young people, Zhironovsky thought to himself. They were worthless. At sixty-eight years of age, he still had to resolve everything on his own. He knew what had to be done.

"Can you find her?" Zhironovsky grumbled into the phone.

"Hypothetically, yes. We were able to pinpoint her general area. But once we're there, we'll have to ask questions. That will draw some attention. We'll be discreet. But it's your call."

Zhironovsky paused a moment to give the dilemma some thought.

"Find her," he sentenced. "But don't do anything there. I don't want any loose ends lying around in the United States. I have enough of those right here."

"So?"

"I'll send a plane over tonight. It will be there by your daytime tomorrow. Get her on the airplane. Quietly and cleanly. I'll have her dealt with here."

"No problem. Have your pilot file a flight plan with the general aviation terminal at Dulles International Airport. It's only an hour away from where she is now. Give him my cell phone number and tell him to call when he lands. We'll deliver her."

Both men hung up without saying good-bye. Conversations like these did not require the usual niceties.

Zhironovsky leaned back in the Mercedes's rear seat. He took a moment to relight his cigar before calling his secretary to arrange for the airplane. All in all, it was a good day, he thought. The phone call from Mikhail was like his meeting today with Packard. Not conclusive, but heading in the right direction.

Yes, a good day, he thought again. With that positive notion lodged in his brain, he let out a large, blue stream of smoke.

MOSCOW
SEPTEMBER 4, 8:10 P.M.
THE METROPOL HOTEL

Anthony Ruiz was standing in front of the mirror of his hotel room. In the last ten minutes, he had tied, untied, and redone his fish motif yellow tie four times. It was not the tie that bothered him. What disturbed him was the wishy-washiness of indecision.

Anthony Ruiz was a success story, a symbol of what could still happen in the United States when things went right. Steeled by his poverty-stricken parents' dogged determination to pass on a better life to their son, Tony had grown up understanding that hard work, loyalty, and moral clarity were the clear keys to victory. It wasn't that his parents had ever objected to a little fun. They were Mexicans. Latinos. Life was supposed to include laughter.

The easy charm and tough determination that had taken him a long way from the protection of his dad's calloused hands were gone now. He wished he could talk to his father. But Mario Ruiz would never have been able to understand what had happened last night. His father's world revolved around certitudes. Mario Ruiz didn't make stupid mistakes. He didn't fall into traps. He didn't allow himself to become blinded.

No, for once, Tony Ruiz wasn't smiling. He could feel a

lump in his throat. How had he fallen for such a primitive trap? He was a former cop, damnit. He should have known better. Knowing that Nina had been beautiful *and* smart, beguiling him with her antigovernment banter and self-assured laughter, didn't lessen the blow. He should have seen it coming.

And the fact that he had been smart enough to undo the evil knot Nina had tied around his neck was certainly no consolation. Sure, it was better to owe Packard than to be in debt to the Russians. But the bottom line was—and would always be—that the Tony Ruiz of infinite potential was gone forever. Tony knew the moral scars he now carried would drag him downward for the rest of his life.

Yet, as strange as it might sound, the question Tony Ruiz was struggling with was whether he should call Nina. He shouldn't; he knew that. It would be dangerous. Don't compound your mistakes; let it go, he told himself.

In a fit of anguish, Tony Ruiz tugged hard on his necktie, feeling its thin end softly whip his neck as it spun around his collar. He crumpled it in his hands and threw it on the floor. Dejected and staring down at the crumpled yellow tie, he realized that the silken heap was a metaphor for his own life.

Oddly, that silly symbol was just the push Tony needed to finally spur a decision. He smiled, realizing the choice had been the obvious one. There was no other way. He was going to see her again. One last time.

Leaving the wrinkled mound in its place as a caution against any doubts, he walked over to the phone. He needed to make two phone calls.

The first was to Martha Packard. She was, thankfully, still in her room.

"General," Tony declared upon hearing her voice, "I'm not coming tonight. I don't feel well. Do you think they'll be offended?"

She hesitated for a long moment. Tony presumed she would be wondering whether the excuse was true. He imagined she would probably surmise that he was headed for another round of weakness with Nina. He shrugged; it didn't matter what Packard thought.

Next, he reached for the phone number in his jacket pocket.

"Nina, it's Tony Ruiz."

He could nearly touch her surprise. He resisted a chuckle. This woman could never have expected that an ensnared animal would return to its trap.

She was cautious.

"Tony, how are you? Did you have a good day?"

"Excellent. We made a lot of progress. Nina, can we talk?"

"Of course, Tony."

"Look, I know what happened last night. I get it. I understand that whatever doubts I may have had about the tunnel needed to be silenced. You did your job effectively."

Nina must have been blown away by his blunt honesty because she remained silent.

"I'm guessing that somebody told you my story. I'm from a poor Hispanic family," Tony said, his voice plaintive. He presumed she knew it all. Why not use it to his advantage?

"And you are the most exciting, wonderful woman I've ever met. Sure, I wish that what happened last night had ended differently. But I still want to see you again. I haven't been able to stop thinking of you. Not for one minute. I need to see you again."

Nina was formal. "We should not see each other, Tony. I'm very sorry. It would not be, umm, appropriate."

"Nina, don't shut me out. Please. You don't have to tell anybody. I know that yesterday was a job for you. But I also know you had fun. We had fun. I saw it in your eyes. Come on. I want to see those eyes again."

He heard her hesitating.

"I won't call again. I won't make you uncomfortable. But let's get together one last time."

"I never imagined getting this call. You are a strange man."

It was a small opening. He pushed through it with all the strength he had.

"I know. I know. It's completely strange. I can't believe I'm doing this either. But you are unforgettable. I'm coming to pick you up right now. You pick the place for drinks."

"I don't know, Tony . . ." she said. But it was too late. He had already put down the phone and was hurrying out of the room.

As the taxi rounded the corner of Nina's street, Tony's fingers nervously swiveled the bottle of champagne he had ordered at the lobby bar on his way out of the hotel. He felt a pit in his stomach. There were two scenarios he hadn't considered until climbing into the cab.

The first was that Nina wouldn't be home. Not knowing Moscow's dialing system, he had realized that he wasn't sure if his call of ten minutes ago had been to her cellular or her home phone. This circumstance left him some hope. If she wasn't here, he could still try the other number she had scribbled on the paper.

The second one was much worse. As he paid the driver, his police-trained eyes darted furtively up and down the street. Cars were parked on both sides. Otherwise it was empty. He heard the front door of Nina's building open. His heart stopped. A couple with a dog walked out and crossed the street to the opposite sidewalk.

Had she been waiting for him at her building's front door, he wouldn't have known what to do. He didn't really have any intention of taking Nina out. He wanted her alone. In her home. Close together, sharing the bottle of champagne.

He rang the intercom, 6C. He hadn't forgotten last night's kisses in front of her apartment door. The number was etched in his brain.

"Tony, is that you?" Her voice was clear, welcoming.

"Yes, we're here." Tony smiled.

"We?" The question crackled over the intercom.

"Yes, we. Dom Perignon and I. We came together."

He heard a giggle as the door buzzed open.

He could see her waiting for him on the landing as the elevator door opened. It was the exact place where he had left her the previous evening. She wore a green army-imitation cotton blouse and tight-fitting blue jeans. The high heels accentuated the jeans' length. Her light hair was different today. It was parted on the far left of her scalp, falling sideways down the right side of her beautiful face. Only one of the large hoop earrings was visible; the other remained hidden behind her blond hair.

Tony looked down the short hallway beyond her and noted with relief that her apartment door was open. He kissed her tenderly on the cheek, not wanting to go too fast.

She looked at him, wanting to say something. He held up his hand.

"Look, I know it's crazy. But what's done is done. Come on; let's open the champagne before it gets warm."

Today, he took a moment to look around the apartment. The Asian furnishings were straight out of *Elle Décor* magazine. Except for a few black-and-white photographs, the walls were bare. The two sofas, set opposite each other with only a small round glass table in between, were close to the ground. Beyond the living room, a low, pale-colored, Japanese-style wood table was surrounded by eight plush cushions. The setting was hyperminimalist.

And expensive. He tried not to think about where the money came from.

They sat next to each other on the sofa, her legs curled under her. Smiling at his transparent infatuation, he could tell she was finally relaxing. That was exactly what he wanted. They talked easily for a half hour.

"Where do you want to go out and eat, Tony? Aren't you hungry?"

"I'm hungry, but I don't want to go out. What do you have in that refrigerator? Give me pasta, olive oil, and cheese and I will make you a dinner that is better than anything you can get in those fancy Moscow restaurants."

She laughed, now totally at ease. "Okay, pasta sounds good. I have tomatoes, mozzarella, olive oil. What can you do with that?"

"Show me the way and you will see the miracles I can create."

Twenty minutes after putting the pasta water on the fire, he ordered her to cut the mozzarella and tomatoes in small cubes as he dropped a couple of pieces of garlic in hot oil. Once they were cooked, he discarded the garlic into the metallic garbage can.

"Why are you taking the garlic out?" she asked.

"Because I just want the scent of garlic in the oil. I don't want the bitter garlic taste. Here, try." Dipping a finger gingerly into the still-warm oil, he lifted his outstretched finger in her direction. She took the finger in her mouth.

Tony didn't remove it. He let his finger roam inside her mouth, spreading the viscous oil slowly over her lips. Her eyes grew warm.

They kissed lusciously. With their mouths still connected, Tony reached under her and lifted her onto the kitchen counter next to the boiling pasta pot. It was going to be a repeat of last night, but this time it would be in the kitchen instead of the bathroom. Steam bulged out of the pot of boiling water, covering them with a translucent trickle of vapor.

"I can't hold on until after dinner," Tony whispered in her ear.

"You are certifiably crazy," Nina pretended to scold. But she offered no resistance.

He unbuttoned her blouse and slipped it off. Her neck was immediately obfuscated by the pot's roiling vapors. He unhitched her bra and leaned over to kiss her right breast as his left hand found and immersed itself in the pan's olive oil. He put his oily hand on her left breast, leaving it glistening as he stroked her to excitement.

"What are you waiting for?" she muttered.

"I wanted an invitation," he said, chuckling as he reached for his belt.

Tony Ruiz quickly unholstered the belt from his pants loops with one fast pull. Once free, he reconnected the end through the buckle in tight, sure movements. With her eyes closed in pleasure, Nina wasn't able to react fast enough to what happened next. As taught by his teachers at the Criminal Justice Academy, just north of Tacoma, he swirled the belt's loop around Nina's wrists in one deft swoop. Once he hands were completely encircled, he yanked hard to fasten the belt tight. The jerk forced her eyes open, but it was too late. Confusion overtook her.

Pulling hard at the belt, he took hold of Nina's imprisoned arms and submerged both her hands in the boiling water. She screamed in pain and writhed off the counter. He managed to cut off the anguished shout with one hand over her mouth. Just fifteen more seconds and he would be finished. Holding the belt with his left hand, his right worked deftly to stuff a single sheet of paper towel in her mouth. The shrieks subsided immediately into muffled yelps.

She was fighting now, pulling her arms and trying to run away. Her eyes were wild with terror. Forcing her onto the floor, Tony pulled her heavy cotton army blouse toward him and used the shirt's two sleeves to tie her feet together tightly. Nina was now immobile. Dragging her arms forward with the belt, he tied the belt's free end to the oven door's handle.

Tony's breathing was labored but he marveled at the fact that his heart was beating rhythmically. He stepped back a moment to survey the situation, looking down at her. Nina was now prone on the floor, lying on her back. The belt was pulling her arms tightly behind her head, raising them toward the oven door.

Nina swerved and jerked. But it only caused the oven door to swing open forcefully and bang her on the head. Sensing slack, she tried to wrench herself to a sitting position. Her burned hands were beginning to turn a crimson red. Already some of the scalded skin was shriveling backward.

"Nina, stop moving. You're rocking the stove. That pot of water is going to tip over and fall on your head."

He saw her eyes peel upward and backward to the still-boiling spaghetti pot. The sight calmed her down.

"Nina, look at me. Look at my eyes. This will be over soon. If you behave and do things right, nothing more will happen to you. Do you understand?"

Her eyes, bloodshot from tears and strangled screams, communicated understanding.

"I want you to move your head to tell me that you understand," he ordered. Her contorted face nodded positively.

"Okay. I have only three questions. This will be over quickly. Who hired you to do me yesterday? Who paid you? If it's Daniel Uggin, I want you to nod yes."

After the minutest of pauses, she nodded affirmatively.

"Good. Two to go. Who does Uggin report to? I'm going to take out the paper towel from your mouth long enough for you to say one name. But, Nina, listen to me. If you scream, I will drop the boiling water on your face. Your hands will be scarred, but you can still have your life with blistered hands. Dariya and you can continue being successful models. But once the water hits your face, you will be out of business forever.

"Are you ready?" Her head bobbed sideways as she pulled again on the oven door. The pot rattled on the stovetop.

"Listen, damnit. If you keep moving, I will start with spoonfuls at a time. First on your eyelids. Then your lips. I will disfigure you step by step."

He walked a few steps to the counter to find a spoon. She yelped through the paper towel.

He leaned over and pulled the wet paper towel out of her mouth. She tried in vain to create some saliva by swiveling her tongue around in her mouth.

"The name, Nina?"

"It's Rudzhin, Piotr Rudzhin. He's the one who told Uggin to organize our evening together last night. Please let me go. My hands hurt so much. Please."

Tony returned the paper towel to her mouth. He was close to the end.

"Nina, there is one more thing. Give me Rudzhin's phone number. I'm going to take out the paper towel again and you're going to give me his mobile phone number. Do you know it by heart or do I need to get your phone?"

He saw her eyes open wide. Far too quickly.

He picked up the cordless telephone on the kitchen counter.

"Nina, be careful. You need to be sure that you give me

his correct number. If I sense that you've given me a wrong number or are using an emergency code, the entire pot falls on your face. Remember, I'm an American official. I have immunity. Even if Rudzhin arrests me, I won't spend a second in jail in this country. What you do now dictates whether our problems are over and done with.

"Now tell me the number to dial."

MOSCOW
SEPTEMBER 4, 10:00 P.M.
THE CDL RESTAURANT

Sitting next to Stuart Altman, Piotr Rudzhin sat back to enjoy the troupe of gypsy troubadours who had just entered the CDL's second-floor Pushkin Room. Wearing bright-colored billowy costumes and knee-high leather riding boots, the three musicians swayed and meandered dramatically through the room as they played their violins.

The meal had been spectacular. Caviar and blinis were followed by Siberian wild salmon and goat cheese terrine. The main course, served by white-gloved waiters, had followed—wild boar and tangy red cabbage. Plates of crème fraîche–stuffed napoleons were now placed in front of each guest as the gypsy fiddlers played the haunting, high-pitched tunes of Russia's steppes.

To set the festive tone, Zhironovsky and Packard had exchanged heartfelt toasts as the group sat down to dinner. Even Packard had spoken genially about "new winds of warmth coming to the frigid constellations of the polar north." It was hard for Rudzhin to believe it was true; to be sure, he had harbored doubts. But one look at the mood around the dinner table was enough to convince him that Zhironovsky was on his way to getting what he wanted.

Midway through the gypsy violinists' second ballad, Piotr Rudzhin's phone rang. He did not hear it above the din of the music, but he could feel the vibration in his pants leg. His leg ratcheted outward, and Piotr dug his hand into his pants pocket, straining to drag out the phone. Looking at the display, the identity of the inbound caller puzzled him.

It was Nina's number. Over the past year, he had taken her to bed a couple of times. She was a sex goddess; Lord, this woman knew how to make a man scream in joy.

But those few times they had jumped in the sack together had always been on his terms. Only when he had wanted. When he had called. Nina understood the drill; seeing her had always been his decision, not hers. Their relationship was a business exchange. She needed to be available. He paid for her high lifestyle.

So why the hell was she calling him? He would have ignored the call if it hadn't been for her excellent work with the American the previous evening. Piotr had the videotape safely stored in his office. He had even watched a couple of pathetic minutes.

This evening, Nina's call deserved answering.

Apologizing to Altman, Rudzhin walked slowly toward the door and pressed the answer button just as he entered the quiet of the CDL's grandiose upstairs dining room. The second floor was only half full of guests. He picked out a free table, still elegantly set to serve late-night diners, and sat down.

"Hi, Ninoushka dear. I can't talk long; I'm with the Americans. But I wanted to thank you again for last night."

He was appalled to hear a man's voice.

"Mr. Rudzhin. This is Tony Ruiz. I hope dinner is going well. I'm sorry I'm not there."

"Why, Mr. Ruiz." Rudzhin's voice strained to sound even-keeled. "I am surprised to hear that it is you. I understood from General Packard that you were not feeling well. Where is Nina?"

"Nina is right here next to me, lying on the floor. She got burned. And I'm feeling better." Tony's sarcasm was sharp and crisp.

Every nerve in Rudzhin's body was now at full attention. Something was very wrong. He pressed the phone against his ear. Even the hushed dining room seemed disruptive and loud.

Rudzhin struggled to remain calm. "I'm not sure I understand, Mr. Ruiz. You clearly have something you would like to say."

"Well, I thought we could chat, since I presume you know me intimately by now. I'm guessing you couldn't resist watching Nina and me going at it all night long."

Rudzhin felt his temperature rising. What the hell did this American want?

"Mr. Ruiz, I don't have time for this. I would remind you that you have called the deputy minister of the interior of the Russian Federation. It seems that you have barged into the house of one of my fellow citizens and she is harmed. There are one million six hundred thousand police at my disposal in this country. Shall I call just five of them?"

Realizing he had just threatened a White House official, he revised the threat by quickly adding, "After all, it sounds like Nina requires some assistance."

"Don't threaten me, Mr. Rudzhin. You are at a disadvantage."

"What? You are in my country as a guest. You have dismissed our invitation to dinner and are calling me from the house of an employee whom you may have hurt. You are behaving erratically and dangerously. Why would you think it is I who is at a disadvantage?"

"Because I know about Humboldt."

Piotr Rudzhin could not have heard correctly. It couldn't be. There must be some mistake, he thought, as a searing chill went up his spine.

"What did you just say, Mr. Ruiz? I didn't understand."

"You understood perfectly. I know about Humboldt. About Peru. About your fraud with Anfang. And, Mr. Rudzhin, I know about Senator Matta's death. As I was saying, you are at a disadvantage."

"I don't know . . . don't know . . . what you are talking about." Rudzhin couldn't remember ever stuttering.

"Of course you don't, Mr. Rudzhin. Nonetheless, here is my message. Unless you want what happened in Peru all over the front pages of every newspaper in the world, you and your boss Zhironovsky are going to slow-walk the rest of the negotiations with General Packard. You are not going to sign any agreement. You will tell Packard that the Kremlin has had some second thoughts about the tunnel."

Rudzhin was silent. Tony continued.

"General Packard will be disappointed, but she'll get over it. We both will go back to Washington and think about it a little harder. I will talk to the president about what I know. We'll let him decide if he wants to deal further with people like you."

Piotr Rudzhin needed desperately to say something. Anything. But no words left his mouth.

"Good-bye, Mr. Rudzhin. I'm sorry to have missed dinner. Please transmit my apologies to Mr. Zhironovsky."

MOSCOW
SEPTEMBER 4, 10:15 P.M.
THE CDL RESTAURANT

It took Deputy Minister of the Interior Piotr Rudzhin a full ten minutes to compose himself enough to figure out what to do. Dressed in a business suit and tie, Rudzhin felt small beads of sweat accumulating in his blond hair. One small rivulet of perspiration rolled down his forehead and onto his nose.

Try as he might, he couldn't figure out how Anthony Ruiz had acquired the information about Peru. He couldn't connect the dots. But it didn't matter now.

Ruiz's call was more than an omen of problems to come. It was a full-scale emergency declaration. There was no way to stop the American. He was a representative of the United States government on an official mission in Moscow. He couldn't be arrested. He couldn't be tortured. He couldn't be exiled to a wintry jail in Siberia. He couldn't even be thrown out of the country fast enough. Rudzhin could think of no obvious path to derail Tony Ruiz from dictating the terms.

Information was a terrible thing, thought Rudzhin, disgusted. One man. That's all. One damn man had found out too much and the tables had turned. Try as he might, Rudzhin couldn't figure out how to rotate the disaster back to neutral. Zhironovsky's grand plan was draining away. Irretrievably.

His cell phone tossed on the elegant place setting in front of him, Piotr Rudzhin sat in stunned silence at the empty table, staring blankly at the wall. The four well-dressed men having dinner just a few feet away had taken notice of his bewildered demeanor and were talking about him, pointing his way. He recognized one of the diners, a senior official at the justice ministry. Knowing that his furious glowering would attract further unnecessary attention, Rudzhin forced himself to get up.

Going back into Zhironovsky's music-laden private dining room was the only option. But the thought of facing Volga Gaz's chairman with news of Ruiz's call only agitated him further.

Feeling the underarms of his shirt pasty with dampness, he gathered up the mobile phone and put it back in his pocket. Rudzhin got up, dazed, and stumbled over the chair. He was attracting more attention, but he couldn't help it.

Opening the door to the Pushkin Room, Rudzhin immediately saw Daniel Uggin's curious glance. His friend was now occupying the seat next to Stuart Altman. The call and its aftermath had taken a full twenty uncomfortable minutes. During his absence, Daniel had moved to sit next to the deputy CIA director, believing that Rudzhin's unusual departure had become too noticeable.

The musicians had played their last song and were now pontificating excitedly about the history of gypsy music to Packard and Zhironovksy. Their broken English sounded like Indians talking in a bad cowboy movie. Frozen next to the door, Piotr Rudzhin didn't know what to do. Sit? Stand? Ask Zhironovsky for a private moment?

Daniel Uggin noticed that something was amiss. He had known Rudzhin long enough to recognize the rare sign of trouble on his friend's face. Rudzhin saw Uggin getting up, apologetically excusing himself to Altman, to head his way.

"You look like you've seen a ghost." Uggin's brow furrowed as he put a hand on Piotr's shoulder.

"Worse than a ghost." Rudzhin's face was covered in worry. "I've just seen the devil himself. We're in trouble, Daniel."

"What happened?"

Rudzhin took a moment to tell his friend about Ruiz's call. As he finished, he looked Uggin straight in the eyes.

"Daniel, I'm not going to sugarcoat this. The leak came from your wife."

"What? What are you talking about? You don't know what you're saying."

"Anne-Sophie told her friend, the environmentalist Blaise Ryan. Ryan confessed it all to Luis Matta." Rudzhin spat out the chronology with cold precision.

"Who told you this?" Uggin's tongue swiped over his lips. He had now lost all the saliva in his mouth.

"Our person in Matta's office told us about Ryan just before the senator went to confront Schutz." Rudzhin looked sad. "Daniel, Matta is dead. Schutz had to finish him."

"Oh, Jesus." Uggin was practically in hysterics. "What are you going to do?"

"What choice is there? We need to talk to Zhironovsky." Piotr's voice was leaden with weight. He had included his friend in the coming conversation. Two was better than one. Anything was better than having to face Zhironovsky alone.

"Piotr, please. Try to keep the connection with Anne-Sophie out of it. Out of respect for our friendship, don't ignite Zhironovsky's rage against me."

"No choice, Daniel. No choice," he repeated emptily, not knowing how to accede to Daniel's request. Rudzhin rubbed his cheeks in preoccupation.

Rudzhin walked over to the chairman, now in animated conversation with Packard. He leaned between them and spoke in formal English, hoping that the demonstration of transparency would reduce Packard's inevitable suspicions about the coming unusual break in protocol.

"Mr. Chairman, pardon me for breaking in. I just received a worrying communication that requires us to speak privately for a minute." Looking at Packard, he formally added, "Please forgive the interruption, General."

She opened her hand in a sign of acknowledgment and Rudzhin could tell she was about to add an elegant "Of course." But Zhironovsky reached over and brought her extended hand down.

"I'm not a man who leaves the company of beautiful ladies," Zhironovsky said, his eyes crinkling in a compulsory smile. Glancing at Rudzhin with the same frozen grin, he added in Russian, "Later, Rudzhin."

Piotr hesitated for a moment.

"Mr. Chairman, we need to talk. Now." It was an order, not a question.

Viktor Zhironovsky's head spun backward. Nobody talked to him that way. Rudzhin thought he was about to be dismissed, like a misbehaving child, but Zhironovsky stopped cold when he caught the young deputy minister's eyes. The chairman immediately understood that something was seriously amiss.

Excusing himself with florid apologies in Packard's direction, he walked behind Piotr and Daniel. There was nowhere to go but back into the open dining hall.

As the three men gathered around the same table Piotr had just used to take Ruiz's phone call, Rudzhin shot a look toward the four diners at the nearby table. They were in full gossip mode, turning their heads and speaking in hushed tones. It was clear to them that Rudzhin's disconcerting behavior five minutes earlier had resulted in dragging the vaunted chairman of Volga Gaz away from his dinner guests. The four men knew something out of the ordinary was happening; their Russian nose for scandal was on high alert.

"It better be good, Rudzhin," snapped Zhironovsky.

"Believe me, I would not have interrupted you for something trivial," Piotr began haltingly. It took him five minutes to relate the details of Ruiz's call. The connection with Peru. The threat to go to the press.

Rudzhin tried to recount the conversation in a steady voice. He forced his delivery into a flat, emotionless monotone. But the words had their effect. Piotr could see the bulge growing on the vein crossing Zhironovsky's aging forehead. The more Rudzhin went on, the more pronounced it became. By the time Piotr wound up his narrative, the swelling above the chairman's right eye was literally pulsing visible heartbeats.

Rudzhin was desperate to conclude. "I've tried as hard as I can, Mr. Chairman, to figure out how he has acquired this knowledge. But I have been unable to find the link." Rudzhin hoped his pretension of ignorance would work. For Daniel's sake.

Viktor Zhironovsky silenced him with a long, cold stare. Rudzhin thanked his lucky stars they were in public. He was momentarily safe from physical aggression.

"You stupid boy," growled the chairman. "It's obvious how he got the information. It is the woman, the environmentalist. She gave it to him. She has gotten to him."

"How do you know this, sir? How can you be sure?"

"Did you think I would take your inane advice to let her be until the Americans were gone? I had her tracked, you idiot. It was obvious she was a loose cannon, a free agent who could unravel everything I have put together. Unlike you, I wasn't going to leave it to chance. And, thank God, this afternoon I found out she had made a long phone call. Now we know with whom she talked."

Rudzhin ignored the multiple insults that had just been hurled his way. Something was strange about Zhironovsky's assurance. There was none of this morning's out-of-control screaming.

"Why do you say thank God? If it's true that she made the call, we continue to be in danger from her as well. She could tell others."

"No, Rudzhin, she can't. She won't. Ever again. She will be on a plane to Moscow in a few hours."

"What? You've arranged to kidnap an American citizen from American soil?"

Rudzhin knew he shouldn't have blurted out his aghast surprise. But he hadn't been able to hold it back. Zhironovsky was out of his mind. Could he not imagine the consequences if something went wrong? Tough tactics were one thing. Rudzhin was fine with hardheaded tactics. But criminality on foreign soil was something else completely. It was sheer recklessness. It could put the nation in danger.

"Yes, Rudzhin. And you are about to do something worse still. Until a moment ago, I thought she was the only loose end. The last thing that could go wrong. But unfortunately, I was mistaken. Ruiz is now the remaining impediment."

Rudzhin looked at him quizzically. What was Zhironovsky talking about?

"We have to deal with him, Rudzhin. *You* have to deal with him." Zhironovsky's voice was now fully in the imperative. "It's time to show some balls. Tonight you will learn that power isn't all heaven and joy. It's also hell. Are you man enough to exercise raw power? He is here, Rudzhin. In Moscow. It can't be too difficult."

Rudzhin couldn't believe what he was hearing.

"Make him disappear," Zhironovsky spat out in flat finality.

Piotr looked at the chairman of Volga Gaz. He didn't need to answer; the distraught look on his face said it all.

Until now, Daniel Uggin had remained quiet, his face white with growing worry. Rudzhin looked at him for support and noticed that his hands shook as he opened his mouth.

"What choice is there, Piotr?" Uggin's voice was trembling in a near whine. "The chairman is right. If we don't silence Ruiz, we risk our country's reputation. It is terrible that things have gone so wrong. Even if the chairman were to desist in the dream of the Bering Strait, we still cannot allow Ruiz out of Moscow. He knows too much. He is a ticking time bomb."

Rudzhin had trouble forming words. He forgot all pretensions of respect and formality. Until now, he had done his best to protect Uggin. Now Daniel was turning on him, becoming more Catholic than the pope. He was saying anything—doing anything—to save himself with Zhironovsky.

"Are you both mad? It's bad enough to have risked kid-napping a woman in the United States. Now you want to 'disappear' a senior advisor to the president of the United States. Do you think this is so easy? Do you think the Americans will just walk away, smiling, from this? Just think about what you're asking. It's preposterous."

"Rudzhin, you son of a bitch, don't you dare talk to me like that." Zhironovsky furiously reached out to grab Rud-zhin's shoulder. But Piotr managed to take a step back in the nick of time.

Rudzhin stared at the chairman. The older man's breath-ing was labored, forced. Zhironovsky was out of control.

Uggin made another plea. He was now arguing full force for Zhironovsky.

"Look, Piotr, getting rid of Ruiz is not as outrageous as you say. I have sat through two days of meetings with these people. I have seen how the chairman has intelligently se-duced Packard with the excitement of a tunnel. She is now convinced it could open up a whole new moment in our bi-lateral relations. Packard will not risk the undoing of the Bering Strait deal; she trusts our chairman. As long as we provide a plausible excuse, she won't rock the boat."

"Damnit, Daniel, what's the excuse?" Rudzhin's question lashed out.

"Nina," Daniel answered simply. "We'll invent a love quar-rel. We'll find a former lover of hers who sees them in a bar and, in an attack of insane jealousy, kills her new American lover. We'll arrest the man. We'll arrest Nina. We'll arrest whoever you want. The story doesn't need to be perfect, just plausible enough. Think about it, Piotr. This is something we can do."

Zhironovsky looked over at Uggin with newfound admi-ration.

"Follow your friend's advice, Piotr. Follow it closely. You are the deputy minister of the interior, boy. You can arrange this."

The chairman's face suddenly softened. He reached out for Rudzhin's arm, but this time it was to pat it softly. Piotr couldn't tell if this sudden lowering of tension was real or just an act.

"Go, Piotr. Arrange this. Daniel and I will say good-bye to our guests. And then we will both go to my house to wait for your news. Come by whatever the hour."

Zhironovsky took Uggin by the arm and began making his way back to the waiting guests in the Pushkin Room. He stopped after a few steps and turned around.

"And, Piotr, don't concern yourself with our harsh words. I've already forgotten them."

CULPEPER, VIRGINIA
SEPTEMBER 4, 6:30 P.M.
THE IT'S ABOUT THYME INN

Blaise awoke to the sound of commotion below her window, abutting Culpeper's Davis Street. She glanced at the night table's radio clock and was stunned to find that she had slept nonstop for six hours. Blaise was sure the clock was wrong until she glanced at her window and saw the waning light. Since arriving in Culpeper, apprehension had created sleep-impeding adrenaline over the past two days. Blaise had not been able to close her eyes longer than an hour or two without waking up to the self-absorbing fear that filled her mind.

Slowly kicking back the sheets, it dawned on her that this morning's phone call to Anna Hardaway must have had a therapeutic effect. It had given Blaise a plan, a direction. A hope. It had been enough to momentarily allow Blaise to tune out. And with that change in frequency, sleep had taken over.

Blaise climbed out of her bed and stepped onto the room's small, wrought-iron porch. It was twilight. The evening's cool, early autumn breezes played with her red hair. A smile slowly grew on Blaise's lips as she looked down on Davis Street below.

The Virginia piedmont was known as "horse country." Only four counties—Loudoun, Fauquier, Rappahannock, and Culpeper—claimed the right to host the exclusive clubs of fox hunters, show jumpers, and steeplechasers.

Culpeper had long been the poorest of the four exclusive counties. The wide-hat ladies of Middleburg and The Plains had always sniffed that Culpeper was on the fence, unable to decide if it was horse country or hick country. But while the northern counties pooh-poohed their poorer neighbor, its cheaper real estate prices had brought Culpeper a plethora of spanking-new gastronomic eateries, elegant country shops, and fancy beauty spas.

As Blaise looked below, she considered how lucky she had been to find a room at the inn. The street and the sidewalks below were fast filling up with two seemingly incongruous things. Animated men and women, each dressed to the nines in herringbone and leather, were spilling out of oversize pickups with large, attached trailers.

Blaise understood immediately. Elegance and dirty rural vehicles came together only under one condition. Early September meant one thing in the horse world. The fall steeplechase season—beginning with the Middleburg Classic and ending with the International Gold Cup—was coming. Owners and riders from all over the country—indeed, from all over the world—were now pouring into Virginia horse country.

Blaise chuckled at the scene. She suddenly felt a little life returning to her body. Turning away from the balcony, she quickly showered with the inn's English lavender soap and dressed. She was going to go down and join the crowds.

She walked out of the inn and looked up and down Davis Street. Crossing to the opposite sidewalk, she entered an odd store with a life-size, stuffed camel in its window and perused the jumbled assortment of artisan shampoos, artsy porcelain, and tweed jackets. The store was filled with horse-show shoppers. One of the out-of-towners described to his wife a fried egg and Virginia ham sandwich appetizer he would soon be ordering at the recently opened, trendy restaurant down the street.

"Excuse me," Blaise asked the spiffy gentleman. "I don't know this town all that well. But the dish you just described sounds delicious. Where is the restaurant?"

"Are you alone?" he asked as she nodded. "Alone on the days before the fall racing season begins is impossible. Come on with us, young lady; we're heading there now."

The three men and four women, horse owners from Kentucky in town for the competition, were a lively and happy group. They walked together to the restaurant. As Blaise headed to the bar to eat alone, they insisted she join them at their table. Nothing matched the outgoing nature of horse people before a race.

Sitting in the exposed-brick bistro, Blaise realized it was the first time in days that she would eat a proper meal. She was famished and hugely grateful for the relaxed company.

Two hours later, as the Kentucky crowd ordered their fourth bottle of wine, Blaise decided it was time to go. It was one thing to temporarily forget about Matta, the Russians, and the mysterious White House advisor in Moscow. Quite another was allowing herself to get tipsy with endless bottles of alcohol.

Wrangling for ten minutes about leaving money for her meal, the Kentucky crowd finally accepted a paltry forty dollars for her share of the food and wine. In return for the discount, she had to fib, promising to join their tailgating picnic table this Saturday two furlongs from the cup's finish line.

Blaise turned left out of the restaurant and slowly walked the two blocks back to her bed-and-breakfast. A quick surge of apprehension jolted through her body. It was 9:30 P.M.; Blaise didn't like the fact that Culpeper's streets were considerably quieter now. Horse people were boisterous, but went to bed early. They tended to get up with the roosters.

There was only one store still open, a chocolate shop called the Frenchman's Corner. It was halfway back to the inn. Blaise entered it, feeling the need for one more injection of reassurance before tackling the remaining block to her room. She chose a couple of squares of Belgian black chocolate with hazelnuts that cost a fortune and began to nibble on the dark cocoa. As she walked out, she noticed two men opening the back of a double-parked horse trailer. One of them looked her way and smiled.

"Excuse me, miss. Would you give us a hand closing the trailer door? I'll get inside and pull Sasha in. He's seventeen hands and his butt is too big. On top of it, he hates trailers."

Smiling her assent, she put the chocolate in her purse and swung the bag's strap over her head. Walking around the open door, Blaise peeked into the trailer to look at the large horse. The trailer was empty.

It took only a split second to realize what was happening, but by then it was too late. She felt the second man reach over her shoulders and cover her mouth. In his hand was a damp cloth that smelled vaguely of solvent. Blaise struggled at first. But she didn't stand a chance against the chloroform's vapors. Her heart rate rocketed forward at the same time that she lost her balance. With the cloth still pushing against her nostrils, she felt herself being loaded into the trailer. She heard the man who had first asked her for help barking muffled orders in a foreign language.

She was still awake when she hit the floor of the hay-strewn horse transport, but her auditory perception was almost gone. The world was going nearly silent. Just as Blaise felt her body going under, she made one final effort against her waning consciousness to identify the language.

It was Russian.

**DULLES INTERNATIONAL AIRPORT
SEPTEMBER 5, 6:25 A.M.
A PARKING LOT**

Lying on her side on the trailer floor, Blaise came to slowly. A strip of weak sunlight was streaking in from the left-hand window. As her mind struggled to reconstruct what had happened, she felt a searing pain deep in her nostrils.

She tried to make the profound mental fog dissipate. But she had trouble beating back the double strain of the chloroform's aftereffects and the stabbing hurt deep inside her nose. The acute pain seemed like a dagger into her sinuses. Overcome with terror that the men were subjecting her to some type of torture, Blaise jerked her head backward in a violent panic.

The movement of Blaise's face against the trailer floor matted her eyes with dry grass. The dusty, broken hay encrusted every millimeter of her eyelid, blinding her momentarily. As painful as that was, it made her realize that the sharp object stabbing her nostril was nothing other than a large stem of hay. She slowly moved her hands to remove the sticklike grass from her nose and was surprised to find them free.

Gathering her wits about her, she swiveled her head imperceptibly from side to side to inspect the inside of the trailer. This time she ignored the rough scratching of the hay on her face and eyes. There was nobody in sight.

She now strained to listen for any sounds and heard nothing. Still, Blaise decided not to move. The men might be just outside. She was lying there for a moment considering what she should do when she heard the loud, mechanical noise. The roar of the machine gathered and accumulated into a deafening pitch. She inadvertently closed her eyes, bracing herself for some type of impact.

But as the noise passed overhead, it converted into the recognizable whine of a jet engine. The realization that she was at an airport filled her with a trembling terror. There was only one possible conclusion. Her kidnappers were taking her to Russia.

Jumping to her feet, she heard the telltale sound of the jet's wheels skidding onto the ground. Blaise moved to the sunlit window and saw a long runway behind a chain-link fence. Two planes were at the top of the runway, awaiting takeoff clearance. She couldn't see a single human being.

Blaise was now fully awake. Wiping more grass from her eyes, she ducked across the trailer's separation barrier and looked out the other window. Peering out the left side of the trailer, all she could see was a large parking lot full of cars, still awash in darkness.

She didn't hesitate. She had to escape. Pushing on the trailer's rear gates, she could tell the doors were locked from the outside. Blaise looked at the narrow windows, calculating whether her body would fit through the small, rectangular opening. Not a chance.

She suddenly remembered that horse trailers usually had an opening at the front where owners could provide hay for the animal at mouth height. Scrambling forward, she saw a door handle and pulled slowly. It opened. There was no way to avoid the loud noise of heavy metal parts scraping against each other. To Blaise's jumpy ears, the noise seemed almost as loud as the passing airplane.

She slipped out. Keeping as low as she could, she crouched for a moment to get her bearings. Now she could see the airport buildings. She knew where she was instantaneously. The prizewinning architecture of Washington's Dulles International Airport's undulating roof was unmistakable.

Questions started to pop up in Blaise's head, but she shook them away. She had only one mission. She had to get to the passenger terminal. Watching the sun slowly rise in the eastern sky, she knew that the airport would be packed. Dawn brought an early morning rush hour to Dulles. And those crowds meant safety.

Swinging around the trailer, she began moving—still crouched, slowly at first and then gathering speed—among the rows of parked cars. This couldn't be one of the airport's main parking lots because there were no travelers getting in or out of their vehicles. Blaise figured it must be an employee parking area.

Reaching a grassy knoll, Blaise crawled up the side of the hill and, at the top, saw the expanse of the passenger lot below her. People were everywhere, snaking their way to the terminal's check-in counters. She began to descend, still bent over. By the time she'd reached the concrete of the parking area, Blaise had broken into a full-scale run.

She didn't slow down until reaching the walking passengers. Only when she was strategically placed between a family of four with a trolley full of vacation-bound suitcases and a businessman pulling a rolling bag, did she dare ask herself the only question now forming over and over in her mind.

It was clear to Blaise that the two men who had taken and drugged her last night were professionals. They had probably stolen the trailer from the streets of downtown Culpeper. People like this did not make mistakes. She hadn't escaped. Not at all.

Instead, something had clearly caused them to abandon their plans. They had just walked away.

The question was, why?

RUSSIA

Piotr Rudzhin walked out of the Central House of Writers
and zigzagged his way among the jumble of expensive Jag-
uars, Porsches, Mercedeses, and Ferraris parked haphazardly around the restaurant's entrance. He called his driver
with his cell phone.

Once in the Saab 9000, Rudzhin told the chauffeur to just
move. For the moment, his destination didn't matter; he just
needed sufficient distance from the restaurant to think. Rudzhin lit a cigarette and inhaled from the Saab's backseat.

Taking out his cellular phone, he pondered his choices.
There were two calls he could make. One was to the police's covert-operations unit. The half-Chechen half-Russian
former KGB interrogator in command of the unit was accustomed to urgent middle-of-the-night telephone calls. Rudzhin had required his help twice before and the service had
been impeccable. These people were used to taking quick
action and asking no questions of senior ministry officials.

The other call was vastly different. Infinitely riskier.

Rudzhin hesitated for a moment, weighing the options. Smiling inwardly, he told himself not to bother rehashing his debate with Zhironovsky. There was really no choice.

Rudzhin pulled up his phone's contacts list and pressed Dial. Waiting for the line to connect, it occurred to him that his request was not a matter for the telephone. He would have to go and explain personally.

"Yes?"

"Good evening. This is Deputy Minister Piotr Rudzhin." He had met the personal secretary only once before.

"Deputy Minister Rudzhin, this is a rather late phone call."

"Yes, yes, I know. And I'm sorry about the hour. I need to see him. There is a serious problem that needs attention."

"When?"

"Now. I know he doesn't go to bed early."

"Now is impossible. He has guests."

"I wouldn't ask if it weren't urgent."

"Hold the line please."

Rudzhin waited thirty seconds. The voice came back.

"All right, fine. You can come. He will see you for five minutes. I will advise the personnel of your arrival."

Rudzhin barked the destination to the driver and settled back into the dark blue leather. He didn't give his mission further thought. He was committed. There was no turning back.

The car slowed as it drove by the first guard dressed in a sharp green uniform. Rudzhin was quickly waved through the gates. They drove farther, along the neoclassical walls, as other guards, flashlights in hand, motioned him forward. The illuminated majesty of Nikolas's Winter Palace appeared and passed on the left side. The driver slowly applied brake pressure as the car rounded the expanse of the Cathedral of Christ the Savior.

Just ahead, another guard was signaling the car to a parking place in front of the opulent old Senate residence, constructed by Catherine the Great in 1773. Once the Bolsheviks had taken over in the early 1900s, Lenin decided to convert the building into the office of Russia's president.

The spacious and luxurious Senate residence had been the workplace of Russia's head of state ever since.

He slowly curled his body out of his car. Looking at the building, he could see the personal secretary descending the stairs to meet him. Most people visiting this place would have felt at least a touch of nervousness. He felt none. What he was about to do was the right choice for Russia. And it was the right choice for Piotr Rudzhin too.

He had arrived at the Kremlin.

MOSCOW
SEPTEMBER 5, 12:44 A.M.
THE KREMLIN

It was past midnight. The requested five-minute meeting with Russian president Oskar Tuzhbin had gone on for over an hour. And he was walking out of the meeting more apprehensive than he had been going in. Descending the Senate residence's steps, toward his car, Rudzhin anxiously lit another cigarette. He hadn't been able to smoke inside the building.

It didn't make him feel any better knowing that the result of the meeting had been inevitable. It could not have gone any other way. He had met President Oskar Tuzhbin only twice before. In those meetings, the president had never changed or modified his demeanor. Tonight, Tuzhbin had been a caricature of himself. Cold and calculating. Distant.

Rudzhin had entered Tuzhbin's ornate office with one simple argument in his head. Logging the details and filling in the blanks for the president had taken some effort. But throughout the conversation, Rudzhin had always come back to a single, consistent premise.

Zhironovsky was out of control. His actions could imperil the president himself. He had to be stopped.

He had repeated those words again and again throughout his time with Tuzhbin. But during their hour together, discerning the president's reaction had been impossible. Nobody ever knew what Tuzhbin was thinking; his lips had remained pursed, except for the occasional request for clarification. His pale eyes had been empty of all emotion.

Until the end. That was when Tuzhbin had revealed his cards.

"It took considerable courage for you to come here. Yes?" the president had asked toward the end, his face impassive. He was smoking but had not offered his guest a cigarette.

"Yes, sir. It did. I believe in loyalty. Chairman Zhironovsky has been a mentor to me. Like a father. I did not take the decision to come here lightly."

"And?"

"And I will always be grateful to him. But even if you decide to take no action, I will also always feel that I have done the right thing tonight. I'm a Russian patriot, Mr. President. Ultimately, my duty is to you as Russia's leader. We have many mentors. Teachers. Patrons and bosses. While we must be faithful, our devotion to the important people in our lives cannot be blind. In my mind, sir, loyalty should not come at the expense of my ultimate allegiance to my country and my president."

"That is wise thinking for a relatively young man."

"No, sir, it is just practical. I was convinced that you would have to pay the price for the erroneous actions I was asked to undertake this evening."

"Thank you for that concern. I will handle this from here on. We will take care of your problems. Let me tell you how we will deal with this."

It had taken Oskar Tuzhbin only three dispassionate minutes to deliver his verdict. The president's words had come out slowly. Clearly. With enormous calm. Once he had begun speaking, there had been no opportunity for Rudzhin to argue, cajole, or correct.

Tuzhbin had issued an edict. Once that was done, the forward motion of his decision was unstoppable. Its direction could not be changed.

MOSCOW
SEPTEMBER 5, 1:00 A.M.
VIKTOR ZHIRONOVSKY'S HOME

Daniel Uggin was two steps behind Viktor Zhironovsky as they walked into the chairman's sumptuous apartment. Uggin had tried during the fifteen-minute car ride to engage the old man in a dialogue. Nothing had worked. Zhironovsky was in an impenetrable, self-combusting cloud of darkness. There was only one thing he wanted. To hear from Piotr Rudzhin.

After pacing in silent circles for five minutes, Zhironovsky ordered Daniel to take a seat and announced he was going to his room to change. Uggin was left alone in the library of his boss's penthouse in Moscow's Rublevka district.

In Moscow, the neighborhood was known, with good reason, as the "Golden Mile." Rublevka was so coveted an address that Russia's NTV channel produced a weekly reality show about its rich residents. Apartments in the Rublevka district were the highest priced in the city, but few owners lived there permanently. The rest of the time, owners were in their various country dachas and Italian beach homes.

Zhironovsky's library was a breathtaking room. The ceiling was made of sequential square-framed dark walnut with recessed halogen lights in the woodwork. The floor was of light pine, laid in a diagonal pattern along the length of the room. Art books and sculptures filled dark-wood library shelves.

Uggin fidgeted in the chair. He was alone for the first time in hours. He tried not to think but couldn't keep his jumpy mind under control. Every second thought came back to the same fearful question. How would Zhironovsky extract revenge for his wife's betrayal?

It had been close to two years since Piotr had first brought him into the rarified air of Moscow's power centers. Zhironovsky and Rudzhin had given him a chance. He had struggled hard to demonstrate the wisdom of their gamble. Yes, he was still an outsider. But he had proved his worth. Again and again.

Now it was all about to end. Sitting in Zhironovsky's library, Daniel Uggin knew he could not escape the inevitable consequences that would pour down on his head. No matter what happened with the two Americans, there was no shirking the hard truth. The detonator for the implosion of Zhironovsky's dreams was none other than his wife. He would pay for her sabotage. He had no doubt about it.

He felt his fingertips tingling from the rabid anger rising in his soul. His mouth trembled with the taste of sour resentment. How could Anne-Sophie have done this to him? Without thinking, he flipped out his cellular phone and dialed his home in Kursk. He heard a sleepy voice answer the line.

"It's me," he snapped.

"Daniel, it's past one in the morning. Where are you?"

"In Moscow. In Zhironovsky's apartment. Waiting to know what will happen to me."

"What are you talking about? What's happening to you?"

"I know what you've done. Damnit, they all know what you've done. Now, because of your deceit, I'm here waiting to hear what will happen to me."

Anne-Sophie said nothing. Her silence was like a slap in the face. She had become the enemy.

"I don't care why you decided to throw me to the wolves by telling Ryan everything about my life. I don't give a damn anymore about you or your stupid worries about our marriage. All I want to know is how you did it. How did you find out? About my involvement in Latin America. About Anfang."

He expected more silence. Instead, Anne-Sophie began to talk.

"I no longer recognized the man I was married to, Daniel. Suddenly, I was living with a stranger. My husband had become an outsider. My best friend had disappeared. You became just like Russia—paranoid, mysterious, inscrutable. I didn't have a choice; I set out to find out who my husband had become."

"This is nothing but psycho-garbage, Anne-Sophie. Who are you to—"

She cut him off.

"Daniel, I no longer want to be married to you. I've known it for months, even though I tried my best to reach out to you. Your own daughter told me about your travels to Bolivia. I then had you followed in Frankfurt. All the way to Anfang's offices and back. After that, Blaise and I figured out Volga Gaz's ruse in Latin America. The moment I was forced to spy on my husband was the day I knew we had no future."

"You had me followed? I can't believe it." Uggin felt an uncontrolled rage. "I want you to go. Leave Russia. Leave us."

"Don't worry, Daniel. We'll leave. I won't make it hard; I just want to go. You have my promise that you can see the kids as often as possible."

He chuckled into the phone.

"Did you say *we'll* leave? No, no. You can go back to Germany. To your silly causes and your stupid friends. The children will never go, Anne-Sophie. Ever. Listen carefully to that word again. 'Ever.' They are staying here. With me. In Russia, where they belong."

He heard her choke.

"Daniel, don't do this. Don't punish Giorgi and Katarina because you are angry with me." Anne-Sophie was sobbing now. "Please. Think about it. You're never home. You are obsessed with your job. With your country. There is no room for children in Daniel Uggin's life. Let them have at least one parent!"

Her tears had a calming effect. They only increased his self-assurance.

"Since you think you understand so much about Russia, you must know that I will use every means, every law, every friend I have to stop you from taking them. They are going nowhere."

A thought suddenly occurred to him. Smiling into the phone, he delivered his last blow.

"Of course, there is another option. You can stay in Kursk with them. I want nothing to do with you, but you can have them. But only here. In Russia . . . the country you hate so much."

He clicked the Off button on his phone.

MOSCOW
SEPTEMBER 5, 1:10 A.M.
VIKTOR ZHIRONOVSKY'S HOME

Five minutes later, Viktor Zhironovsky walked back into the library and resumed pacing. Other than having taken off his tie, Daniel could not identify any other change in the chairman's clothes.

Suddenly, the apartment's phone rang loudly. The noise jolted both men out of their disquiet. Uggin jumped up. Zhironovsky strode to the phone, muttering only the word "finally, finally" over and over.

"Rudzhin, where the hell are you?" He didn't wait for the caller to identify himself.

"I'm on my way, sir." Rudzhin's voice was tense.

"I expected you here ages ago. I expected a report. What are you doing, you shit?" Zhironovsky was again losing control. His shouting trembled with fury.

"I am sorry, Chairman Zhironovsky. I'm on my way; you won't be pleased, sir. But I'm coming to explain. I've been to the Kremlin, Mr. Chairman."

"What? The Kremlin? You are a fool, Rudzhin," Zhironovsky screamed. It was clear to him now that the young man from Kursk who had apprenticed at his side for so many years had broken ranks. But what never occurred to Volga Gaz's chairman was how far Rudzhin had gone.

Zhironovsky could never have fathomed Rudzhin reaching all the way to the top. And even if he had known of Rudzhin's meeting with the president, the chairman would have dismissed it as insignificant. Zhironovsky and Tuzhbin were well known in Moscow's political circles as inseparable alter egos. The chairman would not have been able to bend his mind around the reality that Oskar Tuzhbin had just countermanded the orders of his longest and closest collaborator.

"I will have you jailed for insubordination." The rants were still pouring out. "You will spend the rest of your life cold and hungry for this treason. And for what? I will get somebody else who will accomplish the mission. Someone else will finish off the two Americans. But tomorrow, once Ryan and Ruiz are gone, as God is my witness, I will deal with you. Personally."

"Ryan isn't coming, Mr. Zhironovsky. Your plane was turned around midway across the Atlantic. The orders were canceled," said Rudzhin.

The phone line went quiet. Silence.

"Hello?" Zhironovsky screamed into the handset. "Hello?"

Piotr Rudzhin had hung up on the chairman of Volga Gaz.

The next few moments were sheer bedlam. Viktor Zhironovsky's rants were uncontrollable. Uggin, who had until now watched from the chair as his boss rocketed out of control, became infused with worry. He wanted desperately to get out of the apartment. The last thing he needed was to become the next target of Zhironovsky's rage. But Uggin couldn't figure out an exit strategy.

Zhironovsky stormed out to the foyer and strode back in with a dilapidated old address book. Rummaging through its yellowed pages, he finally found what he had been looking for. It was the phone number of a former KGB colonel, a man who could handle difficult jobs with discretion.

"I will do this myself, damnit. It always comes back to me. Alone. They are all gutless, fearful shits." His loud shouts were directed at nobody in particular. And at everyone.

Zhironovsky reached for the phone.

At the exact moment he started dialing, the apartment's two-tone chiming doorbell rang through the room. Dressed simply in jeans and sport shirts, the two men outside the penthouse's door were in an irritable mood. It had taken them far longer than expected to get here. They had walked for twenty minutes to find a car expensive enough to park in Rublevka without attracting attention.

The fact that the housekeeper was sleeping at this hour meant that Zhironovsky had to open the door himself. This small endeavor only aggravated his angry feelings. The chairman moved slowly to the door, muttering under his breath about how a man of his age and position still had to tackle the big and the small things of life all alone.

In his confused state, Zhironovsky fully expected to see Rudzhin at the door. Instead, he felt the onset of another wave of irritation upon finding two unknown men outside the penthouse.

"Who are you? And how the hell did you get into the building's front door?"

The shorter of the two men standing in the doorway had an oval, angelic face with a perfectly round patch of baldness in the middle of his head. He looked up at his taller colleague, who nodded imperceptibly.

The short man raised his hand in one clean, arcing motion. He held an OT-33 Pernach pistol in his hand. Equipped with a one-hole compensator near the muzzle to reduce barrel climb, the Pernach had a cylindrical sound suppresser attached to its end. The gun was standard issue.

The 9-millimeter Markov high-impact bullet entered cleanly through Viktor Zhironovsky's nose and expanded precariously in the chairman's brain. He was dead instantly.

The two men were about to turn around when they heard a yelp from inside the home. Standing in the library's open doorway, Daniel Uggin's hand was covering his mouth in terror.

The larger man shrugged mindlessly. He raised his own pistol. And fired. Once, right through the heart.

MOSCOW
SEPTEMBER 5, 10:00 A.M.
VOLGA GAZ HEADQUARTERS

After the next day's breakfast, the American delegation filed into the Volga conference room. By now, they felt at home in its wood-paneled officiousness. Two days of ten-hour meetings had accustomed the American guests to the room's offerings. The visitors went straight to the coffee and pastries, set up—as usual—on the marble sideboard along the far wall.

Somewhat surprised to see the room empty of their hosts, Martha Packard and Stuart Altman took their respective seats. The CIA director's assistant, Betty, sat in her customary place along the back wall, directly behind her boss. Tony Ruiz instinctively took a new seat; three chairs of distance now separated him from the intelligence officials.

Ruiz, dressed in a blue suit and with his familiar yellow tie firmly under his collar, felt butterflies roaming through his stomach. He saw Packard rereading again the same document she had been carefully studying in the car on the way over. In large block letters, the words MEMORANDUM OF UNDERSTANDING were spread across the cover of the four-page document.

Tony Ruiz glanced at Volga Gaz's daily meeting agenda, which, like in each of the past two days, had been meticulously placed in front of each setting. He found the entry he was seeking. The agenda slated the signing ceremony for midday.

Tony saw Packard looking up and smiling wanly in his direction. She looked at her watch just as the group heard a rustle outside the conference room's private entrance. He watched as his colleagues shuffled their papers in quiet certitude. Only Tony Ruiz was unsure of what would happen next.

Dressed in an elegant gray pin-striped suit, Piotr Rudzhin strode purposefully into the boardroom. He walked around the table to shake each participant's hand. The slightly longer pause with Tony Ruiz's handshake was imperceptible.

Rudzhin sat down across from the Americans. The visitors exchanged some trite pleasantries with Rudzhin. Over the past two days, they had become accustomed to the Russians flowing one by one into the room at the start of each day. But their hosts had never before dared begin the formal meetings without Viktor Zhironovsky in the room.

It was therefore no surprise to see the American delegation's stunned reaction when Piotr Rudzhin cleared his throat to address the group. He rapped a pencil on the table.

"General Packard, may I have your attention? As you know, my job is at the ministry of the interior. It is why I have attended your meetings sporadically. I have not had the pleasure of working with you as closely as others on Volga Gaz's team. Yet it falls to me to be the bearer of bad news.

"I am afraid that one of my country's great luminaries was killed last night. Chairman Viktor Zhironovsky and Daniel Uggin were in the chairman's apartment yesterday evening preparing for today's meeting when hoodlums entered the building. Both men—both dear friends of mine—were shot dead."

The Americans all sucked in air. A murmur went through the four-person delegation from the United States.

"This morning I spoke to President Oskar Tuzhbin and he has asked me to deliver a few messages. First and foremost, he wants you to know that while Russia has lost a leader, the president has lost a friend. This morning, President Tuzhbin posthumously conferred the Order of Merit for the Country on our chairman.

"Second, he has asked me to communicate to you my appointment as acting chairman of Volga Gaz. I will now be in charge of Russia's role in our continuing efforts to use our mutual interest in gas to improve bilateral relations. Third, the president has requested that I beg your understanding for our need to request a temporary suspension of our negotiations. We need to bury our chairman. We need to reflect and consider."

Martha Packard jumped to her feet. She knew the Russians. She had studied them, followed them, and eavesdropped on them all her adult life. Things never happened by accident in this country. Things were never as they seemed. How had Churchill said it? Russia is a riddle wrapped in a mystery inside an enigma.

Somewhere, somehow, Martha Packard's instincts, honed by twenty-five years in the intelligence business, were telling her that she had been had. Duped. Somebody had derailed the tunnel, at the cost of Zhironovsky's life. But who? How did it happen? A man as powerful as Zhironovsky was nearly impossible to kill.

Packard's eyes careened toward her right, seeking out Tony Ruiz. She couldn't see his eyes; they were locked on Rudzhin. Things had been going swimmingly until he had come in and confessed his sins. Hints of the tunnel's unraveling had begun afterward. Packard recalled his absence at last night's strange dinner. For an instant, she weighed the possibility that Ruiz had subverted her negotiations. No, it wasn't possible. This little Latino boy was too young, too inexperienced.

Standing, she struggled for words to bring the tunnel back on track. But what could she say? It was impossible to lodge formal protests at a time of mourning. The tunnel's potential as a major coup—a single, unique mechanism to solve America's energy deficit for years to come—was evaporating before her very eyes.

She cleared her throat. "Mr. Rudzhin, umm . . . Chairman Rudzhin, I can speak for all of us in telling you that the deaths of Chairman Zhironovsky and Daniel Uggin come as a shock to our delegation. It is a great loss. We offer the profoundest of condolences to you, to President Tuzhbin, and to the Volga Gaz family.

"However, your decision to postpone our negotiations is, frankly, disappointing. The future has a way of dissipating momentum. I am fearful that we will lose the progress made as each of us is forced to return to our daily grind. But I am hopeful that we will be back at this table again. It is in both of our nations' interests."

She was about to sit down. A last thought seemed to occur to her. Her question appeared designed to test Rudzhin's reactions. Glaring at him from across the room, she locked his eyes in a stare.

"Pardon me, one last thing. It is the express hope of the United States government that justice is done in the sinful killing of Messrs. Zhironovsky and Uggin. We want to see the killers brought to trial and punished."

Rudzhin thanked her and responded. But while his words

were directed at her, there was no doubting the barely disguised shifting of his eyes. He was looking at Tony Ruiz, Packard noticed, as she struggled to understand the hidden meaning of his tortured phraseology.

"I could not have said it better myself. Our hope is the same as yours. And may I say that it is the Russian government's aspiration that Americans such as yourself, General Packard, continue to prosper and multiply. There are many people in your country who still believe that Russia can be manipulated and trifled with. We were hopeful that this great tunnel project would have encouraged more people like you, more leaders with opinions such as your own, to come forward. This brilliant dream would have provided new voices in the United States strong enough to counter the continuous anti-Russian propaganda of your press and your elites. That this will not happen is surely one of the most unfortunate consequences of our project's postponement."

The realization seemed to hit her like a brick. It was clear that Rudzhin was talking to Ruiz. The Russian knew exactly who had forced his hand. And now, reading between his lines, he was telling her.

Tony Ruiz had done this.

Overcome with anger, General Martha Packard closed her eyes momentarily. Everyone on her side was waiting for a signal that the meeting was over. She would have to get up soon. There was little else here for her.

But General Martha Packard stood still for just one moment. A tiny second. She needed to calm her fury. Revenge was a dish best eaten cold. She still had an ace up her sleeve; only she knew about Ruiz's one-night stand with the beautiful Russian spy.

Martha Packard didn't know how the young man from Washington State had sabotaged her mission, but she would find out. And when that happened, she would bury Tony Ruiz.

UNITED STATES

The sound was muted on Isaiah J. Tolberg's television set as Tony Ruiz sat in front of his customarily cluttered desk. A plate of Mary Jane's Southern-style chocolate chip cookies was set between them. Tony hadn't touched them. The Senator was on his third.

A month had come and gone since Ruiz's return from Russia. Within twenty-four hours of his arrival, Tony had sat Tolberg down and told him everything. Throughout the hour-long narrative, Tolberg had remained impassive. Silent. He had let Tony speak, uninterrupted, not asking a single question.

As the young advisor wound up the details of his harrowing trip, Tolberg had been able to foresee where Tony was going. He had been in Washington too long not to recognize the telltale signs. Tony Ruiz was succumbing to the capital's sad, unwritten personnel rule. When good people make mistakes, they become shaken, unsure of themselves. They resign honorably, believing they must pay a price. When bad people make mistakes, they dig in. They scrap and battle. Hang on. And never leave.

Listening to the young former Washington State cop tell his story, Tolberg had sat behind his desk, waiting for the predictable sequence of events to unfold. Right on cue, during the inevitable long pause following the end of Tony's chronicle, Tolberg had watched Ruiz reach down to open the red folder resting on his lap. Ruiz had taken out a piece of paper and handed it across the desk.

Tolberg had known what it was without looking at it.

"Senator, I'm handing you my resignation. It's effective immediately," Tony had said, his words choked with emotion.

"Thanks but no thanks." Tolberg had been prepared for this.

Tony had insisted. Tolberg had rejected. So it had gone. Back and forth. For over an hour. In the end, Tony had kept his letter, with the promise that Tolberg would discuss it with President Gene Laurence.

In the ensuing weeks, Tony had tried to resign two more times. Each time, he had argued passionately that the story would eventually leak. Each time he had been rebuffed. He was now about to undertake the conversation again; Tolberg could see it coming and tried to head it off by offering Ruiz one of the cookies.

"Senator, I don't want one of the damn cookies. I want you to reconsider my offer," Tony sputtered, glancing at the clock on the bookshelf. "You have twenty-three minutes left to do it safely before all this hits the airwaves."

A voice from the doorway interrupted the conversation. Both men stood up as President Eugene Laurence walked into Tolberg's office.

"Ruiz, learn how to take no for an answer." Laurence smiled, patting Tony on the shoulder as he walked by.

Tony had seen the president a few times since his return. Each time he had considered bringing up the matter of his resignation, but had held his tongue in the end. Tony wasn't the most experienced Washington insider, but he understood the rule of plausible deniability. If you didn't actually talk to the president about a delicate subject, you left him the option of saying that nobody had told him. All White House administrations functioned under this rule. It ensured that others took the heat for the president.

"Tony, seriously, Isaiah has talked to me about it. I know your thoughts. I appreciate them. But I'm not accepting your resignation." The president's bifocals were perched on the edge of his nose. He looked his usual New England preppie chic. Penny loafers, buttoned-collar oxford shirt, and a simple blue suit.

"Mr. President, with all due respect. This will come out. She is a fighter. I cost her the project. And her job. She will not let go."

President Eugene Laurence sat down and crossed his legs. He pointed to the chair in front of him as an order for Tony to also sit.

"Look, I asked Packard to resign because she had become blinded by her single-minded belief that the tunnel was worth any price. She had, umm, a case of tunnel vision." Eugene Laurence smiled at his silly pun before continuing.

"Tony, she should have packed it up the minute she found out the Russians were trying to blackmail you. Instead, she thought she could use it to force your adherence. It was bad judgment at its worst."

"Yes, I know. But then again, I should have told her what I had learned about Volga Gaz's meddling in Peru. She might have made the right decision at that point."

"Possibly," Tolberg interjected. "But I wouldn't bet on it. And you sure didn't believe that you could trust her, right?"

Tony was silent.

"Young man," Tolberg addressed him, looking him straight in the eye, "can you search your mind and remember what we discussed when you asked why you were being chosen to go to Moscow?"

"You said the president believed that it would be beneficial to have a young person along. Somebody not contaminated by the fifty years of Cold War antagonism."

"That is correct. I also said that your presence was necessary because you had no agenda. Your loyalties were to the president. To this man alone," Tolberg said, pointing to

President Eugene Laurence. "Well, you learned some nasty things on the trip and I think you acted courageously to protect the president of the United States."

"I appreciate that vote of confidence, sir. I really do," Tony answered, switching his view to directly address Laurence. "But you both know as well as I do that to continue protecting the president, I should resign. You can't keep this bottled up. A White House official fell into a Russian trap. It is destined to come out. This office needs to inoculate itself. The only way to do that is to let me go."

"Forget it, Tony," said Tolberg. "We made a decision. We're sticking to it. We're going public. The leak is done. The story is coming out today."

Tolberg drew in a breath before continuing.

"I've been here many times before. The CNN woman has our exclusive; it's airing in twelve minutes. We'll be ahead of the news cycle. That means that our version of events—the true version—will dominate the news. Neither Packard nor the Russians nor anybody else is going to be able to do much about it. That's the way Washington hardball works. Whoever has the guts to leak first dictates the debate."

Those last two sentences seemed less a statement of fact than an attempt to reassure the big boss. Tony looked the president's way. If Laurence was in any way worried about how the news story would play out, he sure wasn't showing it.

"Tony, bring Blaise Ryan in before the program starts," ordered the president. "You asked Isaiah to meet her. I want to join in."

Tony was grateful to both men. He had asked Tolberg to make five minutes to meet Blaise Ryan. After all, she was the genesis of the Bering Strait tunnel's defeat. If it hadn't been for her, nobody would have known of the deceit being perpetrated by Volga Gaz's robber barons.

As Tony walked to his office to get Blaise, the president waited until Ruiz was out of earshot to look down over his bifocals to meet Tolberg's eyes.

"You think this is going to work, Senator?"

Raising a hand, Tolberg curved his middle finger over his

index and shrugged. "Yes, it should, Mr. President. Fingers crossed."

Tony walked back in with Blaise. Introductions were made.

"Young lady, we owe you a whole heap of gratitude. You went through a lot. How is your friend?" asked Isaiah J. Tolberg.

"Thanks for making the time to meet me," Blaise answered, startled to be in the presence of the president of the United States. "Anne-Sophie is fine. She left Russia a few weeks ago. They probably would have let her go anyway, but I told her to take advantage of the confusion surrounding her husband's death to get out. She is back in Germany with her children."

"You stumbled on this only because you were trying to help her, right?" said President Gene Laurence, watching her nod her agreement. "Life's serendipity is amazing. We've learned a lot of hard lessons because of your friend's ugly marriage."

Tony looked at his watch and, gently pulling Blaise with him, started for the door. "It's nearly eight. We'll leave you alone. I've got a television in my office."

"Forget it; stay here," said Tolberg. "Let's watch it together." Hitting the button on the remote to release the television's sound, he picked up the plate of chocolate chip cookies and made his way to the couches. They all sat around him.

It was eight o'clock sharp.

CNN's logo appeared on the screen as the baritone crescendo of the CNN announcer intoned, "This is CNN.

"Good evening, I'm Alan Riding and this is *Witness to the World*. Thank you all for watching. As most of our viewers know, this program's objective is to bring you in-depth analysis of the week's top stories, investigative insights, and fresh looks at old subjects. Tonight we will do all three things together.

"Nearly four months ago, on June twelfth, a national saga began when the first light went out in the state of California. We were all riveted to the tragedy for over three weeks. Throughout those twenty-one days, CNN's prizewinning

Los Angeles correspondent, Anna Hardaway, had the entire world in rapt attention with her detail-laden reporting.

"The repercussions of the crisis in the nation's largest state are still not over. Its effects are spreading across America and overseas. Tonight Anna reports a CNN exclusive story. It is a story which will leave each one of us breathless.

"Anna, over to you . . ."

Anna Hardaway appeared on the screen. It was immediately clear that something was out of place. The reporter wasn't in California. Behind her was an ocean. But the desertlike, deep escarpments in the land were nothing like Southern California's sandy beaches.

"Alan, thank you. Today CNN will break two exclusive news stories. Both will point to one inescapable conclusion. The echoes of California will be heard for a long time to come.

"If you thought California was over, you were wrong. Just ask President Eugene Laurence. Tomorrow President Laurence will deliver a speech outlining a bold new energy proposal to reduce the United States's energy dependency on foreign nations. And fasten your seat belts; this plan is sure to be controversial."

Anna Hardaway was picking up steam now. Her recognizable staccato was forceful and clear.

"President Laurence's plan combines a daring set of incentives for alternative energies with stark disincentives for the consumption of fossil fuels. Tomorrow, President Laurence intends to send Congress a thirty-page bill that will turn the U.S. energy economy on its head. But while many of his proposals will be seen as controversial, one item, in particular, is sure to become a national tinderbox. The president is recommending the creation of a cap and trade system on all carbon emissions. Translated: Under the president's plan, gasoline, natural gas, home-heating oil, diesel, and propane will all become more expensive.

"Let's hear just a small part of my interview with the president . . ."

Gene Laurence, sitting comfortably on a sofa in the subdued elegance of the Oval Office, appeared on the screen.

"Anna, we can't get stuck forever depending on others for our energy. I'm not going to sit and duck any longer. Too many of my predecessors have done that. The buck stops here, as Harry Truman said. We have two duties. One is to lower the greenhouse gases that imperil our environment. The other is to protect our land from foreign dangers—too much of our energy today comes from people who wish us harm. Sacrifice is not something that someone else does for our country. We're all going to have to be in this together. My proposal is not easy; change is hard. But the time for change is now."

Blaise Ryan looked at Gene Laurence. "Thank you, sir, the environmental movement has been waiting two decades for a statement like that one."

Laurence smiled back at her. He playfully put his finger on his lips, signaling silence. It was a sin to distract a politician from a news show that contained his image.

The monitor cut back to Hardaway, in her strange location. Where was she?

"We will have more of the president's interview later in the broadcast. The question you may be asking yourself is, 'What has spurred the president to take such a political risk and why is his proposal so radical?'"

Hardaway paused for dramatic effect. She wasn't good-looking in the traditional sense. But she was keenly aware that, on camera, she had a unique magnetism. Hardaway used it skillfully, to her benefit.

"It's a good question. The right question." The reporter's finger was pointed toward the camera, as if to acknowledge a good student's response. "And I've come far to look for the answer. Today I'm walking along the coastal road in Lima, Peru. If you look behind me, you will see that the word 'beach' is a misnomer for this city's austere, rocky coast. Out there, in the Pacific Ocean just beyond, there are some kids surfing, determined to catch a few after-school waves."

As the camera tilted outward toward the surfers, Tolberg muttered something under his breath about CNN's willingness to have paid the high cost of sending her to Lima.

"Things may look serene here in Lima. But that conclusion would be a mirage. Because a few weeks ago, a famous Peruvian senator and his assistant were murdered in a hotel not far from this very place. The senator was in charge of approving a project that would have sent millions upon millions of cubic feet of natural gas to the United States for decades to come."

Anna Hardaway began to pace, the camera following her closely.

"What Senator Luis Matta did not know—nobody knew—was that a sham company controlled by Russia was bidding on Peru's natural gas. Why Peru? you ask. Don't the Russians have a lot of gas of their own? Yes they do; Russia is the world's biggest producer of natural gas. It turns out that Russia's biggest gas company, Volga Gaz, wanted the gas for the sole purpose of controlling its transportation to the United States."

Tony leaned forward to listen closely. He knew the story; after all, Blaise and Ruiz had helped Anna put together the diffuse strands of her narrative. Still, he was captivated, like everyone else, by the tension the reporter created as she asked and answered her own questions.

"What they intended to do with that control is anybody's guess. But what we do know is that when Senator Luis Matta found out about Russia's control of the sham company that was about to win control of his country's gas, he was assassinated. Shot.

"If this isn't interesting enough," said Hardaway, the Pacific Ocean's wind whipping through her auburn hair, "there is more. The plot gets thicker.

"As we reported a few nights ago, Martha Packard, the U.S. national intelligence chief, tendered her resignation, ostensibly for personal reasons. But CNN has now learned that, at the very moment Luis Matta was discovering Volga Gaz's deceit here in Lima, General Martha Packard was in Moscow negotiating a secret deal with Volga Gaz to expand Russia's supply of gas to the United States. Nobody knows exactly what was happening in those negotiations, but there are two questions that need answering.

"Why was the CIA negotiating in Moscow for gas with

an entity that clearly had the intention of doing harm to the United States? And why did the CIA not know about what was going on here in Lima?"

Tony looked over at Tolberg. His eyes were glued to the television, but his face had contoured into a sly smile. His fist was clenched into a punch. It occurred to Tony that he was imagining his own uppercut landing on Packard's jaw.

"We will explore those two questions in the next half hour," Hardaway said, turning to face the camera. Suddenly, her pacing stopped. For the smallest of pauses, she seemed to hesitate. Television magnified even the slightest of mannerisms. And, for that split second, Anna Hardaway looked as if she didn't want to continue.

"But first we should be clear." Hardaway's delivery suddenly lost its luster. She slowed to a monotone. It was so unusual for her that it left the impression that something important was coming.

"It is CNN's policy to protect sources. There is, however, an exception to that rule. If another news organization is reporting the same story with a name attached to it, it is our obligation to give you, our viewers, the widest-angle view possible.

"We must report, therefore, that the *New York Times* Web site is tonight running a story sourced to unattributed CIA officials for publication in tomorrow's newspaper that Central Intelligence director Martha Packard was not alone in Moscow. According to the *New York Times,* with her in Russia was Anthony Ruiz, a White House official presently under questioning by his superiors for illicitly passing official information to Russian government officials."

The four persons in Isaiah J. Tolberg's office sat in stunned silence, eyes glued to the television. It didn't matter anymore what Anna Hardaway was saying. None of them was listening.

Tony Ruiz looked from the president to Tolberg and back again to the president. Gene Laurence's hand was in his hair, holding on to the firmament of his scalp. Tolberg never raised his eyes from the floor.

Tony had warned them, begged them. It had been obvious

that a story this big couldn't be locked away in a box. Not when Martha Packard was the enemy. But they had refused to listen. What was it about this city that made powerful people believe they were impregnable?

The only one not surprised was Tony Ruiz. He had come prepared. Tony got up and went to his briefcase, parked on the floor next to Tolberg's office doorway. He took out the red folder and tossed it on the coffee table. Without another word, he turned and walked out, leaving Blaise Ryan in the office with the two men.

Tony ambled down the hallway toward his office. In a strange way, he was relieved; a huge weight had been lifted off his shoulders. But he felt sorry for Tolberg and the president.

They would be the ones to deal with this mess, Tony thought, as he followed the cubicle-lined passage to his office. They would be the ones to fight the energy battle with Congress. And with this scandal hanging over the White House, Gene Laurence's effort to liberate America from its dependency on the fossil fuels of hostile outsiders would become hell on earth. Hand-to-hand combat.

No, thought Tony. The energy wars were far from over. A new Cold War had just begun. And as Tony made his way toward the White House's east elevator, he wondered how long he could really stay out. In the past months, he had learned that the coin of leadership had two sides—the beautiful and the unsightly. But Tony Ruiz had now been bitten by the bug of politics. He was hooked. As he smiled at the uniformed Secret Service guard overseeing the traffic at the black-painted, wrought-iron gate, he knew that somehow his role in all this was far from finished.

ACKNOWLEDGMENTS

I write these words with difficulty as they are the first to be drafted such a short time after my mother's death. My mom was a graceful, wonderful woman; intelligently loving life and her family in ways that I can only hope to emulate.

It gives me great comfort and makes me enormously happy to know that she still had the time to read the final manuscript before leaving us. Seated in the dark green easy chair—in my old bedroom, now converted into her study—she rolled through the book in three or four days.

Obviously, she told me that she loved it. Not that she is a fair critic. But now those words of approval sure make a world of difference to me.

Second novels are notoriously harder than first ones. This book is no exception. The now-adolescent author has gone through the full process at least once. Experience naturally raises the bar and creates higher demands than those imposed on the happy-go-lucky first-time writer. Yet even with these heightened challenges, my own novel-writing experience continues to be one that is enormously fun and fulfilling.

And so, there are some people to thank for making this experience positive and uplifting.

As with most things in my life, the first and foremost smile of gratitude and kiss of thanks goes to my wife, Rosa. It is she who has to tolerate my moods and read the countless drafts over and over again. She is the toughest of critics. Yet she always finds a way to say what needs to be said with clarity and mirth. I am the luckiest of men.

René Alegría is my talented, multifaceted editor at Harper-Collins. Part coach, part businessman, part intellectual, and part dramatic showman, René has astutely used his various hats to deliver direction and advice to me throughout the process. At every moment, his wise counsel and teasing cajoling have been spot-on. Thank you, René, for another opportunity to have the benefit of your talents and for your support and confidence.

Andrea Montejo was my first book's editor and the close relationship we built has not waned. Though no longer my "boss" at HarperCollins, she was generous enough to continue reading and providing me with her talented advice. As usual, her wise insights were delivered patiently and generously.

There are a number of dear friends who also deserve my gratitude. To begin, a particular word of appreciation to that special friend, you know who you are, for bringing alive the oft-conflicting poles of Russia's economic, social, and political reality. Your insights were not only impeccable but they were delivered with uncanny creativity.

To Miguel and Ornella, who read a couple drafts of the manuscript and gave me their straight and useful opinions, once again you have my deep thanks.

I try to write about international events affecting our world. In the future, our children's understanding of what we broadly call "energy" will differ greatly from our own. How we, as citizens, relate to what we use to drive our cars, fuel our factories, heat our homes, and brighten our computer screens will change radically over the next twenty-five years. America's leaders face choices today that will decide whether tomorrow this transition will be traumatic and impoverishing or deliberate and enriching.

New York Times bestselling author

ELMORE LEONARD

UP IN HONEY'S ROOM

978-0-06-072426-9

U.S. Marshal Carl Webster wants to have an official "chat" with Honey Deal about two German POWs who escaped from an Oklahoma internment camp.

THE HOT KID

978-0-06-072423-8

Carl Webster wants to be Depression-era America's most famous lawman as he chases down the likes of Dillinger and Pretty Boy Floyd.

MR. PARADISE

978-0-06-008396-0

In hindsight, Victoria's Secret model Kelly Barr thinks maybe it wasn't a great idea to accompany her callgirl roommate to Tony Paradiso's house.

TISHOMINGO BLUES

978-0-06-008394-6

Daredevil Dennis Lenahan's riskiest feat was witnessing a mob hit while atop his diving platform.

PAGAN BABIES

978-0-06-000877-2

Father Terry Dunn thought he'd seen everything on the mean streets of Detroit. Until he fled to Rwanda to evade a tax-fraud indictment.